I0616718

THE LORD OF THE SEA

THE LORD OF THE SEA

M.P. SHIEL

WILDSIDE PRESS

THE LORD OF THE SEA

This edition published 2009 by Wildside Press, LLC.
www.wildsidebooks.com

I

THE EXODUS

In the Calle Las Gabias — one of those by-streets of Lisbon below St. Catherine — there occurred one New Year a little event in the Synagogue there worth a mention in this history of Richard, Lord of the Sea.

It was Kol Nidrè, eve of the Day of Atonement, and the little Beth-El, sweltering in a dingy air, was transacting the long-drawn liturgy, when, behind the curtain where the women sat, an old dame who had been gazing upward smote her palms together, and let slip a little scream: "The Day is coming . . .!"

She then fainted, and till near ten lay on her bed, lit by the Yom Kippur candle, with open eyes, but without speech, her sere face still beautiful, on each temple a little pyramid of plaits, with gold-and-coral earrings: a holy *belle*. About ten P.M. three women watching heard her murmur: "My child, Rebekah . . .!"

She was childless, and whom she meant was not known. However, soon afterwards there was a form at the amulet-guarded door, and Estrella sat up, saying: "Rebekah, my child . . ."

A young lady of twenty-two ran in and embraced her, saying: "I have been to Paris and Madrid with my father — just arrived, so flew to see you. We leave for London tonight."

"No: I shall keep you seven days. Tell Frankl *I* say so. What jewels! You have grown into a rose of glory, the eyes are profounder and blacker, and that brow was made for high purpose. Tell me — have you a lover?"

"No, mamma Estrella."

"Then, why the blush?"

"It is nothing at all," Miss Frankl answered: "five years ago when at school in Bristol I thrice saw through a grating a young man with whom I was frivolous enough to speak. Happily, I do not know what has become of him — a wild, divine kind of creature, of whom I am well rid, and never likely to see again."

The old lady mused. "What was he?"

"A sailor."

"Not a common sailor?"

"I fancy so, mamma."

"What name?"

"Hogarth — Richard."

"A Jew?"

"An Englishman!"

She laughed, as the old lady's eyes opened in sacred horror, and as she whispered: "Child!"

Within three months of that night, one midnight the people of Prague rose and massacred most of the Jewish residents; the next day the flame broke out in Buda-Pesth; and within a week had become a revolution.

On the twelfth morning one of two men in a City bank said to the other: "Come, Frankl, you cannot fail a man in this crisis — I only want 80,000 on all Westring —"

"No good to me, my lord," answered Frankl, who, though a man of only forty — short, with broad shoulders, — already had his skin divided up like a dry leaf; in spite of which, he was handsome, with a nose ruled straight and long, a black beard on his breast.

But the telephone rattled and Frankl heard these words at the receiver: "Wire to hand from Wertheimer: Austrian Abgeordneten-haus passed a Resolution at noon virtually expelling Jewish Race. . . ."

When Frankl turned again he had already resolved to possess Westring Vale, and was saying to himself: "Within six months the value of English land should be — doubled."

The bargain was soon made now: and within one week the foresight of Frankl began to be justified.

Austria, during those days, was a nation of vengeful hearts: for the Jews had acquired half its land, and had mortgages on the other half: peasant, therefore, and nobleman flamed alike. And this fury was contagious: now Germany — now France had it — Anti-Semite laws — like the old May-Laws — but harsher still; and streaming they came, from the Leopoldstadt, from Bukowina, from the Sixteen Provinces, from all Galicia, from the Nicolas Colonies, from Lisbon, with wandering foot and weary breast — the Heines, Cohens, Oppenheimers — Sephardim, Aschkenasim. And Dover was the new Elim.

With alarm Britain saw them come! but before she could do anything, the wave had overflowed it; and by the time it was finished there was no desire to do anything: for within eight months such a tide of prosperity was floating England as has hardly been known in a country.

The reason of this was the increased number of hands — each making more things than its owner could consume himself, and so making every other richer.

There came, however, a change — almost suddenly — due to

the new demand for land, the "owners" determining to await still further rises, before letting. This checked industry: for now people, debarred from the land, had only air.

In Westring Vale, as everywhere, times were hard. It was now the property of Baruch Frankl: for at the first failure of Lord Westring to meet terms, Frankl had struck.

Now, one of the yeomen of Westring was a certain Richard Hogarth.

II

THE FEZ

Frankl took up residence at Westring in September, and by November every ale-house, market, and hiring in Westring had become a scene of discussion.

The cause was this: Frankl had sent out to his tenants a Circular containing the words:

". . . tenants to use for wear in the Vale a *fez with tassel* as the Livery of the Manor . . . the will of the Lord of the Manor . . . no exception . . ."

But though intense, the excitement was not loud: for want was in many a home; though after three weeks there were still six farmers who resisted.

And it happened one day that five of these at the Martinmas "Mop," or hiring, were discussing the matter, when they spied the sixth boring his way, and one exclaimed: "Yonder goes Hogarth! Let's hear what *he's* got to say!" and set to calling.

Hogarth twisted, and came winning his way, taller than the crowd, with "What's up? Hullo, Clinton — not a moment to spare today —"

"We were a-talking about that Circular — !" cried one.

At that moment two other men joined the group: one a dark-skinned Jew of the Moghrabîm; the other a young man — an English author — on tour. And these two heard what passed.

Hogarth stood suspended, finding no words, till one cried: "Do you mean to put the cap on?"

He laughed a little now. "*I*! The whip! The whip!" — he showed his hunting-crop, and was gone.

His manner of speech was rapid, and he had a hoarse sort of voice, almost as of sore throat.

Of the two not farmers, one — the author — enquired as to his name, and farm; the other man — the Moghrabîm Jew — that evening recounted to Frankl the words which he had heard.

* * * * * * *

One afternoon, two weeks later, Loveday, the author, was leaning upon a stile, talking to Margaret Hogarth; and he said: "I love you! If you could *deign* —"

"Truth is," she said, "you are in love with my brother, Dick, and you think it is me!"

She was a woman of twenty-five, large and buxom, though neat-waisted, her face beautifully fresh and wholesome, and he of middle-size, with a lazy ease of carriage, small eyes set far apart, a blue-velvet jacket, duck trousers very dirty, held up by a belt, a red shirt, an old cloth hat, a careless carle, greatly famed.

"But it isn't of your brother, but of *you*, that I am wanting to speak! Tell me —"

"No — I can't. I am a frivolous old woman to be talking to you about such things at all! But, since it is as you say, wait, perhaps I may be able — But I must be going now —"

There was embarrassment in her now: and suddenly she walked away, going to meet — another man.

She passed through stubble-wheat, disappeared in a pine-wood, and came out upon the Waveney towing path. On the towing path came Frankl to meet her.

He took her hand, holding his head sideward with a cajoling fondness, wearing the flowing caftan, and a velvet cap which widened out a-top, with puckers.

"Well, sweetheart . . ." he said.

"But, you know, I begged you not to use such words to me!" — from her.

"What, and I who am such a sweetheart of yours?" — his speech very foreign, yet slangily correct, being, in fact, *all* slang.

"No," she said, "you spoke different at first, and that is why — But this must be the last, unless you say out clearly now what it is you mean —"

"Now, you are too hard. You know I am wild in love with you. And so are you with me —"

"*I?*" — with shrinking modesty in her under-looking eyes. "Oh, no — don't have any delusions like that about me, please! You said that you liked me: and as I am in the habit of speaking the truth myself, I thought that — perhaps — But my meeting you, to be frank with you, was for the sake of my brother."

"Well, you are as candid as they make them," he said, eyeing her with his mild eye. "But what's the matter with your brother? Hard up?"

"He's worried about something."

"He must have some harvest-money put away?"

"He has something in Reid's Bank at Yarmouth, I believe."

"Well, shall I tell you what's the matter with him? He's *afraid*, your brother. He has refused to wear the cap, and he thinks that I shall be down upon him like a thousand of bricks . . . But suppose I exempt him, and you and I be friends? That's fair."

"What *do* you mean?"

"Give us *one* —"

"Believe me, you talk — !"

"Don't let your angry passions rise. I am going to have a kiss off those handsome lips —"

Before she could stir he was in the act of the embrace; but it was never accomplished: for he saw her colour fade, heard crackling twigs, a step! as someone emerged from the wood ten yards away — Richard.

The thought in Margaret's mind was this: "Father in Heaven, whatever will he think of me here with this Jew?"

Hogarth stopped, staring at this couple; did not understand: Margaret should have been home from "class-meeting" . . . only, he observed her heaving bosom; then twisted about and went, his walk rapid, in his hand a hunting-crop, by which, with a very sure aim, he batted away pebbles from his path, stooping each time.

III

THE HUNTING-CROP

Along the towing path to the farmhouse. He did not look behind: was like a man who has received a wound, and wonders whence.

A pallor lay under his brown skin, brown almost as an Oriental's, and he was called "the Black Hogarth" — the Hogarths being Saxon, on the mantel in the dining-room being a very simple coat — a Bull on Gules. But Richard was a startling exception. His hair grew away flat and sparse from his round brow; on his cheeks three moles, jet-black in their centre. Handsome one called his hairless face: the nose delicate, the lips negroid in their thick pout, the left eye red, streaked with bloodshot, the eyes' brown brightness very beautiful and strange, with a sideward stare wild as that sideward stare of the race-horse; and the lids had a way of lifting largely anon.

He passed through Lagden Dip orchard into the old homestead, into the dining-room, where cowered the old Hogarth, smoking, his hair a mist of wool-white.

He glanced up, but said nothing; and Richard said nothing, but walked about, his arms folded, frowning turbulently, while the twilight deepened, and Margaret did not come.

Now he planted a chair near the old man, sat, and shouted: "Listen, sir!"

Up went the old Hogarth's hand to push forward the inquiring ear, while Richard, who, till now, had guarded him from all knowledge of the Circular, snatched it from his breast pocket, and loudly read.

As the sense entered his head, up the old man shot his palms, shaking from them astonishment and deprecation, with nods; then, with opening arms, and an under-look at Richard: "Well, there is nothing to be said: the land is his. . . ."

Hogarth leapt up and walked out; he muttered: "The land is his, but he is mine. . . ."

The question at the bottom of his mind had been this: "Does *Margaret*, too, go with the land?" But he did not utter it even to himself: went out, fingering the crop, stalking toward the spot where he had left the man and the woman. But Margaret was then coming through the wood; Frankl had gone up to the Hall; and Hogarth crossed the bridge and went climbing toward the mansion.

It was a Friday evening, and up at the Hall the Sabbath had commenced, two Sabbath-tapers shining now upon the Mezuzzah at the dining-room door, Frankl being of the Cohanîm, the priestly class — a Jew of Jews. As he had passed in, two Moghrabîm Jews had saluted him with: "Shabbath"; and mildly he had replied: "Shabbath."

But swift upon his steps strode Hogarth: Hogarth was at the lodge-gates — was on the drive — was in the hall.

But, since Frankl was just preparing to celebrate the *kiddush*, "He cannot be seen now," said a man in the hall.

"He must," said Hogarth.

As he brushed past, two men raised an outcry: but Hogarth continued his swift way, and had half traversed a *salon* hung with a chaos of cut-glass when from a side door appeared the inquiring face of Frankl in pious skullcap.

"What is it?" he cried — "I cannot be seen —"

He recognized the man of the towing path, and on his face grew a look of scare, as he backed toward a study: but before he could slam the door, Hogarth, too, was within.

"Who are you? What is it?" whined Frankl, who was both hard master and cringing slave.

Hogarth produced the Circular: but of Margaret not a word.

"Caps-and-tassels, you?" — flicking Frankl on the cheek with a fillip of his middle finger.

"You dare assault me! Why, I swear, I meant no harm —"

Down came the whip upon the Jew's shoulders, Frankl, as the stings penetrated his caftan, giving out one roar, and the next instant, seeing the two Jews at the doorway, groaned the mean whisper: "Oh, don't make a man look small before the servants," crying out immediately: "Help!"

Soon five or six servants were at the door, and, of these, two Arab Jews rushed forward, one a tall fellow, the other an obese bulk with bright black eyes, the former holding a slender blade — the knife with which "shechita," or slaughtering, was done: and while the corpulent Jew threw himself upon Hogarth, the other drew this knife through the flesh of Hogarth's shoulder, at the same time happening to cut the heavy Arab across the wrist.

Now, there was some quarrel between the two Arabs, and the injured Arab, forgetting Hogarth, turned fiercely upon his fellow.

Hogarth, meanwhile, had not let go Frankl, nor delivered the intended number of cuts: so he was again standing with uplifted whip, when his eye happened to fall upon the doorway.

He saw there a sight which struck his arm paralysed: Rebekah Frankl.

Two months had she been here at Westring — and he had not known it!

There she stood peering, of a divine beauty in his eyes, like half mythical queens of Egypt and Babylon, blinking in a rather barbarous superfluity of jewels: and, blinded and headlong, he was in flight.

As for Frankl, he locked that door upon himself, and remained there, forgetting the sanctification of the Sabbath.

The Hebrew's eyes blazed like a wild beast's. The words: "As the Lord liveth . . ." hissed in whispers from his lips.

He took up a pinch of old ashes, and cast it into the air.

As Shimei, the son of Gera, cursed David, so he cursed Richard Hogarth that night — again and again — with grave rites, with cancerous rancour.

"I will blight him, as the Lord liveth; as the Lord liveth, I will blight him . . ." he said repeatedly, his draperied arms spread in pompous imprecation.

As a beginning, he sat and wrote to Reid's Bank, requesting the payment in gold of £14,000 — to produce a stoppage of payment at the little Bank in which were Richard's savings.

Afterwards, with mild eyes he repaired to the dining-hall, and sanctified the Sabbath, blessing a cup of wine, dividing up two napkined loaves, and giving to Rebekah his benediction.

IV

THE SWOON

Hogarth went moodily down the hillside to the Waveney, across the bridge, and home, his sleeve stained with blood.

In the dining-room, he threw himself into an easychair in a gloom lit only by the fireglow, in the room above mourning a little harmonium which Margaret was playing, mixed with the sound of Loveday's voice.

The old man said: "Richard, my boy . . ."

Hogarth did not answer.

"Richard, I have somewhat to say to you — are ye hearkening?"

Richard, losing blood, moaned a drowsy "Yes."

And the old Hogarth, all deaf and bedimmed, said: "I had to say it to you, and this night let it be: Richard, you are no son of mine."

At this point Hogarth's head dropped forward: but many a time, during long years, he remembered a dream in which he had heard those words: "Richard, you are no son of mine . . ."

The old Hogarth continued to ears that did not hear:

"I have kept it from you — for I'm under a bargain with a firm of solicitors in London; but, Dick, it doesn't strike me as I am long for this world: a queer feeling I've had in this left side the last hour or two; and there's that Circular — I never heard of such a thing in all my born days. But what can we do? You'll have to wear the cap — or be turned out. Always I've said to myself, from a young man: 'Get hold of a bit of land someways as your own God's own': but I never did; the days went by and by, and it all seems no longer than an after-dinner nap in a barn on a hot harvest-day. But a bit of land — the man who has that can make all the rest work to keep him. And if they turn me out, I couldn't live, lad: the old house has got into my bones, somehow. Anyhow, I think the time is come to tell you in my own way how the thing was. No son are you of mine, Richard. Your mother, Rachel, who was a Londoner, served me an ill turn while we were sweethearting, hankering after another man — a Jew millionaire he was, she being a governess in his house; but, Richard, I couldn't give her up: I married her three months before you were born; and not a living creature knows, except, perhaps, one — perhaps one: a priest he was, called O'Hara. But that's how it was. Your father was a Jew, and your mother was a Jew, and you are a Jew, and in the under-bottom of the old grey trunk you will find a roll of papers. Are you hearkening? And don't you be ashamed of being a Jew, boy — *they* are the people who've got the money; and money buys land, Richard. Nor your father did not do so badly by you, either: his name was Spinoza — Sir Solomon Spinoza —"

At that point Margaret, bearing a lamp, entered, followed by Loveday, and at the sight of Richard uttered a cry.

V

REID'S

By noon Hogarth knew the news: his hundred and fifty at Reid's were gone; and he owed for the Michaelmas quarter — twenty-one pounds five, his only chattels of value being the thresher, not yet paid for, half a rick, seed, manure, and "the furniture." If he could realize enough for rent, he would lack capital for wages and cultivation, for Reid's had been his credit-bank.

After dinner he stood long at a window, then twisted away, and walked to Thring, where he captained in a football match, Loveday watching his rage, his twisting waist, and then accompanying him home: but in the dining-room they found the lord-of-the-manor's bailiff; and Loveday, divining something embarrassing, took himself away.

The same evening there were two appraisers in the house, and the bailiff, on their judgment, took possession of the chattels on the holding except some furniture, and some agricultural "fixtures." The sale was arranged for the sixth day.

From the old Hogarth the truth could no longer be hidden . . .

Two days he continued quiet in the old nook by the hearth, apparently in a kind of dotage doze; but on the third, he began to poke about, hobbled into the dairy, peered into the churn, touched the skimmer.

"You'll have to wear the cap," Margaret heard him mutter — "or be turned out."

As if taking farewell, he would get up, as at a sudden thought, to go to visit something. He kept murmuring: "I always said, Get a bit of land as your own, but I never did; the days went by and by. . . ."

Margaret, meantime, was busy, binding beds with sheets, making bundles, preparing for the flitting, with a heaving breast; till, on the fifth day, a van stood loaded with their things at the hall door, and she, with untidy hair, was helping heave the last trunk upon the backboard, when the carman said: "Mrs. Mackenzie says, mum, the things mustn't be took to the cottage, except you pay in advance."

Now Margaret stood at a loss; but in a minute went bustling, deciding to go to Loveday, not without twinges of reluctance: for Loveday, with instinctive delicacy, had lately kept from the farm; and to Margaret, whose point of view was different, the words "false friends" had occurred.

Passing through an alley of the forest, she was met by a man — a park-keeper of Frankl's — a German Jew, who had once handed her a note from Frankl. And he, on seeing her, said: "Here have I a letter for your brother."

"Who from?" she asked.

"That may I not say."

When he handed her an envelope rather stuffed with papers, she went on her flurried way; and soon Loveday was bowing before her in his sitting-room at Priddlestone.

"You will be surprised to see me, Mr. Loveday," said she, panting.

"A little surprised, but most awfully glad, too. Is all well?"

"Oh, far from that, I'm afraid. But I haven't got any time — and, oh my, I don't know how to say it, — but to be frank with you — could you lend Richard two pounds — ?"

Loveday coloured to the roots of his hair.

He could not tell her: "Open that envelope in your hand," for that would have meant that it was he who had sent the £50 it contained; and he had now only one sixpence in Priddlestone.

"That is," she said — "if it is not an inconvenience to you —"

He could find no words. Some fifteen minutes before, having enclosed the notes, he had descended to the bar to get mine host to find him a messenger, and direct the envelope — for Hogarth knew his handwriting. Mine host was not there — his wife could not write: but she had pointed out the Jewish park-keeper sipping beer; so Loveday had had the man upstairs, had made him write the address, and had bribed him to deliver the envelope with a mum tongue.

"I'm afraid I've taken a great liberty —" she said, shrinking at his silence.

Then he spoke: "Oh, liberty! — but — really — I'm quite broke myself — !"

"Then, good-afternoon to you," said she: "I am very sorry — but you will excuse the liberty, won't you — ?"

In the forest she began to cry, covering her eyes, moaning: "Why, how could he be so *mean*? And I who loved that young man with all my heart, God knows — !"

Her eyes searched the ground for two sovereigns. Then she happened to look at the envelope: and instantly was interested. "Why, it is the Jew's hand!" she thought, for the letters were angular in the German manner, making a general similarity with Frankl's writing.

Curiosity overcame her: she opened, and saw . . .

"Oh, well, this is *generous* though, after all!" she exclaimed.

And now she ran, coming out from mossy path upon wide forest-road: and there, taking promenade, was Frankl, quite near, with phylacteried left arm.

"Why, sweetheart . . ." said he.

She stopped before him. "Well, you can call me what you like for the time being," said she, laughing rather hysterically; "for I am most grateful to you for your generous present to my brother, Mr. Frankl!"

She had still no suspicion of Richard's visit of chastisement to the Hall!

"Now, what do you mean?" said Frankl.

"Why, you might guess that I know your handwriting by this time!" she said coquettishly, and held out the notes and the envelope.

His eyes twinkled; he meditated; he had, more than ever, need of her; and he said: "Well, you are as 'cute' as they make them!"

"But instead of sending us this, which I am not at all sure that Richard will touch, why couldn't you pay it to yourself, and not turn us out —"

"I let business take its course: and afterwards I do my charity. But it wasn't for your brother, you know, that I sent it — but for *you*."

"I must be running —"

When she reached the farm, she gave the carman a secret glimpse of the notes, while Hogarth, who was now there, went to seek the old Hogarth, for whom a nest had been made among the furniture in the cart.

He was found above-stairs in an empty room, searching the floor for something.

"Come, sir," said Hogarth, and led him step by step.

But as the old man passed the threshold, he fell flat on the slabs of the porch, striking his forehead, printing a stain there.

And the next day, the day of the sale, he still lay in the old chamber, on the ancient bed, dead.

VI

"PEARSON'S WEEKLY"

"**R**ose Cottage" was without roses: but had a good-sized "garden" at the back; and here Hogarth soon had a shed nailed together, with bellows, anvil, sledges, rasps, setts, drifts, and so on, making a little smithy.

He engaged a boy; and soon John Loveday would be leaning all a forenoon at the shed door, watching the lithe ply of Hogarth's hips, and the white-hot iron gushing flushes; while Margaret, peeping, could see Loveday's slovenly ease of pose, his numberless cigarettes, and hear the rhymes of the sledges chiming.

As to Loveday's £50, she had dared to say nothing to Richard, but kept them, intending to make up the amount already spent, and give them to Frankl. Loveday, meantime, she avoided with constant care.

So two weeks passed, till, one day, Loveday, leaning at the forge-door, happened to say: "Are you interested in current politics? The East Norfolk division is being contested, one of the candidates, Sir Bennett Beaumont, is a friend of mine, and I was thinking that I might go to the meeting tonight, if you could come —"

"I invite you to supper here instead."

"Not interested?" queried Loveday.

"Not at all. Stop — I'll show you something in which I *am* interested."

He ran to a corner, picked up a *Pearson's Weekly*, and pointed to a paragraph headed:

"FIVE HUNDRED-POUND NOTES!
"FIFTY TEN-POUND NOTES!!
"ONE HUNDRED FIVE-POUND NOTES!!!"

— a prize for "the most intelligent" article, explaining the cause, or causes, of "the present distress and commercial crisis."

Loveday read it smiling.

"Ah," said he, "but who is to be the judge of 'the most intelligent' article? Pearson must himself be of the highest intelligence to decide."

"True," said Hogarth. "But the man who offered that prize has indicated to the nation the thing which it should be doing. If I was able to form an Association to enter this competition — and why not? Stop — I will go with you —"

So that evening they walked to Beccles, and took train for Yarmouth.

The candidate to speak was a Mr. Moses Max, a Liberal Jew; the chair to be taken by Baruch Frankl; and in the midst of a row, the stately great men entered upon the platform and occupied it, hisses like the escape of steam mixing with "He's a jolly good fellow." Midway down the pit sat Loveday, and with him Hogarth, whose large stare ranged solemnly round and down from galleries to floor.

Frankl sipped water, and rose, amid shouts of: "Circular!" "Caps-and-tassels!"

He made a speech of which nothing was known, except the amiable bows, for a continual noising filled the hall; and up rose Mr. Moses Max, a stout fair Jew, whose fist struck with a regular, heavy emphasis. After ten minutes, when he began to be heard, he was saying:

". . . Sir Bennett Beaumont! Is *he* the sort of man you'd send to represent you? (Cries of: "Yes!") What is he? — ask yourselves the question: a fossilized Tory, a man who's about as much idea of progress as a mummy — people actually say he's *got* a collection of mummies in his grand fashionable mansion at Aylesham, and it's only what we should expect of him. (Cheers, and cries of: "Oh, oh!") And what has he ever done for East Norfolk? Gentlemen, you may say as you like about Jews — Jews this, and Jews that — and every man has a right to his opinion in this land of glorious Saxon liberty — but no one can deny that it's Jews who know how to make the money. (Cheers and hisses.) They know how to make it for themselves (hisses) — and, yes, they know how to make it for the nation! (Loud triumph of cheers.) *That's* the point — *that* touches the spot! (Cries of: "Oh, oh!") Righteousness, it is said, exalteth a nation: well, so do Jews —"

"That is false," said a voice — Hogarth, who had stood up.

The words were the signal for a shower of cheers swept by gusts of hisses; and immediately one region of the pit was seen to be a scrimmage of fisticuffs, mixed with policemen, sticks, savage faces, and bent backs; while the two galleries, craning to see, bellowed like Bashan.

Moses Max was leaning wildly, gesticulating, with shouts; while Loveday, who had turned pale on Hogarth's rising, touched Hogarth's coattail, whereupon Hogarth, stooping to his ear, shouted: "We will have some fun . . ."

"The paid agents of Beaumont!" now shouted Moses Max; "sent to disturb our meeting! Englishmen! will you submit to this? The nation shall hear —"

At that point Moses Max, in his gesticulation, happening to touch a switch in the platform-rail, out glowered into darkness every light at that end of the hall: at which thing the audience was thrown into a state of boisterous lawlessness, a tumult reigning in the gloom like the constant voice of Niagara, until suddenly the platform was again lit up, and the uproar lulled.

And now again Moses Max was prone to speak, with lifted fist; but before ever he could utter one single word, a voice was ringing through the Assembly Rooms:

"*Where* was Moses when the light went out?"

This again was Hogarth; and it ended Moses Max for that night.

Hogarth had not sat since he had called out "That is false": his tall figure was recognized; and, with that electric spontaneity of crowds, he was straightway the leader of the meeting, men darting from their seats with waving hats, sticks, arms, and vociferous mouth, the chairman half standing, with a shivering finger directed upon Hogarth, shrieking to the police: but too late — Hogarth had brushed past Loveday's knees — was dashing for the crowded platform steps — was picking his way, stumbling, darting up them.

Crumpled in his hand was a *Pearson's Weekly.*

Now he is to the front — near Frankl.

"Friends! I have ventured to take the place of our friend, Moses, here — no ill will to him — for with respect to the question before us, whether we elect Beaumont or Max, I care, I confess, little. I'm rather an Anti-Jew myself" (hissing and cheers) "but it strikes me that the Jews are the least of our trouble. To a man who said to me that the cause of all our evil days is the inability of England to feed these few million Jews I'd answer: 'I don't know how you can be so silly!' Why, the whole human race, friends, can find room on the Isle of Wight — the earth laughs at the insignificant drawings upon her made by the small infantry called Man. Then, why do we suffer, friends? We *do* suffer, I suppose? I was once at Paris, and at a place called 'the Morgue' I saw exposed young men with wounded temples, and girls with dead mouths twisted, and innocent old women drowned; and there must be a biggish cry, you know, rising each night from the universal earth, accusing some hoary fault in the way men live together! What is the fault? If you ask *me*, I answer that I am only a common smith: *I* don't know: but I know this about the fault, that it is something simple, commonplace, yet deepseated, or we should all see it; but it is hidden from us by its very ordinariness, like the sun which men seldom look at. It *must* be so. And shall we never find the time to think of it? Or will never some grand man, mighty as a garrison, owning eyes that know the glances of Truth, arise to see for us? Friends! but, lacking him, what shall we do to be saved? — for truly this 'civilization' of ours is a blood-washed civilization, friends, a reddish Juggernaut, you know, whose wheels cease not: so we should be prying into it, provided we be not now too hidebound: for that's the trouble — that our thoughts grow to revolve in stodgy grooves of use-and-wont, and shun to soar beyond. Look at our Parliament — a hurdy-gurdy turning out, age after age, a sing-song of pigmy regulations, accompanied for grum kettledrum by a musketry of suicides, and for pibroch by a European bleating of little children. We are still a million miles from civilization! For what is a civilized society? It can only be one in which the people are proud and happy! The people of Africa are happy, not proud; not civilized; the people of England have a certain pride, not a millionth part as superb as it might be, but are far from happy: far from civilized. The fact is, Man has never begun to live, but still sleeps a deep sleep. Well! let us do our best, we here! I have here a paper offering a prize to the man of us who will go to the root of our troubles, and my idea in usurping the place of our friend, Mr. Max, was to ask you to form an association with me to enter that competition. There is no reason why our association should not be large as the nation, nor why it should not spread to France and Turkey. For the thing presses, and tomorrow more of the slaughtered dead will be swarming in the mortuaries of London. Will you, then? The understanding will be this: that each man who writes his name in a notebook which will lie at Rose Cottage, Thring, or who sends his name, will devote sixty minutes each day to the problem. I happen to be in a position to use a chapel at Thring, and there I will hold a meeting —"

At this point Frankl rose: Thring was *his*, his own, own, own; and now his eyes had in them that catlike blaze which characterized his rages.

"Here, police! police!" he hissed low, "what's the use of police that don't act!" And now he raised his voice to a scream: "Jews! Shew yourselves! Don't let this man stay here . . .!"

About twenty Jews leapt at the challenge; at the same time Hogarth, seeing two policemen running forward from the back, folded his arms, and cried out: "Friends! I have not finished! Don't let me be removed . . ."

Whereupon practically every man in the pit was in motion, for or against him, the galleries two oblongs of battle.

As up the two curving stairs stormed the mob, by a sudden rush like an ocean-current he was borne off his feet toward the side, and was about to bring down his sharp-pointed little knuckles, when his eye fell upon the face of a lady who had fainted.

He had had no idea that she was there! — Rebekah Frankl.

She had quietly fainted, not at the rush — but before — during Hogarth's speech.

Hogarth managed to fight his way to a door at the platform back with her, entered a room where some chairs were, but, seeing a stair, could not let her go from his embrace, but descended, passed along a passage and out into a patch of green.

She, under the dark sky, whispered: "It is you," her forehead on his shoulder; and added: "My carriage, I think, is yonder."

Hogarth saw the carriage-lights at the field's edge, bore her thither, laid her with care on the cushions, kissed her hand: and this act Frankl saw — with incredulity of his own eyes. As he approached, Hogarth walked away.

Frankl mastered his voice to say blandly in Spanish: "Well, how did you get through, sweet child? Who was that man — ? But stay: where are those two fools?"

This meant the two familiars — the Arabs, Isaac and Mephibosheth, one of whom had come as footman, the other as coachman — and, as he went raging about the carriage, with stamps, his boot struck against a body. There was enough light to reveal to his peering that it was Mephibosheth, whom Isaac had stabbed, and fled . . .

Frankl lowered his ear — doubted whether he could detect a breathing; and though scared, he being a Cohen, and the presence of death defilement, yet he stayed, bending over Mephi several minutes, thinking, not of him, but of Hogarth.

"It is that fool, Isaac, has done it," he thought; "and if the man be dead —" What then? "*If* he be dead, I've got you, Mr. Hogarth, in the hollow of this hand. . . ."

His fingers passed over the body: there, sticking in the breast, was a cangiar which Isaac, in his panic, had left, and Frankl's hand rested on the handle; if he did not consciously press the knife home, very heavily his hand rested on it, eyes blazing, beard shaking. . . .

Then he drew out the knife carefully, to hide it in the carriage, listened again close, felt sure now that death was there, and now scuttled, as if from plague, guiltily hissing: "Putrid dog . . .!"

Presently he led his carriage to the station, and made a deposition of the murder.

Asked if he had any suspicion as to the culprit, he said: "Not the least: I left the man alone with the carriage, and who could have had any motive for killing him beats me."

VII

THE ELM

Hogarth, meantime, had made his way to the front of the room, then vomiting its throng, discovered Loveday, and, deciding to walk home, they were soon on the cliffs.

And suddenly Loveday: "Tomorrow will conclude my fifth week in Westring. What, do you suppose, has made me stay?"

"I have wondered."

"I work better here . . . Hogarth, you inspirit me."

"Is that so?"

"It is, yes. Merely your presence is for me a freshness and an enthusiasm: I catch in the turn of your body hints of adventurous Columbuses, Drakes, nimble Achilles; and sibylline meanings in some glance of yours infect my fancy with images of Moses, blind old Homers — prophet, lawgiver, poet —"

They were passing along a stretch of sand, with some lights of Lowestoft in sight, arm in arm; and Hogarth said: "Well, you speak some big words. But my life, you understand, has been as simple and small as possible. I will tell you: my father sent me to an extraordinary school — where he got the coin I could never find out — Lancing College at Shoreham. There I did very well — only that I was continually *getting* it! What was the matter with me when a boy I can't understand: I was the devil. One summer vacation (I was fourteen) I stole three pounds from the old man, and ran away one Sunday night. Passed through London and soon was apprentice in a blacksmith's shop in a Kent village called Bigham. But in six months I had the forge at my fingers' ends, and was off: nothing could hold me long. One day I turned up before the Recruiting Office of Marines in Bristol — just of the right age for what they call 'second-class boys' — and decided upon the sea — that sea there — which, from the moment I saw it at the age of four, caused me a swelling of the breast with which, to this day, it afflicts me. Well, I got the birth-certificate of another boy, scraped through, was entered into a District Ship, and finally sailed in the *St. Vincent* to the Pacific Station.

"However, my trial of His Majesty's ships was not a success: twice I was in irons, once leapt into mid-ocean; nor could the battleship hold me when she had nothing to teach me; so I did to the King what I had done to the old man — cut and ran.

"It was at Valparaiso, and I made my way across the continent to Buenos Ayres.

"I forget now what took me to Bristol: but there I was one day when I happened to see — what do you think? — a girl — sixteen — I a stripling of nineteen, or so — but she most precocious, spoke like a woman — a grating in a wall between us. Ah, well, God is good, and His Mercy endureth for ever. But she said it could never be — she a Jewess: though that, by the way, is nonsense, for she is a Jewess, and a Parisienne, and a Hindoo, and a Negress, and a Japanese, and the man who marries her will have a harem. My friend, I have seen her this very night!"

He was silent. Suddenly he broke out: "I came home raving! The old man was scared out of his wits by my frenzy — I drank like ten men — in a month was the terror of Westring. One midnight, going home through the beech-wood — I don't know if you have noticed a hollow elm tree which stands to the right of the path?"

"I think I have," said Loveday.

"We shall pass near it presently; and at the moment when we approach it, I shall feel a little thrill in my back: always it is so with me. But I was saying: that midnight, as I passed the tree, drunk as I was, I saw a naked black man with a long beard run out; I took to my heels; he was after me; till I reached the bridge, when I stopped, faced him, fired a blow into his eyes, and he vanished.

"During the week I continued to see apparitions. My groans were heard in the farm yard: Lord have mercy upon me! Christ have mercy upon me! I was visited by the Methodist preacher at Thring; and finally I found solace: I became a class-member, a leader, a local preacher.

"For some time I have been conscious of dissatisfaction among the people with my preaching, who say that my God 'is not a personal God', and that my Christianity is 'rum stuff': I am therefore meaning to give it up. But I still preach every second Thursday night.

"It was about that time that, by accident, I found out the power of my hand to cure headache, and things like that, and the sensation among these villagers was enormous, I can tell you, six years ago; now they come to be touched without the slightest sense of the unusual. But what I have done well in was — the farming. I knew little of agriculture —"

At this point they turned into the lane to Westring: and Loveday went with him a little beyond Priddlestone to see the fatal elm.

VIII

THE METEOR

The next morning, after breakfast, Hogarth went down old Thring Street, and spent a penny for a notebook to contain the signatures of his association.

But this was no day for interest in that scheme: for under the projecting first-floor of the paper shop were newspaper placards bearing such words as:

THE EARTH IN DANGER
SHALL WE PERISH TONIGHT?

and Hogarth was soon bending in the street over a paragraph, short — but in *pica*.

M. Tissot, the astronomer, had, at half past ten the previous night, observed through the 40-inch telescope of the Nice observatory a body which seemed a tiny planet or aerolite of abnormal size. It was sighted at a point two degrees W. of *a* Librae at an angle of 43½° with the horizon, and had been photographed, its elements calculated, its spectrum taken. The ascertained diameter was 3° 17, or about 73 miles, and its substance seemed to consist of ironstone mixed with diamond.

By noon a fresh light was thrown upon the little world, the Yerkes observatory and Greenwich both uttering their voice, the Astronomer Royal announcing that the so-called planet was merely a meteor — not more than 400 yards in diameter, with a low velocity of two miles a second; and its distance was less than a tenth of that estimated by Tissot. The Yerkes observatory fixed the diameter at 230 yards. All, however, agreed in the opinion that it must strike the earth between ten and twelve that night.

These later announcements so much allayed the panic, that by one o'clock Hogarth, on peeping into the notebook on the box before the smithy, saw six signatures; and a young man who came about six P.M. to sign, cried out: "Hullo! the book is filled up!" on which Hogarth ran out, saying: "Don't run away on that account, I'll run and get —" darting into the house to ask Margaret where a certain account book was.

"Didn't I throw it into the box of rubbish in the cellar at Lagden, when we were leaving?" she asked; on which he threw off his apron, and was off toward Lagden Dip to get it.

He had almost cleared the village when he was blocked by a crowd before a cottage, from out of which were coming screams — a woman's; and he ran in, found a man named Fred Bates beating his wife, planted a blow on his chest.

The next morning the wife of Bates was found dead, greatly disfigured about the face, whereupon Bates was arrested, and Hogarth, as we shall see, was subpoenaed to give evidence of the beating.

In ten minutes he was at the old farm house of the Hogarths.

The new tenant was a Mr. Bond, a bankrupt metal-broker, who had two hobbies — farming and astronomy; and, as Hogarth approached the yard-gate, he saw Mr. Bond, his two daughters, his servants, grouped round an optic tube mounted on a tripod. He asked permission to get the account book, got it, in a few minutes was again passing through, and, as he went by, bowing his thanks, Mr. Bond said: "But — have you seen the asteroid?"

"No — whereabouts?"

"Not quite visible to the naked eye yet: but come — you shall see."

He himself looked through, fixing the sight, turning the adjuster; then with fussy suddenness: "Now, sir —"

Hogarth put an eager eye to the glass.

"You see her?" said Mr. Bond, rubbing his soft old palms; "straight for us she comes — in a considerable hurry by this time, I can tell you! and if she happens to break up in the air, then, pray, sir, that a splinter of her may fall into your back yard — not too big a one! but a nice little comfortable *piece*" — he rubbed his palms — "for you know, no doubt, of what her substance is composed? Diamond, sir, in extraordinary evidence! in conjunction with specular iron ore, commonly called the red haematite, and the ferrous carbonate, or spathic iron. You see her, sir? you see her?"

Hogarth whispered: "Yes."

There, fairest among ten thousand, sailing the high seas she came; and longer than was modest he stopped there, gazing, then ran, wondering at her daisy loveliness, not dreaming that between himself and her was — a relation.

She broke up with a European display soon after eleven that night over the North Sea.

IX

HOGARTH'S GUNS

At the moment when Hogarth was peering through the telescope, a man was loitering before his cottage — one of the Hall's park-keepers; and when Margaret put out her head to look for Richard's coming, the man whistled.

In a moment a note was in her hand.

> "DEAR MISS HOGARTH,
>
> "This is to ask you to be certain sure to meet me this evening at 9 P.M. on the towpath. It isn't today that you are well aware of the state of my feelings toward you: but it is not to talk sweethearting that I wish to see you now, but about your brother, and the matter is about as important as can be. If I were in your place, I should destroy this letter.
>
> "Yours, with my respects,
> "BARUCH FRANKL."

Margaret tore it up, and "My goodness!" she thought, "what is anyone to do? If I only had the money to make up those fifty pounds! May the Holy Spirit guide me now . . .!"

Later in the evening she stole out, and met Frankl.

He assumed a very respectful tone.

"Miss Hogarth," said he at once, "have you heard?"

"No, sir."

"You have not been told that your brother has been to the Hall?"

"What in patience for?"

"He came — you couldn't believe — to beat me!"

"Richard! I don't understand. When?"

"Yesterday." (In reality it was four weeks before.)

"But what about?"

"Revenge! Blind, murderous revenge for turning him neck and crop out of Lagden!"

"You *are* in a temper! But I can't understand a word of it!"

"Well, that is what I had to tell you. He came to my house — And how good have I been to this man! Didn't I send him the fifty pounds — ?"

"Well, that *was* kind. But I must tell you, Mr. Frankl, that Richard knows nothing of the fifty pounds —"

"Well, then it is *your* fault! Oh, he did not know of the fifty pounds? Then it is your fault entirely, this rage of his against me — He threatened to shoot me dead — thrice he threatened — soon, he said —"

"Not Richard?"

"Yes, Richard! — your nice Richard! But what did I want you for tonight? It was to let you see that I have it in my power to let your brother in for three months hard — not less. But you know, my dear, don't you, that I wouldn't do anything to give you pain? That is why, so far, I've taken no steps. But your brother must be unarmed. I can't have my life exposed, after his threats, and all."

"Unarmed. . . ."

"Yes. I have it on good authority that your brother has guns. I must have those guns put into my own hands by you . . ."

"But I couldn't! He would find out . . ."

"Then I must act, that's all. Or no — I give you another chance — tell him of the fifty pounds I sent — that may disarm him in another way —"

He was sure that this she would not now do, yet felt relieved when she cried out: "I couldn't! Not now! Can't you see?"

"Well, there is nothing to be done, then. I must act, that's all."

"But don't be *hard*! What can I do? Sooner or later he'd be sure to miss them!"

"Poh! he is not always shooting, I suppose? And after a few weeks I'd give them back. Anyway, think it over: and I'll be here on Tuesday night next at nine to receive them. Good night —"

She looked palely after him, her feet in a net, new to her, woven of concealments and deceit.

At eleven that night she was sitting in their diminutive parlour, — Hogarth at a table inscribing the association's names received by post that evening; and at last, bending low over her sewing, she said: "Richard, is it true you have been to the Hall?"

He started! "Yes. Who told you?"

"I heard it."

He looked at her piercingly. "*Answer*!"

"I heard it," she said with a stubborn nod, quite pallid.

He turned upon her a stare of displeasure; but in that second they heard a shouting down the village, ran to the front, and saw heaven all like cancer and cracked windowpanes, for from a central plash of passion the shattered asteroid had shot long-lingering ribbons of lilac light over the bowl of the sky.

X

ISAAC

On the Tuesday was the inquest on the murdered Mephibosheth; ending in a verdict of wilful murder against some
person unknown.

The same night at nine Frankl had Hogarth's two guns from
Margaret on the towing path, she now well inveigled into his net,
and under his commands.

"I want you," he said, "to meet me—here again on Thursday
night, at 7:30."

"But you will tell one why, I suppose!"

"When you come you will hear. And don't let anything keep
you away — not *anything*, mind — if you take my hint."

She left him with her head hung, praying for deliverance, but
consenting.

The next (Wednesday) morning Frankl was in a high room of
the Hall, in a corner of which cowered the Arab, Isaac, and he said
in his strong bass in Arabic: "Well, Isaac, well."

A groan broke from the obese heap of grief; down each side of
his kefie streamed waves of trembling; on his square-cut beard of
ritual flecks of foam.

"Isaac, why did you kill Mephibosheth?"

Vigorously sputtered Isaac, spitting out the ill-omened words.
He said: "Your servant did not kill Mephibosheth."

"Well, there was an inquest today, the Court decided that you
did, and has sentenced you to be hanged by the neck like a dog."

The Arab sprang up, his thick bluish underlip shivering.

"An eye for an eye," said Frankl solemnly: "it is written in the
Torah."

"*Mercy* My father served your father —"

"I have remembered that: that is why I have saved you from
hanging like a dog at the hands of these *Goyim* vermin: but, Isaac,
you must die —"

"God of — !"

"You dare raise your voice! Blood for blood —"

"*Mercy*! — I did not mean to kill — !"

"Blood for blood, you dog! Raise it, and I fell you! Raise it, and
the noose sinks into your fat swine's-throat! Can't you understand? — you have been tracked by the avengers of blood! and you
may swing lingeringly, with a crowd of Christian boys and girls

mocking round you, or you may shoot yourself in one painless flash. Which shall it be?"

Isaac, again dropping a-heap, covered his face, without answer.

"Well," said Frankl, walking away, "I can't wait all day. The detectives are at this moment downstairs —"

Now the Arab leapt up, and, in a movement of great dignity, with an outrush of both arms, rent his caftan from the top to its muslin girdle.

"I will shoot myself," he said quietly.

Frankl took snuff.

The same night he took his secretary's typewriter, and spelled out the following note:

"SIR,
   "Permit me to ask you as an old friend of your father's if you are aware that your sister Margaret is the lover of the lord of the manor? Everybody seems to see it, but yourself. I have reason to know that the very day you receive this she will be meeting him at about 7.30 P.M. under the old elm in the beech-wood near the Hall-park.
   "ONE WHO SHALL BE NAMELESS."

Hogarth received it by post the next morning.

He had to think, as he worked, of something to say at the service that night on the text: "God's way is in the Sea," but the glare of forge and heated metal swam vaguely, a fog of red, about his consciousness. And mixed with those recurring words: "the old elm," "God's way," something with a voice shouted inside him — a name — *Margaret*! Anon his face flushed to a dusky turbulence, and he hurled the sledge high to shatter the earth, like Thor.

Suddenly he had the thought that he would clean his rifle, and, dropping a hot iron which vanished with a stifled cry into black water, he tossed his tongs clattering, and almost ran toward the cottage.

He had not, however, reached the back door when he heard his name called from behind.

And now happened to him the most momentous event of his life — though nothing could have seemed more commonplace.

It was an old fellow named Tom Bates who had called him — father to that Fred arrested for the murder of his wife — a Yarmouth fisher and herring-curer.

And when Hogarth twisted round, with that stare of his large and bloodshot eye, "Here," said the old man, "take them" —

holding out a basket of herrings.

Hogarth seemed not to understand, but then said: "All those for me?"

"Every bloomin' one!" answered Bates, with the dropped jaw of pantomime, and a far-away look of blue astonishment which he had.

"It is extremely handsome of you. Can you spare all that — ?"

"Spare, *ya'as!* They're easy enough come by, for that matter. Why, the day's work of a fisherman gives him enough fish to live on all the week, and he could lie around idling the other six days, if he chose, only anybody can't live on nothing but fish ."

These words, destined to produce a horror of great darkness, and a cup of trembling of which all the nations should drink, hardly affected Hogarth at the time. He *did*, indeed, shoot an interested glance at the old man, but the next moment his mind, numb that morning, was left dark.

"Here — take them — they are yours," said Bates. "But with regard to that God-forsaken son of mine: you'll be givin' evidence agen him, I'm told —"

When his sleeve wiped a tear, Hogarth promised to make his evidence mild, and was left alone.

Now his purpose of cleaning the rifle was turned: he went back to the forge, and worked till Margaret, at one o'clock, called: "The dinner is on the table."

At that table, for a long time, silence reigned, Margaret's eyes fixed on his face, his on his plate.

Toward the end he said: "Are you going to chapel tonight?"

Her bosom heaved; she cleared her throat: she had to meet Frankl by the towing path.

"I don't think I shall . . ."

Margaret!

"Why not?"

"I have something to do."

"*What?*"

Silence.

"*What?*"

"Something" — with a stubborn nod, and pallor — "if I tell you *something* that should be enough."

"You will go to chapel tonight."

"That I shan't."

"Yes"

Silence.

A little before seven they left the cottage together for the chapel, Hogarth taking his hunting-crop — from habit; he had also a little Bible; in his jacket, tight at the slight waist, unbuttoned at the breast, lay the anonymous letter, and a little poetry book, neither moon nor star lighting the night, bleak winds swooping like the typhoon among the year's dead leaves.

The chapel was a paltry place, though in the wall to the right of the preacher was a slab bearing the inscription:

ON THIS STONE
JOHN WESLEY PREACHED
IN THE VILLAGE, ON THE
9TH JULY 1768

And they sang a hymn; Hogarth "prayed"; read a chapter; once more the harmonium mourned; Hogarth gave the text: "God's way is in the sea . . ."

Even as he uttered it, he happened to glance toward the "mission-pew" — a square pew rather behind the pulpit: Margaret no longer there.

A paleness as of very death — then a dreadful wrath reddened his dark face.

He seized his hunting-crop; and, without a word, sped bent and thievish down the steps — and was gone.

Upon which Loveday in a middle pew, perceiving here something sinister, like a still wind flew to a back door, before ever the amazement of the people had given place to a flutter like leafage; and running fast, he came up with Hogarth by a stile twenty yards behind the chapel, touched his shoulder.

"To the devil with you . . .!" shouted Hogarth, running still, and there Loveday stood.

Margaret, meantime, was hurrying toward the towing path, while Richard, in a direction at right angles to hers, was pelting toward that spot terrible to him — the elm.

At the moment when he entered the deep darkness of the beeches, he heard what sounded like a pistol shot, rain now falling drop by drop, and through the forest with an uplifting whoop, like batsmen, swooped the tomboy winds.

Now, approaching the elm, again he felt that thrill which the spot had for him, and came peering, at slower pace: no sound but the gibbering rout of the stiff-stark beech-leaves. Some steps more, and now he was at the mound which surrounds the tree: stood, listened: silence, sightlessness: Margaret not there.

One more forward step: and now his foot struck a body.

As he stooped, his hand touched a revolver — which was his

own; another moment, and he saw running lanterns borne by two park-keepers, and by their light saw the body of Isaac, who but now had shot himself with the weapon that was in Hogarth's hand.

The park-keepers had just been urged by their master to the spot, he having, he told them, heard a pistol shot; and before anyone could speak Frankl himself was there, defiled with the presence of the dead.

He looked from Hogarth to the corpse, and from the corpse to Hogarth, then, snatching the weapon from Hogarth's hand, exclaimed: "Why, bless my heart, you've *murdered* the man. . . ."

XI

WROXHAM BROAD

In a cottage in Thring Street, marked "E. Norfolk, E. 58, Constabulary," Hogarth passed the night, having been arrested the moment he returned home from the elm.

A few minutes afterwards Margaret, who had found no Frankl at the towing path, came home to the ghastliest amazement throughout Thring, so that sleep overcame the village only toward morning.

At 7.30 A.M. Hogarth was marched to Beccles, then after an inquest-verdict appeared before the magistrates' court, and was committed.

One of the witnesses in the summary-jurisdiction court had been Loveday, who had deposed that Hogarth, on leaving the chapel, was, beyond doubt, in a passion; and mixed with the crowd was Margaret, who, standing thickly veiled, heard that evidence. And thought she: "Is it possible that he can be giving evidence against Richard like that? And smiling, the mean, false thing —"

She had disappeared on the morning after the arrest: and Loveday was now racked by disquiet, wondering how she was living, though she and he were in the same train, unconscious of each other, when he followed Hogarth to Norwich; and, as Margaret stepped upon the Thorpe platform there, a Jew, who was watching the arrival of every train, spied and shadowed her to the old Maid's Head, this intricate city being now crowded, the Assizes all in the air, mixed with the Saturday cattle-market.

At ten the next morning Margaret learned at the Guildhall the address of her brother's defending solicitor, and set out to find him, the wretchedest woman on earth now.

But as she passed by the archway in the tower of St. Peter Mancroft, Loveday stood before her; and she started like a shying horse.

"Good morning" — she went on past him.

He took two steps after her. "Are you in a hurry? Can I come with you?"

"It is quite near. Thank you — I'd liefer go alone."

He, a delicate being, all nerves, was repelled; lifted the old cloth hat; but then again stepped after her, saying: "But are you angry with me for something?"

"Why should I be? I have no right to expect anything from you, Mr. Loveday."

"No right? You *have*, a little, I fancy!"

He said it at her ear with such a lowering of the eyelids, that it pierced to her fond heart, and she smiled with a "H'm!" uncertain, half turned to him; but said: "I must be getting on —"

"But it is most important that I should talk to you about everything. Where are you staying?"

"It is some distance from here," she answered, undecided whether or not to give her address.

"Ah — in that case — but still — will you meet me? Say here — this evening?"

"I will see if I can."

"At seven?"

"I will see."

So they parted, she to tread that intricacy of streets round the Market, with stoppages for enquiries, till she found the office, where she presently sat in an inner room, veil at nose-tip, and before her at a grate stood Hogarth's solicitor.

What, till now, for shame, she had concealed, she revealed: showing how Richard could not possibly have taken the revolver with him to the elm, since she, two days previously, had secretly given it to — someone.

Mr. Carr, the solicitor, frowned, elaborating his nails.

"This is very extraordinary," he said. "Whyever did you keep us in the dark as to all this before? And to whom was it that you gave the revolver? and why?"

"Am I bound to tell that?"

"No, but you may be sure that the truth will be got from you. Stay — I must ask you to excuse me now. But tomorrow morning at this hour — will you? As for your brother, have no fears at all: he is now absolutely safe."

Margaret went rapidly away, not knowing whither, only returning toward late afternoon to her inn. As she entered, a letter was handed her from Frankl.

"Dear Miss Hogarth:

"It is only due to you that I should see you at once to explain the mystery of this affair, so as to clear your brother, and as it would not do for me to call upon you for obvious reasons, the only thing for us to do is to meet tonight on Mousehold Heath at 7 P.M. without fail . . ."

What now was she to do? At "7 P.M." she had half promised Loveday to meet him.

And what had her meetings with Baruch Frankl, innocent as they were, brought upon her and hers!

Yet Frankl *must* be kindly intentioned, she reasoned — since he had sent them the £50; and she thought of that agony of humiliation when she had asked Loveday for £2, and he had refused.

And he had given evidence against Richard with his down-turned smile.

But he had said a word at her ear — and her crushed heart had leapt. She did not know what to do, fell by her bedside and prayed to be taught which of the two was Richard's best friend.

As she passed over the inn-threshold, she decided in favour of Frankl: and a few minutes past seven was on Mousehold Heath.

Frankl hurried to meet her, and the hand which he held out was rather cold; but she did not take it.

"No, Mr. Frankl," said she, "before I give my hand, it is only what is due to me to hear how Richard's pistol, which I trusted to you, was found where it was —"

"Well, that is only fair," answered Frankl; "that is only fair. But I have a carriage there, let us get into it, and sit as we talk."

She could see no carriage in that dark, yet it stood only some yards away — Frankl's own.

"I think I prefer to stand . . ." said she.

"As you like. But with regard to the gun, I should have thought that you could have guessed how it was — but no, you always mistrust me instead — the Jew. Don't you know that the dead man was a servant in my house? Well, I left the two guns in my study, and he, wanting to shoot himself, stole one, that's all."

"It was *he* shot himself?"

"Why, who else? You don't suppose Richard shot him! You are as cool as they make them."

"Well, that was how it was! But couldn't you say that at the police-court — ?"

"I am *going* to at the big trial, of course. But I was ill, am ill now, and here have I been running about all day on your brother's behalf, and dead tired — and ill, and all — and you won't let me have a rest in the carriage —"

"Well, as you put it in that way . . ." she said.

So they walked to a motor-brougham, sat within, and as they commenced to talk again, the brougham moved.

"Tell me," said Frankl, "have you mentioned to anyone that you had given the guns to me?"

"I told Richard's solicitor this morning —"

"That was horribly imprudent, without consulting me!"

"I think I have been silent long enough, don't you? I didn't mention your name, but —"

"Oh, you didn't mention my name! That's all right, then! Look here, do you know — ?"

"Well?"

"I believe you love me in your heart. Can't help yourself."

"Oh, Mr. Frankl, do I look as if I was in the mood for that kind of fun tonight, a poor wretch like me, steeped in misery, my God knows."

"*I* love *you*!"

He suddenly grasped her wrist, his eyes blazing.

"Stop — let me get out of this —" she said.

"Wait! — I give you your chance! — Listen: I am not a man whose mind you can read right off like a book, I twist like an eel, I am deep, I am tricky, and I never yet met the man that I didn't hoodwink. Ninety-nine per cent of what I say is a lie; even when it is the truth, it is a lie just the same. But at this particular moment I am talking the God's truth: I want you! You shall be my little girl! Chuck Richard! — chuck the swine's-flesh! — I'll take you right away — to Paris — this very night —"

She had arisen, alarmed by his hissed fury. "But, you are stark, staring, raving mad," she said proudly, "that is what you are."

Frankl struck the side of the brougham, it flew, and Margaret tottered backward with an exclamation. The next moment she sent forth a scream, the grip of Frankl on her wrist agonizing her bones.

"Where are we going?" she cried out.

"I gave you your chance!" was Frankl's fierce answer.

"Let me get out! — you must be a wretch — to take advantage —"

He put his mouth to her ear till it touched. "Your nice Richard flogged me like a dog! I felt the cuts to the marrow of my damned soul! Now I've got him in the hollow of this hand! Why, you helped me! you helped me! That's good! And I've got you, too."

Blackness and swiftness bound her; a dizziness overcame her. Soon they were by a great pool of gloomy water — Wroxham Broad — where hern, wild duck, and the mast of the darkling boat brooded among bulrush; and now in three minutes more the brougham was sweeping over the lawn of a lonely building, surrounded by walls.

She, peering, saw with joy both lights and a well-dressed man and woman; and, as the carriage stopped, she sprang out with alacrity, Frankl with her, still grasping her wrist.

"Sir," she blurted out at once, "you will help me, I know. I am a poor unfortunate woman — my name is Margaret Hogarth —"

"We know!" said the gentleman, and, approaching Frankl's ear, asked in Yiddish: "How long has she had her delusion?"

"Only about a week, I think. She may be violent at first, but —"

"Come in, Miss — Hogarth," said the gentleman.

Margaret passed the threshold; the doors closed upon her . . .

XII

THE ROSE

On the third morning of his confinement in Norwich, Hogarth was hurried into the hall of justice and the witness-box — in the dock Fred Bates.

Bates had denied — with sufficient impudence, it seemed: for his wife had been found dead, battered and burned about the face, Bates' own hand also burned by the poker with which, *red-hot*, he was presumed to have beaten her.

The same afternoon Bates was sentenced to death: but, having had sunstroke in Egypt, was afterwards reprieved.

And two mornings later Hogarth heard the bar of the prisoner's dock clang behind himself.

The speech of leading counsel for the Crown was short: a letter, found on the prisoner, would be produced, in which some busybody had falsely informed the prisoner that Mr. Frankl would meet his sister under a certain elm-tree: and the prisoner, in a crisis of passion, had hurried from the pulpit to that tree, on observing that his sister had left the chapel (to keep a real appointment with Mr. Frankl elsewhere). Under that tree the prisoner had encountered the murdered man, whose Oriental dress on a dark night would give him a resemblance to Mr. Frankl, himself a Jew. The prisoner had then shot the deceased, mistaking him for Mr. Frankl, and had been found holding the smoking weapon, which he admitted to be his own. It was a painful case; but the chain of inference was not assailable.

"Not assailable" found an echo in the minds of solicitor and counsel for Hogarth, who with growing anxiety were awaiting the coming of Margaret with her story of the weapons. Margaret was where her name was changed to Rachel.

Now was the régime of examining counsel for the prosecution. The usher called: "Baruch Frankl!"

A voice in the gallery shouted: "Caps and tassels!" while Frankl, in the witness box, bowed largely to both bench and bar. He put his palms on the red-hot rail, caught them up, put them again, caught up, put them; and still he bowed, while a trembling of the chin gave to his beard a downward waving.

"Now explain to the court the reasons for the state of the prisoner's feelings toward you."

"For one thing I had turned him out, because he could not pay his rent; for another, his sister was inclined, my lord, to be a little bit weak on my account —"

"A little bit *what*?" asked his lordship.

"Just a little bit weak, my lord."

"A *reciprocal* weakness?"

"Well, my lord, you know the world — so do the gentlemen of the jury —"

"And of the Jewry!" screamed his lordship, amid laughter from the merry wigs.

As Frankl stepped down, a name was called at which Hogarth went cold as a ghost: "Rebekah Frankl."

And in she stepped splendent, to stand like a Nubian woman, with that retreat of the hips, her ears torn with their load of gold, her throat and breast ablaze, she bringing into that English court the gaudy heat of the Orient, Baal and Astarté, orgies of Hindoo women in temples of Parvati, the pallid passion of Bacchantes. Though not tall, she was lofty, and her ebon eyes had that very royalty of the stare of the bent form in the dock, whose heart throbbed quick like paddle-wheels that thrash the sea, she his wild divinity, wild wife of his wild youth. . . .

At her shocking beauty the Court stood hushed.

She suggested the East: but in her speech was the energy of the West — sharp — a bass almost like her father's.

"You recognize the prisoner?"

"Yes." She smiled.

"You were present on the day of the 11th November when the prisoner entered your father's house, and attempted to strike him?"

"Did strike him."

"He did?"

"Yes."

"Did he seem in a passion?"

"Seemed severe."

"Severe! But was he not highly excited?"

"He did not seem so. Frowned and flogged."

"By whom was he ejected?"

"Went of his own accord."

"But — try to remember. What made him go?"

"He suddenly saw *me*, and fled."

Laughter droned through the court, in which she naïvely joined, while Hogarth's eyes and hers met one instant, blazed outrageously, and dropped. . . .

That was all. Counsel bowed.

The day grew toward evening, and still the stuffy Court sat.

But Margaret Hogarth did not come; a defending counsel finished examination, counsel on the other side again addressed the Court, and again defending counsel. The judge then held the scales, the jury trooped away, the crowd buzzed.

The light in the room seemed to brood to a denser yellow, and anon to grow dim; the stuffed court festered; voices spoke, but low. The King of Terrors was here.

When the jury came, the judge was called, Hogarth stood up, and the clerk of arraigns put a question to the foreman.

The foreman said: "We find the prisoner guilty: but beg to recommend him to the mercy of the Crown."

"On what grounds?" asked his lordship.

"On the grounds of past good conduct and strong provocation."

The judge then placed on his head a square of velvet and passed the sentence of the Court.

During the reign of stillness that followed, while the court clock's ticking was still loud, something which was thrown struck Hogarth on the arm, a red rose, black at heart, that had lain on the breast of Rebekah, who, when Hogarth looked round at her, was calmly drawing her mass of cloak about her throat.

XIII

OUT OF THE WORLD

A week later a governor and a chaplain together entered Hogarth's cell with news of his reprieve.

Eight months later he was being trundled in "Black Maria" to Paddington Station amid a Babel of escaped tongues, when, sitting in his pigeonhole, he heard the unknown voice before him cry: "Well, Jim, we're away to the mountain's brow!"

Jim, nothing but a voice, was heard: "Worse luck! I knows Colmoor, and I knows the Scrubs, and I knows Portland; and of the five I say — give me Jedwood. Who's the guy in front o' you?"

"Hi, you in front there, who *are* yer?" cried the first, pounding.

He was answered by a deep voice, which said:

"I AM WHO I AM."

"All right, keep yer 'air on, if you've any left! It's the Lawd Chief Justice, mate! 'E says 'e's 'oo 'e are!"

"''Old on! *I* knows who it is: it's that newcomer, 33. They say he was once a priest —"

But now speech was swallowed up in hubbub, as the van ran battering down a rough street near the station.

Then again Hogarth was whirled into night and space, and, toward morning, after the bumping climb of a van, was bidden to alight on moorland, where he spied, far off, set on a hill, a mighty palace of Romance, all grim, aloof, which was Colmoor.

The next morning while the outdoor gangs were being searched on parade before the exit, Hogarth saw a face which he knew; and "You, Bates," he said, "I thought you were in Eternity!"

But no: there stood Bates, all capped and arrowed, cropped and neat, not wearing the filthy old scarf of liberty any more.

The neighbor of Hogarth now was a stout man, with black hair, and grey eyes.

He it was who had been — a priest: and in "Black Maria" had given that answer: "I am who I am."

XIV

THE PRIEST

A year passed, during which John Loveday exhausted the resources of civilization, (1)in seeking Margaret, and (2)in investigating the innocence of Richard.

He had, however, a sprightly, adventurous nerve in the mind, and would pull his velvet sleeves busily up — such was his little way. He began to plot.

About the same time the ex-priest, in that far-off world of Colmoor, said one day to Hogarth: "*You* won't be here long!"

"You jest," Hogarth answered; "if I had the chance of escape, I should never take it. I am here by due legal process."

"Tut, if I say that you will escape, it is not because I am a prophet, but a man of the world, and know what happens in it."

Converse with this deep, world-wise, and fluent man had now become to Hogarth like manna, or rather a vice, like opium: for in those grey eyes of the cleric was hinted anon the baleful glint of the cobra's.

That day, a Saturday, outdoor gangs were recalled early, to "clean up" for Sunday, and out across the heath rang the great bell, Colmoor being famous for its bell, its tone and great size, larger than even the eight-ton "Mighty Tom" of Christ Church, for though its thickness was only six inches, it weighed, bell and clapper, ten tons, and was seven feet high and seven in diameter.

A busy Saturday afternoon ensued, and whatsoever Hogarth's hand found to do he did it with his might, though his face now seemed all eyes — brown, bloodshot, imperially large, morbidly staring.

He was giving the finishing touches of order to his wooden spoon and salt-cellar, his tin knife, plate, and pint cup for gruel, when a Warder Jennings peeped in with, "No. 76 — you are to follow the assistant warder at once," and Hogarth descended to an anteroom where an official handed him a letter, which had been read and initialed by governor and chaplain.

An event! — a letter in Colmoor, like a shark's fin on the voyages of old sailing ships.

It was from Loveday, and concluded with a reference to Hogarth's "poor old grandmother."

So Hogarth, who had no "grandmother," propped his forehead to ponder that thing; and presently said: "Oh, it is a cypher."

And by noting little peculiarities in the shapes of the letters, a double cross to a t, a q like a g, etc., he soon had "flemecops-leftquary" — which he took to mean: "flee to me in the copse to the left of the quarry."

He smiled with tenderness at the dear heart planning and daring so very much for him. But in his smile was a touch of disdain also, he not intending to "flee."

XV

MONSIGNOR

Hogarth's first thought, as getting-up bell clattered réveille through the gallery, was of Loveday's cypher, and by the time the warder came to ask if he would see governor or doctor, a thought of Monsignor O'Hara had somehow mixed itself with the thought of the cypher; when an orderly handed in the day's brown loaf, he was thinking, "Strange that he never told me what he has done"; eating his pint of gruel, he thought: "If I will not escape myself, I might perhaps let another."

"What!" said O'Hara on the march out, "you still here?"

"Where should I be?" answered Hogarth, dull and sullen.

"Where palaces stand open for you, and bank-notes — have you ever realized something very charming in the Helen pallor of a bank-note, Hogarth? And gold-yellow, sparkling gold! Hogarth, I — *love* gold! It is a confession —"

"Is it that love which brought you here?" Hogarth asked with his sideward stare.

Whereupon the priest turned a cold gaze upon him — had regarded Hogarth as a well-bred man, or would hardly have conversed with him.

"I had a motive for asking," said Hogarth, eyeing the face of the prelate — a man of very coarse feature; a small head, made to receive the tonsure, with a low brow; a stern bottom lip, and long upper; a fat neck held majestically erect; and up stuck his double chin. In profile, the part between the sharp edge of the bottom lip and the chin-tip was divided, down near the chin tip, by an angle and crease; and the lower face seemed too massive for the size of the head.

Nothing could be more exquisite than the contrast between his air of force, authority and importance, and the knickerbockers, the coarse cap, the canvas slop-jacket, which he wore.

Outwardly calm, he was yet very excited by that "I had a motive"; he said to himself: "Suppose this man has some plan! He could invent ten, if he only knew it. And suppose he would tell me it, if I make him believe me innocent! It would be like him!"

When the eleven o'clock dinner-bell rang, and they two were again together, O'Hara said: "Hogarth, I have for some time been intending to give you my story. Have I in your eyes the air of a guilty man?"

"God knows," answered Hogarth, with a shrug; "you talk nicely, and you know much."

"So much for the hollowness of friendship!"

"Don't be sentimental," said Hogarth: "I never pretended to be any friend of yours; but I do respect your talents, do pity your misery: and if I knew the solid facts of, as you have said, your 'innocence', I might —"

"*What?*" whispered O'Hara with a thievish, fierce glance.

"Help you."

"*In God's truth?*"

"I might."

O'Hara said: "I don't find it so cold as it was this morning. You must have observed a certain peculiarity of moorland climates — the same being true of the Roman Campagna, and of Irish peat-lands — that they are colder than elsewhere in the absence of the sun, and warmer in its presence. This afternoon — *I will tell you —*"

They had reached the great gates, and were marched to parade-ground for the second of the four daily searches; then, after three ounces of fat mutton and forty minutes' rest, the third search, the second march-out.

And immediately beyond the gates O'Hara began: "In order to paint you my life, Hogarth, I must give you at once to understand what has been its mainspring and secret: my passion for my Church —"

He paused, while his lips moved in prayer, and he crossed himself.

"From boyhood my dream was to see my Church supreme in the warfare of the world, I being a King's College and Maynooth man, at twenty-three was Senior Chancellor's Medallist, and seven years later, sent to Rome was quickly received into the Vatican household. It was recognized that I had a future: both gifts and graces; piety; a versatile tongue; a powerful voice; some learning; could dine, I could look august; above all, I knew my man and could talk him over. My great day came when, one morning, in St. Gregory the Great on Mount Coelius, I was consecrated Bishop Coadjutor to his Eminence the Archbishop of Westminster. Now I was on the heights. My life during the next ten years was a life of bustling action — and was led always with one unselfish object. No man ever spoke a greater number of words than I, Hogarth. I have breakfasted with the Prime Minister, lunched with a President of the Conference, and dined with the Bishop of London: between the three meals I have written a hundred letters and pitched into ten cabs. Such a life is very exhilarating, in comparison, for example, with quarrying. Oh, my God what am I fallen! Most of that time I was running over Europe: from Madrid to Vienna, from Rouen to Rome. It happened that the Archbishop of Paris was organizing a scheme of Church-workhouses in France, in the absence of municipal ones, such as we have here. . . . Well, it was a grand thing, but was falling through for lack of funds: so I, on my way to Rome, undertook the mission to plead the cause before his Holiness, and succeeded to this extent that, on my return, I had with me a casket from the good old man containing seven diamonds, which I might either dispose of personally, or hand over to the Paris fund. Now, it was during my stay at Rome that that series of events, culminating in the Jewish exodus from Europe, occurred; and on my journey home I was seized with the mighty thought that, since many of the Jews were perishing of want, *that* was the moment to reach their spirit through the body, and add their race to the trophies of the Church. Was it not a thought? You yourself, who are a Jew —"

Hogarth's eyes opened in surprise. "*I* am not a Jew."

"No? I should have said that there was a hint of expression somewhere — But to resume. I retained those seven diamonds, and disposed of them."

"Honest behaviour!"

"Perfectly honest! I acquainted the Pope — he sanctioned it! And now, I, single-handed almost, threw myself into that task. I hired, I built, I begged, I borrowed, I formed committees, I haunted Religious Houses, I sweated, I ran, I wept, I visited dens, I smoked opium, I drank gin, I framed memorials, I learned Yiddish, I read the Mishna and Gemara, I interviewed Rabbonim, I wrote tracts: I was busy. In the midst of it, I had to visit Rome ceremoniously, to assist at an interview between the Duke of York and his Holiness — arrived on the Monday, and on the Wednesday, I remember, attended a Court Ball in the suite of his Royal Highness. That night, when I returned to the Vatican, I found all the Piazza di San Pietro crowded. I do not know if you were free at the time when my friend, M. Tissot, startled everybody by predicting the collision of an asteroid with the earth? Tut, the silly being — he should have known from the body's response to the spectroscope that its condition was too friable to resist our atmosphere. But I never yet knew an astronomer not imbued with sensationalism they acquire a certain megalomania from their intercourse with space. But, at all events, the people, dreading the destruction of everything, had crowded toward the Vatican. The Duke of Genoa,

I, and some of the College of Cardinals, stood watching from a balcony; and very imposing, I remember, was the moment when a glare appeared — I must stop —"

They were at the face of the rock, and the "halt" and "set to work" parted them.

But again on the final march back at 5.15 when nightshades were falling fast like snow, and the arm now felt the pick a load, O'Hara began his muttering:

"I was telling you about the asteroid," he said. "Now this body, it was given out, contained diamonds in large evidence, and the mere thought of such a thing bursting in mid-air, and scattering itself about was, I — I confess, a little fascinating to my mind. A man might let his soul gloat upon such a hope till he went lunatic with lust! I — I confess, the thought was alluring to me. Diamond, my son: lucid — But when the body burst, and none of it came my way, I drove it from my mind: in fact, I never heard of a trace of it having been seen — hissed itself into gases in mid-air. Except in one instance — one instance.

"When I reached Calais on my homeward way, stopped there a day, awaiting the coming of Rouen, for whom I had nuncio communications, and in the evening went to visit a cottage where I had once been a great favourite with an old fellow called Santé- you know those Calais fishers, with painted sabots, and ochred trousers. And 'What!' said I to Santé, 'the nets already spread at this hour?' 'Nothing to be done today, my Father', he answered, and explained that he had attempted to pick up a stone before his door, and — it had burned him: he showed it me: it had the appearance of a piece of ferruginous rock, stuck with pieces of dirty glass; and it had burned Santé on the midnight of the asteroid's scattering.

"Imagine my excitement: 'The asteroid', I thought, 'may add fifty thousand Jews to the Church'. I asked Santé for the stone — Do you blame me?"

"Go on," said Hogarth.

"That day two months I had the diamonds lying polished in a casket in my house. My evil destiny, Hogarth, ordained that the casket was the one given me for Paris by the Pope, the number of the new diamonds the same — seven: and one day, about that time, the Vatican organ, the *Osservatore Romano*, published a dreadful article, hinting that I had applied to my own purposes seven diamonds entrusted me for Paris: the Pope, just dead, must have left some record of his gift. My friend, before I had heard a whisper of the attack upon me, the casket, whose lid was mosaicked with the Papal fanon, was secretly searched by a secretary in my house: the seven diamonds were seen.

"Imagine the horror of what followed: I was abandoned by all — superior and inferior; the story of the meteor was received with sneers. The scandal reached the public papers — the public prosecutor. And here now is the wretch, Patrick O'Hara."

The latter part of this narrative was fiction! The Pope's diamonds O'Hara had duly handed to the Archbishop! and though there was such a man as Santé, no asteroid had ever fallen at his door. In fact, O'Hara was "serving time" for an assault upon a lady in a railway compartment between Whitchurch and Salisbury.

But Hogarth spent that night in meditating the pros and cons as to O'Hara's escaping; and, in a moment of destiny, said at last: "If he is undeservedly doomed —" and swooned to sleep.

The very next day was foggy. . . .

On the march out O'Hara said: "Here is something like a fog. On the Carinthian Alps, where you have dense woolly fogs, there is a race of goats, which —"

"Would you like to escape?" whispered Hogarth.

"*Who?*"

"You."

"Hogarth — ! My God — !"

A trembling seized the priest's leathery left cheek, he at that instant seeing a vision of the world — Andalusian wines, hued ices, the opera-house, and great greyhounds of the sea, and a snuff which his gross nose loved at Gorey.

"Hogarth, you are not mocking me?" chattered the priest's jaws, hurrying like a jarred spring.

"I am quite serious. You will have to run for it though."

"*Run!* I am not such a young man! Have pity Hogarth."

"Bah! Be a man."

The priest approached his mouth to Hogarth's ear: "*I should die of fright!* My heart —"

"What would it matter? I thought you had more beans."

"But have you — a plan?"

"Yes. You must run to the copse —"

"I shall be shot!"

"Probably."

"I *could* not —"

"Then, do not."

"Tell me, boy! Tell me, Hogarth . . ."

"Within the copse to the left of the quarry there is almost certainly at this moment waiting a man who, as soon as you pronounce my name, will help you —"

"You say *almost* certainly."

"I can't see him, O'Hara. But I should say he is there on a morning like this."

"*What* a risk! *What* a risk!" went the priest with lifted eyelids each time.

"You cannot escape from prison without risk. But I, personally, would venture upon ten times as much, if I thought it becoming. There is, however, another risk: that you may not strike the part of the copse where he is. But near the 1 middle it is high —"

"Why, it is nothing but risks!" whined O'Hara with opening arms.

"You are not bound to try it. By the way — can you swim?"

"Yes — I suppose so — yes."

"Then lift yourself to it, and risk it. I should, if I were you. Think of liberty, activity. Prick your spirit, grip at it, and spring it."

"Do you think I shall be shot?"

"No! It does not matter! Crush your doubts, martyr yourself to your aim, and your aim will give you the crown of martyrdom."

"Well — God reward you — I will think of it —"

"*Do* it!"

"I will!"

"In that case, don't trust to your own eyes — *I* will give you the signal with my handkerchief — so: you keep your eyes fixed on me. Then run, zigzagging. And tell Loveday for me to look after you, and not make any more plans for me. Good-bye, O'Hara! All this is very unselfish of me, for I lose my old talky-talky O'Hara —"

They parted at the rock, and set to work.

As minutes, half-hours passed, the condition of O'Hara became piteous, hideous. His knees knocked together. Like death he dreaded, like life awaited, that signal. He said to himself: "This Hogarth will be my ruin . . . God deal not with me after my sins . . .!"

Hogarth was waiting that the warders' morning watchfulness might yield to the influence of use and time; but near nine, when the morning fog showed signs of thinning, he approached the water-can to ask for a drink, O'Hara being then two yards from him, wheeling a barrow.

As he stooped to the water, his huge stare ranged the moor, took in the truth of it, and, after waiting ten, fifteen seconds, he upset the can. As two officers, at the outcry, ran toward the spot,

Hogarth, his eyes fixed upon them, waited — and all at once, with a flourish, drew his handkerchief.

O'Hara, with a heavy but impassioned run, was away . . .

He had not run five yards when a chorus of whistles was shrilling.

And quick, that monotony reels into a very frenzy of sensation: it is no more the same world, the same men. Lo, in the Palace of Continuity is an Event.

33 was off.

Five hundred pairs of eyes lit up, and the flurried warders ran in random dismay to see to it! How if all the five hundred should do the like, simultaneously? — a possibility underlying, through all its breadth, the little social "system" which has produced Colmoor.

But the five hundred, exhorted, stamped at, shouted at, remained quiet, though restive, only the wild eye showing the wild thought, while two of the warders pursued O'Hara who had also to run the blockade of two pickets of the civil guard.

The escaping convict, however, has this advantage: that his mind is strung to a far higher pitch than his pursuers'; and, given a certain ecstasy, everything can be accomplished.

So O'Hara separately dodged the two pickets, and was making bolt for the copse before three rifles, aimed at a large vague ghost, rang out, and did not hit. He plunged madly into the brambly bush.

Immediately a bleating like a child's trumpet was heard from its midst; and in a few seconds, not one, but *four*, men were seen to rush toward the river, all in convict knickerbockers, stockings, caps, all in black overcoats: and one carried a bundle.

Beyond the river one was shot in the leg — a black sailor, who, with two roughs, had undertaken the risk for lucre. The rest escaped.

XVI

THE ROPE

Soon after this Hogarth was taken with vomitings, his heart retching at Colmoor. His dark cheeks jaundiced; those mobile nostrils of his small bony nose yawned, like an exhausted horse's; his face was all a light of eyes.

Whether or not some suspicion of his complicity with O'Hara had occurred to the authorities, he now found himself transferred to another "graft": from quarrying was set to trenching.

Four things are inexhaustible in the earth: the hope of a gambler; the sea; the lip of a lover; and the capacity of Colmoor to be trenched and quarried.

And in Hogarth's new gang was — Fred Bates.

One day, Hogarth, intent upon his work, heard a sob and, glancing, saw that Bates had dropped his spade and buried his face in his hands.

"What, Fred, not giving in?" He went quickly and pressed his palm on Bates' brow, saying: "Patience! Stiffen your back: look how *I* slip into it!"

"Ah, Hogarth, you don't know. I am an innocent man."

"So am I."

"Yes, but *I* was certain in my own mind to be out within anyway, six months; *you* wasn't. That makes a difference, don't it? That touches the nerve, don't it? Ah!"

"And how did you expect to be out?"

"I had a brother-Bob-in the 9th Lancers in Punjab and his regiment was ordered home just a week before I was arrested. Well, the morning after the missus was killed, I went early — for I knew I'd soon be arrested — to a stableman at Beccles — you know old Harris — and I made him swear to give a letter to Bob the moment Bob put foot in Southampton, and to nobody else. In the letter I told Bob where he was to look for so-and-so, and how he was to prove my innocence —"

"But I don't understand a word of what you are saying," interrupted Hogarth.

"I'll tell you. I did not kill my Kit. The burn on her face, and on my hand, wasn't any red-hot poker. Did you ever hear such bosh? Look here, you mind, don't you, the talk that week about the world getting blowed up by some comet? Well, about 3 P.M. on the comet day, as I was walking home through Lagden Dip, an old gent, the same as took the farm over after you, he comes up to me, and he says: 'If you should happen to see anywhere in your travels', sez 'e, laughin' and rubbin' his hands, 'a piece of hot iron after eleven tonight, you bring it to me, and I'll put a cheque for One Thousand Pounds there in the middle of your palm'. Well — I said it was a Wednesday, didn't I? And Wednesday bein' the pay-day on the Eastern, me and the missus had a drop o' beer that afternoon, and you know 'ow you come and catched me a-paying of her — dirty dog that I was those days. But, Hogarth, you hadn't hardly gone when we made it up between us, and the rest of that evening we was just like — well — two bloomin', cooin' doves! kissin', blubblin', havin' drinks, and doin' our week's shoppin' together. Well — stop, here's Black —"

They were interrupted, and for two days found no other chance.

Two days during which Hogarth received another letter from Loveday, of which one paragraph was as follows: "The fifteen pounds which you left in Lloyd's Bank I have managed to with-draw for you on the authority of your aunt, Miss Sarah Hogarth," and at once he scented a cypher, having no fifteen pounds, and no aunt.

When he had unravelled it as before, he had: "Why you failed? Expect — Balloon — Rope."

He was astounded: and could only conclude that O'Hara had not delivered his message.

And as the image of O'Hara had mixed itself with his thoughts of the copse, so now the image of Fred Bates mixed itself with the balloon.

It was partly through *his* evidence that Bates was here . . .!

On the third day Bates, as though he had just left off, resumed his story:

"You know Seely's, the general shop, at Priddlestone," said he; "it was there we always did our Wednesday-night marketin' — nobody would believe what high old jinks those Wednesday pay-days was to us Great Eastern blokes! By the time we reached Priddlestone, we had a quart of four-ale down us, let alone what we'd had before, and, as the saying is, one glass leads to another. By now we was feeling just nicely, thank you, and instead of going to Seely's, we took a short cut to 'The Broom', and it was going on for past eleven when we found ourselves in — you know the beech-wood between Priddlestone and Thring — she singing all the time with her head thrown back, at the top of her voice.

"Hogarth, it gives me the creeps to think of! Suddenly it

looked as if the whole wood was lit up: there was the sky all cut up with streamers, I saw my Kit quite plain, then all at once there was a whishin' and a rushin' among the trees, like steam — and I saw my Kit drop smack. In two ticks my head was sober: but, as I ran to her, I staggered sideways upon my left hand, and I let such a *yell* out of me — had put my hand upon something flamin' hot.

"The minute I bent over my old woman I knew she was a deader; and I dropped down, and I called of her, and I shook of her, and it was quite two hours before I come to myself properly, by which time the affair what struck her down was gone out in darkness. Of course, the first thing I thought of was the old gent at Lagden. 'This should mean a cool thou', says I to myself. But I knew I should be arrested first thing in the morning, except I told plain out what had happened: and that, you bet, I didn't mean to do, for if once I mentioned that there piece of iron before I had it safe off the lord-o'-the-manor's land, I knew it 'ud be taken from me. But to take it off before another day or two was out of the question — it was too hot. So says I to myself: 'I'll *get* convicted; and tonight I'll write a letter to Bob, telling him where to find the affair, how to get the thou, and *after* he's got it, how to set about gettin' the case retried.'

"Well, so said, so done. You know that old elm in the beech-wood? I dug a grave at the foot of it, and managed to kick and roll the affair into the grave, then I took up my Kit, carried her home, and by the time I pegged out the letter to Bob, I saw day breakin'. So I made paces for Beccles, knocked up old Harris, and gave him the letter for Bob. By eight o'clock I was arrested —"

At this point the 5.15 recall-bell rang out, and there was falling into line.

The next time that they had speech together, Hogarth said: "And were you such a clown, Fred Bates, as to imperil your life for a paltry thousand pounds?"

"*Paltry* thousand pounds?" answered Bates, surprised: "Hark at this! Didn't I peril my life ten times more in Egypt for a bob a day? I tell you I was certain in my own mind of getting out in a few weeks!"

"Well, what happened to prevent you?"

"Only this: Bob died on the troop-ship coming home; that's all."

"But you could write old Harris to open your letter to Bob, and act on it, or else hand it over to your father."

"My word, but haven't I wrote? Old 'Arris is either dead and buried, or gorn away, or somethin'. I've waited a year and nine months — good God! and no answer yet."

"Poor Fred! I could weep blood for you. Believe in God!"

"More Devil than God about Colmoor, it strikes me."

"As though *you* knew! Suppose I strike you blind — *now* — with a flash of Him?"

"I don't take your meaning, sir," said Bates, with a strange heart-bound and sense of awe.

"Do you remember 33 of the quarry-gang, Fred?"

"Yes."

Hogarth whispered: "It was *I* who got him off."

Bates whitened to the lips. "I — I thought as much."

"There is yet another chance, which *you*, if you like, may take."

Bates saw heaven opening; but with this vague hope was left two days.

On the third, Hogarth explained what he assumed to be the new plan of Loveday.

"I take it," he said, "that he will pass over the moor in a balloon trailing a rope, which will have a loop to be slipped under the arms. I tell you, there are dangers in this scheme: you may be shot. Are you for trying it?"

"Trying it, aye," said Bates, with fifty times the boldness of O'Hara.

And now began for these two a painfulness of waiting days, the sleep of both, meanwhile, being one nightmare of confused affrights, balloons and deliriums.

Ten times they re-discussed every possibility of the scheme, Hogarth giving messages for Loveday, heaping counsels upon Bates. Nothing remained to be said, and still the days passed over the time-worn hearts, till a month went by.

At last something was observed in the sky — afar to the N.W. — in the afternoon turn, about two o'clock, a mist on the moor, but the sky almost cloudless.

Whereupon Hogarth, who first saw the object, stepped, as if looking for something, close to Bates, hissing: "*Goodbye*! Keep cool — choose well —"

Bates shovelled on steadily, as though this was a day like others; but twice his knees gave and bent beneath him; and there was a twitching of the livid under-lip, piteous to see.

It drew nearer, that silent needle, while Bates worked, delving, barrowing, making little trips; plenty of time; and no one noted his lip which pulled and twitched.

Without visible motion it came, wafted on the breaths of high heaven: half an hour — and still it was remote, fifteen hundred feet up. Bates and Hogarth peered to see a rope, but could none.

After fifty minutes it was actually over the moor, all now conscious of it; but the rope was indistinguishable from the air.

Yet it was there, walking the ground, at its end a horizontal staff. . . . Hogarth, with wiser forethought than Loveday's, had predicted, not a staff, but a loop.

It passed twenty yards from the quarry, Loveday no doubt imagining that Hogarth still worked there; but the quarry was some hundred and fifty yards from the trench.

Its course, nevertheless was toward the trench: and on walked deliberately the fluctuating rope, the staff now travelling the gorsey ground, now bounding like a kangaroo yards high, to come down once more yonder.

A moment came when Hogarth, with intense hiss, was whispering to himself: "If I were he, I should dash *now*."

But Fred Bates did not move.

Hogarth suffered agonies not less excruciating than the rack.

"Oh, whyever does he wait?" he groaned.

But now — all suddenly — it was known, it was felt, deep in five hundred ecstatic hearts, that a convict was gone — a man overboard — a soul in the agony — battling between life and death.

Like tempests the whistles split the air.

Where is he? Who is he? What mother bare him? It is 57! And he is *there*! — on high — caught, to the skies.

The tumbling of four ballast bags from the balloon was marked: the balloon darted high, wildly high; and with her, seated on the bar, the cord between his thighs, darted high Fred Bates.

Exultant! the five hundred faces wax fire-eyed, each heart a flame of madness. But yonder is Warder Black taking trembling, yet careful, aim: now the report is echoing from the two Tors, the granite-works; and that smoke no sooner thins than a whole volley of crackling musketry is winging toward that dot under the clouds.

And it was hideous — pitiful — the quailing heart waited and was still to see the dot dissever itself from its rod: he had been hit: was in the middle of the vast and vacant air: and wheeling he came.

A shockingly protracted interval did that fall fill up: the five hundred, gazing as at some wonder in heaven, did not, could not, breathe: the outraged heart seemed to rend the breast in a shriek. Would it *never* end, that somersault? Wheeling he came.

In reality it occupied much less than a minute: and now he is no more ethereal, but has grown, is grossly near, attended by the raving winds of his travelling: is arrived. And the thump of his coming was heard. As he touched the earth he jerked out circular. . . .

Here was a tragedy remembered many a year at Colmoor, and always with feelings of the deepest awe.

XVII

OLD TOM'S LETTER

The fate of Bates filled Hogarth's mind with a gloom so fune-real, that now his strength, his great patience, all but suc-cumbed.

One evening, while his broom lay stuck out under the notch of his cell-door in order that Warder Black might count him, he took his tin knife, and began to scratch over the hills and valleys of his corrugated wall some shining letters:

    VEN

He was now, after long reflection, convinced that he was the victim of a plot of Baruch Frankl's: yet in his heart was little ran-cour against Frankl, nor, when he wrote his "V E N," was he thinking specially of Frankl — hardly knew of whom, or what. It may have been of the system of things which had given to Frankl such vast powers over him; but, the "N" finished, he pshawed at himself, and threw the knife down. If something was wrong, he knew not at all how to right it, supposing the world had been his to guide.

But a simple incident was destined to transform his mood — a letter from old Tom Bates, the father of Fred.

And as hitherto we have seen him passive, bearing his weight of pain with patience, after that letter we shall find him in action.

Old Bates' letter was handed him three weeks after the scratching of his vague "VEN."

"DERE MISTER HOGARTH:
    "thise fu lines is to ast you how you er getn on, and can you giv a pore old feller ane noos ov that godfussakn sun ov mine hopn they ma find you as they leave me at present wich i av the lumbeigo vere Bad and no Go the doctor ses bob wot you no was in the ninth lansers he dide comen home so ive only fred left out of the ate. I rote to im fore munths agorne, but no anser, no doubt becos i cum to london soon arter, so no more at present from
    "Yours trule,
      "TOM BATES."

The old fellow, Hogarth saw, did not know of Fred's fate: Fred, the last of eight. He would find it hard to answer that letter.

When "beds down" was called, his head was still full of one

thought: old Tom Bates; and he could not sleep; heard the bell ring for the change of warders; the vast silence of the prison's night; and still his brain revolved old Tom.

The stealthy slipper of the night-warder passed and re-passed. Anon a click of metal on metal, and the bull's-eye searched him.

Suddenly he remembered that visit to the forge at Thring, and the present of herrings which old Tom in his guernsey, had brought.

"Here — take 'em — they're yours," old Tom had said.

He had just then, he remembered, been on the point of going into the cottage to examine his guns, when the old man came, and stopped him — a fatal, appointed thing, apparently. Had he actually gone, he would have found the guns vanished, and would never have been condemned. . . .

And what was it that the old man had said about fish, and fishermen, and the sea?

He bent his brow to it, and finally remembered: "The day's work of a fisherman gives him enough fish to live on all the week, and he could lie round idling the other six days, if he chose; only anybody can't live on nothing but fish all the time."

Was it true? Yes! He remembered facts of Yarmouth. . . .

But since true, it was — strange.

Was the sea, then, a more productive element for men to work in than the land? No, that was absurd: the land, in the nature of things, was more productive.

Then, why could not *all* men procure an easy superfluity by one day's work, as the fisher could, if he chose to live naked in a cave, eating fish alone? In that case the fisher could change some of his day's-work fish for the shore people's day's-work things, and so all have a variety as well as superabundance.

At the interest of this question, he leapt from his hammock, peering into that thing, and his fleet feet were away, running after the truth with that rapt abandonment that had characterized his hunting and football. This was clear: that there was some difference between land and sea as working-grounds for men. Shore people, like a shoemaker, did not have for themselves enough shoes from even five, or six, days' work on which to live in plenty for a week: and hence would take nothing less than an enormous quantity of the fisher's fish in exchange for a pair of shoes, making him, too, poor as themselves. But since land work was as productive as sea work, and far more so, it could only be that the shoemaker did not get for himself all the shoes which he made, as the fisher got for himself all the fish which he caught: some power took from shore people a large part of what they made, a power which did not exist on the sea. That much was sure.

What was this power, this inherent difference?

He could think of no inherent difference except this: that shore workers paid rent for land — directly and indirectly — in a million subtle ways; but fishers paid none for the sea.

So, then, if shore folk paid no rent, they would have a still greater superfluity of shoes, etc., from one day's labour in six than the fish-rich fisher?

So it seemed. So it *was* — as with savages. He started! But one minute's reflection showed him that it was in the very nature of the shore to pay rent: because one piece of land was better than another — City land, for instance — and those working on the better must pay for that benefit. Civilized land, therefore, was bound to pay rent.

So that the shore people could never have the easy superfluity of the fish-rich fisher — because land was bound to pay rent? And the fisher must buy the shore things so dear with his easy-got fish, toiling, he, too, all the week — because land was bound to pay rent?

The wretchedness of Man, then, was a Law?

Hogarth, confronted by a wall, groaned, and while his body was cold, his brow rolled with sweat, he feeling himself on the brink of some truth profound as the roots of the mountains. . . .

"Land was bound to pay rent": he reached that point; and there remained.

"But suppose the workers on shore paid the rent *among themselves*. . . ?"

At last those words: and he gave out a shout which begat mouths of echo through the galleries of Colmoor.

"If the workers on shore paid rent among one another" — then they would — on the whole — be in the very position of the fish-rich workers on sea, who paid no rent at all, the nation — as a whole — living on its country rent-free: England English, America American, as the sea human: and our race might then begin to think, to live!

It seemed too sublime — and divine — to be true! Again, point by point, he went over his reasoning with prying eye; and, on coming back to the same conclusion, hugged himself, moaning. At last — he knew.

And away now with the dullness and lowness! That blithe and hand-clapping day! Good-bye, Colmoor! the daily massacre, the shame and care. Men could begin — if in a baby way at first — to think, to see, to sing, to live.

He saw, indeed, that that would hardly have been fair business if he, for example, had paid his rent to the English Nation instead of to Frankl, Frankl having bought Lagden with money earned. But he thought that Frankl would hardly be slow to resign that rent, if once he was shown. . . .

But if Frankl *was* slow — what then?

The oblong of ribbed glass over his flap-table showed a greyness of morning, as he asked himself that thing.

In that case — Frankl could be argued with.

But if he still refused?

Then the question could be gone into as to whether that which is good for forty millions, though apparently bad for Frankl, is not *forty million times* more just than unjust, goodness being justice; also, as to which had the primary right to England, Frankl or the English.

But if he still refused?

Suddenly Hogarth giggled — his first laugh in Colmoor.

That could be arranged. . . .

For him, Hogarth, the great fact was this: that he saw light. Into that humble cell the rays of Heaven had blazed.

After standing motionless a long time, he dropped to his knees, and "O, Thou, Thou," he said. . . .

An hour later, when asked by an orderly if he wished to see doctor or governor, he replied: "The Governor."

XVIII

CHLOROFORM

(Captain Bucknill, the Governor, was making his morning rounds, when he heard that among the convicts claiming to see him was 76.)

A little man, prim, snappy, compact: an army officer, with moustachios stuck upon him, to curve and finish him off.

"Well, what is it, 76?" said he busily at the cell door.

Hogarth struck a hand-salute — his old habit on His Majesty's ships.

"Sir, I wished to tell you that I have determined to escape from this prison — if I can."

"Indeed, now! This is a most refreshing candour, 76!"

"I have said what I had to say," said Hogarth. "You keep a sharp eye on me, and I, too, will keep a sharp eye."

The Governor puffed a breath of laughter, turned on his heels, walked away, and that day spoke to three officials with regard to Convict 76.

And during a week Hogarth lay deep, chained, in a punishment-cell.

But during its first four days he had invented three separate plans of escape, and had determined upon the one which seemed the surest, though longest.

When he again came up into the light, he was a marked man, under Warder Black's constant suspicion.

Now, however, his expression was changed: he no longer belonged to Colmoor, though he was there. Sometimes he felt like shouting at the burden of his secret. In his impatience to proclaim it, he pined to write to Loveday — but now his punishment had lost him that privilege.

Meantime, the problem was to get ten good miles beyond Colmoor: a hard one; but his brain had already accomplished a task far harder: and the greater implied the less.

His first thought, when he had begun to plan, had been Loveday; his second, that on no account could he permit Loveday to incur further risk, or expense, for him; his third, that he might yet use Loveday to any extent not involving risk or expense.

At the next weekly "School" he sat near a Thames-works hackle-maker, who, though he could write, was no scholar, and was laboriously spoiling a second letter-sheet, when Hogarth whispered him: "Can I help you? I see it's to your mother. I could get her a quid from a friend of mine."

"Well, I'm much obliged. . . .!"

The laborious letter, after half an hour, had in it:

"If you go to 15, Cheyne Gardens, the gentleman will give you a sovereign which he owed me for cutting down the elm in the beech-wood at Teddington for him."

Now, Loveday lived at 15, Cheyne Gardens, and had only to see those words "*the elm in the beech-wood*," to scent a cypher from Hogarth.

He offered five pounds for that letter: but it was two weeks before he decided upon the intended words: "Small chloroform — trenches — rock."

There were several trenches, many rocks: yet one midnight, when a blustering wind huddled the bracken, and the prison stood darkling, wrapped in mystery, a lonely figure in an ulster was there; and under each of three rocks he deposited two vials: for the formation of only three gave the least chance of concealment.

What Hogarth's plan could be he racked his brain in vain to dream, guessing that prisoners, on returning from the moor, must be searched, even to the ears: Hogarth, therefore, could never use the vial within the walls, and must mean to use it without — a sufficiently wild proceeding. But the finding of the vials, was sure: for the "rock" which Hogarth had had in mind was one of those granite ones common on Colmoor, standing five feet high on a small base; and one day he swept his hand among the gorse under it, and, with a glad half-surprise, touched two vials.

Three days later he again swept his hand among the gorse, touched the vials, breasted his handkerchief, laid the vials on it, and presently contrived to tie them together with a twig.

At his feet now was a wheelbarrow full of marl, and two yards off Warder Black, waiting for him to roll the barrow; but, inserting his spade between a wheel and a side of the barrow, his back toward Black, Hogarth, with a tug, bent the spade: then walked to Black.

"Look here," he said, "that spade isn't much good now. . . ."

Black strode to look, Hogarth a little behind him: and at the instant when the officer was a-stoop to lift the spade, Hogarth took the vials from his breast, and laid them upright in the little pocket of Black's tunic, near his bayonet-sheath and cartridge-box, above the belt.

By the time the matter of the spade was settled, the great bell rang, the gangs went marching over the old familiar level, up the old path in the grass-mound on which the Palace stands, and so, in lax order, like shabby French conscripts, powdered, toil-worn, into the gates.

Then the search on parade: during which, as Black busily searched him, Hogarth said: "Search well."

They were then led up to cells.

And the moment Hogarth's door closed upon him, he put his skilly-can on the floor, and, with one stamp, stamped it out of shape; also he broke his cup, and pocketed two fragments of it.

A few minutes afterwards, before cocoa, Black, trotting in heavy haste here and there in the gallery, looked in to say: "Bath tonight."

And Hogarth: "Warder! a word with you! sorry, I have trodden on my can. . . ."

Upon which Black went stooping to look, the can now standing on the low shelf; and as he said "I shall report this," Hogarth, stooping, with quick deftness had the vials picked from the thick pocket.

"Well, fall in," said Black to him; "better take your precious can, and give it to a bath-room warder for the store-keeper to change."

Hogarth, as he passed out, placed the vials on the shelf over his door, where they were secure, since cells were never searched; and, the bathers having formed in single file, five feet between man and man, away they moved and down — away and down — lost in space, treading the journey of galleries, till, at the bottom, they passed up a vaulted corridor, monastically dim, across a yard open to starry sky, and into the door of a semi-detached, steep-roofed building, which was the bath-house.

A row of thirty-five baths; a very long bench for undressing; in the space between bench and baths three warders walking: such was the bath-house: all whitewashed, galvanized iron, and rigour; but for its old record of uneventfulness a scandal was preparing that night.

Outside the door a fourth officer paced, and a cord within rang a little bell in one click, to tell when, the bathing over, the door should be unlocked outside.

After giving up his can near the door to a warder, who laid it on the bench, Hogarth undressed slowly; got off his boots; and now had on only knickerbockers and stockings: he got off his stockings.

And the moment his bare soles touched the floor, he felt himself once more agile on the ratlines, larky for a shore-row, handy in any squall. Let them all come, therefore! He smiled; passed his palms down his crib of lean ribs.

"Good gracious, why don't you hurry up there . . .?" an officer came asking, stooping.

At "there" he saw stars-and-stripes, dropped upon his back: Hogarth was away toward the door, while the bathers started with shouts, though in no bosom arose any impulse to follow, the bath-house being the centre of a maze of twenty unscaleable walls, prison within prison.

But as for Hogarth, in such a dazzling flash did he dash toward the door, that he had struck down the second officer before the outcry of the first, and had pulled at the door-bell before the third could cry "Don't open!" — a cry muffled into his maw by a cuff prompt as thunder.

This third man, however, grasped the fugitive by the middle: and while the overthrown two were running up, and the key without seeking the lock, a short, venomous tussle was waged just near the door, till Hogarth, wringing his naked body free, tossed his antagonist by the knees to slide into the path of the two on-comers; at the same time, catching up his battered can, and smashing it into the face of the door-orderly, who now peeped in, he slipped through, and was gone into a yard, small, of irregular shape, and dim, with one wall-lantern, and but one egress (except the egress into the prison-hall), namely a blind-alley between the laundry and carpet-makers' building on one side, and stables on the other: blind alley, yard, and all, being shut in by big buildings.

By the time the door-orderly opened his eyes, and one of the inside three had rushed out, Hogarth had vanished; and these two, shrilling whistles to reinforce the bath-room guard, pelted down the blind-alley to effect, as they thought, a sure capture. But Hogarth was not there.

Back they came trotting, breathless, rather at a loss. One panted: "He must have run back into the great hall. . . ."

The other panted: "He'd hardly do that — hiding in the yard still, *must* be. There's that little nook. . . ."

The "little nook" is a three-sided space in a corner, very dark, formed by one wall of the campanile, or bell-tower, together with a wall of the laundry-house, and a third wall which shuts in the yard; the entrance to it narrow, and one looking up within it seems to stand at the bottom of a triangular well, split at one corner. It is not far from the bathhouse, and into it Hogarth had really darted; but when the officers came peering, no trace of him.

He had, in fact, gone up the lightning-conductor, which runs down a bell-tower remarkably high, Colmoor having been built during the Napoleonic wars for French prisoners at a time when the theory was accepted that a lightning-conductor protects a space whose radius is double the height of the conductor. The tower is a five-sided structure with a Gothic window into which it is impossible to get from the conductor, because a corner intervenes, and it is a feat to swing from the conductor to the laundry-wall coping, and thence, leaping up, to grip the window: at each of which ordeals Hogarth hesitated, pierced with chills; to his observations from afar it had seemed so much less stupendous; but in each case he dared, and reached.

All this time the can was between his teeth.

Arrived on the window, his arms out groping, he felt a slanting beam — climbed it — found it short-mounted upon a horizontal one, all here, as he had expected, being a chaos of beams, raying every way. Thrice he sneezed low, and felt cobwebs in his face.

And groping he went, seeking the great Bell of Colmoor, which he had doomed, hearing sounds of the to-do, echoes that ran below, and the vague shout of somebody, till he touched the flat top of the bell, clamped to the swing-beam on which he sat astraddle; felt also that along the top of the beam lay an iron bar; made sure that this was in actual contact with the clamps of the bell: and, no longer hesitating, set to work upon the can.

Tugging with his dog-teeth under the upper rim, he got a loose end, and wrenched the rim off; then, tearing along the solder, got the cylinder separated from the bottom; and, opening it out, had a sheet of tin. And now, by the help of his fragments of cup, he set to hack-sawing, breaking, tearing this into strips, no easy thing, in spite of the thin-worn condition of the can: but finally had six strips.

The edge of one strip he inserted under an end of the bar of iron on the beam; then connected that strip with another by loops, slid again to the window, and there lay connecting the six strips by a smith's-trick, with skew loops, non-slipping, getting a tin string five feet long. He then took the leap to the laundry coping, and thence the spring to the conductor, this being all the more ticklishly perilous because he could barely see it.

Hanging away now from the conductor by the left elbow, he reached out the right arm across the corner to catch the tin, which stuck toward him from the window: and he wound its end round the conductor, electrically connecting the bell with the conductor.

And now, standing with one foot on a staple below the tin, he twice sawed the conductor's soft metal with the fragments of cup, cutting and tugging out three inches of it, thus isolating the conductor's point atop from its earthing; then he tossed the piece cut out behind the laundry-coping.

This done, he listened, cast a searching eye below, slid down the rod.

The yard was at present silent, but as he moved to give himself up in the prison-hall, five night-warders with bull's-eyes fell out, still seeking him.

And as he knelt with clasped hands of supplication and bent bare back, like a captured slave, they fell savagely upon him, and cried one: "Well, of all the idiots . . .!"

XIX

THE GREAT BELL

The next morning Hogarth was not marched out, and near dinner-time was summoned before the Governor. Here he stood in a cage of bars in a room of "No.1" prison, devoted to prison-offences; and before him, at a littered table, sat governor and chief warder, with the witnesses of the outbreak near.

The case was gone into, the report made: whereupon the Governor looked up and down the length of Hogarth, and suddenly gave vent to a laugh.

"So, No. 76," said he, "this was the threatened escape?"

Hogarth was now all contrition and hanging head.

"I beg for mercy," he said, with a little smile.

"Oh, I am not your judge . . . Where were you when the officers were looking for you in the yard?"

"I was hiding in that little nook."

"Confounded carelessness on someone's part . . . And what cut and swelled your mouth?"

"I bashed into the wall in the nook" (The can had cut him!).

"You must have been mad!"

"Yes, sir."

During the next two weeks he had round his ankles a chain which, rising in two loops, was fastened to a band round his waist; and he was set to turn "the crank."

Finally, he was led forth to stand before the periodic Director, who, after reading the report, turned to a volume of writing in which was Hogarth's record: good — till lately; and the Director addressed him with sternness, which yet was paternal: he would sentence him to one month in a punishment cell, to two months in chains, and to one dozen lashes.

And two days later he was led to the flogging-hall, which, as he approached it, sent forth screams; the doctor looked at him and consented; the Governor said: "Get it over."

Hogarth stripped to the waist, his teeth chattering: but not with fear. On the contrary, he felt a touch of exultation.

The wrists of his outstretched arms having been bound to "the triangle," the Governor gave the sign, the cat rose, and sang, and fell.

Slowly up, and whistlingly down, rasping, reaping. At the seventh shock he fainted: and thence onward had a long dream, in which he saw Rebekah Frankl in Hindoo dress and jewellery, and she threw at him a red rose black at heart with passion, and her body balanced in dance, and her hands clapped at him.

During the next month he tholed the cold of that same punishment-cell; and during the next was in his old cell, but in chains, picking oakum. All this time, if he was aware of high winds by night, he was in an agony, till the next day the great bell rang its treble.

About the middle of February he was once more trenching in the open air.

But a fear had stolen into his mind: for the string of tin was not strong, and the winds of the last month may have dislocated it. In any case, he might have to wait a year, two, ten. . . .

Occasionally he would redden with suppressed and turbulent energy.

But on the 17th of March, toward evening, England was visited by a storm long remembered, lasting three days, during which the poor prisoners were comforted with rations of hot soup and cocoa.

On the morning of the fourth day when the gangs were once more taken out Hogarth was hardly conscious of frigid winds or agued limbs: for three days the great bell of Colmoor had not rung; and his ears were open.

Of the prisoners, who, by practised instinct, get to know the moment at which it should sound, three presently straightened up, spade in hand, to glance at the prison: and suddenly heard — a sound.

A dull something somewhere — from the prison? unless it was some shock of the wind . . . Hogarth gazed piteously into the faces near him . . . No one seemed to have heard.

A few seconds, like eternities . . . Then he saw a warder look at his watch; then — another! and — they glanced at the prison; and — they approached each other; and — they laid whispering heads together.

Then — joy! — came five officers, wildly running from the prison gates, calling, waving. . . .

And now he knew, and smiled: the babble of that lalling tongue was dumb.

And the very next day, when the afternoon-gangs were marching out, they saw descending from a carriage before the Deputy Governor's house a gentleman with a roll of diagram-paper — a bell-foundry expert, summoned by telegraph from Cardiff.

Hogarth resolved to act that night.

XX

THE INFIRMARY

As soon as the cell-door clicked upon him, he commenced to work: first took off his boots; then felt over the doorshelf for the chloroform; wet his handkerchief with some of it: then inserted the vials across the toes of his boots, which were a succession of wrinkles, far too large; then put on the boots again.

He then lay on the floor, close to the low shelf; and, pressing the handkerchief over his mouth and nose, breathed deep, knowing that in four minutes, when he did not obey the order of "brooms out," his cell would be opened.

As he sank deeper and deeper into dream, it was with a concentration of his will upon one point — the handkerchief, which, if smelled by anyone, would ruin all; and finally, as he drew the last gasp of consciousness, he waved it languidly from him under the shelf; then, with a sigh, was gone.

He had known that he must have about his body the unmistakable signs of an abnormal condition in order to sleep a night in the infirmary — which was what he wanted. And thither, when shakings and the bull's-eye had sufficiently tested him, he was swung away, and the doctor's assistant summoned.

Hogarth's pupils were hurriedly examined, his heartbeat tested; and the freshman frowned, smelling an odour which, in another place, might have been chloroform, but here was pharyngitis; and he muttered, "Digitalis, perhaps. . . ."

From a table Hogarth was swung to a bed by two of those well-behaved convicts who act as hospital-orderlies, and there two hours later had all his wits about him, and a racking headache.

His first thought was his boots — expecting to find them under his stretcher, and himself in flannels; but he had them still on, and also his work-clothes, humanity to the sick in the first stages not being in the Colmoor code.

He spent half an hour in stealthily tearing a square foot from his shirt-tail; then, weary and sick, went to sleep.

When, soon after 3 A.M. his eyes again opened, all was still. He lay in a long room, rather dim, in the midst of a row of stretchers which were shut in by bars containing locks and gates, and on the other side of the room a row of stretchers, shut in by bars. At a table in the middle, on which were bottles, lint, graduated glasses, sat a warder, with outstretched legs and fallen head:

near him, standing listless, a convict hospital-orderly, who continually edged nearer the stove; and, halfway down the room, another.

Occasionally there were calls from the sick-beds — whispered shouts — apologetic and stealthy, as of men guiltily conscious of the luxury of being ill; but neither night-warder nor orderlies made undue haste to hear these summonses. There was, beside, an octagonal clock, which ticked excessively in the stillness, as though the whole place belonged to it.

Hogarth took off his boots under his blanket, and from them took out the vials; then, sitting up, commenced to call the warder, at the same time wetting the torn piece of shirt with some of the fluid.

"All right, I'm coming — shut up!" said the warder, but did not come.

So Hogarth grew loud; and the warder, presently rousing his drowsy bulk, unlocked the gate of that compartment, as Hogarth said to himself: "Do it handy . . ."

And as the warder stooped, Hogarth clapped the rag upon his mouth and nose. A struggle followed a muffled sob, both standing upright now, till the warder began to paw the air, sank, toppled upon the bed, whereupon Hogarth slipped into the blanket again, and called out in the voice of the warder: "Come here, Barrows — see if this man is dead."

He had now drawn the warder over him, holding up his chest with one arm, had also poured chloroform upon the rag, and when the convict-orderly came, Hogarth, by means of a short struggle, had him asleep, then seized the warder's truncheon and keys, and ran out in his stockinged feet.

At that sight, the sick, the dying, the two rows of stretchers, were up on elbow, gazing with grins. To the second convict-orderly who came running to meet him Hogarth hissed: "Not a word — or I brain you with this! If I tie your feet, you won't have to answer for anything. Come along. . . ."

He was an old fellow, and when he realized the impending truncheon, the menace of Hogarth's eyes, and the silence of the warder, he permitted himself to be dragged toward Hogarth's stretcher; and his feet were quickly knotted in his own stockings.

Now again Hogarth ran: but not many steps, when he felt himself tapped on the back, and, glancing in a horror of alarm, saw one of the two patients who had occupied with him his cage of bars — a wiry, long-faced Cockney shop-boy, who had had his ankle crushed by a rock at the quarry.

"Are you off?" he asked.

"That's *my* business —"

"No, you don't. Part, or I give the alarm."

"What is it? Do you want to come with me?"

"That's about it."

"But — your foot's sick, you fool."

"You'll carry me in your awms, as a father beareth his children. . . ."

"You are cool! What are you in for?"

"Murder, my son-red, grim, gory murder!"

"Guilty?"

"Guilty, ya'as. What do *you* think?"

"Then you may go to hell."

"'*Ell* is it? I'm *there*: and if I linger longer loo in it, you linger, too, swelp me Gawd!"

Hogarth was nonplussed.

"But the foot . . ."

"Never mind the *foot*. Foot's still good for a run. Do we go shares?"

"Come along, then."

"But you ain't 'alf up to snuff, I can see, though you are pretty smart in your own way: I'd 'ave felt the confidence of a son in you, if you 'adn't overlooked that wine —"

To Hogarth's dismay, he turned back to the table, put a black bottle, half full, to his lips, and with tilts anc stoppages set to gulp it, while eager jokes, touched with jealousy, began to jeer from the beds.

"Lawd Gawd, that was good!" said the Cockney with up-turned eyes, "and what do I behold? — broth, ye gawds!"

Now a saucepan of cold broth was at his lips; and not till he had drunk all did he run after Hogarth into the other arm of the ward, where one of the keys unlocked the door at its end, and they passed out into the infirmary exercise-hall, now dark, Hogarth dragging the Cockney, who limped, and kept up a prattle of tipsy ribaldries.

Then, emerging upon a platform of slabs, from which the jump into the infirmary exercise-yard is twenty feet, Hogarth leapt. The Cockney stood hesitating on the brink.

"As sure as my name's 'Arris, you'll be the bloomin' ruin of me . . ." he said aloud.

"*Sh-h-h*," went Hogarth, "one more word, and I leave or knock you speechless."

Now at last Harris jumped, Hogarth catching him, and they

ran across the yard northerly, Harris complaining of cold, being in hospital flannels, his feet bare, Hogarth bitterly regretting the burden of this companion, meditating on deserting him. Accordingly, when they had run down a passage, and were confronted by a great gate, spiked a-top, Hogarth said: "I'll get up first," and, forcing the small end of the truncheon into the space at the hinges, he got foot-hold from which he caught the top hinge and scaled, a feat of which he considered Harris incapable; and, instead of helping him up, leapt down with a new feeling of lightness, hearing from the other side "Dastardly treachery . . .!"

Again he ran through dark night wild with winds wheeling snowflakes; and, seeing in the unpaved court in which he now was a clothes-line supported on stakes, he seized both, to run with them to where the court is bounded by the great outer wall: for though it is thirty feet of sheer rock, the mere fact of stakes being found there, and of a vanished rope, would furnish grounds for the belief that he had scaled it: he therefore leant the stakes against it, and kept the rope.

About to turn, he felt his back touched; and, spinning round, saw Harris panting.

"There's a friend that sticketh closer than any bloomin' brother, Mr. 76," Harris said. "Try that game on again, and I give myself up; and where will *you* be then?"

"You silly wretch!" said Hogarth: "before I am free, there'll be a hundred difficulties and pains. Are you prepared to undergo them? You couldn't, if you tried."

"Bear ye one another's burdens, it *is*," said Harris: "with thee by me what need I fear? Lawd Gawd, that wine was good! it's got into my poor 'ead, I believe. On, general; where thou leadest, I will follow."

Hogarth looked at him, half inclined to knock him down, and half to shelter, and save.

"All right," said he. "Can you climb?"

"Climb, yes, like a bag of monkeys."

"Come, then."

He mounted three low steps before four doors at the north end of the infirmary buildings, where, as he had observed from the moor, a spout runs up the wall at its east end; and up this he began to climb.

"'Old on!" called Harris: "I can't do that lot."

"*Sh-h-h*! — you must! — come —"

Harris made three attempts before he reached the first foot-rest, and there stuck, vowing in loud whispers that he would no further go, and Hogarth had to come back, and encourage him up. Finally, they went running southward on the leads between the infirmary roof and its coping, and had hardly reached the south end when a whistle shrilled, and they saw a warder run across the exercise-yard with a lantern.

"Stoop!" whispered Hogarth.

Crouching, they stole along the south coping, and thence dropped to a flat cistern-top, Hogarth, with a painful "*Sh-h-h,*" catching Harris as he fell, for the signs of alarm and activity every moment increased.

Up a series of little brick steps, the base of a chimney over the kitchen — then across another stretch of leads beneath which is the tailor's shop — then, stealing in shadow under the beams of overhanging eaves by a garret window, behind which was a light, and someone moving — then a spring of three feet between two cornices — then a running walk at a height of a hundred feet along a beading four inches wide, holding on with the upstretched arms — then, with course changed from south to east, along more leads — then a climb of ten feet up a glazed main — and now they were skulking behind the coping of the great No. 2 prison.

Now, contiguous with the back of the bath-house is a wall which runs from No. 2 prison to the bell-tower, dividing the bath-house yard from the bell-yard; but the top is not horizontal, being lower at the bell-tower end, neither is it broad, and to reach it from the prison coping a drop of seven feet is necessary: this Harris refused to do. "Not for Joe," said he: "I've already run my 'ead into enough perils by land and sea on your account. If this is what you've brought me out moonlighting here for. . . ."

Hogarth did not wait, but disappeared over the side: and Harris, after five minutes' pleadings, followed. They then drew on the belly to the bell-tower; and here again Harris refused the leap to the conductor. When finally he dared, and Hogarth sought to steady him, as he came sprawling upon the rod, both went gliding down, till checked by a staple.

But they climbed again; Hogarth undid the half-fused string of tin from the conductor, swung to the laundry coping, caught Harris, leapt to the window, drew up Harris; and was ensconced far up among the beams in thick darkness in the belfry an hour before daybreak.

At this time the great gates were open, and the moor being scoured for the two.

XXI

IN THE DEEP

They had not been ten minutes in the tower when Harris began to whine of the cold; whereupon Hogarth took off his slop-jacket and waistcoat, and put them upon the Cockney.

As from two sound-escapes far down near the bell some twilight came in, near eight Hogarth descended, working from beam to beam, to find that on one side the bell-metal had been melted into a lumpish mass, its rim shrivelled up, leaving an empty space under the motto *Laudate Domino* (mistake for *Dominum*) *omnes gentes*; and on the opposite side ran a crack from top to rim. Sliding still lower on a slanting beam, he could look obliquely upward into the bell's interior, and see the clapper, a mass weighing eight hundredweight, and so long, that quite down at the bell's rim were two hollows where it had constantly struck. It, too, had been blasted; but the bell-rope hung intact from a short beam at right angles to the swing beam; and, having found this much, he searched where he had left the bottom of his tin can, and clambered back with it into the upper regions.

About eleven, lying along two beams, they could see the portal below opened, and four men came in, looking unreal and small; whereupon the leverage wheel was pulled, the swing-beam swung, the bell struck the clapper, and throughout the tower growled grum sounds: after which the four stood talking half an hour, and went away.

A little later — it must have been after the forty minutes' dinner-interval — about twenty convicts entered with two warders, bearing three ladders. When these had been fastened together and set up, and the leverage wheel removed, they went away.

It was evidently to be slow work. Not till about four did a solitary man mount the ladder, and take stand, far down under the bell, gazing up a long while, with stoops, and changes of posture. Hogarth thought that it was the bell-foundry expert whom he had seen; but could only guess: for all here was dim and remote.

By now he had sawed the clothes-line into two pieces with the tin, one piece eight feet, the other much longer — had intended tearing his clothes into strips for ropes, but the clothes-line was still better. In both ropes he made knots for hand-hold, a large knot at one end of the short one, and he attached the string of tin to the other end. Descending now, he tied the longer rope round the swingbeam, let himself down to the rim of the bell, and with the right hand pushed the tin into the hole in which the clapper swung, reaching up, until the tin over-balanced, ran, and toppled down beside the clapper; drawing the tin now, he brought the rope down till it was stopped by the knot; and now, by a swing off from rope to rope, could climb into the bell. He then reascended, taking the longer rope, and the tin, with him.

As night fell, he judged that by the next he would succumb. Happily, Harris, who had eaten later than he, was snoring in a nook; but toward morning began to whine again, and sulk, and kept it up all the day. Not a soul now entered, and as the blackness of night once more filled the place, Harris threw up the sponge, with "Here goes for this child. . . .!" Hogarth flew across the space which divided them, and a quarrel of cats ensued, both being under the influence of the fury called "hunger-madness." It was only when Harris felt the grip of Hogarth at his windpipe that he squealed submission, whereupon Hogarth threw himself away; and half the night they sat, nothing but four eyes, eyeing each other.

That night what was a revival of the great gale took place, belling like bucks about their heads, and noising through the tower in many a voice. This so increased their sense of desolation, that even the heart of Hogarth fainted, they like castaways on some ocean whose glooms no sunrise ever goldens; and now a doubt arose whether, even if the bell were removed on the morrow, Harris would have strength to cling on during the descent.

However, early the next day hope revived when five men entered, four mounting among the beams to the swing-beam with tools, one at the ladder-head shouting up orders; and Hogarth, when they had gone, whispered Harris: "They have been unscrewing the sockets in which the bell-beam swings."

"Let them unscrew away," said Harris, his chin shivering on his hand.

Five more hours; during which only once did three men enter, seeming to do nothing but talk, with upward glances.

But at three it was evident that there was considerable to-do, though above there the row of the winds drowned all sound. A crowd, chiefly of convicts, passed in and out; then twelve men, one after the other, ran up the ladder, and thence climbed among the beams, with six cables. Half went to the east, half to the west, side of the bell; and three of the cables were fastened round the swing-beam near one end, three near the other end; one three were then cast over a beam higher than the swing-beam, to the north of it; the other three cast over a beam to the south of it; and the six ends lowered — operations which Hogarth, lying on his face, could just see; and the twelve had hardly begun to descend, when he saw a lorry backed into the gateway, filling half 1 the area of the tower; whereupon over a hundred convicts were swarming over and round it.

"Now," said Hogarth; and he hurried down, tacking his way with slides and runs among the intricate beams, tied the rope to a beam above the swing-beam, and let himself down to the bell's rim; reached out then, caught the knotted rope that was within the bell, and climbed, the clapper now so rough, that hand and knee found grip; and he spent a minute in estimating his power of holding on with one arm, and with both, to its support-shaft.

And now he whispered Harris, and caught and half-sustained the Cockney.

Now they could hear echoes of the tongues below; and now Harris, clinging alternate with Hogarth, arms and legs, face to face, by rope and shaft and clapper, whispered: "But-good Lord- look 'ere — there are some people coming up!"

Four convicts were indeed climbing: but even directly beneath the bell, where it was impossible to come, they would hardly have distinguished the forms huddled in its dark cavern, and their aim was higher, to stand ready, when the beam should lift, to swing it diagonally across the square of beams which had supported it, so that it might find space to descend. And soon the bell-beam stirred at the tightening ropes: the fugitives felt them- selves swinging, rising, poised — descending.

They were dizzily aware of shouted orders, the creaking of the toiling, slipping ropes, little jolts and stoppages, two hundred eyes blinking up, not seeing their cringed-up limbs — unnecessary cautious: for the nearer they descended toward the half-light, the surer did the area of the lorry make their invisibility. At last they were near; the bell lingered, swinging; babel was around them; the Governor's voice; a cheer: the bell was on the lorry.

Someone struck the bell with a hammer, there was talk, swarmings round it, then shoulders pushed at the lorry wheels, which squealed and moved amid a still fussier babel drawn by four horses, and seven yoke of cattle. The fugitives could hear the opening of the great gate, the laborious exit, and, in a moment's pause, again the Governor talking, it seemed far off, to the expert. . . .

Wearily creaked the cart — beyond the moor — to a country road.

Now chattering words came from Harris: "All damned fine! I don't deny that you know your way about —"

"Way out," said Hogarth.

"Yes, a gamesome sort of cock you are in all weathers . . . but what next?"

"'Next' is to fall upon your knees and worship me, you cur."

"Thou shalt worship the Lawd thy Gawd," chattered Harris; "no bloomin' fear! This is only a new kind of punishment cell. You've got me in; 'ow are you going to get me out?"

Hogarth believed that the lorry was *en route* for the railway, and hoped to escape in the transfer of the bell; but that night lorry and bell slept in a shed outside a village *en route* for the sea.

At four A.M. they were again *en route*, and at intervals during the day, opening their now feeble and sleep-infected eyes, could hear the hoots of the two cattlemen, the sound of winds, the rowdy gait of the crooked-legged oxen, and stoppages for drink or rest, and anon an obstruction, with shouting and fuss. It was night before the waggon came to rest on a jetty, the elaborate day's journey done.

The fugitives were then deep in sleep, and only awoke at the rattle of a steam-crane in action above them, to find the bell beginning to tilt, lift and swing; then they were on a deck; and soon afterwards knew that it was a steamer's, when they heard the bray of her whistle, and presently were aware of blaring winds, and billows of the sea.

Harris was for then and there crying out, but Hogarth, now his master, said: "Tomorrow morning"; and they fell again into their morbid slumber.

When they again awoke, uproar surrounded them, voices, a heaven-high shouting of quenched fires and screaming steams; moreover, the bell was leaning steeply, they two huddled together at its edge.

Harris began to bellow: but he was not heard, or not heeded. . . . There had been a collision.

"If you can't swim, better catch hold of me," Hogarth shouted — "there will be —"

But the earth turned turtle, and Hogarth felt himself struck on the shoulder, flung, and dragged down, down, into darkness.

After an upward climb and fight to slip the clutch of the ship's suction, in the middle of a heavy sea he managed to get off his clothes, and set to swimming, whither he did not know, a toy on mountains of water.

Exultation raged in him — a crazy intoxication — at liberation attained, at the sensation of warmth, at all that water and waste of Nature.

But within ten minutes it is finished: he shivers, his false strength changing to paltriness, the waves washing now over his head; and now he is drowsing . . . drowning . . .

XXII

OLD TOM

He continued, however, to swim after his conscious efforts ceased: for his body was found next morning on a strip of Cornish sand between Gorran and Mevagissey, washed by every sheet of surf.

His rescuer, a shrimp-fisher, occupied one of three cots perched on a ravine; and there on the evening of the second day he opened his eyes on a settee, four children screaming in play around him; he so far having been seen only by a reporter from Mevagissey, and the doctor from Gorran, who, on his wide rounds, had been asked into the cottage.

The same night Hogarth spoke to the fisher: told him that he was not a wrecked sailor, had reasons for avoiding observation, and would pay for shelter and silence: whereat the fisher, who was drinking hot beer, winked, and promised; and the next day took for Hogarth a telegram, signed "Elm Tree," to Mevagissey, asking of Loveday five pounds.

Finally, one midnight, after two weeks of skulking, he reached Whitechapel, where, the fact of his brown skin now giving him the idea of orientalizing himself, at a Jew's, in a little interior behind the counter, he bought sandals, a caftan, a black sudayree, an old Bagdad shawl for girdle, and a greenish-yellow Bedouin head-cloth, or kefie, which banded the forehead, draped the face like a nun's wimple, and fell loose. For these he discarded the shrimp-man's clothes; and now dubbed himself "Peter the Hermit."

For he meant to start-a Crusade.

At a police-station on the third day he saw a description of himself: three moles, bloodshot eye, white teeth, pouting mouth; but over the moles now hung the head-cloth.

For several days he lay low in a garret, considering himself, abandoning himself to sensuality in cocoa, vast buns, tobacco: rioting above all in the thought of the secret truth which lay in his head.

Up to now, not a word to anyone about it; but on the seventh night he spoke.

It was in some "Cocoa Rooms" in a "first-class room," strewn with sawdust, where, as he sat alone, another man, bearing his jug, came and sat; and soon he addressed Hogarth.

"Talk English?"

"I am an Englishman," answered Hogarth.

"What, in those togs? What countryman?"

"Norfolk."

"Know Manchester?"

"I was there one day."

"Difference between Manchester and London, isn't there? I am a Manchester man, I am. All the difference in the world. This cold, stiff, selfish city. Londoners, eh? A lot of peripatetic tomb-stones!"

And so he went on; this being his whole theory of God and Man: that Londoners are peripatetic tombstones, but Manchester-men just the other way — seemed a mechanic, brisk-eyed, small; a man who had read; but now, evidently, down on his luck.

"Then, why come to London?" — from Hogarth.

"Looking for work," — with a shrug — "looking for a needle in a bundle of hay. What would you have? the whole place overrun with Jews. England no longer belongs to the English, that's the long and short of it."

Hogarth looked him in the face. "Did England belong to the English before the Jews came?"

"How do you mean? Of course it did."

"Which part of it?"

"Why, all of it."

"But fix your mind upon some particular piece of England — some street, or field, that you know — and then tell me: did that belong to the English?"

"Belonged to some Englishman."

"But you don't mean to say that some Englishman is the English?"

"Ah, yes, I know what you are driving at," said the mechanic, with a patronizing nod: "but the point is this: that, apart from vague theorizing, a man did manage to make a good living before these dogs overran the country."

"But — a *good* living? How much did you make? — forty shil-lings a week? toiling in grime six days, sleeping the seventh? I call that a deadly living."

"Well, I *don't*, you see. Besides, I made, not forty, but forty-*five* shillings, under the sliding-scale."

"Yes, but no brave nation would submit one day to such petty squalors after it was shown the way to escape them."

"There *is* no way," said the mechanic: "there are the books, and the talkers; but the economic laws that govern the units like you and me are as relentless as gravitation. Don't believe anyone who talks to you about 'ways of escape'."

"But suppose someone has a new thought?"

"There can be no new thoughts about *that*. The question has long since been exhausted."

"Well, come" — with sudden decision — "I will tell you a thought of my own." And he told.

If the English people paid the rent for England to themselves — to their government — instead of to a few Englishmen, then, by one day's labour in six, Englishmen would be much more rich in all things than a fisherman, by one day's labour in six, was rich in fish.

The expression which he awaited on the face before him was one of illuminated astonishment; but, with a chill in his nerves, he saw the workman's lips curve.

"Bah!" said the Manchester man, "that is an exploded theory!"

Exploded!!!

Hogarth was rather pale.

Yet he knew that it was true. . . . Who, then, could have been exploding the Almighty?

"Who has exploded it?"

"Been exploded again and again!" said the Manchester man; "of all the theories of land-tenure, that is about the weakest: *I* should know, for I've studied them all. The fact is, no change in the system of land-tenure will have the least effect upon the lot of the masses; would only make things worse by unsettling the country — if it didn't mean a civil war."

"I begin to see."

Hogarth got up, walked home meditating: and suddenly blushed.

It was known! by mechanics in cocoa-rooms! — that secret thing of his secret cell. And it was not believed!

As for him, what was he now doing outside Colmoor? That question he asked himself, as he sat unsandaling his feet; and he commenced to dress himself again: but paused — would first see Loveday.

Accordingly, the next night, the two friends met at Cheyne Gardens.

And a long time they sat silent, Loveday feeding his eyes upon his friend's face, that hard, rounded brow which seemed harder, and frowned now, that gallant largeness of eye which seemed now wilder, and that manly height, which seemed Mahomet's in the Oriental dress.

"But where have you been for five weeks?" asked Loveday.

"Skulking, and thinking. But about my sister. . . ."

"Do not ask . . ." said Loveday.

There was a long silence.

"Did not O'Hara tell you to make no more efforts for my escape?" asked Hogarth.

"Who is O'Hara?"

"Why, the priest who escaped, instead of me, through the copse."

"O'Hara was not the name he gave me; and no, he said nothing about that. I got him off to America, and only saw him twice. I thought him rather — But why didn't you escape youself?"

"I thought it improper."

"But you did finally?"

"For a reason: you remember the association which I was forming to answer the question as to the cause of misery? Well, that question I have answered for myself in prison."

"Really? Tell me!"

Hogarth absently took up a water-colour drawing from the table, and turned it round and round, leaning forward on a knee, as he told how the matter was. Meantime, he kept his eyes fixed upward upon Loveday's face, who stood before him.

In the midst of his talk Loveday scratched the top of his head, where the hair was rather thin, and said he, twisting round: "Forgive me-let me ring for some brandy-and-soda —"

Hogarth stood briskly up.

"What I say, I can see, is not new to you?" said he.

"No, not new," Loveday confessed: "I believe that it is quite an ancient theory; there are even savage tribes whose land-tenure is not unlike what you advocate — the Basutos, for example."

"And are these Basutos richer, happier, prettier fellows than average Englishmen?"

"Oh, beyond doubt. Don't suppose that I am gainsaying you: I am only showing you that the theory is not new —"

"But why do you persist in calling it a *theory*? Is the fact that one and one make two a *theory*?" — Hogarth's brow growing every moment redder.

"What can one call it?"

"Call it what you like! But do you believe it?"

"It is quite possibly true; and now that you say it I believe it; but I have never seriously considered the matter"

"Why not?"

"Because — I don't know. It is out of my line."

"Your line! Yet you are a human being —"

"Well, partly, yes: say — a novelist."

"Do not jest! It is incredible to me that you have written book after book, and knew of this divine thing, and did not cram your books with it!"

Loveday flushed. "You misunderstand my profession; and as to this theory of land-tenure, let me tell you: it will never be realized — not in England. Anyway, it would mean civil war. . . ."

Again those words! "Civil war. . . ."

And as, for the second time, he heard them, Hogarth dashed the picture which he held to the ground, shattering glass and frame: which meant that, then and there, he washed his hands of the world and its wagging; meant also his return to Colmoor.

He dashed from the room without a word; down the stairs; out into the street.

As he ran along the King's Road, he asked a policeman the way to the nearest police-station, then ran on through a number of smaller streets, seeking it, till, at a corner, he stopped, once more uncertain, the night dim and drizzling.

He was about to set off again, when, behind him, he heard: "Excuse me, mister — could you give a poor man a penny to get a night's lodging?"

Turning, he saw — old Tom Bates: still in the guernsey; but very senile and broken now.

The fish-rich fisher . . .! he had come to this . . .

Hogarth had twenty-eight shillings about him, and, without disclosing himself, put hand to pocket to give them all, just as the old man reached up to his ear to say: "It's the lumbago; I got it very bad; but it won't be long now. It wur a bad day for me as ever I come to Lunnon! I'm Norfolk born, I am: and I had eight sons, which the last was Fred, who, they say, met his death in Colmoor. . . ."

At that word, "Fred," Hogarth started: for under the elm in the beech-wood between Thring and Priddlestone Fred had concealed a thing fallen from heaven, which could be sold for — a thousand pounds.

That would keep the fisher rich during the few days that remained to him!

But the old man could hardly go himself; if he could, would bungle: the thing was heavy — on the lord-of-the-manor's land. . . .

Do a kind act, Hogarth. He would see the old place, his father's grave; and there was a girl who lived in the Hall at

Westring whom it was a thrilling thing to be near, even if one did not see. . . .

"Here are two shillings," said he, in an assumed voice: "and if you be at this spot, at this hour, on Thursday night coming, you shall have more. Don't fail."

Again he ran, and took train, two hours later, for Beccles.

XXIII

UNDER THE ELM

His risk of arrest here, round about his old home, was enormous, and he drew the Bedouin kefie well round his face, skulking from the station to the "Fen," northward, where he got an urchin to buy him a paper lantern in a general shop, and now trudged up to Priddlestone, then down through meadows to the beech-wood, the night rough with March winds.

It was not the winds, however, which made him draw close his Arab cloak, but his approach to the elm: there, one night, he had seen a naked black man! there had fallen the Arab Jew.

He stood twenty yards from the tree, till, with sudden resolution, he strode, soon had the lantern ruby, and since the grave of "the affair" had been digged with a piece of wood, for such a piece he went seeking, having thrown off his caftan.

Instead, he found the rusted half-blade of a spade, and commenced to dig round the roots, the lantern shine reddening a face strangely agitated, uncertainty of finding what he sought heightening his excitement: for the earth showed no disturbance, and since three years had passed since that night of Bates in the wood, the object might have been already unearthed. After an hour his back was aching, his hands dabbled, his brow beaded, while the night-winds blew, the light now was commoved, and now glowed a steady red; and still he grovelled.

Presently, as he shovelled in a circle, always two feet deep, moving the light as he moved, he saw on the top of a shovelful of marl — a twig: barkless, black, cracked — *scorched*!

To an immoderate degree this thing agitated him — some whisper in the back of his head — some half-thought: he began now to root furiously, with a frowning intentness.

But suddenly he shuddered: a finger seemed to touch his shoulder behind; and he twisted with wild eyes, caught up the light, peered, saw no black man — nothing: but quite five minutes he stood defiant, with clenched fists; then resumed the work, though with a constant feeling now that he was being watched by the unseen seers.

After two new strokes he struck upon something hard, and, digging eagerly round it, found a quart-can, full of earth. And instantly all doubt vanished: for this must have been the beer-can carried by Bates.

Strong curiosity now wrought in Hogarth, a zeal to lay eyes upon that object which had careered through the heights of space to find that beech-wood and that elm-tree; and during fifteen minutes his little implement digged with the quick-plying movement of a distaff-shuttle, he fighting for breath, anon casting a flying wild glance behind, but still digging.

Now, frequently, he came upon burned objects, twigs, cinders. Even the marl had a scorched look; and his agitation grew to ecstasy.

Something very singular had happened to his mind with regard to this "affair" of Bates: Bates had said that it had fallen on the asteroid night; and O'Hara had told him — falsely, indeed — that a piece of the asteroid, fallen upon the French coast, had had diamonds; yet, somehow, never once had his mind associated the Fred Bates "affair" with the thought of diamonds, but only with the "thousand pounds" which Bates had been promised by old Bond. So at the moment when he had begun to dig, his whole thought was of "a thousand pounds"; but, somehow, by the time his implement at last grated against something two feet down, that word "diamonds" had grown up in his brain.

But diamonds! In the midst of his shovelling the thought flashed through him: "The world is God's! and to whom He wills He gives it. . . ."

Now at last the thing lay definitely before him: he grated the spade from end to end, scraping away the marl; and it was very rough. . . .

The size and shape of a man's leg, and red, anyway in the red lantern-shine — his sight dim — he moved and saw in an improbable dream; and when he tried to lift the object and failed, for a long time he sat on the edge of the trench, passing one palm across and across his forehead, till the lantern-light leapt, and went out.

He sprang upright then — awake, sure: they were diamonds, those bits of glass, big celestial ones, not of earth, in hundreds; when he passed his hand along the meteorite he felt it leprous, octahedron, dodecahedron, large and small: if they were truly diamonds, he divined that their owner must be as wealthy as some nations.

About three in the morning he managed to raise the meteorite; refilled the trench; and since it still rained, rolled the meteorite to the hollow of the elm, put on his caftan, and with his back on the interior of the tree, his feet on the meteorite, tumbled into a wonderful slumber.

XXIV

FRANKL SEES THE METEORITE

He was awaked by a footstep, and, starting, saw rocking along the forest path one Farmer Pollock, wearing now fez and tassel, and he saw his clothes all clay, and, with a smile of fondness, saw how, even beneath its grime, the meteor dodged and jeered, with frolic leers, in the beams of a bright morning that seemed to him the primal morning, a fresh wedding-morning, swarming with elves and shell-tinted visions, imps and pixy princes, profligate Golcondas.

Going first to the spot where he had digged, to give to the surface a natural look, he trampled the lantern into the mire, threw the tin can far, then, taking a quantity of marl, plastered the meteorite, to cover its roughness; then boldly left it, starting out with consummate audacity for Thring, where everybody, police and all, knew him well.

A singular light now in his eyes, an evil pride; and he had the step of a Prince in Prettyland. Corresponding to an inward majesty, of which, from youth, he had been conscious, he now felt an outward, and had not been awake eight minutes when his brain was invaded by plans — plans of debauchery, palaces, orgy, flying beds of ivory arabesqued in fan-traceries of sapphire, in which Rebekah Frankl lolled, and smiled; and on toward Thring he stepped, prince new-crowned, yet by old heredity, high exalted above laws, government, and the entire little muck of Man.

At one point where the path ran close to Westring-park proper, the park on higher ground, a grass-bank seven feet high dividing them, he saw a-top of the bank in caftan, priest-cap, and phylacteries, taking snuff — Baruch Frankl.

Hogarth skipped up, and stood before the Jew, having drawn his face-cloth well forward.

"What's the row?" asked Frankl.

"Could you give a poor man a job?"

"You a Jew?"

"Yes," replied Hogarth, not dreaming how truly: "London born."

"A Froom?"

"I keep the fasts."

"What you doing about here?"

"Tramping."

"Fine mess you are in."

"I slept in a hollow tree down yonder — an elm tree."

"Well, there's many a worse shake-down than that. Who are you? Ever been about here before?"

"I was once."

"You put me in mind of an old chum of mine. . . . Well, here's half-a-crown for you to go on with."

"Make it a crown," said Hogarth, "and get me to clean up down there; in a shocking state with mast and leaves."

Frankl considered. "All right, I don't mind."

"I shall want a spade, and — a barrow."

"Go down the path yonder, till you come to the stables, and tell them."

Frankl resumed his musing stroll, and Hogarth ran for the barrow.

In twenty minutes he was again at the elm tree, and, with a scheme in him for seeing Rebekah, heaped the barrow with refuse, pushed it between a beck and the wood, till, wearying of this, he was about to get the meteorite into the barrow, when he had the mad thought that Frankl must be made to see and touch it, so set off to seek him: and a few yards brought him face to face with Frankl.

"Well, how goes it?" asked the Jew.

"There is a weight there which I can't lift," said Hogarth. "Then you must do the other thing. Don't lift it, and you don't get the pay. What weight is it?"

"It is here."

Hogarth led him, led him, pointing. Frankl kicked the meteorite.

"What is it?" he asked.

"It can't be a branch," said Hogarth; "too heavy — more like a piece of old iron."

"Well, slip into it. A strapping fellow like you ought to be able to do that bit."

"But suppose it's valuable?"

"I make you a present of it, as you are so hard up."

Now Hogarth, by tilting the barrow, with strong effort of four limbs, got the meteorite lodged, while Frankl, his smile lifting the wrinkles above his thick moustache, watched the strain: then, with arms behind, went his contemplative way.

Hogarth rolled the barrow toward Thring.

XXV

CHURCH ARCHITECTURE

It was already eleven o'clock, the sun shining in a bright sky, under which the country round the Waveney lay broad to the hills of mist which seemed to encompass the valley; yet, when one came to them no hills were there, but were still beyond. When Hogarth came out from the wood upon a footbridge, to his right a hand-sower was sowing broadcast, with a two-handed rhythm, taking seed, as he strode, from his scrip; and to the left ran a path between fields to an eminence with a little church on it; straight northward some Thring houses visible, and north-east, near the river, Lagden Dip orchard. Only two stooping women in fields near Thring could Hogarth see; also, still further, a gig-and-horse whose remote motion was imperceptible; also the trudging two-handed process of the sower nourishing the furrows. But for these, England, supposed to be "overcrowded," seemed a land once inhabited, but abandoned.

To Hogarth the whole, so familiar, looked uplifted now, the sunlight of a more celestial essence. Westring he would buy — though one memorable night in Colmoor he had arrived at the knowledge that it was not just that Westring should be anyone's; but then what one bought with his own diamonds was surely his own — his name being Richard.

He had passed the bridge, when, glancing to the left, he saw a fifth person in the landscape — a man under a sycamore near the church, gazing up, with hung jaw, at the apse window — dressed in a grey jacket, but a clerical hat, and he had a notebook, in which he wrote, or drew. Hogarth, whose mind was in weathercock state, rolled the barrow to the hill, left it, went stealing fleetly up, and gripped the man's collar, to whisper: "In the King's name I arrest you."

The man's hand clapped his heart, as he turned a face of terror.

"There is — some mistake — My God! Are you — ?"

"Yes."

"Hogarth?"

"Who else?"

"But you have killed me! My heart —"

"Serves you right. Why didn't you give your right name to Loveday? And what are you doing here?"

"I was just examining this lovely old church, with its two south aisles, and one north, like St. John's at Cirencester. When the church fell in England, architecture was abolished — But as to why I am in Norfolk at all, I am skulking: and here is as another place. Your friend packed me off to America; but for some reasons I should prefer Golmoor — old Colmoor, eh? I fear I am a voluptuary, my son, fond of comfort, and old things, and pretty things. And all that I shall have yet! Tut, O'Hara is not done with the world, nor it with him. As to Norfolk, I once knew — a person — in this neighbourhood —"

The priest paused, regarding Hogarth with a smile, the "person" meant being Hogarth's mother; and he said: "But you are quite the Jew in dress: do you know now, then, that you are of the Chosen Race?"

"Singular notion! This is a mere disguise."

"Ah. But you look quite radiant. You must have come into a fortune. When I heard of your escape, I said to myself —"

"How did you hear?"

"Why, from Harris."

"Harris is drowned."

"Harris is now under that little roof down there — there" — the prelate stabbed with his forefinger: "Harris is my shadow; Harris is my master. He was picked up naked by the ship which ran down your vessel, recognized me one day in Broadway, and threatened to give me in charge if I did not adopt him 'as my well-beloved son'. Well, from him I heard all, how you called fire from Heaven — it was gallant. But aren't you afraid of capture down here in your own country?"

"I cannot be captured."

Those stony eyeballs of O'Hara, bulging from out circular trenches round their sockets, surveyed Hogarth, weighing, divining him, while his bottom lip, massive as the mouth of Polynesian stone gods, trembled.

"How do you mean?"

"I can buy King on throne, Judge on bench, Governor and Warder, the whole machinery. Even O'Hara I could buy."

"I am for sale! Hogarth! I *smelled* it about you, the myrrh of your garments! And didn't I prophesy it to you years ago? What a development! That beast, Harris, will dance for joy! Oh, there is something very artistic to my fancy, Hogarth, in the metal gold — brittle, bright, orpimented —"

"And diamonds?"

"Hogarth, have you diamonds?"

"Yes," said Hogarth, smiling at the effect of ecstasy upon O'Hara.

"Prismic diamond!" cried the prelate: "but how — ?"

"Do you want to enter my service?"

"Do I *want?*"

"Well, I want a tutor, O'Hara; and you shall be the man. Undertake, then, to teach me all you know in two years, and I'll give you — how much? — twenty thousand pounds a year."

"My son," whispered O'Hara, "what a development — !"

"Good-bye. In Thring Street there is a little paper-shop. Come there tonight at seven."

He ran down the hill: and as he went northward, pushing his barrow, O'Hara had a lens at his eyes, saw the meteorite, and wondered.

XXVI

FRANKL AND O'HARA

Mrs. Sturgess, of the paper-shop, a clean, washed-out old lady, held up both averting hands at her back door, as Hogarth threw back his kefie, finger on lips; but soon, her alarm warming into welcome, she took him to a room above, to listen to his story of escape.

"And to think," said she, "there is the very box your sister, poor thing, left with me to keep the day she went away, which never once have I seen her dear good face from that day to this. Anyway, *there's* the box —" pointing to a trunk covered with grey goat's-hair, the trunk to which the old Hogarth had referred in telling Richard the secret of his birth, saying to deaf ears that it contained Richard's "papers" — a box double-bottomed, on its top the letters "P. O.," with a cross-of-Christ under them.

"But, sir," said Mrs. Sturgess, "you must be in great danger here. I hope" — with a titter — "I shan't be implicated —"

"Don't be afraid, Mrs. Sturgess, it will be all right, and, for yourself, don't trouble about the paper-shop any more, but buy a little villa near Florence, where it is warm for the cough — don't think me crazy if I tell you that I am a very rich man. Now give me a steak."

Mrs. Sturgess served him well that day with a pang of expectancy at her heart! Always, she remembered, Richard Hogarth had been strange — uplifted and apart — a man incalculable, winged, unknown, though walking the common ways. He *might* be a "very rich man" . . .

His meal over, Hogarth threw himself upon a bed, to dream another trouble of bubbles and burden of purples; woke at four; and, with a procured cold-chisel, hammer, and a calico bag, went to the fowl-house where he had left the meteorite, shut himself in.

Sitting in the dust there, he set to chisel out the gems from the porous ore, and as the chisel won the luscious plums, held them up, glutting his gaze, scratched his name on a fragment of window-pane, and was enchanted that the adamant rim ripped the glass like rag: the whim, meanwhile, working in him to purchase Colmoor, to turn the moor into a paradise, the prison into a palace; where his old cell stood in Gallery No. III to be the bedroom of Rebekah.

To see *her* that very night was a necessity! and when it was dark he set out.

But that plot failed: on presenting himself at the front of the mansion, he was sent round to the back, where he received payment, and was dismissed; and when he again started for the front, intending to force his way in, he decided upon something else, and walked back to Thring.

He reached the Sturgess cottage soon after six, ate, with a candle returned to the lean-to to resume his work, and was still intent upon it at seven, when Mrs. Sturgess ran out to tell him that "the gentleman had come." He said: "Show him up to my room."

The first thing which O'Hara noticed in that room was the goat-hair trunk, with the initials and cross, the initials his own.

After some minutes he furtively turned the key, dived into a mass of things, paused to remember the whereabouts of a spring, found it, and, lifting the upper bottom, peered beneath; saw a bundle of papers; and, without removing the band, ferreted among them, and was satisfied — Hogarth's "birth-papers."

He presently went to a back window, and saw ruddy streaks between the boarding of the shanty, while sounds of the hammer reached him.

He would go and meet Hogarth: no harm in that; but it was stealthily that he hurried down the stair and carried himself across the yard, grinning a grimace of self-conscious caution, to peep through a cranny.

Hogarth's back was toward him, the iron leg lying near a box in which was a sitting hen, on its top a candlestick, the calico bag, and a lot of the gems: at which the priest's palm covered his awed mouth, and with a fleet thievishness, like a cat on hot bricks, he trotted back to the cottage.

Ten minutes later Hogarth entered, nodding: "Ah, O'Hara ..." and he called down: "Mrs. Sturgess! pen, ink, and paper!"

When these came, he sat and wrote:

"I have escaped from prison, and come into great power. I summon you to meet me at the elm in the beech-wood tonight at nine. I beseech you, I entreat you. I burn to ashes. Rebekah! My flames of fire! I am dying.

"R. H."

He enclosed, and handed it, without any address, to O'Hara.

"O'Hara," said he, "I want you to take that for me. Come — I will show you the place. You ask in the hall to see 'the young lady': her name does not concern you; but you can't mistake her: she is so-pretty. Give the note to no one else, of course: it mentions my escape, for one thing. I know you will do it well."

He conducted O'Hara, till the two towers of Westring were visible; pointed them out; then went back, and in an hour had finished his work on the diamonds.

O'Hara, meantime, going on his way alone, muttered: "You go fast, Hogarth: prelates of the Church your errand boys? But there is a little fellow called Alf Harris . . . if he had seen what I have seen tonight, you would be a corpse now."

In twenty minutes he was at Westring, which he knew well, for twenty-five years before he had lived in the Vale: but he supposed that Lord Westring de Broom was still the inmate.

He asked to see "the young lady," persisted, and after a time Rebekah came with eyebrows of inquiry.

The moment O'Hara saw her well, his visage acquired a ghastly ribbed fixity. Even before this, *she*, by one flashed glance, had known him.

But she took the envelope with easy coolness. And, instead of then returning upon her steps, went still beyond, and whispered to two men in the hall: "Do not let that man pass out!"

As she again returned inward past O'Hara, she remarked: "You might wait here a little."

She travelled then, not hurrying, down the breadth of a great apartment to a side room where her father sat, capped and writing; and she said: "Papa, the man who assaulted me in the train is now in the hall. As his sentence was three years, he must have escaped —" She was gone at once, the unaddressed envelope, still unopened, shivering a little in her hand.

Frankl leapt up, rather pale, thinking that if the man had come *here*, he must mean mischief; but remembering that the man was a gentleman, a priest, he took heart, and went out.

O'Hara, meantime, stood at bay, guessing his exit blocked, while the terrors of death gat hold upon him, the flesh of his yellow jaw shivering. But he was a man of stern mind — stern as the rocky aspect of his face, and the moment he saw Frankl coming (he had seen him in the Court), he started to meet him — stooped to the Jew's ear, who shrank delicately from contact.

"There isn't any good in running me down, sir," he whispered in sycophant haste. "I pledge you my word I came here without knowing to whom. O do, now! I have already suffered for my crime; and if you attempt to capture me, I do assure you, I strangle you where you stand! Do, now! I only brought a letter —"

Frankl, half inclined to tyrannize over misery, and half afraid, swept his hand down the beard.

"Letter?" said he: "from whom?"

"From a friend."

"Which friend?"

"A man named Hogarth."

O'Hara said it in an awful whisper, though not aware of any relation between Hogarth and Frankl.

Whereupon an agitation waved down Frankl's beard. The news that "a man named Hogarth" had written to his daughter would hardly have suggested *Richard* — safe elsewhere; but, one night at Yarmouth, he had seen Richard Hogarth inexplicably kiss his daughter's hand.

"Hogarth?" said he: "what Christian name?"

"Richard."

The agonized thought in Frankl's brain was this: "Well, what's the good of prisons, then?" — he, too earnest a financier to read newspaper gossip, having heard not a word of the three escapes from Colmoor.

He said: "Well, sir, generally speaking, I'm the last to encourage this sort of thing; but, as yours is a special case, I tell you plain out that, personally, I don't mean a bit of harm to you. Just step into a room here, and let us talk the matter quietly over."

He led O'Hara to his study; and there they two remained locked half an hour, conferring head to head.

XXVII

THE BAG OF LIGHT

Rebekah, having excused herself from three ladies, her guests, alone in her room opened her letter.

Glanced first at the "R. H.," and was not surprised. He had "escaped," had "come into great power": that seemed natural; but he "summoned" her to meet him, and she saw no connection between his "great power" and his right to summon her.

She held the paper to a fire, and, as it began to burn, in a panic of flurry extinguished the edge, and hustled it into her bosom; then perambulated; then fell to a chair-edge with staring gaze; then, rocking her head which she had dropped upon a little table, moaned: "He is mad. . . ."

"My flames of fire! Rebekah! I am dying. . . ."

He suffered; and a pussy's wail mewed from her; but with a gasp of anger which said "Ho!" she sprang straight, and went ranging, with a stamping gait, through the chamber, filling it with passion. "I *won't go!*" she went with fixed lips, as something within her whispered: "You must."

To escape herself, she went again to see what had happened with regard to the convict, whose face would carry to the grave the scars of her nails.

There were no signs of any disturbance; and she asked a footman: "Where is the man who was here?"

"With your father in the study."

That seemed a strange proceeding: she felt a touch of alarm for her father, and, passing again by the study, peeped; could see nothing for the key, but heard voices.

This messenger of Hogarth, she next thought, was a criminal: he might betray . . . so she stole into an adjacent room, to peep by a side door of the study, and though a key projecting toward her barred her vision, the talkers were near this point, and she could hear.

"The diamond block," O'Hara said, "is the same which he rolled across the bridge this morning; to that I'll swear."

"Then it must be the very same block he showed me," Frankl said in a whisper; "that thing was worth millions. . . .!"

"Undoubtedly it was the same."

"Oh, but Lord," groaned the Jew in an anguish of self-deprecation, "where were my *eyes?* where were my *wits?* I must have been *dreaming*! No, that's hard!"

"Well — *nil desperandum*! Let us be acting, sir!"

"My own land — !"

"They are still safe enough: come —"

"He may have lost one or two — in his excitement. Thousands gone! He may have hidden some!"

"Tut, he has hidden none," said O'Hara; "we may have all. Let us make a move."

"But he is a strong man, this Hogarth. Why do you object to the assistance of the police?"

"What have the police to do with such a matter? Hogarth would simply bribe. And there are three of us —"

"Who is this Harris?"

"He is a Cockney — assassin."

Frankl took snuff, with busy pats at alternate nostrils.

"What will you tell him is in the bag?"

"Anything — rings — something prized by you for sentimental reasons. We offer him a thousand — two thousand pounds. And he will not fail. He strikes like lightning."

"And we share — how?"

"Come — let us not talk of that again, sir. What could be more generous than my offer? You divide the diamonds into two heaps, and I choose one; or I divide, you choose; and, before I leave you, you give me a declaration that it was by your contrivance that I escaped prison, and that the gems which I have, once yours, are duly made over to me."

"And you collar half!" gibed the Jew with an ogle of guile; "that's about as cool a stroke of business as I've come across. You don't take into account that the whole is mine, if the concern fell, as you confess, on my own land! And just ask yourself the question: what is to prevent me handing you over this minute to the police, and grabbing the lot? Only I'm not that sort of man —"

O'Hara drew a revolver.

"You talk to me as though I was a schoolboy, sir," said he sternly. "Be good enough to learn to respect me. I am not less a man of the world than you are, and quite competent to safeguard my own interests. Supposing I was weak enough to permit you to send for the police, the moment they had me I should tell of Hogarth in hiding; they would go for him, and he, after bribing, may be trusted to take wing with the stones, leaving you whistling. Or perhaps you would care to tackle him in person? He would wheel you by the beard round his arm like a Catherine-wheel, I do assure you. All this you see well, and pretend not to. Do let us be honest with each other!"

"Well, I don't want to be hard," said Frankl, looking sideward and downward, plotting behind an unwrinkled brow, intending to have every one of the diamonds; so did O'Hara, who already had his plot.

"No, don't be hard," said O'Hara: "*I* am not. I give you an incalculable fortune; I take the same. Live and let live! Why should two shrewd old fellows like you and me be like the dog which, wanting two bones, lost the one he had? Come, now — give me your hand on it."

"Well, I'm hanged if you are not right!" cried Frankl, looking up with discovery: "Share and share alike, and shame the devil! That's the kind of little man I am, frank, bluff, and stalwart — Ha! ha! Give me your hand on it, sir!"

"Ha! ha! you are very kind. That is the only way — absolute sincerity —" and they shook hands, hob-nobbing and fraternizing, with laughs and little nods, like cronies.

"Stop — I'll just ring for a drop of brandy —" said Frankl.

"No! no ringing! — thanks, thanks, no brandy —"

"Well, you are as cautious as they make them. Oh, perfectly right, you know — perfectly right" — he touched O'Hara's chest — "not a word to say against that. I am the same kind of man myself —"

"Come; are you for making a move?"

"Agreed. Where is my hat? I suppose a man may get his hat! — ha! ha! — I can't very well go in this cap —"

"You use mine — with the greatest pleasure. I do not need — Ah? quite the fit, quite the fit."

"Why, so it is. Ha! ha! why, it's a curate's hat, and — *I'm a Jew*!"

"Excellent, excellent, ha! ha!"

So they made merry, and, with the bitter lip-corners of forced merriment, went out, while Rebekah, who had caught a great deal of that dialogue, crouched a long time there, agitated, uncertain what to do.

That her father should coolly look on at an assassination for a fortune was no revelation to her: she had long despised, yet, with an inconsistency due to the tenderness of Jewish family ties, still loved him; the notion of appealing to the police, therefore, who might ruin Hogarth, too, did not enter her head.

She ran and wrote: "Your life and bag of gems are *at this moment* in danger"; and sent it by a mounted messenger addressed to "The Guest at the Paper Shop."

But in twenty minutes the messenger returned to her with it, Hogarth having gone to the *rendezvous* at the elm — long before the appointed time.

When, accordingly, Frankl, O'Hara, and Harris arrived at the paper-shop back yard, and Harris had stolen up the back stairs, he presently, to the alarm and delight of the others, sent a whisper from the window: "No one 'ere as I can see!"

And the search for the diamonds was short: for Hogarth had actually left the bag containing them on the trunk, and Frankl and O'Hara returned with it to Westring, holding it out at arm's length, one with the right, one with the left hand, like standard-bearers.

Hogarth, meantime, was striding about the elm, and once fell to his knees, adoring a vision, and once, at a fancied step, his teeth-edges chattered.

Rebekah! He called, groaned, hissed that name, while his to-and-fro ranging quickened to a trot.

And now, fancying that he heard a call "*Come!*" he stood startled, struck into a twisting enquiry to the four winds; but could not locate the call, ran hither and thither, saw no one.

"Come to me, little sister," he wailed tenderly, while to swallow was a doubtful spasm for him, her name a mountain in his bosom.

When he was certain that it must be nearer ten than "nine," he set out in the sway of a turbulent impulse to spurt for the Hall: but as he reached the point of proximity between path and park, just there where her father had stood that morning he saw her patiently waiting — ever since that "*Come!*"

He flew, and was about to skip up the bank, when, with forbidding arm, she cried: "Don't you approach me!" — and he stood checked and abject, one foot planted on the bank, looking up, ready to dart for her in her Oriental dress, flimsy, baggy at the girdle, her arms bare, her fingers clasped before her, making convex the two tassels of the girdle, from her ears depending circles of gold large enough to hoop with, a saffron headdress, stuck backward, showing her hair in front, falling upon a shawl which sheltered her frank recumbent shoulders. She did not see Hogarth at all, but stood averted, implacable, unapproachable, looking across the park, while Hogarth occupied a long silence in gazing up to where, like a show, she stood, illumined by the moon.

At last he sent to her the whisper, "Did you call just now? Did you say '*Come*'?"

"What is it you want with me, Hogarth? You have '*summoned*' me: but be very quick."

"I told you: I am wealthier than all the princes —"

"Well, let me inform you that your life is in danger here; if you are a wise man, you will not fail to leave this neighbourhood this night."

"But no one knows —"

"It is known, Hogarth: your friends are false, and your enemies crafty. You will have to walk with your eyes open, my friend. What will you do with all the money?"

"I will buy the world, because *you* are in it."

Now she flashed upon him one glance, in which there was astonishment, and judgment.

"You said that so like my father! Hogarth among the dealers? I thought you would be more squeamish, and arduous, and complex."

"But if a man is famished, he is not complex, he runs to the baker's. You can have no conception how I perish! And I cannot be contradicted-I claim you-I have the right-I am the lord of this lower world —"

"But you do not see the effect of your words: you disappoint me Richard. How of what the poet sings:

> . . . this is my favoured lot,
> My exaltation to afflictions high?

"That is more in your line, you know, but you are dazzled, Hogarth — fie. To *buy me*! And how would you like me afterwards, having renounced my obligations? And how would I like *you* — I whose name is Rebekah, who will mate with none but a wrestler, a fellow of heroic muscle? I feel certain that you are dazzled. It is natural, I suppose — But are all the people in the world so happy, that *you* too, can find nothing to occupy you but the market-place, with its buying and selling? And to buy *me*? I am *not* for sale! How dare you, Hogarth?"

With this she walked off; but, having a creepy instinct in her back that he was on the point to follow, catch, and snatch her away, she span round again, crying: "Do not follow me! Mind you! If you like, be at the elm-tree again at half past ten-and I will communicate with you. Goodbye —"

Now she did not once look back; and he had not heard that fainting "Good-bye," it had fainted so.

He found himself presently in his room at the paper-shop, and lay biting the bed-clothes, spasm after spasm traversing his body.

Then, turning on his back, he lay with his face now toward the trunk, and a little clock ticked ten more minutes before the fact stole into his consciousness that the bag was not on the trunk.

For some time the disappearance was too stupendous to find room in his brain. He got up and paced, stunned, just conscious of a feeling of unease.

Now he was searching the room mechanically. It was not there. . . .

And again he paced, tapping his top teeth with a fingernail; and now he called down the stair: "Have you seen, Mrs. Sturgess, the calico bag you gave me today?"

"Why, no."

"Has anyone been in my room?"

"Why, *no*, sir! Only myself."

Again he began to pace, and suddenly the grand reality stabbed his brain like a dagger: he was poor. . . .

O'Hara! Where was he. . . .?

His forehead dropped upon the mantel-board, and he leant staring downward there, a miserable man.

But suddenly the man said quietly aloud, raising himself: "All right: better so. O, I have not been myself — virtue has gone out of me — !"

Presently he noticed that it was near the hour of her unexpected *rendezvous* under the elm. . . .

And nearly all the way he ran — wild to see her again — until he neared the tree, when, descrying a female form, he came stooping with humility, but soon saw that it was a girl, her head in a shawl, whom he did not know.

And she, coming to meet him, said: "What is your name, sir?"

"Why?"

"I am Miss Frankl's messenger."

"My name is Hogarth."

"Will you turn this way that I may see your eyes? . . . All right: Miss Frankl directs me to give you these."

The girl, who had been weighted down toward the left, handed him an envelope, and a steel box.

Never was he so bewildered! On the way home, he observed that the box had three knobs of gold, surrounded by rays, and, inlaid in the top, the letters "R. F."; when he tore open the envelope in his room he found in pencil on one half-sheet:

"Turn the 10 of the right knob to the ray 5; the 5 of the middle knob to the ray 0; the 15 of the left knob to the ray 10: and the box will open."

No more. When he had set wildly to work, and the lid turned back, his eyes beheld the calico bag.

Rebekah had, in fact, before setting out to the *rendezvous* at nine, seen her father and O'Hara return to the Hall, bearing the bag between them; and, she, crouching at the side door, as before, had heard them talk, arranging details. Her father had then said that before he could write any document, he must either ring or go search for paper: and suddenly she had heard an oath, a thud, a scuffle, had turned the key, softly entered, seen the men struggling against the other door, a revolver, held by the muzzle, in O'Hara's hand; and before she had been sighted by the two desperate men, had had the bag, lying near on an escritoire, and was gone. She had then sent some servants to the scene, and hurried to her chamber.

Later she had heard that O'Hara had escaped through a window, and that her father was raving below in a sort of fit: for Frankl supposed that O'Hara had the jewels, as O'Hara that Frankl had them; and after tending her father, she had dashed out to the *rendezvous*, the jewels then in her room.

As for Hogarth, he did not neglect her warning: and, having left a note for O'Hara, telling him where to find him, at Loveday's, took a late train southwards.

By what marvel Rebekah had become possessed of the jewels he did not even seek to fathom; but one of his uppermost feelings was shame for having suspected O'Hara of stealing them: and for years could never be got to believe in the bad faith of the prelate, his tutor.

Near midnight, on reaching the obscure townlet of Hadston, he there took a bed — not to sleep.

At the tiny inn-window he made periodic arrivals, looked out unseeing at a cart, a wall of flint and Flemish brick, and a moonlit country, then weighed anchor, and swerved away on another voyage; then arrived anew, looked out, saw nothing, and weighed.

He walked now in the dark of the valley of humiliation, with those words written in flame in his brain: "This is my favoured lot — my exaltation to afflictions high": he had allowed a woman to say them to him, and he went "*I!*"

He, the richest of men, was, therefore, that night poorer than any wretch, brought right down, naked, exposed to death, and he filled that chamber with his moans: "God have mercy upon me! a vulgar rich man . . . a dreadful contented clown. . . ."

But toward morning he lay calmer, weeping like Peter, and at peace.

Being without money, he sent the next day a small stone to Loveday, asking him to sell it; also to meet old Tom Bates on the night appointed, and keep him till he, Hogarth, came to London.

Four days later he received the money in the name of "Mr. Beech," but the old Bates had not kept the *rendezvous*; and a month later a detective agency discovered that the fisher was dead.

At Hadston Hogarth remained two months, the most occupied man anywhere, yet passing for a lounger in the townlet.

Here and now he was descended deep into himself, aspiring to greatness, set on high designs; and, as the days passed, his thoughts more and more took form, though sometimes, with a sudden heart-pang, he would flinch and shrink, pierced by a consciousness of the unwieldy thing which he was at; and he would mutter: "I *must* be mad." Anon he would start and cower at a distinct sound of cannon in his ears.

Usually, during the day, he had with him an atlas, a pair of compasses.

One day he took train, to see the sea.

Another day, happening to look into the goat-hair trunk, he saw that account book, containing the addresses of the signatories to his old "association," and was overjoyed. "Quite a little army," he tenderly said: "I won't forget them."

After two months he left Hadston for London, having in his head a new age hatched.

XXVIII

THE LETTER

It was night when Hogarth broke into the presence of Loveday at Cheyne Gardens with a glad face, crying: "Forgive me, my friend, for being a boor!"

"You are forgiven," Loveday answered with his smile, hastening to meet him: "the broken picture, you see, is in a better frame, and so are we. What could have made us invent a quarrel about — land, of all things!"

"Come, let us talk," said Hogarth: "not long — all about land, and sea, too. I suppose you have nothing to tell about my sister? Never mind — we shall find her. Come, sit and give me *all* your intelligence. You are not interested in land, then? You *will* be in ten minutes — it is interesting. Listen: all the land of the earth is *mine*, and all the sea especially — a good thing, for, for a hundred years Europe, especially England, has wanted a master: the anarchy of our modern life is too terrible! it cannot arrange itself; and now the hour has struck, though none has heard the bell."

"Hogarth! but you gabble like a mad god," cried Loveday. "I am all in the dark —"

"I will tell you."

And he spoke, first going into his discovery at Colmoor, frowning upon Loveday, ploughing the truth into his brow; proving how modern misery, in its complexity, had its cause in one simple old fault, sure as the fact that smoke ascends, or apples fall. And when he saw conviction beam in Loveday's face, he next told what had happened at the elm-tree, and what would happen soon; whereat Loveday, like a frightened child, clung to his arm, and once gasped: "Oh no — my God!" and once felt a gory ghost raise horror in his hairs.

An hour afterwards they were bending over a sheet of paper, Hogarth in his shirt-sleeves, writing, Loveday overlooking, suggesting, when two men were announced, and in stepped O'Hara with bows and polished hesitations, followed by his shadow, Harris; and, "Ah, O'Hara . . ." cried Hogarth, still writing, "who is that with you?"

"A friend of mine," said Loveday, for O'Hara had introduced Harris to him, and he had adopted Harris as a human study, horrid, but amusing.

The moment O'Hara saw the face of Hogarth, he started,

muttering: "He has the diamonds back! God! is he a magician?"

And Harris drawled nasally: "Of course, you wouldn't know me now, Mr. 76! Were there not ten cleansed, but where are the nine, it *is*."

Hogarth was silent — had not yet decided what to do with Harris.

"This is my tenth call here, Hogarth," said O'Hara, "in the hope of seeing you, and the streets, you know, are no small risk. You see how I am muffled up, and this gentleman, too. By the bye, I have selected a cargo of books for you —"

"No study for a month," said Hogarth, "but I shall want you all the same. Just come over here and watch me write this thing. You, Harris, sit right over there."

Harris cursed, but obeyed, while O'Hara came and bent under the golden glow of the silk shade a brow puckered with a care of puzzlement, as he read.

Then he fell into the work, and was soon the director of it — invaluable! knew everything! remembered forgotten points; explained technicalities; the proper person in each little State to whom the document must be directed, the style of addressing him. Of one sentence he said: "That will never do — lacks formality"; and of another: "Tut, they will laugh at that — it is provincial and insolent," distracted between the work and his brandy glass. At last, about eleven, the three brains had produced a letter.

Hogarth laid claim to the sea as his private property, and warned the nations.

XXIX

PRIORITY OF CLAIM

A gentleman — a Permanent Under-secretary — stood one noon, his back to a fireplace in a bright-carpeted room at the Foreign Office, letting his eyes move over some opened letters submitted to him, and presently came upon the following document, its crest a flag, containing in blue the letters "R. F.":

"17 LEADENHALL STR., E.G.
"To the Most Hon.,
"The Marquis of Hallam, K.G.,
"Foreign Office,
"Westminster, S.W.
"MY LORD MARQUIS:
    "I have the honour hereby to make formal announcement to Your Lordship that I am on the point of setting up in the midst of the world a new Power, whose relations with the King's Government will, I trust, be relations of friendliness.
    "It is my desire that Your Lordship forthwith convey to the King's Most Excellent Majesty the announcement which is the subject of this Memorandum.
    "My purposes and policy in the establishment of the new Power will hereafter appear; and my properly accredited Ministers will, in due course, present themselves at the Chancelleries of the world.
    "Hitherto a British subject, it is my will to acquire diplomatic recognition — as soon as such shall comport with the dignity of the Great Powers — as an Independent Sovereign, under the title of: 'Lord of the Sea'. (Address: 'Your Lordship's Majesty', or 'My Lord King'.)
    "The domain of my Power will be the sea: and to the sea I hereby set up claim as far as such points of latitude as have been attained by Man, and over all degrees of longitude. Provided only: that nothing in this claim shall be held to infringe upon the prior claim of any nation to a 'three-mile limit' round its coasts, nor to any national fisheries whatsoever, nor to any claim of the Kingdom of Denmark with respect to the Sound.
    "The validity of my title to the sea must be considered to rest on the same basis as the title of any private owner to any area of the earth's crust: namely, Priority of Claim. If one is valid, so, necessarily, is the other, this title to land, based on

Priority of Claim, being admitted in the Law of all civilized Nations.

"This my claim will come into operation on this day three years hence.

"I have the honour to subscribe myself
"Your Lordship's
"Obdt. Servant,
"RICHARD HOGARTH."

The Under-secretary, a pale, distinguished man, read this letter with a little lift of one eyebrow, then let it drop from him into a waste-paper basket.

At the German, the Turkish, capitals it met much the same reception. Nowhere did it reach the eye of a Departmental Head. It went to Siam, to the Prince of Monaco, to Ecuador, and was tossed to cumber a basket, or moulder on a file.

But Hogarth, who knew that it would be instantly forgotten, had written it so as to be able to say that he had written it.

At that time he was lodging in a top room in Bloomsbury, and had an underground den in Leadenhall Street, on its doors the words: "R. Beech & Co." Thither in a brougham he drove daily, lying very low, but holding in that den interviews with all sorts and conditions of men, and feeling his way toward operations of dimensions so immense, that their mere project had a modifying influence upon industry.

XXX

MR. BEECH

During six weeks Hogarth lived that life of daily passage between Keppel Street and his office, unknown to the general world, but spreading a noise of rumour through certain circles of the business world. All day in the den the gas-jets brawled upon him, he not for minutes casting a glance, if a clerk brought a caller's name. And here was no novice modesty in the tackling of affairs; as O'Hara, who would be there, said: "You must have been *born* in the City; you have the airs, the very tricks, of Threadneedle Street, you — Jew." In a day the prelate counted seven hundred and thirteen telegrams from the Terni Cannon foundry, many a diamond dealer, polisher, cutter, the Vulcan Shipyard of Stettin, the Clydebank, Cramp of Philadelphia, the Russian Finance Minister, San Francisco, Lloyd's, metal brokers, the Neva, and one night, the eve of a dash to Amsterdam, he, with O'Hara, Loveday, and five clerks, sat swotting till morning broke, sustained by gin and soda-water. The priest lived with wide eyes at the easy fleetness with which Hogarth rolled off him the greatest affairs: as when on the day after his return from Holland he stood, his thumbs in his waistcoat armholes, with quite the right air of serene City-king, his tallness possessing considerable natural courtliness, and the De Beers' Secretary sat before him, saying, "Well, Mr. Beech, I have spent the morning with your brokers, and have felt that I must see you personally before calling a meeting. This proposition is so tremendous —"

"I only wish I had some time," said Hogarth, "I would invite you to dine upon the matter; but it is really so simple — everything at bottom is merely twice two are four. And you are not obliged to turn over Kimberley to me: only, in that case, as I have said, I shall be compelled to flood the market with diamonds as cheap as cat's-eyes —"

When De Beers stared, Hogarth shrugged, saying: "I suppose I must convince you —" and, unlocking a safe, he took out an *écrin* which contained three stones. De Beers appeared to see Titania peering in their fairy painting.

"Of stones of this water and carating," said Hogarth, "we have two hundred and eleven in the Bank of England, two hundred and thirty-eight in other English and Continental banks, and seventy-five in safe-deposit. The carating of these three is 111-1/2;

and in the sixties, such as this one" — he took a stone from among coppers in his pocket — "we have three hundred odd on hand, all flawless, and an equal number cutting. When I point out, what you know, that our mine is as yet without the delicate plant of Kimberley, the stones being simply picked from the blue-earth by three inexpert friends of the firm on the spot, you will recognize that the wealth of a mine can no further go. . . ."

He was rid of the visitor within six minutes, and within three weeks, by knack and organization, had gathered into his hands most of the reins necessary to the control of the world's trade in diamonds.

In an outer room sat O'Hara, writing, reading Theocritus, or a little book on mediaeval embroidery, forefinger on cheek; and anon, absolutely without motive, he would rise, creep, and peep through a keyhole at Hogarth, then on stalking, bowing tiptoe, grinning a rancid grimace of stealth, get back to his seat, and read — the tutor falling over head and ears in love with his pupil: one of those passions that end tragically.

One day, as he so sat, the bell *pinged*, the door opened, and O'Hara jumped to find himself face to face with — Frankl, who had come to see the new diamond king, in the firm belief that Mr. Beech was none other than O'Hara; and, "I thought as much!" said he.

"*Sh-h-h*," went O'Hara bitterly — "for God's sake! he is *in there* — !"

"Who is?"

"*Hogarth!*"

"Well, but —"

"Outside — in the passage —"

They stepped out; and Frankl, his eyelids red, said: "I have only this day crawled from bed with the blow you struck my temple, or I should have had you before this —"

"*Sh-h-h.* Your own fault, sir. *You* played false first —"

"Played false with my own diamonds? You hand me over this day one-half those stones, or I bring a civil action for the whole, hound you to beggary, and drag you back to your convict-cell where you come from."

"Don't lift your voice, I beg of you. Tut, you rave. You can't bring a civil action against a great millionaire who doesn't care to defend; and as for me, I do assure you, I haven't fifty pounds today. *It is Hogarth who is Mr. Beech!*"

"*Who?*" — Frankl obtruded a startled ear, frowning his eyes small.

"Hogarth. He has the diamonds back!"

"Which diamonds? How did he get 'em?"

"He is — *in* — *there*: better go and ask him! He got them by black art — by the aid of the legion of mediaeval witches which wait on him — *God* knows how he got them! *You* gave them to him! *I* gave them to him! but he's got them — *in* — *there*! Better go and ask him — don't be afraid — just for the roaring fun of it —"

"Hogarth?"

"Yes — Hogarth, Hogarth."

"Cheated the gallows? And out of prison? And rolling in my wealth, my riches, my diamonds? Oh, no! — is that fair? A dog? Is that how the world is run? God of Israel!"

"There is this to be said for him: that he *deserves* to be rich —"

"Who? So you are taking his part now?"

"Tut — !"

"There is no *tut* about it! You confess that you are nothing more than a penniless hanger-on: well, then, I have *you*! back to prison you go this hour —!"

O'Hara's cheek trembled; but he said: "A sufficiently vain threat, sir: I am Hogarth's tutor: he won't let me be taken. Don't waste your time, you impotent Jew —"

"Tutor? That's good! What you teaching him? — murder? *outrage*? He *ought* to have a tutor, he! That's good! Tutor! Well, suppose I drop a line first post to your nice *pupil* to let him know that it was his *tutor* who stole his diamonds —"

At this threat O'Hara felt himself outflanked; and though his eyes surveyed the Jew unflinchingly during a silence, inwardly he had succumbed.

"A man in Hogarth's situation," he slowly said, "is always liable to attack. Why should two sharp old fellows like you and me, whose interests are identical, quarrel?" — and instantly Frankl took note of that surrender, that weak spot, and knew that the man was his.

"Well," said he, "so true — two old gaol-birds like you and me, eh? So true, so true. But what beats me — who runs Beech's? Hogarth is only a young farmer: he can't operate all the big things I hear about this Mr. Beech —"

"Tut, you do not conceive the man as he is at all," said O'Hara: "perhaps you cannot. High finance, the first day he looked into it, ceased to mystify him, for he goes always to the ground of things, touches bottom, where first principles lie, and first principles are simple as two and two. It was because he had discovered a first principle that he escaped from Colmoor. And he is as nimble as six twisting minnows: what you or I learned in a year he learns in an hour, and if he does not know the usual way, not an instant does he hesitate to invent a way. You know about Owthwaite's: how the recent shake-out of the market threatened their collapse, like so many others'. Owthwaite's, in fact, had already declared, when Hogarth decided to help them over. And how? Not Bills! He filled up a call-in of two millions and a half by the India Council, resettled loans and short-discount business, cheapened money, and in twelve hours his *protégés* were off the rocks. And now I hear —"

"But why not buy a chapel, and preach about him? I hate —"

"Stop! O Lord — he is calling —"

"Here's my card; I want to see you tonight at that address at eight."

And that night at Frankl's town-house in Hanover Square Jew and prelate conferred, O'Hara for some time resisting, but finally again taking sides against his saviour. He disclosed that Hogarth, beyond doubt, kept a few diamonds in a goat-hair trunk in his room — enough to make two ordinary fortunes, and also carried two or three, with some hundred-pound notes on his person; and this was made the basis of a scheme for bringing about the arrest of Hogarth, the first step being to get from Hogarth the sum he carried about him, leaving him in a situation where he would find himself powerless to bribe.

This Frankl undertook; and O'Hara promised to lend Harris, and some friends of Harris.

Now, during these weeks Hogarth was living in some fear, haunted by insecurity and a vision of Colmoor; and, remembering the theft at Thring, with a consciousness of Frankl somewhere in him, he went not only with diamonds on his person, but a revolver as well, and a puñal of Toledo.

But three evenings after the conference in Hanover Square, he received this letter:

"Dearest Richard:

"It is long since we have met. This is to let you know that I have heard of your getting out, and your coming into great things, which has made my heart rejoice. I, alas, am just the other way about. I am staying for the next two days at Woodfield Cottage, Wylie Street, Finchley Road, N. I understand that you are lying low, so better not come to see me perhaps, but send me something.

"Your loving

"Margaret."

And at sight of these words such a whirlwind transacted itself in the brain of Hogarth, that he hardly awoke to sense till he found himself in a railway compartment, going northward. It was only then that, reading the letter again, he started.

The handwriting was hers! he was sure. But the words . . .?

"I, alas, am *just the other way about*" — "better not come to me perhaps, but *send me something.*" There was a tone here not in character. But her handwriting! This was no forgery. If she had written *from dictation* that might explain it.

In this uncertainty he left the train, and took cab, scenting trouble ahead.

The difficulty was to find Wylie Street, which was a half built street of five cottages in a new neighbourhood of brick, and when what was supposed to be Wylie Street was discovered, the cab had to stop, for across it lay bricks, hods and barrows in mud. So Hogarth alighted, and, peering, stumbled forward: no lamp; above, a labouring half moon riding a sky of clouds, like a poor ship riding the bleak morning after a hurricane, her masts all gone by the board: and Hogarth could just see that three of the five cottages were roofless brick, the fourth unfinished, so the fifth, alone on the other side, must be — "Woodfield"

"Woodfield" was unlighted: and the moment he ascertained this, he felt himself the victim of a plot; but not all the whispers of prudence could hold him now from seeing the adventure through. Loudly he flung back the little gate, with rash precipitancy entered: and as he sprang up the three steps to ring, he was seized.

They were five, three being big fellows, two masked.

His main sensation was gladness that none, apparently, was a policeman; and he set hilariously to work with his knuckles. This, however, could not save, soon he was on his back, striking his head; but when he saw that the object was to rifle his pockets, letting be, he managed to steal out the *puñal* from his breast, and presently with a sudden upheaving and scattering rage, was staggering to his legs. Before he could be stopped, he was making for the gate, but close upon him ran one of the five — a slim man, masked — who fired Hogarth's own pistol at his legs, but missed: whereupon, Hogarth, with a backward twist, struck at random with the dagger, which entered the man's breast. But at the same time a whistle shrilled, and from an opposite cottage rushed out at last what he dreaded — three policemen.

These had been placed there on the understanding that it was thither that Hogarth would go, the object of the plot being to rifle his pockets before he was officially taken; and it succeeded to the extent that his pockets *were* rifled: but he knocked down one officer, and dodged the other two, reaching his taxi; and, having previously arranged with the cabman, got off racing.

But the masked man whom he had struck down was Harris, who for weeks lay raving in fever — an ill-fated stroke, for Harris had a memory.

As for Hogarth, he rushed home to Keppel Street, hurried down the trunk, and was off to Cheyne Gardens.

"Well," he cried, breaking in upon Loveday, "this phase of our life is up! Look at my clothes: I have had a fight — Frankl, I suppose. I wanted to live a simple life for two years: but they won't let me, you see. Ha! — then the other thing. From this night we bury our identity under mountains of splendour. It is disgusting to me, this life, skulking, thinking to bribe honest men. Meantime, you must find me some room to hide in with the trunk — mustn't stay here tonight. And tomorrow you buy me a boat to take us off from some point of the coast — Come —"

XXXI

THE HAMMERS

Within six months Hogarth, as distinct from "Beech," had risen upon the consciousness of Europe, say like the morning sun: and the wearied worker, borne at evening through crowded undergrounds, might read his name with a listless incomprehension.

He impressed the popular fancy, especially in Paris, where he was best known, as erratic: as once when, by a stroke of financial sleight-of-hand, he got the young Government of Russia into a tight place, then refused them a loan, except on condition of the lease to him of the Kremlin: and for three months squalid old Moscow was the most cometary Court anywhere — acts savouring of a meteorite waywardness which impressed him, more than anything, upon the everyday world; and he won a tolerant wonder.

However, an outcry, led by the *Intransigeant*, denounced his acquisition of the site of royal St. Cloud for his Paris residence on the ground that he was a Jew, betrayed by his face — an accusation which caused the buying up of hundreds of thousands of his photographs — and on the ground that his design was to familiarize the people with the idea of his sovereignty, and by a *coup* to seize the Government; at which Paris was in a ferment, and a midnight mob traversed the *Bois* and demolished some of his mason-work. The next day, however, the Minister of the Interior announced from the Tribune that Hogarth was no Jew, but an Englishman *pur sang*; and, on the whole, Hogarth had his way: the noise died down; and where parterres and avenues had stood on the old palace site, there arose one of those enchanting fabrics, which, from the Bosphorus to London, bore the name of "The Beeches."

At this time he had dependent upon him a retinue, serving him in multifarious ways from electrical adviser to spy, and from chancellor to recruiter, numbering many hundreds. He knew five thousand faces by sight; in England had two armies — a small one collecting data as to acreages, tenures, trades, scales, wages, prices, crimes, mines, and a large one, numbering five thousand, doing gun-practice in Westring Vale: for, England being for sale, he had bought at thrice its market value that part of it called Westring; and on the sea also he kept a little army of a thousand, borne in old cruiser-hulks bought from the English Admiralty, hulks whose crews, in rotation, changed places with drafts from the Westring barracks.

Once he disappeared from Europe, and when he returned the President of the Republic of Ecuador, thenceforth one of his closest friends, was with him; whereupon, through newspapers in the pay of Beech's, the rumour commenced to appear that the Ecuador Government was giving orders for coast-defence on an unparalleled scale, in view of probable hostilities with Peru.

In the midst of which activities O'Hara said to him one morning: "You can now be called a mathematician."

"I have many admirers, and but one teacher, O'Hara," Hogarth answered: "teach me."

O'Hara cut a secret grimace.

After the failure of the Finchley Road plot he had had another repentance, and had set himself earnestly to the cultivation of Hogarth's mind; but the priest's spirit was not "erect"; he had "falls"; maintained a correspondence with the Jew, whose eye of malice never slept; and once at Cairo, twice in Paris, Hogarth had to use words like these: "I must tell you, O'Hara, that I have heard of your recent behaviour. Naturally, there are those that see for me, and I do not mean to be compromised by your low revels."

"Wretch that I am!" broke out O'Hara with smitten brow, and for half a day was on his knees in an affliction of self-reproach. Yet the same night he wrote a letter to Frankl containing the words: "You do not know, *you cannot dream*, the high and slippery road which H. has chosen for his feet: the future is *big* with events. Wait: his sublime path is not without pitfalls. . . ."

Study with O'Hara was in the morning; at night, when possible, that other study of the working world: and often then Hogarth would withdraw from opera in the St. Cloud palace, or from some "crush," to give an hour to the river of statistics with which he was inundated.

Till these years he had never seen into the sea of things as it is: his life so isolated — had not even read newspapers.

Now he saw and knew. There below him blazed some masque of beauty and majesty, moving under a moonlight of blue-darting jets of electric light all among colossal columns of alabaster robed in vine and rose; or there below some Melba voice, all trembles and maze of wobbly trebles, warbling: and the thronged hall sat tranced; but before *him* — figures: parents killed their children for insurance-money — keeping children in cellars till their flesh grew green, keeping sore the stumps of children's legs; with some trades certain comic-sounding names had got to be associated, "potter's rot," "phossy jaw," — enormous horror; each day in England one million people had to seek pauper-relief, many perished; of aged persons 40 per cent were permanent paupers; children were paid 2-1/2d. for making 144 match-boxes; pretty girls (though pretty girls were detestably rare) were allowed to work, nay *forced* to — far harder than any ten savages ever dreamt of working; in Glasgow 41 of every 100 families lived in one room: fathers, for weeks, did not see their children, except asleep; girls took emetics to vomit up cotton-dust — enormous horror, comic-opera in Hell: and below in the "crush" the voice of the warbler, cooing, shook.

Sometimes he would mutter: "But that can't be true!" There, though, the figures lay; and presently he would take heart, and say: "Well, not for long now, God help me. . . ."

Whether God helped him or not, certainly Man was helping him: ten thousand and ten thousand hammers — from Spezzia to Belfast — in model-office and mould-loft and rolling-mill — in foundry and yard and roaring forge — were ringing upon metal for him, their clamorous industry clattering over Europe and America carillons of his name.

XXXII

WONDER

Almost suddenly that noise of chiming hammers reached the general ear.

First in the German Admiralty was wonder when a spy, engaged as a workman at Birkenhead, sent to his Government information that the British Government was up to something: something of a novelty so extraordinary, that as yet he could form no conception as to its object. That it was intended for the sea one must suppose: yet it was evident that nothing of such odd draughtsmanship — of such mastodon proportions — had ever yet taken the water.

He had been clever: had penetrated even the model-office, peered at detailed draughtsman's-plans, developed from the original specifications, as well as at orders for Krupp plates, frames, etc.; had listened in the yard to the talk of four naval men acting as a Board of Inspection; was able to give details of the machining of enormous processed plates to sizes determined by templates, the length of pan-headed rivets, the specific gravity of an average cubic foot, the scarfing of edges, the accumulation of prepared material. The wooden half-model, he said, was a one-ninety-sixth, instead of the usual one-forty-eighth; yet, even so, it was 5 ft. 7-½ ins. long, as much broad, and 1 ft. ¾ in. high. This meant that the structure would measure 180 yards square — over one-tenth of a mile — with a depth of 34 yards. Already the far-reaching chaos of scaffolding had run up eight yards, with stringers and frames to a like level. There were no keel-blocks, for there was no keel — or rather, the keel was a circular plate a yard in diameter, resting on a single block, the shape of the structure to be a perfect square, along the sides of which four battleships might lie like toy-boats: the bottom, from circular keel to upward bend, having the same shape as a battleship's seen in midship section, only with four faces instead of two. From the knee-bend the sides ran up perpendicular; but at the level evidently intended to be the water-line they struck inward, so that the flat roof was smaller than the area below; the position of this water-line giving a definite clue to the intended displacement; and this again showing that the whole — roof, sides, bottom, and all — would be one wall of Simmons armour — steeling and backing — layer on layer — no less than 4ft. 9-1/4 ins. thick.

Yet this stupendous ark, or citadel — so simple was its plan — would be turned out in less time than a second-class cruiser; and its cost, apart from yard-modifications and groundways, small in proportion.

This, and much else, the spy reported: but the new fact was obvious as the sun; the British and French Intelligence Departments, too, were soon conning it; and a week later it was established that, not one, but at least eleven, such structures were a-building in the world.

There went the rumour: "It is the Government of Ecuador's order. . . ."

This was at the end of April; Hogarth, obeying some instinct which continually drew him toward Asia, then loitering alone in Trebizond tea-gardens and bazaars, buying a braid-bag, mule-trapping, or silver sword of the Khurdish cavaliers; while Trinity House gave the alarm that if ever the steel monsters, whatever their object, were launched, "they would constitute, in the absence of proper precautions, a serious danger by night to the world's mercantile marine," and while Lloyd's, the Maritime Exchanges, the Hydrographic Offices, lived in a species of amazement, and were already putting the steel islands into the gazetteers and manuals; the newspapers, too, inundated with the views of the public, took sides, maintaining, some of them, that it was the part of Governments to ascertain the objects of the new works, others that any tampering with their progress at this late stage might even mean revolution, so profound was their intimacy with industry. Hogarth, meanwhile, having come to El Khiff, the camp of the Bedouin pilgrims, there spent some days, and then, passing between Jerusalem and Jericho in a caravan of Moabite sheiks, went visiting the holy places of Israel, everywhere examining the country, especially its agriculture, with great minuteness. It was only on his return to Jerusalem that he heard of the agitation in Europe: and at once set off Westward from Joppa.

From his arrival at Paris toward the end of May the wildest legends, originated by him, began to be printed, the most persistent relating to the diamond and banking House of Beech, which, it was given out, had discovered diamonds within the crust of a Pacific rock-island: the new structures, ordered by them, being designed to blast the coast-wall with dynamite guns. Cavillers pointed out that diamonds never occur in nature in this fashion, and that, even so, it did not need a fort made of armour five feet thick to fire off dynamite guns; but so continuously was the thing repeated, explained, and puffed, that when the London manager of Beech partially admitted it, the most incredulous acquiesced; though at the very same period it was proclaimed that the President of the Ecuador Republic, Hogarth's friend, had admitted to the Great Powers that the forts were to his order (as, in fact, they nominally were); and anti-climax was reached when a naval expert, asked to do a hurried article for the Times, made some error in calculation, and came out with the statement that the fort-things would sink of their own weight. This article was headed "Beech's Folly"; and even when the error was detected, the roar of merriment retained its momentum and rolled: so that, to the hour of the first launch, the enterprise was commonly referred to as "Beech's Folly," and scarf-pins, ink-stands, etc., in the shape of the forts, were sold with that superscription: "Beech's Folly."

This, translated into French, became that horrible gallicism: *la bêtise Biche*.

Gradually, however, the Ecuador-Beech rage died down the hammers, heard for nine days through the turmoil of the world, were again drowned in it. The scarf-pins ceased to sell. The 'buses rolled, the Bank cashed notes, the long street roared — and all was as usual.

Only, in the valley of Westring there was drill and target-practice and barrack-life routine, the Westring-eccentricity being associated with the millionaire, Hogarth, the island-eccentricity with the House of Beech: and in the popular mind Beech and Hogarth were two notions. Islands were building in Italy, France, Germany, Russia; in England, Scotland, Ireland; at Maine, Baltimore, Newport News: but the Governments, lacking the machinery, and also the initiative, and judging tomorrow by yesterday, gave no sign from their Olympus.

In June, John Loveday being then at Westring, one morning O'Hara arrived, he, too, having left mediæval chasubles to grind at war, and though he no longer taught Hogarth, a relation persisted between them; and always not far from O'Hara was to be found Harris, living now on the pinnacle of dandy bliss, twisting a dandy stick.

It was on the last night of this visit to Westring that O'Hara at a late hour went with stealth and hesitations along a corridor of the Hall, and finally tapped at Loveday's door, who, detesting the priest, and reading in bed, disgustedly dashed off his cigarette ash, as he called: "Come in."

And a long time they spoke of things other than the real object of O'Hara's visit, till O'Hara said: "But — may I ask you something?"

"Do."

"Well, now, you are a fellow more in the counsels of Hogarth than another. I want to ask you right out frankly — is it a fact that Hogarth is choosing Admirals for the islands?"

"I believe it is," answered Loveday with his long-bow smile of amusement: "I already know, for example, that Saltoun will admiral the *Homer* in the Indian Ocean, Vladimir the *Ruskin* in the Atlantic Crescent, and the young Marquis of Erroll the *Justice* in the Yellow Sea."

"Those all?"

"All I know of. I believe, however, that Hogarth is in the throes of decision as to the rest."

"I see."

There was a silence full of Loveday's smile.

"But," said O'Hara, "what I meant is this: you know what I have been to Hogarth; without me, what could the poor fellow have done, after all? I have taught him to think, to dance, and to dine. Now, then, I ask you right out frankly — am *I*, my son, in the list of Admirals?"

Loveday, flushing, started upright, and sank back. "No, I don't fancy that your name is among those entertained, O'Hara."

"We will see about that. Woe to Hogarth, and to his advisers, if he dare slight O'Hara, my son! What! after preparing myself with toilsome zeal for this post? and after two promises from Hogarth's own lips — ?"

"I deny the promises on Hogarth's behalf."

"Oh, you! Hogarth looks upon you as a plaything. I do assure you, you are not taken seriously, Mr. Loveday. How should such as you know what Hogarth promises or designs?" — his cheeks trembling.

And, Loveday, smiling again, though pale: "Well, if we admit the promises . . . but — have you accurately acquainted Hogarth with your past, sir?"

"Most decidedly, sir!"

"If you have not, I think he should know it."

"Your threats do not affect me, sir! In three days I shall be in Petersburg with Hogarth, and shall take a pleasure in writing you the name of the island to which I am appointed."

"In three days I also — !" He stopped: but O'Hara understood.

Now the door rushed open, and in looked Harris in undervest and drawers, beneath his arm a bundle of walkingsticks, which he had been caring and telling.

And "'Ere," he drawled, "when are you coming to 'ave that bit of cold mutton? It's past twelve o'clock as it is."

"I am coming, boy," said O'Hara, rising with brisk obedience.

"Then, come, why don't you! There were shepherds watching their pretty little flocks by night, but to leave a man watching the cold animal is a bit out. Come along!" — and O'Hara went.

He reached Petersburg twelve hours before Loveday, his reason for choosing that time being his knowledge that Frankl was in Petersburg, and with him Rebekah, Frankl being in a deal with the new-régime Minister of Finance.

For, as O'Hara had been asking himself the agonized question: "By what absolute *finesse* can I, *just now*, win Hogarth?" the mere presence of Rebekah in the same city with Hogarth drew him thither.

But the next day, when Loveday came, nothing had been done — no chance of *tête-à-tête* with Hogarth: and that day was O'Hara an anxious and tremulous man, living on the tiptoe and *qui vive* of lynx-eyed keenness.

The same night at a masque at the Palace of Peterhof Loveday got a chance of dialogue with Hogarth, they seated amid greenery and coloured gleams, Hogarth groomed to the glittering glass of his shoes, his legs stretched, arm akimbo; and presently Loveday led the talk to things of the sea. "What an extraordinary activity! The British Government launches the *Peleus* next Monday at Deptford — the first 28,000-ton war-boat; and seven cruisers on the slips. Then the French, Austro-German, Russian —"

"Ha! — I know. They won't build long."

"Still the confidence?"

"You can only ask, my dear boy, because you do not yet see what a thing the battleship really is — much more than half a sham. The march of invention is from the complex to the simple: for simplicity is strength; but to the moment when I began to construct, naval construction had not followed this law: for from the old smooth-bores, aimed with tackle and quoin, to the present regime of electric wires, you have had a continual advance in complexity — always within the same little arc of thought — till now the most complex of things is a battleship; and if you ask me which is the weaker, a battleship or a watch, I answer a battleship — *weak* meaning liability to the injuries which they were built to resist. In such a case as that of the *Maine*, sunk at Havana, one might fancy that the task of naval constructors is to turn out a thing to sink with a minimum of trouble; and you remember the

Camperdown and *Victoria*, how, playing about together, one happened to touch the other, when down plunged that other. These ships are a compromise between three *motifs* — speed, resisting attack, and attacking: and the first is so antagonistic to the second, and also to the third, that the net result is almost a Nonentity, or No-Thing. Nothing, in fact, could be more *queer*, unfounded, than these ships; and the future will look back upon them with pity. Hence the simple islands, following the law: and don't think t hat their efficacy is a thing riskier than arithmetic itself"

"Good," went Loveday. "But, Richard — captain your islands with decent men."

"You have something on your mind: what is it?"

"It is — delicate. Have I your permission to speak?"

"Why, John, yes."

"Well then — is O'Hara to be an Admiral?"

"Old Pat? Hardly, I think. He may. But no — I don't think. Poor old talky-talky. He has worked hard for us, John: and his fund of experience, in one way and another, has been invaluable. Well, I don't know: I have had the idea, but I don't suppose that, in reality — Still, I am fond of him, John. Such a tongue, and such a versatile brain, is he! He was my comfort for many a sombre day in prison —"

Listening near with rancid grin behind some greenery, O'Hara kept nodding emphatic assents of satisfaction to Hogarth's praise.

"But, stop," said Loveday: "do you know why he was in prison?"

"He was innocent."

"Of what?"

"Of stealing some diamonds entrusted him by the Pope."

"Bah! he lies. His trial was a *cause célèbre*, and hence the false name he gave me at first: the moment I heard you say 'O'Hara' I knew the man. He had committed an assault upon a lady in a train —"

"Beast that he is," went Hogarth, while O'Hara's eyes started from his head: "and liar, too, it seems. Ha! — he gave me the most circumstantial story. Why didn't you tell me this before?"

"It was delicate —"

"Beast that he is. Yet how complex is character! the man's tenderness for his Church is so charming —"

"Fiddlesticks! Look here, Richard, I am come all the way from Westring to tell you this thing. Don't you give vast powers to that man: it isn't decent; and I have a feeling that it will be a baleful piece of weakness. And don't get easy, and tolerant, and fat in the eyes, Hogarth. That is a very significant Bible-story — the implacable disaster sent upon old Eli for no greater crime than a *bonhomme* indolence. And in order to arouse your wrath against this O'Hara, I am going now, against my will, to tell you something: the name of that lady in that train."

"Someone whom I know?"

"Yes."

"Who?"

For a moment Loveday's answer hesitated: and in that moment, O'Hara, with lightning decision, had his mouth at Hogarth's ear: "Come with me quick — then fall down and worship me for a month! *Someone is in the Malachite Hall!*"

Like sudden death Hogarth's colour fled his face; in another instant he was a blind, oblivious wight . . . had known that she was in Petersburg; but not that she was at the masque.

In a moment shrubbery, lights, all life, rushed into transformation for him: and with an excitement of the eyes, the bloodshot left looking bloodier, he went after O'Hara, tossing back at Loveday that fatal saying: "*Tomorrow. . . .*"

A little previously O'Hara, having got from Frankl details of Rebekah's dress, had spotted her in primrose silk, black mask and domino, and soon with Hogarth refound her in the crush: whereas Hogarth went about prospecting over the crowd, with that excitement of his red-veined eyeballs, once even entered into talk with a group of four diplomatists, but all the time with eyeballs absent in hankering tracking, out prowling after one morbid form, as the stallion's prowls after his Sally.

After an hour she said in French over her shoulder: "Why follow me?"

And as he bowed compliance, she added: "Are you well?"

He said: "Yes," and bowed, and she nodded twice, smiling a little, as they parted.

He, on the wings of exaltation, made haste to salute the Throne and leave the palace, rushing toward solitude to brood upon that smile, those familiar nods, and the gentle "Are you well?" — in his landau with him O'Hara, who persecuted him even to his bedroom; and when, after an hour, the priest at last reappeared in a corridor, the night-lights there shone upon an exultant visage, like a climber's who, after long clamberings, at last stamps on the Matterhorn, and looks abroad.

When he entered his own room, he stood with a hung head, till, sharply looking up, he ejaculated with amazed, realization and opening arms: "Well, it's done! — I've got it!" Now he put forefinger to nose, and cut a beastly face at himself in the mirror-wall.

The next day Hogarth rather guiltily said to Loveday: "Well, I have promised old O'Hara the *Mahomet* for the Straits. Don't frown — I owe him something, and the clever beast got over me in crazy moment."

"Quite so," Loveday coldly said: and thenceforth, the thing being done, was mum as to the name of the lady connected with O'Hara's crime.

He returned immediately to England, having there many oc-cupations, which multiplied as the islands everywhere neared completion, the first of the launches taking place at Spezzia on the 7th of February.

A fortnight before this event the Beech-fever had revived, the coming launch being no secret, and the doubt whether "Beech's Folly" might be no folly, and the question what, on the whole, Beech's Folly might really bode, filled once more the conscious-ness of the Western world. By the 1st of February a drop was recorded in many general securities, in "governments," rentes, and consols; in Berlin the bank-rate rose one per cent.; it was stated that specie was accumulating in European vaults; while up leapt futures-cotton in the Liverpool market. At last the First Lord of the Treasury, in a speech at Manchester, gave sign of the Gov-ernment's consciousness of the new fact, saying that he could only repeat the answer given by the First Lord of the Admiralty to the recent Deputations of the Chamber of Shipping and of Merchant Shippers, that Britain and the other maritime nations would know how to protect the seas from any nuisance. He anticipated no nuisance. The structures popularly known as "Beech's Folly" (prolonged laughter) would be provided with lighthouses: and until they proved a nuisance on the ocean's fairways, the Govern-ments must permit to private enterprise that free hand which was the characteristic of our age; moreover, a recognized Government had avowed its association with these structures.

Nevertheless, the fever heightened. The light-system of the *Boodah*, now included in the usual alphabetical lists of derelicts, was conned by thousands of mariners, while in the crowded cap-tains', underwriters', and committee rooms at Lloyd's discussion buzzed and speechified in every tone of gravity. Suddenly in the F. G. and S. clause marine insurance underwent a profound modifi-cation; and it was then that the millionaire, Schroeder, at that time a German clerk in the City, managed to borrow five thousand pounds, and quickly cleared his pile by underwriting on larger F. C. and S. terms. And again raged the sale of the islands as penny salt-cellars, finger-basins, etc.; in broker's and sub-editor's office the tape-machine clicked the hourly progress of preparations at Spezzia; while every by-street was dreadful with that music-hall chorus:

"To Spezzia runs the Pullman train;   The Follies soon their sense will teach; We've Beech, O dear, upon the brain,   He brains upon the beach."

Meantime, the question of the drawing-room was "Are you going to Spezzia?" and by the 7th so great a pilgrimage of tourists — experts, idlers, cinematographers, special correspondents, ministers of state, Yankees, officers, social stars — had flocked to the scene, that accommodation failed in the town and surrounding hill-country, from Le Grazie on the west, to Lerici on the east of the Gulf.

The morning dawned bright — Italian sky, tranquil Italian sea — and by nine the harbour was alive with small-craft and Portovenere steamboats, all gala with flags; on the land side, too, over the hills, up the old road called Giro della Foce, and before the villages commanding the town, spread a cloud of witnesses; while the multitude in possession of *permessos* for the dock-region stretched across a hundred and sixty acres, perched on every coign, and murmuring like the sea.

And all in the air a fluttered consciousness of the to-come, the present nothing, an hour hence everything — like the suspense of nature before gales, and that greatness and novelty of marriage-mornings: for such a bride that day would rush to the brine as it had never embraced.

There lay the hulk, all nuptial in colours, her roof looking like a *plaza* of Lima or La Paz at Carnival, flags in mountain-ridges round her edges, flags in festoons, in slanting clothes-lines, in trophy-groups, on bandroled poles, bedecking her; some scaffolding still round her; and three running derricks, capable of wielding guns and boilers of 140 tons, craned their shears about her. A temporary stair under flags ran right up to a ledge above the waterline: from which ledge little steel steps led here and there to the roof; round the edge of roof and ledge running two balustrades, surrounding the hulk; and over that upper portion, four times repeated in white letters ten feet high, the name *BOODAH* boomed itself.

By eleven some seven hundred people stood and sat on the roof — the *élite* of Europe, invited to the luncheon after the launch, seeming to the tract of on-lookers quite dainty and visionary there, like objects mirrored in an eye. And they formed groups, of which some chatted, and were elegant, and some spoke the gravest words uttered for centuries.

"What, really, is the *Boodah*?" asked a Servian Minister of a French: "is she a whim, a threat, or a tool?"

"She is too heavy for a whim," answered the French, "too dear for a threat, and too fantastic for a tool. Time will show."

But this was no answer at all: something more to the point came from a multitudinous tumult of sledges below — the workmen "wedging-up."

At last, soon after noon, Hogarth, with a considerable following, was seen ascending the steps, on his arm the Queen of the Ceremony — a little Bavarian Gräfin, famous for her face: he, princely now with that cosmopolitan polish picked up in Courts, bending above her with laughter, making her laugh also, as they paced up. And at once the invited, including the Board of Verification, entered the hull upon a tour of sight-seeing, conducted by a manager of the contractors.

Already the set-up wedges had raised the *Boodah* from her keel-block, and left her resting on the great braced ground-ways; and now down to the sea's brink the greasers were busy, prodigals in tallow, while, within, the seven hundred trooped from spectacle to spectacle, like a tourist group guided through the Louvre.

An hour, and they anew appeared on the roof, trooping toward that balustrade that faced the sea: upon which the throngs felt the impending of the event, and intently watched. But there seemed no hurry, Hogarth all gay chatter, anon lowering the lids a moment, as he looked over the water; till suddenly hundreds of glasses detected a champagne-bottle with ribbons in the christener's hand; and the consciousness of the moment come moved the hosts when Hogarth, even as he chatted, disengaged a flag, and let it fall: it was a signal; down it fluttered; and instantly, down there, bustle broke loose, as the call "Saw-off!" went forth, and the saws set flurriedly to fret through the timbers which bind groundways to slidingways.

"*Now?*" whispered Hogarth at the christener's ear: and, even as he spoke, the voice of a noising arose and droned from Spezzia, its hills, its villages, and its sea; the *Boodah*, only half liberated, strained in travail; crashed from her bands; slipped down the greased gradient — plunged — and, gathering momentous way, went wading deep, deeper — like Behemoth run mad — amid a wrath of froths and a brawling of waters, into the sea.

There, deep-planted, she stretched: on the surface appeared a reef of steel; and the stirred-up water slapped vapidly upon those flanks, like waters upon the Norway wall.

XXXIII

REEFS OF STEEL

Nothing was ever so scrutinized as the movements of the *Boodah* during the next two months.

One morning three weeks after her launch three steamers took her in tow, with progress so slow, that at nightfall they were still visible from land; but the next morning had vanished.

Two days later they were met on the Genoa-Leghorn *route*, six steamers then towing the *Boodah*, their course S. by W.

Again and again it was met, that funeral of the sea: the prone, tearing steamers, the reluctant bulk. Sometimes a captain's glass might make out a few men lost on the roof like men on a raft, smoking, seated, leaning over a balustrade.

Southward and westward it swam. On the seventh day there arrived at Ajaccio from Marseilles twenty-five bluejackets; and these, in a hired *speronare*, put to sea, and joined the *Boodah* twenty miles from the coast.

Thenceforth, a smoke would be seen at a point of the roof, indicating that she, too, was steaming: for it was known that she had a screw and a rudder; and so closely was she observed, that her now added rate could be fixed — two to three knots a day.

She must therefore have some small engines about 4,000 H. P.: and since their *motif* could only be one thing, resistance to ocean currents, this meant that the *Boodah* was intended to rest always in one spot: a startling conclusion.

Occasionally a Surveying Service warship would peep above the horizon, watching her.

As she passed through the Straits, seventy-five English blue-jackets put out from Trafalgar, and joined her.

With such reports passed the weeks. Occasionally five or six coal-ships would be seen about the *Boodah*; her number of tug-ships might be as low as two; sometimes nine, ten.

At night she made a fine display, and homeward-bound boats from Cape Horn, from Pernambuco, Para, Madeira, spoke highly of her two revolving-drum lighthouses: for these, from opposite corners of the roof, at the rate of a revolution per minute, poured into space two shimmering comets, like Calais and the Eddystone — rapt spinning-dervishes of the sea that hold far converse with the dark, till morning. And between these two ran a festoon of electric lanterns, Japanese and Moorish, cut in ogives; and festoons of coloured moons drooped round the balustrades, so that the blaze and complexity of it presented to ships a spectacle of speckled mystery, fresh to the sea.

After five weeks a hundred and seventeen blue-jackets put out from Portsmouth in a chartered barque and joined her, she still in tow, making now about N. by W.

But by the time this news reached Europe the eyes of Europe were no longer given up to the *Boodah*: for *another Boodah*, called the *Truth*, was a-tow through the North Channel from Belfast; and she had not reached the Mull of Cantire, when a third was launched at San Francisco, so that the interest of the islands became complicated.

What would they do? What could they? Compared with this question, the riddle of the Sphinx was simple, the supposition that they were going to batter coast-walls in the S. Pacific being hardly now tenable. The *Boodah* finally came to rest some miles North of lat. 50° and East of long. 20°: and there — just on the northern rim of the Gulf Stream where it divides, part toward Ireland, and part toward Africa — she remained, precisely in the middle of the trade-route between Europe and Boston, New York, Halifax: a *route* covered for fifty miles — twenty-five north, twenty-five south — by her 19.5-inch guns.

It is impossible to describe with how wild a heart, or thrilling a boding, the world heard this thing: eight days later the International Conference of Maritime Nations met at The Hague.

But nothing happened — or the opposite of what was feared: for, as months passed, the *Boodah*, planted there in the ocean, rapidly became the recognized gathering-point of the fashion and gaiety of Europe, thither flocking the socially ambitious and the "arrived" together, and to have been invited to those revels of taste and elegance became a superiority. Gradually, as the names "Beech," "Ecuador," ceased to be associated with the islands, the name of Hogarth took their place; and Hogarth had engaged Wanda, sweetest of tenors, to a year's stay in the *Boodah*, whose orchestra was the most cultured anywhere; Roche, her *chef*, had two years previously been put into a laboratory to devote his soul to the enlargement of his art; and he and that tenor lived in suites of the *Boodah* such as most princes would consider Utopian.

Hardly anything in her interior suggested *the ship*: no hammocks for marines, rolling-racks, sick-bay, lockers, steam-tables, washrooms, she being just a palace planted in the Atlantic, her bottom going down to a layer of comparative calm, so that hardly ever, in a storm, when the ocean robed her sides in white, washed abroad her slippery plateau, and drenched with spray her light-house tops, did the ballroom below know shock or motion. Into her principal hall, far down, circular, one descended by a circle of steps of marble, round which stood a colonnade of Cuban cedar, supporting candelabra and silks; and from atrium-pools sunk in the floor twelve twining fountains brandished spiral sprays, the floor being of a glassy marble, polished with snakestone, suffused with blushes at the coloured silks and at a roof gross with rose and pomegranates, hanging chandeliers; round the raised centre of the floor stood two balustrades, three feet high, hung with silks, the inner circle thirty feet across, higher than the outer, forty-five across: a roseate room, strewn with cushions, colours, flushes; but that raised space was empty: reserved for — a throne.

The throne, still unfinished, had been three years making in India.

And during nine months the *élite* and joyous yachts arrived, not at the *Boodah* only, but at others of the twelve which, one by one, were launched and towed to position; and a round of events transacted themselves in the fortresses: Marie Antoinette balls, classic concerts, theatrical functions by *troupe* or amateur, cos-tume-balls, children's-balls, banquets of the gods, grave recep-tions. By now there ran right across the *Boodah*'s roof, in the form of a cross, two double colonnades of Doric pillars, at the four ends being Roman arches: and here, some summer afternoon, the passing ship would see a bazaar, all butterfly flutter, feminine hues like flower-beds, cubes of coloured ice, flags, and a buzz of gaiety, and strains of Tzigany music — rainbow-tints of Venice mixed with the levity of the Andrássy Ut of Pesth. Sometimes a fleet of craft would surround the islands. Besides, to each was attached a yacht, and a trawler which continually plied for it between island and land.

At this time Hogarth was deep in debt, and Beech's living upon credit.

So, gradually, a good deal of the awe which the structures had inspired passed off. On the whole, they seemed mere whimsical castles-of-pleasure. The trains of industrious ships grew habitu-ated to their gaudy brightness by night, to their seething reefs, or placid mass, by day. On foggy days the mariner was aware of the islands wailing weird siren-sounds of warning. The islands waved common-code signals of greeting to the passer. Trinity House sent them the usual blanks and instruments for recording meteorolog-ical observations. Their positions were marked in British Admi-ralty Charts, in American Pilot Charts, in "Sailing Directions."

The great greyhounds, racing to Sandy Hook, raved with jest past them. The islands began to seem a natural part of the sum of things. There they lay, stable, rooted, trite, familiar; and the question almost arose: "How came it that they were never there *before*?" — just that object, of that form and colour, seemed so old and natural in that particular spot. So the frogs hopped finally upon the log that God sent them for sovereign.

Meantime, the more thoughtful of men did not fail to observe, and never forgot, that no ship could possibly depart from, or arrive at Europe, without passing within range of some one of the islands' guns. A row of eight lay an irregular crescent (its convexity facing Europe) from just outside the Straits of Gibraltar, where O'Hara admiraled the *Mahomet*, to the 55th of latitude, where the *Goethe* lay on the Quebec-Glasgow *route*: these commanding the European trade with the States and with S. America, as well as with W. and S. Africa, and with Australia by Cape Horn; another in the narrows of the Gulf of Aden, commanding the world's traffic by Suez with the East and with S. Africa; another in the middle of the narrows of the Kattegat, commanding all Baltic trade; another, fifteen miles from San Francisco, and another a hundred and fifty miles from Nagasaki, on the edge of the Black Stream, commanding the Japanese-San Francisco, the Australian-San Francisco trades, and great part of the Japano-Russo-Chinese. These were the principal trades of the world.

Like the despair of Samson awaking manacled and shaven, an occasional shriek would go up from some lone thinker, who perceived that the kingdoms of the world had lapsed into a single hand; and in the privy cabinet the governors drank to the dregs the cup of trembling. But their speech was bold, the matter hung long, the peoples ignored and wrought: there was seed-time and harvest; the newsboy brawled; the long street roared. Far yonder in the darkness and distance of the deep the islands flashed and danced, and were fashionable.

Richard Hogarth held back his hand.

XXXIV

THE "KAISER"

It was the habit of Hogarth, when in the *Boodah*, to rise very early and ascend in flannels to one of the four doors opening upon the ledge — blocks five feet thick, moved by hydraulic motors — and sometimes Loveday would accompany these walks, they always seeing on the plane of the sea some sail, or by a spyglass the fading light-beam of the *Goethe* north, of the *Solon* south; or they watched how the *Boodah*'s galaxy, too, waxed faint and garish as some drama of colour evolved in the East; saw gulls hover and swing, fins wander: and marking that simple ampleness of the plan of sea and arch of heaven, their hearts felt enlargement.

One morning, the 3rd October, Loveday was up even before Hogarth, having started awake from a gory nightmare, this altogether not being a day like others: and when the two friends met on the ledge, they walked a long time in silence.

Only after the dayspring began definitely to dabble in its chromatic chemistries Loveday at last remarked: "Did you ever think why I took such pains to get you to come down with me to Lord Woolacot's last autumn two years?"

"Yes," answered Hogarth: "you wanted me to see the model farms, and how the young ladies fed the poor, and how the tenants loved their lord, and everyone thought himself happy. Only, I didn't see what the pastimes of Lord Woolacot's daughters have to do with the process of the suns, and with the woe of Oldham. Ah, Lord, it is a job, I tell you, pulling this vile thing straight! Of course, the eagle doesn't blink: but I am only one man, and the world, and its stupid sins, are a tidy burden. Ha! — never mind. Look at that big *Boodah* of a sun how he blooms: isn't he launched and handled all right? Let us of this desert bend the knee to him like the old Sabæans. There is hope." . . .

It was known that on that day, at half past eleven A.M., the *Kaiser Wilhelm der Grösste* would pass on her second voyage within some miles of the *Boodah*, this ship being the greatest afloat, having a cargo-carrying deadweight of 45,000 tons, and travelling the waters like a railway-train at 37 miles (32 knots).

So toward noon Hogarth, in a peaked cap, jacket, and white boots, was again on the roof, a glass and book of Costonlights in his hand, while not far off a knot of five officers in frockcoats talked, and near one light-house, where a number of men stood, a flagstaff flew the ensign — blue letters "R. F." on a white ground, looking Russian; on the northern horizon two fox-tails of smoke; on the western three diminutive sails; between the two, quite real and big, a brig becalmed; and now the *Kaiser Wilhelm*: for that yonder could be only she, with so fervent a growth, from the first moment of her upward climb, did she approach. It was twenty minutes to noon, and she was somehow a little late, that punctual strong wrestler with space.

The officers on the *Boodah* spoke of her in low and stealthy voices; looked at her with queer and stealthy glances.

"'As a bird to the snare . . .'" muttered one.

"She comes all right, but will never go," said another.

"She will be always near us," said a third.

"Life is an earnest thing, after all," said a fourth: "there are wrongs, it seems, which only blood can wash out: it comes to that at last."

Now Loveday ran up, looking scared and busy, a quill behind his ear, Hogarth now having the glass at his face, while his eyes struggled with the reek from his cigar-end.

"Is that she?" Loveday asked him.

"Yes, poor boat."

She was nine miles away; in four minutes she was less than seven, and now distinct: — her three staysails; her four funnels; the stretched-out space between her raked masts; her host of cowls and boats; her high victorious hull, silently running.

And all along her lines were lines of faces thick as dahlia-rows in June — globe-trotters; captains of industry; children; the Wall Street operator who plotted a stroke in Black-Sea wool, and to him time was money — I guess; commercial travellers, all-modern, spinning, prone, to whom the sea was an insignificant and conquered thing; engineers; capped enthusiastic Germans, going forth to conquer; publishers, ladies, lords, all the nondescript prosperous: and all ran there blithe, sublime, and long drawn-out; and they toyed with oranges, nuts; and they looked abroad to see the *Boodah* — ship's-surgeons and officers with them — jesting, as they munched or sucked.

But the Captain who had often seen the *Boodah*, was log-writing in the chart-room . . .

As her ensign of greeting ran up her main, her clocks struck twelve, the full noon — like an omen — come; she not then three miles from the *Boodah*.

And simultaneously with the hoisting of that ensign, and the striking of those clocks, the old-worn wheels of Roman Civilization stopped dead.

The *Boodah* ran up the signal: "*Stop!*"

Those who understood rubbed their eyes: it was like a vision at high noon; they could not believe.

At that news the Captain, a handsome fair-bearded man, rushed like a madman from pilot-house to bridge, and the startled passengers saw his lighted eyes. He had some moments of indecision; then down he, too, rang that word: "*Stop.*"

The engines left off; the *Kaiser*'s speed, as from heart-failure, gave in, died away.

By this time all the passengers knew, in a state of tremor saw confused runnings to and fro, and face caught from face dismay; the voyage was spoiled, the record! What, then, had happened to the world? And now again the *Boodah* is signalling: "*Let the Captain come.*"

The Captain's hands were shaking; he could not speak, could only gasp to the first-officer: "By God, no; O, by God, no." Then, as great quantities of black-grey reek, wheeling all convolved, were now enveloping the vessel, resting on the sea, reaching away in thinner fog even to the *Boodah*, and as, the day being calm, there was a difficulty in reading the flags, the Captain gasped: "Take the trumpet — ask them — But don't they pay for this . . .?"

So out brayed the trumpeted query, and back the inexorable trumpeted answer: "*Let the Captain come.*"

So, then, the *Kaiser* would never reach Sandy Hook? To put out boats! — to parley! — while the earth span with quick-panting throbs, every second worth seven thousand pounds!

"But don't they *pay* for it . . .?" so, with a painful face of care, the Captain questioned space.

But he would be mild and patient as a lamb that day! His order went forth: the ship forged ahead; a longboat, hurriedly lowered to starboard, was manned for the first-officer to put off in her, while every heart of the passengers thumped, every face an ecstasy of emotions.

Then a wretched, long interval . . .

The ship's-officers were received on the *Boodah* in a deck-room containing a number of boats with castored keels, capable of being quickly launched down an incline, where Mr. F. Quilter-Beckett, the Admiral, with some lieutenants, awaited them at a bureau on which lay documents, while in the background stood Hogarth and Loveday, and, "Gentlemen, this is a most damned wild piece of madness!" broke out wrathfully the first-officer, as he dashed up wild-eyed to the level: "in consideration of the guns you have in this thing —"

"But your Captain?" asked Quilter-Beckett, a courtly man, with a dark-curling beard, a star on his breast.

"The Captain won't come!" whined the officer in perfect English: "I suppose you realize the terrible consequences of this stoppage, gentlemen?"

"But you are wasting time, sir. You represent your Captain?"

"Of course, I represent — !"

"Then just cast your eye over this" — that so slighted letter, sent years before by Hogarth to Foreign Offices, claiming the sea as his private manor.

The officer read it half through with flurried closeness; then, "Well, but what is all this?" he broke out: "is it a piece of comedy, or what, gentlemen?"

"It is serious; and the last clause comes into operation today: only such ships being held authorized to pass on the sea as pay to the first-reached sea-fort on any voyage a tax, or sea-rent, of 4s. per ton on their registered tonnage, with an additional stamp-tax of 33s. 4d. for receipt, and a stamp-tax of £1 16s. 8d. for clearance. You will see at a glance the clauses of the law, if you cast your eyes over this schedule —"

"Law!" the other broke in: "you talk of *Law*! But doesn't the sea, then, belong by right to all men — ?"

"Not more than the land. Ask yourself: why should it? But I do hope you won't argue: your time must be so precious."

Out shrilled the *Kaiser Wilhelm*'s whistle of recall.

"I must go!" said the officer with a worried hand-toss: "I must go. If you give me those documents, I will show them to the Captain — but he is not the sort of man — this is mere piracy, after all! But, good God, gentlemen, if you only dare touch that ship, I shouldn't put myself in your place this day week for all —"

He snatched the papers, dashed, and his men, in a passion of haste, lay to the oars, the *Kaiser* only four hundred yards from the *Boodah*; and the officer, shaking aloft the documents, pitched up the stair, the centre of five hundred pairs of scared eyes, while the captain bored his way to him.

Two minutes of intense low speech, crowded with gestures: and suddenly the Captain's face, till now haggard, reddened; out went his shaken fist; with eyes blazing like lunacy, up he flew to the bridge; and now he is bending down with howling throat: "Passengers to their berths!"

Simultaneously, above the engine-room stair a bell jangled;

round swung the pointer to "*Full Ahead*"; and ere the decks were cleared of their bustle the *Kaiser*, like a back-kicking hen, scratched up under her poop a spreading pool of spume, which tossed spasmodic spray-showers and spoutings: and she stirred, stretched like a street, churned the sea, and, wheeling to reveal her receding stern, was away.

By which time Hogarth was standing at a cubical cabin of steel on the roof, with him Loveday and Quilter-Beckett, his brow puckered with wrinkles, the sun troubling his eyes.

"I suppose the *chef* is warned?" — he threw away his cigar.

"Oh, yes, my Lord King," Quilter-Beckett answered.

And Loveday: "She sweats like a thoroughbred" — haggard, but assuming calm: "few things could be more profusely expeditious."

"Ah, make phrases, John," murmured Hogarth. . . . "Well, but hadn't you better be getting out the boats?"

Upon which Quilter-Beckett stepped into the little erection, touched a button, and in a minute the water round the southern side was swarming with twenty-three boats whose blue-jackets began to row toward the *Kaiser*.

And presently, "It's no use waiting," said Hogarth, looking in upon Quilter-Beckett: "I should mine and shell her at the same moment, if I were you; tell them to get it in well amidships."

Now a few seconds, full of expectation, passed, the *Kaiser Wilhelm* already two miles away: till suddenly space opened its throat in a gulf to bay gruff and hollow like hell-gate dogs; and, almost at the same moment, close by the *Kaiser* a column of water hopped with one humph of venom two hundred feet on high: when this dropped back broad-showering with it came showering a rain of wreckage; and instantly a shriek of lamentation floated over the sea, mixed with another shriek of steam.

For the moment the ship, enveloped in vapours, could not be seen; but in two minutes glimpses of her hull appeared, shewing the bluff bulge of her starboard bottom: for she leaned steeply to port with a forward crank, her two starboard screws, now free, spinning asleep like humming-tops. A six-inch shell, beautifully aimed, had shattered her engines, killing two stokers, and a torpedo-mine had knocked a hole nine feet across in her port beam.

But as the *Boodah*'s boats, meanwhile, had been racing toward her, and as her own port boats were quickly out, all were got off; in fact, she floated so long, that her ship's papers with £270,000 in specie, and a few hundred-weight of mailbags were saved, and even after the boats reached the *Boodah* she still stretched there motionless, until, with a sudden flurry, she determined to plunge.

Soon afterwards Hogarth had the Captain in his suite, to tell him that he did not wish any intelligence of the event to reach the world for four days, during which passengers and crew would be his guests, and then be sent on to America, his object, he said, being to impress the loss of the *Kaiser* upon the consciousness of all, by making all anxious as to her fate.

So that night her passengers danced till late, for there was no resisting the hospitality of Hogarth, or the witchery of those vistas and arcades, grand hall and lost grot, *salons* and conservatories, there in the dark of the ocean, or such an enchantment of music, and fabulousness of table; the host, too, pleaded prettily for himself; and now they pardoned, and now they pouted, but always they banqueted, kissed, lost themselves in visions, were charmed, and danced.

XXXV

THE CUP OF TREMBLING

It was by the merest chance that Baruch Frankl and his daughter were not on the *Kaiser*: for Frankl was the half nephew of Mrs. Charles P. Stickney, a New York Jewess, and as the marriage of Miss Stickney with Lord Alfred Cowern was only fifteen days off, Frankl had made arrangements to accompany the bridegroom across, but had been detained by stress of business; happily for him — for Lord Alfred, the bridegroom, was a dancing prisoner in the *Boodah*.

Early, then, on the third morning thence, Charles P. Stickney, the bride's father, a natty little Yankee, hurried a-foot to the Maritime Exchange: for, to his infinite surprise, the *Kaiser*'s arrival had not been in the morning's paper: so the little arch-millionaire stepped toward Beaver Street, sure that the *Kaiser* had come in too late for the press.

Early as it was, he found the place as thickly a-buzz as though it was that feverish hour between eleven and twelve.

He pushed his way to the bulletin-board, inscribed with the hours at which ships are sighted and entered into dock: the Kaiser was not there: and with prone outlook he went seeking an assistant superintendent; but, sighting a fellow-operator, come, as usual, to digest the world, from barometer-reports to coffee-quotations at Rio, Charles P. Stickney cried to him: "Funny about the *Kaiser*! Know anything?"

"It's the darndest thing . . ." mumbled the other, still stargazing at a blackboard prices-current of American staples: "raise Hell this day, I guess." . . .

And on through the rooms Stickney shouldered: all in the air here an odour of the sea, and of them that go down to it in ships; pilot, captain, supercargo, purser; abstracts from logs, copies of manifests and clearances, marks and numbers of merchandise, with quantities, shippers, consignees; here peaked caps, and the jaw that chewed once, and paused long, and, lo, it moved anew; Black Books, massive volumes enshrining ancient wrecks; vast newspaper-files in every tongue; records of changes in lightships, lights, buoys, and beacons, from Shanghai to Cape Horn; reports, charts, atlases, globes; the progress of the rebellion in Shantung, and the earthquake last night in Quito; directories, and high-curved reference books, and storm-maps; every minute the arrival of cipher cablegrams, breathless with the day's Amsterdam exchange on London, or with the quantities of tea *in transitu* via Suez or Pacific Railway; and the drift of ocean-currents, and the latest position of the *Jane Richardson*, derelict, and the arrival of the *Ladybird* at Bahia; and the probabilities of wind-circulation, atmospheric moisture, aberrations of audibility in fog; and in the middle of it the pulse of the sun, the thundering engines and shooting shuttles of this Loom; a tiptop briskness and bustle of action; a scramble of wits; a *mêlée* to the death; mixed with pea-jackets, and aromas of chewed pigtail, and a rolling in the gait.

Into this roar of life that word *Kaiser* stole: and it grew to a chorus.

Charles P. Stickney, butting upon a tearing clerk who was holding aloft a bulletin of icebergs and derelicts, tried to stop him: upon which the clerk, who would not be stopped, cried with a back-looking face of passionate haste: "London message just received — *no intelligence of* Kaiser —"

But he had hardly disappeared, when another man from an inner room rushed, waving something: the Navesink Highlands lookout had wired the *Kaiser* in sight! And while the Exchange rang with cheers, Stickney, a colour now in his sere cheeks, went boring his way outward.

The lookout had said it — those blue eyes that never failed there on his watch-tower, he knowing the ships that sail the sea as the Cyclops his sheep, in his heart so knowing them all, that as that sea-glass detected a speck on the horizon, those sea-wise nostrils sniffed its name: for between the *Mary Jane* and the *Mary Anne*, both off-shore schooners, is all the world of difference: if you would not see it, *he* knows. And he had wired the *Kaiser*! — so expectant his outlook: and that day wept like a ruined man.

Swift upon his first wire a second flashed: and one of those craped days of the tragedies of commerce followed, the boding, the loss, flashed everywhere, pervading Europe and America.

The next morning the Exchange, all the exchanges, the Lloyds', the bourses, were crowded from an early hour, but subdued: no news, not a word; but still — there was certainty: for had the *Kaiser* and her wireless been merely disabled, she would undoubtedly by now have been reported: she had foundered.

Foundered! — in the serenest weather in which ship ever crossed the water. . . .

But at eleven the truth came: for the brig which had lain becalmed near the *Boodah* at the moment of the tragedy, and now was nearer England, had flashed the news: "many of the Kaiser's passengers mutilated, many drowned."

Death, then, was in the pottage of Life; the air tainted with specks of blood. . . .

That day Man, as it were, rent his garments, sitting in ashes, and to Heaven sent up a howl of fear, of anguish, and of hissing hate.

Those who lacked the intelligence to feel the fear, felt the hate: every girl, the shirt-maker, the shopman, feeling himself robbed of his very own; the Duke in the centre of his oak-lands felt it; the burglar, the junk-dweller of the Yangtse, the pariah of the Hugli. Lamentation and a voice in Ramah, wail on wail. For God had given the sea to man, and it had been seized by a devil.

God had also given the shore; and it, too, had been seized: but, as that had been before their birth, they had not observed it — in such a numb somnambulism shambles humanity.

But the theft of the sea was new and flagrant, it, and the air, being all that had remained: and a roar for vengeance — sharp, and rolled in blood — rose from the throat of man.

Accordingly, when Mr. C. P. Stickney during the afternoon wired for information to the White House, he received the reply: "Encourage calm on 'Change. Government in touch with Europe. Great naval activity. Await good news, seven P.M."

It was about seven P.M. that what the White House would have considered specially good news occurred: for the *Boodah* then telegraphed through to O'Hara's *Mahomet* at the Straits:

"B. 7651. Begins. After tomorrow (Monday) you begin taxation, as per Order B., 7315, of 2nd inst. But if warships desire to pass out, (not in), permit, till further order. Richard. Ends."

Which meant that if any Power, or Powers, desired to concentrate force upon the attack of any island, the Lord of the Sea granted them facilities.

The *Kaiser* passengers had now been sent off to New York, the *Boodah*'s halls seemed the home of desolation; and, as the night advanced, Hogarth and Loveday walked on the roof: for they could find no rest, the sky without moon or star, the sea making of three sides of the *Boodah* a roaring reef, the wind blowing cold, they two wrapped to the nose in oilskins with sou'-westers, lashed by rages of rain and spray.

Yonder, to the north-west, appeared a ghost, a thing, a derelict brig, driving downhill on the billows, like a blind man gadding aimless with a crazy down-look, the rags of her one sail drumming on the gusts; and near, nearer, within a stone's-throw of the *Boodah*, she swaggered wearily, drab Arab, doomed despondent

Ahasuerus of the deep, nomad on the nomad sea; and on into the gloom of the southwest she roamed, to be again and again re-created by the rolling light-drum, while Hogarth with a groan said: "If I were only dead! I feel tonight like a man abandoned by the Almighty."

Loveday muttered those words so loved by Hogarth:

". . . . this is my favoured lot,   My exaltation to afflictions high." . . .

And Hogarth: "Do you know what is burdening me tonight? It is the curses which the world is at this moment hurling upon me: as when one man, thinking evilly of another, sticks needles into wax, and needles of pain pierce the other . . ." a sense of evil which was deepened the next day by an ominous little accident, when one of his old gunpractice hulks arrived from Bombay, bearing the throne: for as this was being conveyed into the *Boodah* a front leg was broken.

Meantime, the world's trade went on as before: only, night and day, its ships lay-to, to pay rent with threat and curse: in all only thirteen ships being sunk ere sea and earth had learned the new conditions.

And from the very first day of this taxing a deeper sense of pain and hardship pervaded the world, the Lord of the Sea now taxing at 4s. per ton a world's tonnage of 29 millions, 7 1/2 millions in sailing-ships, 21 1/2 millions in steamships, once in a voyage — a little less than the revenue of Britain.

So one night he received message from O'Hara that "British Mediterranean fleet has passed through the Straits, homeward."

It was not for nothing that the nations had allowed three weeks to pass before avenging the Kaiser: soon enough the Cabinets had been in intercommunication; but in the "Concert" had occurred — a hitch.

Britain had proposed the destruction of the islands in detail, the Powers to contribute weights of metal proportionate to their mercantile marines: as a basis for calculation she had offered her force in Home and Mediterranean waters; and, this having been accepted, by the 5th ships were under the pennant, and outfitting.

Now, all this time, things had been in a pretty whirl: oratory from pulpit, platform, stump, eyes on fire, mobs that went in haste, shrieks of newspaper passion, organized burglary, and a strange epidemic of fires: for the modern nations lived by the sea, and it was seized. Moreover, on the 6th, after a meeting at the Albert Hall, organized by the Associated Chambers of Commerce, our Government — "Liberal," under Sir Moses Cohen — suffered a defeat of thirty-four votes on a division.

And it was during the turmoil that ensued upon this that the German Foreign Office (on the 9th) sent to the new Russian the wireless "*Bion*" — meaning — "Let us meet to discuss the subject of England."

That meeting took place at Konigsberg.

It was now that a fort-man — formerly a Nottingham shoe-maker — landed from the Truth's yacht at Frederikshavn, and thence wrote to the Daily Chronicle, to say, briefly, this: That, supposing the European navies joined to batter away with 15-inch guns and torpedoes at five feet of steel, they might finally succeed in mining a hole in it; but if the thick steel happened to have still bigger guns, "*and other things*," with which, meantime, to batter back at the thin ships, then it would be the ships, probably, which would get holes in them: it was a question of Time. Also he said that the islands were defended by devoted men, every one of intelligence and high principle, who knew what they wanted, and meant to have it — their shooting average being 97 per 100. He advised his country not to try it, especially in view of certain political rumours which he had picked up in the Cattegat.

This letter, although badly spelled, aroused a sensation The "high principle" of the fort-men, indeed, met with bitter laughter; but its hearty patriotism, simplicity, technical knowledge, were so remarkable, that now a doubt as to the battleship arose — and with it a gnashing of teeth. The service-clubs, the "experts," wrote this and that; the publics poured forth letters, schemes, plots, inventions — like the brain of the world *versus* the brain of Hogarth. "*Starve Him Out*," was a title in the *Contemporary*: but the reply was bitterly obvious. And into the midst of this racket burst the news that the negotiations with Germany, Russia and France were at a deadlock.

These Powers had raised this question: "In case of the capture of the islands — what shall be done with those most powerful engines?"

Here was a riddle. For whichever nation took even one would score a vast advantage.

If, now, Britain had had the greatness of mind to declare for the sinking, in any case, of all the islands, the difficulty was solved, but the new-Government brooms would score a point and gain a trick, and they proposed the division of surviving forts in the proportion of fighting-power contributed.

The Continent objected: Britain was "*firm*"; whereupon the French Ambassador sent to Downing Street his withdrawal from the crusade.

And so when — on the 22nd — the fleets assembled at Portland and Milford Haven before *rendezvous* at the Lizard, the whole original proposal had fallen through: for here was neither tricolour nor saltire, only three German ships, only five Italian; the "probability," moreover, of the capture of a sea-fort by England was imminent: and on the evening of the mobilisation of the squadrons feverish activity was reported from Toulon; a British Legation *attaché*, seeing fit to stroll round the Caserne Pepinière, beheld in the yard an extraordinary crowd of limbers: and, pitching into a cab, from the nearest *postes et télégraphes* wired to London the word: "Angleterre."

Too late: the British fleets were gone, leaving the Channel and Western Mediterranean desert.

Now the nation awoke to a consciousness of dark skies: cloud of the west rushing to meet a yet lurider eastern — with probability of lightning.

The fleet could hardly return in less than five days — if it returned! Would the hostile nations be good enough to await its return? The lightning would be "near."

A day of fear, in which flash tracked flash: till at 11.30 P.M. the rumour pervaded the crowd round St. Stephen's that the new Ministry had suffered defeat: and the drifting ship was captainless.

And early the next morning a number of *Boodah* boats, out running a regatta, came tearing back, all fluttered; soon after which Quilter-Beckett was hurrying into Hogarth's presence, who was at coffee, to say: "Well, my Lord King, here they come at last — and enough of them, I think."

XXXVI

THE "BOODAH" AND THE BATTLESHIPS

The ships had gone forth in two lines ahead at ten knots, Admiral Sir Henry Yerburgh, K.C.B., being in the flagship Queen Mary, with the capital-ships being nearly all of the five mosquito flotillas, and half the Home submarine; though what was the object of the torpedo craft (unless they were to go within 2,000 yards of the *Boodah*'s guns) was not very evident.

At that news, Hogarth, putting on a wide awake, and lighting a cigar with rough perfunctory puffs, ran along a corridor to call Loveday, whereupon the two went out to the ledge and up to the roof.

There, at the south edge, stood a marine trumpeting something at Hogarth's yacht; and, just landing at the *Boodah* from his gig, a fretful Yankee skipper, register in hand with a bag of £900 sea-rent in gold, while twenty yards yonder rode his smoking ship loaded with grain for Rouen; and on the eastern horizon the armada, in crescent at present, moving with fires banked at two knots, a glare hiding them from the naked eye, but the glass revealing them like toys in the abstract, ethereally hazy.

And now the yacht's cones shewed steam, three of her boats making toward the *Boodah*; soon at the landing-place stood Wanda, some interpreters, Mons. Roche (the chef), women, engineers, paymasters, civil servants, waiters, etc.; and Hogarth, seeing them, approached, questioned them, and, hearing that they had been ordered a day's pleasure-trip round the *Solon*, with lifting hat shook hands all round.

By this time some fifty officers and blue-jackets were about the roof and ledge, some discussing, others unfixing lanterns and festoons, with shouted directions. Leaving which, Hogarth and Loveday descended to an office of Loveday's, and Hogarth was just saying: "Quilter-Beckett could destroy a quarter of those warships yonder — *now*, if he chose — without firing a gun —" when in, with flushed face and stretched stalk, hurried Quilter-Beckett, crying: "My Lord King, I thought you would be here — just look — !"

He held out a Sea telegraph-form-from O'Hara:

"F. 39241. Begins. Almost certainty of war: Germany, France, Russia against England. Three corps massing between Harfleur and Rouen, two upon Petersburg, transports at Havre. England undefended on sea. Ministry fallen. Toulon outfitting. Donald, Admiral. Ends.

Hogarth, with an all-gone gesture, handed the telegram to Loveday.

But with lightning energy he was at a desk, scribbling:

"F. 39242. Begins. To Donald, Admiral, Mahomet. Be in half-hourly communication with Beech's Bank, Paris and Petersburg branches. Send hourly bulletins of news. War to be averted by every means. Let Beech threaten. Warn Cattegat. Richard. Ends."

And "Quick, Quilter-Beckett," he cried, "send that! What is the speed of your quickest picket — ?"

"Fifteen knots —"

"Then, go yourself to the British Admiral. *Make* him fly back: he has years to attack me in, tell him — I'll write a dispatch —"

On which Quilter-Beckett telephoned up for a picket, took the dispatch, and was soon away, while Hogarth watched his flight over the Sea.

An anxious hour passed, and by then a line of ships had been sighted to the west — the Americans at last; ten minutes later, the picket, too, was seen returning.

"Well, now," said Hogarth, watching her, "I wonder. The ships seem to be coming on just the same. You have no idea, John, how the mind of people in office becomes fixed, like hardened putty in a hole: I am sorry now I didn't go myself."

Some minutes more and Quilter-Beckett was pelting up the steps, his face pink as prickly-heat, blurting out: "My Lord King! I have been grossly insulted . . .!"

"Ha!" went Hogarth.

"I met a dispatch-boat coming to make summons of sur-render, and, in spite of my white flag, they took me prisoner! How I restrained myself — and these people in the hollow of my hand! When I got at last to the Admiral — it is Yerburgh on the *Queen Mary* — he 'pirated' me — but I have no time Yonder, you see, are the Americans. British won't go back: I doubt if they believe — 'under orders', and so on. By the way, you shouldn't stay there — no longer safe —"

He was away: for the moment was near, the *Boodah* now sur-rounded with a series of floating squares hanging deep torpedo-nets against submarines, on both horizons effusions of smoke, the ships no more visions, but middle-sized sea-things, seeming fixed in the thick of the sea, though steaming quickly. Hogarth watched them through a hand-glass, while Loveday, ghastly pallid, whis-pered: "Come, Richard, come," but still lingered a little, seeing them grow up — like the infant, the lad, the hairy man — toiling at the bigness of the sea, looking stripped, prepared for tempest They were six miles away — five.

Mute lay the *Boodah*; and, surrounding her, perniciously moved the ships at forty-eight revolutions a minute, hardly a cable's interval between the host of them, they seeming no more the playthings of the sea, but its masters, each a travelling throne of power; and as they pared so taciturn, with baleful aspect they trained their cannon upon the sea-fort in their midst: not a soul visible on fort or ships.

A long while it seems to last, that noonday stillness, a noonday breezy and oceanic, the sea sharp-edged, hard-looking, dark-blue, tossing spray along its ridges, not rough, but restless, shewing against the ships white foams a moment, which silently glide away.

But their Admiral is signalling: *Let her have it!* and in some moments more yonder to the far north the *Florida* breaks into quick-flashing ecstasy, like quick-winking Gorgon glances; and the north-east catches it in a single boom; and in ten seconds more it is as if Nature, with sudden yell, feels to her womb the birth-hour come and rueful throes: and where ships had been appears in one minute nothing but a ring of stagnant smoke, tugged into rays and out-sticking clouds, flushed with glares and rouges.

And no question of missing: the *Boodah* stationary and huge; every shell told. But, the deluge over, that thunder-marred visage again looked grimly forth, a face new-risen from smallpox, an apparition, roof-houses gone, lighthouse tops, one of her great 19.5 inchers in fragments, in her casemates seventeen dead.

But where now is the one-masted *Hercules*, which but a moment since went trembling at the bale of her own bellowing barbettes? The *Hercules* is in a Nessus-shirt of flame. And whither the *Hercules* is going, thither is the *Idaho* going, and the *Dante* gone, and gone the elongated length of the *Invincible*, and twenty destroyers, and the bow-works of the old *Powerful*, which stoops woefully there, screws in air, as the camel of the desert kneels and waits, while into her beam comes crashing the ram of the poopless *Deutschland*.

Yet the *Boodah* has not fired a gun!

But now she fires: as the broadsides drench her anew, she fires, the hulk — all round the horizon — lowing in travail: and as there is no question of missing on the one side, so on the other is assurance, the *Boodah*'s broad-sides of 19.5-inchers and 9.5-

inchers, ninety-two in all, being fired by the hand of Quilter-Beckett, who sits at a table grim with knobs, buttons, dial-faces, in a cabinet near a saloon where Hogarth, Loveday, and five lieutenants are lunching; and where he sits he can hear the band in an alcove rendering for the eaters Beethoven's Ninth Symphony: hear, not heed: for two gunners in each casemate have sighted a ship through pivoted glasses, whose fixing, disturbing an electrical circuit, prints the ship's distance on an indicator before the Admiral: whereupon he touches a button — many buttons — in intense succession: the *Boodah bawls*: and the thrust-back of her resentment becomes intolerable, the ships just like fawns under the paws of an old lion whose grisly jaws drip gore; the sharks that infest her will fare well of her hand.

Of forty-three ships fixed, thirty-nine are hit, eleven founder: wreckage so vast and swift, that the Admiral, still afloat in a *Queen Mary* pierced above-belt, is like a man stung by the tarantulas of distraction: tries to signal flight — flags cannot be seen; fires coloured pistol-lights: "Retire!" — and soon, all round, the circle is in flight.

But hapless flight: the *Boodah* is an octopus whose feelers reach far, and they, within her toils, cannot escape her omnipresence. She sends after them no guns: yet they are blown to atoms; the sea becomes a death-trap thick with pitfalls and shipwreck; one by one they are caught, they fly aloft like startled fowl, or they succumb, and lean, and stoop, and sink: the sea, for mile on mile, proving a hell of torpedoes-dirigible, automobile, mine.

For in the matter of mines the *Boodah* had all the advantages of a shore, and as to dirigible torpedoes more than all.

Her mines, whose weight was adjusted to the specific gravity of salt water, sank till the pressure at ten fathoms arrested them, they, electrically connected with the forts, reaching out twenty miles; and the whole network, charted to an inch, was coordinated with the range-tables.

The ordinary 18-inch Whiteheads, moreover, were replaced by a longer design running 6,000 yards, the added length being occupied by the flask, whose compressed air runs the engine, they not sinking on finishing their course: so, if they missed, there they lay, a trap of 380 pounds of gun-cotton in the course of the numerous moving foe.

With these three forms of the same plague the *Boodah* hunted the fleeing ships, and drove them stumbling through complicated miseries, amazed and thunderstruck: so that seventy-three only, several of them half wrecks, reached her twenty-five mile limit;

and, there, over the mines of the *Solon*, reassembled.

Amid the throng on his ruined roof Hogarth watched their flight and the ever-coming boatloads of blue-jackets through a mist of smoke and the after-smell of war, while under the sea wide eyes in hosts were a-gaze at a windfall of 2,400 bodies.

About half past four captains and commanders of the survivors were in the ward-room of the Second-in-Command on the *Orion* — the *Queen Mary* gone — when he, with splendid infatuation, proposed a return to the attack, with a change of tactics to concentration upon one side only of the *Boodah*; but the foreigners pointed out the obvious added dangers; and in the midst of a wrangle a dispatch-boat from the *Solon*, eleven miles south, arrived, demanding the usual sea-rent, by draft, if not in gold; so out, at this unlooked-for incident, broke a new quarrel, the British for a whole hour resisting the inexorable; till the *Solon* Lieutenant, his eyes moist with pleading, explained their helplessness, adding that war between the four Powers had been declared that day at noon from the Stock Exchange steps: and only then the Vice-Admiral, breaking into tears, yielded to destiny.

Hogarth, meanwhile, was like a wild man, imprisoned, till his yacht returned at dusk with her excursionists; and without delay he was on her, and away for England.

XXXVII

THE STRAITS

In England, meantime, was nothing but dismay.

The Government, whose defeat was accidental, on being hurriedly patched up, threw itself passionately into the work of defence, calling up every enrolled man, while at regimental centres the enlistment of volunteers went forward, Weedon alone turning out 7,000 rifles a day.

But on the night of the Declaration the Under-secretary announced in the House that the Russians were moving down the Baltic, the French toward the Straits: and the next morning dawned with the dreariness of last mornings and days. However, soon after 1 P.M., the Lord of the Sea landed at Bristol, his yacht being one of the swiftest things afloat; there heard the known facts; and thence wired to Beech's London house, to the London Foreign Office, to Cadiz and to Frederikshavn, where he had wireless for the *Mahomet* at the Straits, and for the *Truth* in the Cattegat.

His wire to the Foreign Office was as follows:

"I have come to England hoping to avert European war by fiscal means, not knowing that the passage of ships into open water was of first importance. Since this is so, accept my assurance, there will be no war, except on the part of Britain, which I should much resent. British Government, I suggest, should forthwith allay national anxiety.

"RICHARD."

But the Foreign Office did not publish this telegram, not knowing what to make of it — unless Hogarth were vehemently the friend of England, while every British being regarded him not so much as the enemy of man, as the special Anti-Christ of England. And how came he to be in England, when he should be at the bottom of the Atlantic? The telegram was passed through the agitated departments, but kept dark. . . .

So the afternoon passed without news: and tension grew to agony.

Hogarth spent the evening in his Berkeley Square house with the Manager of Beech's, examining office books and specimens of some new Sea-coins, till near eleven, when, being alone, he put on a mackintosh, shaded his face well with hat and collar-flap, and went out into the drizzling night.

Even his Berkeley Square was peopled, and, as he strolled toward Pall Mall, he found it ever harder to advance, till he became jammed. Never had he seen such a crowd, all in the air a sound, vague and general, which was like a steam of thought-made-audible; till presently, while trying in vain to get away, he was startled by a tumult that travelled, a rumour of woe that noised and swelled, terrifying, the voice of the people, the voice of God: and though he did not know its meaning, it keenly afflicted him.

The fastest of the survivors from the battle with the *Boodah* had wirelessed: on that commonplace bulletin at the War Office the news stood written . . .

But the rumour of that despair had not yet attained its culmination, when another rumour roared after and over it, roar upon roar, like tempest poured through the multitudinous forest, joyance now overtaking sorrow, and a noise of roistering overwhelming lamentation. And all at once a great magnetic hysteria seized them all, and the many became as one, and the bursting bosom burst: men weeping like infants, laughing foolishly, grasping each other's hand, and one cried "Hurrah!," and another, catching it, cried "Hurrah!"

For the French, German, and Russian fleets, in attempting to pass the two narrows north and south of Europe, had been stopped by the two sea-forts there; and though they had been so eager to pass, that they had even offered to pay sea-rent, this, too, had been refused. They had then, at five and at five-thirty in the afternoon, offered battle to the islands: with the result that half their weight had been annihilated before they took to flight. So said the bulletin. . . .

And Hogarth in the midst of the jubilee saw the man who jammed his left shoulder, a broker in spectacles, grip the hand of the man on his right, a ragamuffin, to cry out: "That scoundrel Hogarth! Isn't there good in the damned thief, after all?"

And the other: "Aye, he knows how to give it 'em 'ot, don't 'e, after all! Thank God for that!"

Three weeks later peace was proclaimed by a procession at Temple Bar between England, Austro-Germany, France, Russia, and the Sea.

XXXVIII

THE MANIFESTO

The last effort of Europe to resist the Sea was made on the afternoon of the 14th of October, when the British Prime Minister refused to conclude a treaty of peace.

"Your master is only a pirate — on a large scale," he said to a Minister of the Sea.

That was on the 14th.

On the 15th there was a stoppage of British trade nearly all the world over.

On the 20th England was in a state of *émeute* resembling revolution.

On the 28th the Treaty of Peace was signed.

Its principal conditions were: (1) The undertaking by the Sea not to raise sea-rent on British ships without certain formalities of notice; and (2) The undertaking by Britain not to engage in the making of any railway or overland trade-route, or of any marine engine of war, without the consent of the Sea. And similar treaties were signed by the Sea with the other nations.

Then followed the rush of the Ambassadors to the *Boodah*, and the frivolous round of Court-life revolved, *levée*, audience, dinner, drawing-room, investiture; the Lord of the Sea descended from the throne before the Court to pin a cross upon the humble breast of his best shot and give him the title of Præceps, gave fanciful honours to emperors, received them of them — wore when throned a brow-band of gold with only one stone, the biggest of the meteor octahedrons, that glanced about his brow like an icicle in whose glass gallivanted a fairy clad in rags of the rainbow.

Now the old gaieties recommenced, but more Olympian in tone, as befitted the ruler of rulers, terrible now being the lifting of Hogarth's brows at the least lapse in ritual; and only the chastest-nurtured of the earth ever now stalked through gavotte or pavane in those halls of the sea.

The world now lay at his feet. The dependence upon him of England, of France, of that part of Austro-Germany called Germany, was obvious: he could starve them. But over Austria proper, Russia, Italy, his sway was no less omnipotent: for the panic cheapness of scrip which followed the destruction of the *Kaiser* had, of course, been foreseen, and used by him; Beech had bought up, easily ousting the Rothschilds from their old financial kingship: by tens of millions the process had gone on; and still it continued increasingly, for the wealth of Hogarth now, as compared with that of other rich men, was like a ship to a skiff. If he threw upon the market, the bankruptcy of several nations might follow: it was doubtful if the United States could survive; certainly, Austria, Russia, South America must go under.

Nor was the East less his slave: Japan a mercantile nation, China and Turkey in his fiscal net. So, looking round the globe toward the middle of November, he could observe scarcely a nation which he could not, by scribbling a telegram, crush out of recognition.

It was precisely then that Richard Hogarth revealed himself.

On the 15th of November appeared his Manifesto.

This Charter, which everlastingly must remain one of the Scriptures of our planet, simple as a baby's syllables, yet large like the arch of Heaven, has left its mark on the human soul.

On the morning of the 16th its twenty clauses occupied in *pica* a page of every newspaper, and it was posted up big in the streets of cities.

The document ran:

Richard, by the Will of God. . . . I do hereby discern, declare, and lay down: That:

1. What is no good cannot be owned: only goods can be owned.

2. "*Good*" is *well*, or pleasant; goods is *well*th (wealth) or pleasures: thus, a coal-mine, being no pleasure, cannot be owned.

3. Coal *becomes* goods after being moved, or taken. Moving does not make it good; its nature does not make it good: moving-*plus*-Nature makes it good, ownable. At the pit-head, already, it is a pleasure, fewer pains being now needed to move it to a fireplace. Thus, Nature apart from motion cannot be owned, being no good, as a cave is no good to a caveman outside it: rain is wetting him; if he takes it, moves in, it is good.

Animals and plants, by taking things from the planets presented to them, by moving things, raise Nature into wealth, and own things.

4. For Jack to *own*, have a thing for Jack's *own*, Jack must by his *own* force have subdued Nature, must have taken the thing by moving the thing's atoms, or moving something relatively to the thing, or, negatively, by not evading, but accepting, the thing in motion — a wind, tide, light-wave; else Jack must have taken something (by as much work) to purchase the thing from its (true) owner, or accepted it as a favour from Nature in motion, or from

its (true) owner. To say "own" is to say "take"; to say "take" is to say "motion," i.e., the doing of work: "work done" being FD, i.e., Force used into Distance moved-over. I cannot own the air: it is no good; I own the air in my lungs, having taken, moved, it, done FD on it: it is very good; and I own the air which, doing FD, moving to my face, I do not evade, but accept, take: it is very good.

I say to Jack "take a cigar"; he loudly says "yes!," but does not move it to his mouth, nor moves his mouth to it; instead, he moves a pen to his mouth; this makes me laugh: he has not taken a cigar.

Jack is catching fish in a boat; Tom owns the boat: so Jack gives fish to Tom, until Jack's FD done on the fish is equivalent to Tom's FD done on the boat; and now Jack owns the boat. If "the law" says that Tom still owns the boat, this makes me laugh: for how can Tom come to own two boats' good by the FD done on one only?

Jack is ploughing the sea with a ship: just there he owns the sea, has taken, is moving, it for his good. He does not own the sea before, nor the sea behind, him: for the motions behind made by him have ceased to do good.

Jack is ploughing soil: he owns the soil ploughed, has taken it, and will own it while the motions he has made do good: so that, if Tom who has not moved it says "I own the soil, for 'the law' declares that I have taken it by moving a pen two inches," this makes me laugh. Or, if Jack says "I own it for ever," this makes me laugh. Or, if anyone says "I own both the soil and the site" (relative position), this makes me laugh: for what can one man move to make a relative position good? He can neither move a field toward anything nor move much toward a field. If many men move railways that way, or move things to rear towns round the field, this makes the site good, moving it from outside a community to inside a community; and the many who make it good own it.

5. The site is the field's chief good: so the plougher owes something to those who, making it good, own it, This something is named "rent."

6. Suppose that the plougher, or dweller-on, is an Englishman: he owes rent to the English. And, since the site of England is made good by movements made in America, he owes rent to the Americans.

7. This the mind readily descries to be true: it is a "truism," and is necessarily the Fundamental Principle of Society throughout the universe. So that, summing up, we may define: "Rent" is "right," based on truth when paid to those by whose movements a site is made good.

8. One might readily guess (if there were no example of it) that any violation of a Principle so fundamental would be avenged by Nature upon the planet which violated it.

9. Our planet is such an example: for here Two Separate Violations of the Principle appear; each great in itself; but one small in comparison.

10. Accordingly, for the small violation Nature has not failed to send upon Man a small penalty; and for the great violation great penalties.

11. The small violation consists in the claim by nations to have taken, without having moved, sites called "countries."

12. For this Nature has sent upon man the small penalty of War.

13. To abolish War men must remove its cause.

Therefore let the site-rental of England (i.e., the excess of English goods over what English goods would be, if no other country existed) be handed over to a World Council; and the site-rental of America to the same; and the World Council shall disburse such funds for the majesty and joy of Man: and War shall terminate.

14. This way the Lord of the Sea indicates to the world, though with its initiation he is not personally concerned.

15. Beside the small violation of the Fundamental Principle of Society, there is a great on the earth.

16. The Great Violation consists in the claim by individuals to have taken, without having moved, sites and soils called "estates," "domains," "plots": for, as rent tends to rightness when paid to the fifty millions of a nation, *fifty-millionfold* is its wrongness when paid to one; and as rent is right when paid to the thousand million inhabitants of a planet, *a thousand-millionfold* is its wrongness when paid to one.

17. For this Great Violation of the Fundamental Principle of Society Nature has sent upon Man great penalties: poverties, frenzies, depravities, horrors, sorrows, lowness, dulness.

18. Lowness, dulness: for by far the greatest of these penalties is a restraint on Man's development. Man is an animal, Man is a mind: and since the wing of mind is Pride, Assurance, or Self-esteem, and since the home of an animal is a Planet, and an animal without a home is a thing without Assurance or Pride, so Man without Earth is a mind without wing. Even so, a few, having Assurance, make what we call "Progress," i.e., the discovering of truth — a crawling which might become flight, had all minds but the wing of Pride to co-operate in discovering truth. But Man

lacks assurance and foothold, founded home and domain: his sole heritage, though he is neither fish nor fowl, being sea and air.

19. This is a great violation.

20. And with this great violation of the Fundamental Principle of Society the Lord of the Sea is personally concerned. In the name of Heaven and of Earth he urges upon the nations of men to amend it in the month of the promulgation of this Manifesto: and this summons he strengthens with a threat of his resentment.

As the Lord God Omnipotent reigneth, I will see to it.
RICHARD.

XXXIX

THE "BOODAH'S" LOCK-UP

Three days after the Manifesto the marriage of Miss Stickney of New York with Lord Alfred Cowern was to take place, this having been put off owing to the *Kaiser* tragedy; and so, on the day of the Manifesto, Baruch Frankl, the Jew, was crossing to a wedding which, even in the midst of great events, had stirred up a considerable rumour and sensation, since the American guests were to consist of the *coterie* known as the "Thirty-four," all millionaires, while "the cake" was to weigh three-quarters of a ton, each guest's grub to cost $500, and for that breakfast the Neva had been ravished for fish and Siamese crags for nests.

Frankl, however, was never destined to taste those five hundred dollar mouthfuls. It happened in this way: as the *Boodah*'s searchlights, destroyed in the battle, were not yet repaired, in the interval some lawless ships took the chance on dark nights to skulk past with extinguished lights; now, the captain of Frankl's chartered steamer had that bright idea (being of adventurous turn), when night fell forty knots east of the *Boodah*, so he came to Frankl, and broached the scheme.

"Not for Joe," was Frankl's answer: "pay the Pirate his taxes and be done."

"It could be worked as sweet as a nut, sir!" persisted the skipper, with a watering mind.

"Well, so long us *you* take the risk, perhaps — but no, sir, I'd rather not."

On which the skipper winked self-willed to himself, and, putting out nine miles from the *Boodah* his three lights, went dashing past.

And the attempt would have succeeded, had it not been for the fact that the night was pitch-dark, and that *another* ship was trying that very venture with extinguished lights. And these two ships met, bow to bow, with such an energy of adventurous smartness, that both sharply sank.

The sea, however, being smooth, all hands were saved; and now, since the boats lay forlorn on the vast, with nothing but the *Boodah*'s swarm of moons to move to, for the *Boodah* they started, while Frankl cast twinkling fingers to the sky, and cursed that night, as the oars with slow wash journeyed through turgid murk toward the very den of the devil.

When they reached the *Boodah* they were conducted down to a police-court, and there shivered an hour in a dreary light, till three officials in peaked caps and frock-coats came, sat on a Bench, and, after hearing evidence, pronounced sentence of seven months against the captains, and one against Frankl.

These were led away by police blue-jackets, and Frankl groaned through the night in a box as cold as the cells of Colmoor.

The next morning Quilter-Beckett, making a report in Hogarth's *salon*, mentioned the incident, saying: "Here are the names, with the sentences; I shall send the sailors home . . ." and Hogarth's eyes, resting on the document, chanced to catch that name of Frankl.

At once he turned pale, for his first thought was: "Frankl must have been going to the wedding, in which case *Someone Else* may be with him."

But her name was not there. . . .

He rose and paced; and he said low: "No one else on either of the ships?"

"No, my Lord King."

Then up lifted Hogarth's brow, alight with fun, and he muttered: "All right, Caps-and-tassels."

He said aloud: "Quilter-Beckett, this Frankl I know. Did you never hear anything about Caps-and-tassels at Westring? *He* is Caps-and-tassels. Now tell me, which is your biggest blue-jacket?"

"Man called Young, my Lord King."

"Then, have a suit of Young's sea-clothes put upon this Frankl, and let him be brought before me in the Throne Room this morning after the Audience. He was fond of liveries. . . ."

Accordingly, by half past eleven Frankl entered the Throne Room, where, as soon as its rosy translucency broke upon his gaze, an "Oh!" of admiration groaned from him, in spite of his weight of misery, he not walking, but being lifted forward in successive swings by his armpits — up the first steps to the outer circle of balustrade, forward to the second steps and the inner balustrade, within which shone the throne, and Hogarth, crowned and large in robes, on it.

The two warders, intent upon portering Frankl, and not noticing the cap which still covered his eyebrows, one now in sudden scare whispered: "Off with your cap, you . . .!" on which Frankl snatched it off, grasping through superabundant sleeves, he at the same moment a fury and a dazzled man, the throne before him incredible, like a dream which one knows to be a dream, in structure not unlike the Peacock Throne of Akbar, its length fourteen feet, seating thirteen persons in recesses, standing on a gold platform with three concave steps set with rings of sapphire, and consisting of a central part and two wings, the wings being supported on twisted legs (one had been broken), and made of fretted ivory mosaicked with cabochon emerald, ruby, topaz, turquoise, chrysoberyl, diamond, opal, the large central part, with its recesses, being also of ivory, gold-arabesqued, its mosque-shape canopy (of Hindoo enamel-work on the outside) being supported by eleven pillars of emerald; at the top of each pillar a dolphin (hence the name "Dolphin Throne") made of turquoise, jasper, pearl, sardius, and at the bottom of each pillar a *guldusta*, or bouquet, of gems; the concave ceiling one mass of stones, representing a sea in which sailed three Dutch galleons, and seven dolphins sported.

But all that Frankl saw of it was its opulence: for his terror lest the warders should let him go occupied his mind.

And precisely the thing which he feared came upon him, for Hogarth said: "Warders, retire."

And now Frankl, all unsupported, stood in unstable equilibrium, anon stooping to his finger-tips, then straining doubtfully forward with struggling arms from a too backward poise: for not only did the trousers lie a twisted emptiness far below his feet, but the feet themselves were lost in Young's boots, so he stood like Scaramouch, a mere sack, a working of his chin wobbling down his beard, and there was a blaze in his stare which Hogarth, unfortunately, did not well estimate.

They faced each other, alone, save for the body-guard at the circumference of the room.

"Was it *you* that sent me to Colmoor?" Hogarth suddenly asked in a low voice, stooping forward.

"*Me!*" shrieked Baruch Frankl, pointing a hanging sleeve-end to his breast: "as Jehovah is my witness —"

"Were you about to *swear*? For ever the same? — tyrant and worm? It *was* you. Now tell it me right out: you have nothing to fear: for you cannot be vain enough to imagine that I would harbour enmity against you."

"It wasn't me, I say again, my Lord King!" — Frankl trampled a little backward, then stooped over-poised to his finger-tips: "with what motive? Oh, that's hard — to be accused. They have already given me a month — my God! a month! And only because I am a Jew. But it wasn't me — that I'll swear to God —"

Hogarth rose to his height, descended, put his hand upon

Frankl's shoulder. "Well, leave that. But — *my sister!*"

His hand felt the shoulder beneath it start like fits.

"Your sister!" Frankl screamed with a face of scare: "Why, what of her now?"

"Frankl, you are frightened: you know, Frankl, *where she is!*"

"Me? O, my Good God, what is this! Me, poor sinner, know where your sister is, my Lord King? Why, spare me! spare me, God of Hosts! Why, you've only got to ask yourself the question —"

"Listen to me, Frankl," said Hogarth, bending his blazing brow low over the Jew: "I have searched for that woman through the world, and have not found her. All the time, mind you, I felt convinced that you know where she is; and you may wonder why — years ago — I did not have you seized. I will tell you why: it was because I had a sort of instinct that God, whom I serve continually with tears and prayers, would not fail in His day to show me her face: and today you are here. Do you suppose, Frankl, that you will go away without telling me where she is? And in order to hurry you, listen to what I say to your warders —"

He touched a button in the balustrade, and to the warders said: "If at any time this man should demand pencil and paper, supply them, and take to your Admiral what he writes. Today his food shall be fare from your own table; tomorrow three loaves and water; from the third day one loaf and water; till further orders."

Up shot Frankl's shivering arms, while Hogarth, training his ermines and purples, paced away.

That was on the day following the Manifesto.

XL

THE WEDDING

By the time Frankl's three loaves had become one, that amazement with which men received the Manifesto had commenced to give place to more coherent impressions.

He was not a "Monster"! that was the first realization — no pirate, nor lurid Anti-Christ, nor vainglorious Caesar! And in two days, the first astonishment over, there arose a noise in the world: for the Lord of the Sea had given to the nations one month only in which to do that thing: and the peoples took passionately to meetings.

In England Land Leagues, Chambers of Agriculture, Restoration Leagues, Nationalization Leagues, many Leagues, were organizing furiously, stretching the right arm of oratory; deputations, petitions in wagons, demonstrations *en bloc*, party cannonades, racket heaven-high. Sir Moses Cohen, the Jew-Liberal Leader, appealing to the strongest prejudice in Englishmen, spoke one night at Newcastle of "the interference of a foreign prince in the affairs of Britain"; used the word: "*Never!*," and on this cry secured an enormous following: so that, within a week, he was instrumental in forming the formidable League of Resistance — destined to prove so tragic for Hogarth, and for England.

It was in the midst of this world-turmoil that — on the third day — the marriage-morning of Miss Cecil Stickney dawned; and that same evening Rebekah Frankl, convalescent from influenza, was seated over a bedroom fire in Hanover Square, a cashmire round her shoulders, her sickness cured by herbs, her physician then hobbling with a stick down the stairs — Estrella of Lisbon — her back almost horizontal now with age.

And as Rebekah mused there, two newsboys below, whose shouts pursued each other, went proclaiming through November gloom as it were the day of doom, crying, even in that uproar of Europe, a private event:

**MARRIAGE OF
LORD ALFRED COWERN
AND MISS CECIL STICKNEY
APPALLING TRAGEDY**

And soon a girl ran in, gasping: "Miss Frankl! — this is too awful — your father —"

The news, having been flashed to Paris by Mackay-Bennett cable, now appeared in detail after the *New York Herald*'s French edition, and Rebekah's eyes ran wildly over details as to the "bevy of beauty," daughters of "the Thirty-four," and the church of waiting ladies, the carpeted path between palms and exotics, and how the ticket-holders heard the organ tell the Cantilenet Nuptiale and Bennett's Minuet; and then the multitudinous stir: behold the bridegroom cometh! — the little necessary bridegroom of no importance, and then the white entry of bride and bridal train, while the choir knelt to sing "O Perfect Love."

Perfect love, however, was hardly the order of that day, but rather perfect hate: for in Madison Square — the church being at the upper end of Fifth Avenue — a mob was being harangued on the subject of this very wedding: and when they heard and realized the thing that was being done before their eyes they were swept as by a wind of fire, and under its impulse set out like some swollen Rhone with a rushing sound to pounce upon the church, full of perfect hate: and the choir sang "O perfect love."

What happened now was described as a nightmare. The same elemental instincts of the Stone Age which had exhibited themselves in the $500-worth of food wrought in another form, but with no less savagery, in assassins as in victims: and a massacre ensued, bride and bridegroom passing away like bubbles, of "the Thirty-four" five only escaping. The report ended with the words: "The ringleaders have been arrested; quiet reigns through the city"; then a list of the guests, with asterisks indicating those killed.

Rebekah searched for her father's name, and when she became certain that it was not there, her lips moved in thanksgiving.

But since Frankl was not at the wedding, where, then, was Frankl? She counted the days on her fingers: he could not have been late.

Unless there had been an accident to his ship. . . .

Her brows knit a little; she peered into the fire: and thought of the *Boodah*. . . .

It was possible that when her father's steamer stopped to pay sea-rent, Hogarth might have heard, and seized him. That notion occurred to her.

And at once it threw her into an extraordinary fever, her bosom swelling like elastic in her heavings to catch breath, though she did not realize the wild thought that was working up to birth within her. She rose and paced, furiously fast.

If he was in the hands of Hogarth?

"He is a British subject," she muttered: "Hogarth has not the right . . . Oh, he has not the right . . .!"

She was fearfully agitated! something fighting up and up within her, stifling her, working to burst into birth; she flung the cashmire from her shoulders, her bosom rowing like two oarsmen. "Because we are Jews . . .!" she went.

"If he *dared* do that — !"

What then? Say! Rebekah!

"I would go to him myself —"

All at once that thought was born, and she stood shockingly naked to her own eyes, her hands rushing to cover a face washed in shame. "But, surely," she whispered, "I could never be so *bold*, good Heavens? Why, Never! Never — !"

However, an hour later, with flaming eyes, she was writing a letter to Frankl's manager.

XLI

THE VISIT

Frankl's Bank was scanning the agents' yacht-lists for her, when Sir Moses Cohen, who was closely associated with Frankl, placed his own three-master at her disposal; and she set out from Bristol, with her being three Jewish ladies, Frankl's manager, and a snuffy Portuguese rabbi who resembled a Rembrandt portrait.

It was late at night, and Hogarth, who had lately acquired a passion for those Mathematics which touch upon Mysticism, was bent over Quaternions and the quirks of ↵ in an alcove of his *Boodah* suite hardly fourteen feet square, cosy, rosy, and homely: he sitting at a sofa-head, and, lying on the sofa, Loveday, his head on Hogarth's thigh, escaped from office and frockcoat, in happy shirt-sleeves, between sleeping and waking.

Hogarth was interrupted by a telephone bell.

"Well?" he answered.

"My Lord King," from Quilter-Beckett, "Frankl has handed to his warder something written: will your Lordship's Majesty see it now?"

"Yes!" Then: "John! Frankl has yielded!"

Up Loveday started with "Thank God!" while Hogarth: "When does my yacht arrive?"

"At midnight" — from Quilter-Beckett.

"She starts back immediately for England with me and Mr. Loveday."

Now an officer entered to present an envelope, and the two looked together over these words:

> "Your Lordship's Majesty's sister, Margaret Hogarth, is at No. 11, Market Street, Edgware Road, London. She goes under the name of Rachel Oppenheimer, I don't know why. As God is my witness, I repent in ashes. Won't your Lordship's Majesty have mercy on a worm of the earth? I am an old man, getting on, and starved to madness. The ever devoted slave, from this day forth, of my Lord King.
> "BARUGH FRANKL."

Hogarth 'phoned up: "Give Frankl food now, and put him where it is not cold. . . ." and to Loveday he said, "Well, you see,

she is there: 'No. 11, Market Street'. And under the name of —
what? 'Rachel Oppenheimer' . . . John Loveday, do you fathom the
meaning of that?"

"No — don't bother me about meanings, but shout, like her,
'O Happy Day!' I say, Richard, you remember that singing? how
we would hear her from the forge? All day, washing, cooking —
melodious soul! There was 'O Happy Day', and there was —
By God, how charmingly holy! how English! And, Richard, you
remember — ?"

Another telephone bell: Hogarth turned to hear.

"Just arrived in the yacht, *Tyre*, my Lord King," said Quilter-
Beckett's voice, "four Jewish ladies, a Jewish gentleman, and a
rabbi, who request early audience tomorrow; they lie-to, and have
sent a boat —"

"Rubbish! I shall not be here tomorrow, and even if I was —
Who are they? By the way, no sign of the yacht?"

"Not yet. They are Miss Frankl —"

"Who?"

"Miss Rebekah Frankl —"

"God," went Hogarth faintly, stabbed to the heart.

"Miss Agnes Friedrich, Mrs. —"

But the rest fell upon ears deaf as death, the teeth of Hogarth
now chattering as with cold, that haggard, gaunt yellow, which
was his pallor, overspreading his face. So long was he speechless,
that Quilter-Beckett asked: "Are you there, my Lord King?"

"Quilter-Beckett!"

"Yes, my Lord King?"

"Will you go *yourself* — for me — to them? *Make* them sleep
here, will you? This is most urgent, I assure you. And go quick, will
you?"

That night did not the Lord of the Sea sleep: she under his
roof . . .

Nor did he go that night to find Margaret — nor the next day,
nor the next, though Loveday chafed: for, gyrating through the
giddy air of a galaxy where Margaret was not, he forgot her.

XLII

REBEKAH TELLS

At that time Hogarth, personally, was in close relation with the score of Embassies that inhabited the belly of the *Boodah*, these intriguing incessantly for half-hours at his ear, and in communication, meanwhile, with their Governments through O'Hara's *Mahomet*: so that Hogarth had to get up early, and his mornings sweated with audience and negotiation.

The German and Russian Emperors, with the Prince of Wales (then virtually Regent), had hurriedly met at Vienna — presumably for the discussion of the Manifesto; and immediately after it, the Prince, who had the reputation of being one of the most tactful of men-of-the-world, took a step which hinted that the Royal House, as often before, meant to come to the rescue of the country which loved it however the politicians might bungle: Hogarth was invited to accept the Garter.

He accepted: and the ceremony in the *Boodah* was witnessed, as it were, by Europe, King-at-Arms in a new tabard, with his suite, going to invest him, taking the Statute of the Chapter, with the Great Seal of England, and a set of habiliments — white-silk stockings, gold sword Spanish hat, stars, gloves. And the effect was speedy, the other rulers, dumbfounded before, said now: "England will comply with the Manifesto; and, if before us, the taxed sea opens to her. . . . Yield, moreover, we must: let us make haste!"

But to consent was one thing: the *how* another: the mere suspicion of the willingness of Kaiser or Tsar shook their thrones. Whereupon Russia said to Hogarth: "Recently dispossessed, they cling dyingly now to their lands, so I will *buy* the land from them, and *you* will lend me the money"; to which Hogarth virtually replied: "It is too childish to talk of buying part of a heavenly body from a Russian: have you no sense of humour? You may give the Russian 'nobles' some money, if that pleases you: but without my help. If His Majesty the Tsar is more afraid of them than of me, my only way will be to prove myself more truly terrible than they."

But high words hurl down no hundred-headed hydra: in France — fast, faster — with dizzy vertigo — millions were forming themselves into secret societies, while in England was One only — but stronger than the many of France.

By the date of Rebekah's pilgrimage Hogarth had so far failed and yielded, as almost to decide that from the *Boodah* nothing could be done, unless he went to the extent of ruining and starving. The other alternative was the fixing upon one nation, becoming its recognized ruler, and there furnishing an example both of *modus operandi*, and of a subsequent state of happiness, which others could not long refrain from imitating.

But this modification was still in the air; and, meanwhile, he listened, weighed, revolved: using men, impressing, convincing, extracting for his use the wisdom of their experience, estimating the exact pressure of the Time, the *timbre* of its roar.

So on the morning after Rebekah's arrival his Gold Stick became his rack from the moment of the bow from the throne till noon: name after name — cordons, orders, gold-lace, sashes, stars, tiaras; till enter the four Jewesses, the bank-manager, the rabbi, Hogarth's pallor showing up his three moles and nose-freckles, adding a glare to his eyes, he suffering from the runaway drumming of his heart.

The ladies stoop through curtseys; the men do reverence; Hogarth bows.

There like a Begum of Bhopal stood Rebekah, floridly reflected in the glassy floor, sallow under the eyes, smiling at him, he at her; and very quickly now, she once in his sight, he recovered comparative calm, and the strength of his heart.

"Your first visit to the *Boodah*, I think?" — looking at her.

"Yes, my Lord King" — curtseying.

"Do you like her?"

"Why, yes: she is solid, and mighty, and rich. In my own, and the name of my friends, I beg to thank your Lordship's Majesty for your Lordship's Majesty's kind and good hospitality to us."

"Humbugging little beggar," thought Hogarth, his mind slowly gathering tone, but rushing meanwhile into a species of frivolous assurance after those agitations, his hands still cold.

"Well," he said, "but you have not seen her! I think I know her fairly well, and I propose to be myself your guide, if that will interest you —"

The Rabbi spoke with trembling voice: "It is gracious, my Lord King. We are here, however, humbly to present an urgent petition to your Lordship's Majesty. Baruch Frankl, at present a prisoner in the *Boodah*, a man no longer young, and habituated to comfort —"

"Stay," interrupted Hogarth: "if you have a petition the day and hour must be arranged by negotiation between yourself and my Chamberlain. But surely, meantime, I may consider you my guest? Miss Frankl and I — have met — in the world. Come, ladies — come, sirs — say yes!"

Rebekah, standing averted, flashed a look at him, reading his heart, and Jews and Jewesses laid heads together, whispering a little, until the Rabbi said, bowing: "We bend to your Lordship's Majesty's most gracious will."

"Agreed, then, sir. We might now see the *Boodah*, and if you will luncheon with me — Mr. Chamberlain! direct Admiral Quilter-Beckett to meet me at once in the north corridor."

He rose, master of his limbs now, descended, unrobed in an alcove, and in a corridor above the circular stair came upon Quilter-Beckett, who, acting as guide, Rebekah's hand now resting on Hogarth's arm, led them about the *Boodah*, now walking, now slipping in little trains over eighty-foot rails, rolled in one heat, laid down the vanishing length of dim-lit corridors floored with white tiles, their frieze of majolica, with rows of ceramics; and they saw the armouries, piles of rifles, cutlasses, pistols; ferneries grown by electric light; great cold-storage rooms that struck a chill, for preserving meats, butter, fruit; the doctors' *environ*, the dispensary, and roomy hospital; watched from a railing the working engines that fixed the *Boodah*'s position, Hogarth here saying: "There you have a menagerie of gnome-land: observe those two black beetles, sedately nodding; and there is daddy-longlegs, working his legs gymnastically; and the three pairs of gallant grey stallions, galloping grandly neck to neck; and those two ridiculous beings, rubbing their palms together, round and round: each preoccupied, comically solemn, busied about its own quaint affairs — like a varied gnomeland."

And Rebekah said in a meek tone, like the hen submitting: "Yes, I see now you say it, my Lord King."

Up stairs and down, round semicircles, up lifts, through nooks, corridors: saw the guns, and how by hydraulics everything was done — the hoisting of ammunition, loading, training: guns intact, guns wrecked by the Dreadnoughts; and shimmering kitchens, which reeked a smell of heat, and the dairy-maids, and the line of kine, and the row of prison-doors, and the mechanism of ventilation, fans and blowers, the drainage-system, and the dynamos for lighting, for supplying power to motors, for heating, and for shimmering forth rich in the search-lights; and the central ballroom, the clothes store, the original one-ninety-sixth model, the Ambassador-region, the steaming laundry, and the roof, where Rebekah saw her initials on the breeze, and the vertical pop-guns under shields for dealing with aeroplane attack, and the cream theatre, and the paymaster's suite, and the bunkers, the Government-offices, and the tax-receiving rooms, the telephone system, and the lady-telegraphists — till all were tired, though half had not been seen. They luncheoned together; in the early afternoon there was an Investiture, and she was there; for "five-o'clock" there was a Gounod concert in the theatre, and she sat in his box; at night the Bulgarian Ambassador gave a ball, and she danced a gavotte with him.

When they parted a dying wind sighed his name: "*Hogarth* . . ."; and when Loveday before sleeping happened to ask: "When do we set out for London, Richard?" Hogarth with a laugh turned upon him, replying: "When do we set out for Arcturus and the Pleiades? Do give one time to look round him!"

The next morning Rebekah, led forward from a semicircle of courtiers by a backing Silver Stick, approached within four feet of the Throne, and after the protracted humiliation of her curtsey, said ruefully: "Our party have failed, my Lord King, to obtain audience for our humble petition till after four days."

"Is that too long?"

"We could not wait beyond tonight. Our good Rabbi, and my father's Manager — both must hurry back, and we others with them. This being so, *I* appeal to Your Lordship's Majesty ."

"A *personal* appeal?"

"Yes" — poutingly.

"Then, I grant an audience."

"Where?"

"Here."

"Who will be here?"

"Why — you and I."

"*No*" — very low, with pressed lips.

"I am so sorry," says he: "it is the only chance I shall have; not for long — a few minutes — I am so busy. Otherwise, you will have to stay four days — and your poor father suffering —"

She seemed unsure now, and his hands in the uncertainty of that moment were moist like melting ice.

"So, then, you accept," said he: "a little audience — you grant me? Or rather, I grant you."

"When, my Lord King?"

"At three — No, what folly! At four. Will you? At four? And here? Say at four."

He spoke leaning keenly forward; and she, with a curtsey of acquiescence, retired.

They were near again, and yet far, in the *salle à manger* at luncheon, a function of a hundred guests at small tables, with more of orchestra than of talk; and even as Hogarth and his train entered, and the crowd rose, she saw his eyes, by some power, prowl and find her.

Afterwards there were two hours to wait.

Such a heat of haste now possessed them both! Hogarth locked himself from his attendants into his bed-chamber, and, tumbling a chaos of clothes and uniforms upon the carpet, stumbled bitterly among them, hunting for a cravat whose effect he remembered; wished at the mirror that he had no moles and nose-freckles, or that his father had turned him out rather less black; and anon a delicious chill pang of mingled sugar and peppermint would gash his heart at the thought: "*she consented!*" He broke glass, dropped his watch to fragments, hissing "damn the thing!"; and about half past three the hands of Rebekah, too, in *her* locked closet, were like the scattering sirocco among powder-boxes brushes, jewel-cases, and toilet-toys. What a hot haste was here! She too much blued her eyes, and bruised the skin in wiping, intense the contest between poudre blanche and poudre Rachel, violette and germandrée, she manoeuvring among mirrors to catch each angle of view, but with a blind impatience; and, if she wanted something, she tripped running, breathless: such a disease of flurry, an eruption and conflagration of haste — for nothing; yet, all the while, with a miserable sub-feeling of the penal creeping of time.

At four Hogarth in the Throne-room alone was now afraid that he would not be able to utter a syllable, and wished that she would not come; then, in a minute, began to fear that she would not, and wondered whether he was not a deluded fool ever to have dreamed it, he walking quick, or anon listening like a thief in that half dark: for few lights were shining, the hall like the after-flush of sunset just before the dark.

At four past four he was aware of a rustling train's rush down the steps, and now was like a man with his neck on the block, awaiting the axe. A moment afterwards she was before him, and two moments afterwards he was collected and hot, and a man again.

"*Dear,*" he whispered at her ear, leading her by the hand to an ottoman in a near alcove.

She, in self-defence, was repellent, breathlessly saying with galloping haste: "No — I will not sit: you sit, and I will stand here: do as I say, Hogarth — or I repent and go: I know you, and you know me — or you should. Our talk must be short. You say *dear* to me: that is very gentle, my friend; but it was not to bandy such words that I am here — alone — with you and your strength — Hogarth. I come as a suppliant, to implore you — firstly for the man who is my father — and secondly for yourself, to warn you. You are said to be about to become the sovereign of England —"

"*I* am?" — starting where he sat obediently before her, surprised that she should utter the purpose then forming in his mind: "witch — of Endor!"

"*I* am not the witch, but an old lady in whose predictions many Jews believe, who prophesies the return of the Jews to Palestine — through you. Be that as it may, if it is so that you are about to meddle with the institutions of England, oh beware, the resistence will be terrible!"

"With respect to England I am omnipotent."

"Yes, you can starve it, but *will* you? You won't. And listen to your friend: there is now in London a society, enormously powerful I believe, sworn to your destruction."

"What can they do — assassinate me?"

"Ah! who knows?"

"That would be too childish: I have sown my seed in Time, and it will grow: two thousand little lords could hardly obliterate the ploughing of my wrist. But you know this?"

"Richard, my father is of them."

"Ha! — I forgive him: his daughter seems to be on the other side —"

"Richard, you would not touch my hand? Ah, my friend, I warn you — ! Now — you have agitated — I have been ill — my father is of them. And who is one of the closest associates of my father — ?"

"Who?"

"The person known as Admiral Donald, whom *I* know very well to be Monsignor O'Hara. I think you might have been more — recondite — in your choice of an admiral, Richard!"

"Ah? — you surprise me."

"But why? You once sent that man to me as a notebearer: certainly, a singular selection. You must have known that he had been a convict —"

"I thought him innocent then!"

"But you know now — ?"

"Yes."

"And is it not extraordinary that your ensign bears my initials, while this man is one of your commanders?"

"I confess that I do not see the point —"

"Then you cannot know, I suppose, that it was against *me* that his offence was directed."

Hogarth's left lid lowered. . . .

"But my complaint is of the present: are you not aware of the scandal which the *Mahomet* is now creating in the world?"

"Scandal?"

"Thrice lately whispers have reached me of unnameable iniquities perpetrated there — Alexandria of the sixth century, Rome of the second! I believe the rumour is widely spread in London — no woman of the world now lands on the *Mahomet*."

"It was *you* whom he assaulted . . ." Hogarth laughed and was pale at once.

"Yes, but observe that I must go now, my friend. I have spoken of the things which I had in my mind: there remains — my father."

"He shall go with you."

"I thank you, my Lord King; that must be in an hour: so I say, Richard, good-bye."

"I do not suppose you can dream how dark —" he went woefully.

Of which she took no notice, but with rapid speech said: "How fair this hall is — one supposes that the art of impressions was lost with Solomon — like some chamber under a lake at set of sun, colour without substance, suspended, flushed — I cannot express —"

"Sad, say."

"Ah, Richard."

"Rebekah!"

"Well, Richard, my poor friend?"

"Have pity!"

"Poor Richard!"

"I can't help it, you are all mixed up with my blood, don't go from me. If you think it a sin — the Gentile — God will forgive the charity. Come for ever —"

Now he sobbed once, and, as he sobbed, she was on her knees, in pagan posture, at his knees. "Do not —" distractedly — "see, I kiss your hand-do you doubt that I pity my love — as a mother has compassion — ?"

Now were heaving breasts, a vehement fight for breaths, wild eyes, and a live brand in the marrow.

"You will not go! I have you! In God's name, what a mad thing — !"

"My furious king — you kiss —" the short-winded *mélée* of whispers now suffocated in a passion of inarticulate breaths; but at that moment one of Rebekah's chaperons, wandering out of time and place, stood at the alcove entrance, and they, smitten into two, sprang straight, awaked from trance, Rebekah with half a sob and half a laugh.

And two hours later Hogarth, from the roof, saw the Jewish yacht disappear to the East, on board being the four — and Frankl.

As he descended, he threw up his head with: "Ha! — O'Hara"; announced his immediate departure with only a secretary and two lords-in-waiting, left a mystical note for Loveday, saying that he had decided to go alone in quest of Margaret, and went almost secretly, only the salute informing the *Boodah* as he steamed away. In reality he was in haste to face O'Hara, and the yacht's bows turned, not eastward, but southward, under forced draught, to arrive at the *Mahomet* in early afternoon. As her flags indicated the Lord of the Sea absent, there was no salute, and, landing in a panama and jacket, in the Collector's Office he gave the sign of mum, and, led only by a blue-jacket, went spying the depths of the *Mahomet*.

In many parts, noticing a singular odour, "What is it I smell?" he asked.

"Incense, my Lord King," the man answered.

On the fourth floor he entered the loveliest *bijou* chapel, the coenaculum gold-plated, altar flower-piled, frescoed roof, "stations" in oils, where a lonesome Moorish youth slothfully swung and swung a thurible ruby-studded: but in vestments of no *enfant de choeur* — of an ancient Phrygian.

Another descent and Hogarth reached a region of laugh and harping: whereupon, dismissing his guide, he tracked the music into a nook so rare, that he stood amazed — a Court of Love, or Mahommedan Heaven, or grot of Omar — anything old, lovely, and devil-sacred — the air chokingly odorous, near a fountain some brazen demon — Moloch or Baal — buried in roses, over everything roses, bounty of flowers, a very harvest-home of Chloris, Flora in revel; and smooth youths bearing cups for some twenty others, all garlanded, besides those on the marble stage; and on the stage itself a scene of dancing girls, Sevillian, Neapolitan, Algerian, mixed with masked Satyrs, which made Hogarth pale, while at a Herod's-table buried under fruits, wines, flowers and gold, reclined Pat O'Hara, tonsured now, crowned with ivy and violets, gowned in a violet toga; while under a pendulum whose swings left whiffs of incense behind lay Harris insensible.

As Hogarth descended into it, harp and dance ceased; some

leapt to their feet: but O'Hara sat still, gazing in a dead silence through glairy eyes, while Hogarth, looking about, spied an electric button in a couch, touched it, and soon a man in uniform stood at a door above.

"Who are you?" asked Hogarth.

"John Souttar, head-telegraphist, may it please your Lordship's Majesty."

"Make haste: tell the First Lieutenant and the Chief Constable that the Lord of the Sea is here."

By now all the revellers were on their feet; no sound: only, the clicking pendulum voyaged, landed an incense-whiff, and voyaged, like traders.

Then the Lieutenant appeared, mottled and panting, and immediately the Constable.

"Ah, Royds," said Hogarth: "is it practicable to flood this room quickly with a hose?"

"I — should think so, my Lord King."

"See to it. First set guards at the exits."

He turned to the other: "Mr. Chief Constable, I give all present, except, of course, your Admiral, into custody, on a charge of misdemeanour on the high seas. The General Prosecutor will, in due course, forward the indictment to your Summary Court. Have your men here with handcuffs."

Again silence, till, in four minutes, two men appeared on the steps, ball-nozzle in hand; upon which Hogarth said to O'Hara: "Follow me," and as the two passed up, O'Hara tottery, care hanging on that ponderous nether-lip, Hogarth whispered the hose-bearers: "Drown the room well — man and woman — do not spare."

To O'Hara he said: "Lead to your suite," and, descending, they presently stood in a bed-temple, the bed surrounded with mirrors, and at the other end of the apartment an altar — pyx, six unflickering candles, and flowers, with rail and reredos, and maxims of St. Theresa.

Hogarth said: "Sleep two hours," and went out, turning the key.

But in half an hour O'Hara had started awake, sober, and, clapping his palms over his face, burst into tears.

That Hogarth might be capable of impeachment before a Court of Admirals, followed by death on the block, he feared; and he rolled, groaning, tugging his tonsure-fringe, which, on the forehead, lay a thin grey forelock, thinking: "Guilty wretch that I am! putrid, unwholesome, hopeless, I have befouled the holiest:

how richly do I deserve to die!"; and even as he groaned and smote, his secret mind weighed up the chances of Hogarth's action.

He rose, listened, rushed to the door, found it locked, tossed up despairing hands, and tottered to the altar, at which he knelt, all sighs, and dying fish-eyes, and sideward-languishing face, and weary woe. Ah! how great the mountain of his iniquity: if he might be but once more spared, his evil remainder of days he would bury in some Carmelite retreat, with fastings and prayers; but no — he had too much tempted the Eternal patience, the sword was out against him. Yet he implored, he implored with groans: with half an eye, meanwhile, on the door; and, having with regard to Hogarth a piece of secret knowledge which he guarded deep for some possible emergency and use (the fact of Hogarth's Jewish birth), as he prayed, his brain with complete detachment worked out the question whether he might now reveal this with advantage.

Hogarth found him kneeling, said "Get up," and O'Hara stood, leaning upon the rail, too faint to stand unpropped, Hogarth contemplating him, tapping the toes.

"Well, sir! I know all: your whole past."

"Red as crimson — !" went O'Hara faintly, with tossed hands.

"Red enough, Admiral. You are a bad old man: merit death."

"Ah, God knows it, my Lord King! I do assure you, I am a leprous wretch: and I welcome death — I pray you, I pray Heaven, for it —"

"You should have it, if you were a better, or a younger, man: but I will not stain the Empire of which you were chosen to be a stay, and are the shame, with the blood of such as you. You are beneath judgment: and that clemency which is our scutcheon I extend to you. Live, therefore, and repent, O'Hara. I, however, you understand, now turn from you for ever. And I discharge you like a menial, sir. See to it that within six months you have your affairs regulated, and send in your resignation to the Government."

He turned and went; and, as he disappeared, O'Hara straightened, coolly went "H'm!," and took snuff. He lived, he lived: while there is life there is fun.

Fumbling about, searching for nothing, all relieved and rescued, yet stunned, he suddenly exclaimed: "What a noble fellow is my son Hogarth!," and knelt again.

Hogarth in the same hour was away for England; and on the fourth evening thence, the street-lamps just lit, stood before No.

11 Market Street, Edgware Road, come for Margaret; his carriage waiting at a corner forty yards away; and though within the last hour he had realized vividly that his voyage to the *Mahomet* had given Frankl time to remove her, or accomplish any devilish device in his power with respect to her, he was now all prospect and expectancy.

The house was three-storied, mean, unlighted, with an "area"; from a neighbouring window a woman screaming down to some playing children; and under her a shop sending out that fishy fume which "drove Asmodeus back to hell."

He rapped, received no answer, rapped again without reply, then stepped down and back, looking up: and suddenly, faintly, but distinctly, he heard her voice, high up — *singing*.

"O what a pretty place,   And what a graceful city,   Where the striplings are so gay,   And the ladies are so pretty ."

It was she! He ran and banged at the door: no reply.

Back again he stepped; and now a window on the top floor went up, and she, putting out her head, twice beckoned him — listlessly, it seemed, then drew in; and instantly — again — he heard her sing.

As once more he ran to the door, he discovered now that it was open, darted into darkness, up uncarpeted stairs, making for that upper room, vague light through grimy stair-windows guiding his impassioned dash; and on the third floor entered a room with two doors, beyond one of which was the room he sought: but that door was locked.

At it he pushed, fumbled, called: "Margaret!" No reply. And suddenly he heard her singing, not before, but behind him.

"Happy day! Happy day!
"When Jesus washed my sins away . . ."

When he flew to the other door, and now found it, too, locked, gradually in that gloom all colour faded from his face; and the voice sang on:

"Happy day! happy day." . . .

XLIII

THE LAND BILL

The Manifesto's "month of grace" was passing, yet nothing had been done, second-rate Powers awaiting the Great, while the Great, appalled by the bigness of the demand, fussed and intrigued, consulted, fermented and proposed: but did nothing.

But at last, on the 3rd of December, the First Lord of the Treasury laid a Bill on the table of our Commons — at the end of an Autumn-session!

On the 3rd: and on the 1st the Lord of the Sea had been captured near Edgware Road, the probability being that this Bill was brought forward with a knowledge of that capture.

It consisted of three clauses and two schedules — called The Land Purchase Bill; and it had only to be published to produce the stormiest agitation ever known.

The Opposition was the Jew-Liberal-Labour party; and when the Labour Congress (met at Manchester) denounced the measure, there occurred a "split," a Liberal-Labour cave, the whole body of Jews, numbering 87, retiring to the Government ranks.

The Bill proposed the "purchase" of Britain from its "owners" by the British, the price fixed being 27 times the annual value, to be paid in settled annuities for entailed estates, and in consols for unentailed.

So, then, the Government would buy London alone for 1400 millions and Britain for 8000 millions — a bad lookout for England.

And the authors of the Bill chose a moment when Hogarth was living on bread and poisoned water in Market Street.

It rapidly passed to Committee, and then to the Lords.

But on that night a terrifying rumour for the first time pervaded England: that the Lord of the Sea, having come to London at the beginning of the month, was missing, and that his person had been claimed from our Government by the Sea under menaces.

In fact, when a week, two weeks, had passed, and not a whisper from Hogarth, apprehension had turned into certainty in the breasts of Quilter-Beckett, Loveday, and all: and at a hurried Council called in the *Boodah* on the 19th, when the date of Hogarth's landing at Southampton was determined, and his small train-in-waiting, his coachman, re-examined for the twentieth time, one certainty emerged: Frankl had had time to reach England before him; and the arrest of Frankl was demanded.

Now England in consternation almost forgot the Land Bill; Scotland Yard ransacked Market Street: not a trace of Hogarth; it dissected the country for Frankl: but Frankl was now in the *Mahomet*, safely conferring with O'Hara.

The popular tempest first directed itself against the League of Resistance: and at an attack upon its Offices in Victoria Street during the afternoon of the 21st Viscount Reid (the Secretary), and a girl, were killed by missiles; petitions signed by the nation raining meanwhile upon the Prince of Wales: for, apart from the wreck which threatened, Hogarth's popularity was at present considerable with the masses, whose instincts suspected those above them of knowing more of his disappearance than appeared.

On the night of the 22nd, when things had an air of revolution, fifty-three men met in a house in Adair Street, W. (This runs parallel to Market Street, the backs of the two house-rows facing.)

These were the warders of Hogarth: and the object of that night's meeting was to determine whether he should die, and when, and how; the Land Bill now awaiting the Royal Assent; and on the morrow British high-sea trade to be ruthlessly stopped, failing news of Hogarth.

The room was double, with an arch in the partition, through which ran a rough-board table surrounded with velvet armchairs; the floor richly carpeted, though paper peeled from the walls; down the table a procession of silver candlesticks and typewritten notice-papers and agenda; the windows boarded — a second floor; and in a room near, Hogarth, shackled hand and foot, he having been borne through a subterranean way, made for the purpose, from the cellar in Market Street to this Adair Street.

From eight o'clock men began to let themselves in at the two doors in both streets, and continued to arrive till nine, when a marquis at the table-head rose to speak, the others leaning back with downcast eyes, nearly all pale.

The point before them was plainly put by the speaker on the Question: *viz.*, whether they had more to fear from the life, or from the death, of the Lord of the Sea.

"By a strange Providence," he said, "this man is in our hands: and we have the right to become his executioners. My Lords and Gentlemen, the awful decision rests with you tonight."

Then, one after another, they rose, they spoke: no two views identical; till at ten it was voted that the question be put, voting papers went round, and presently the ballot-result was announced amid a momentous stillness.

Twenty-eight had voted for the death, twenty-five against.

But in that minute a key was heard in the room door, and in rushed two flushed men: Frankl and O'Hara, just arrived in London from the sea; and Frankl burst into speech:

"I hope this is all right, my lords, my coming like this, and bringing into your very midst a gentleman who is not one of us. When I tell you that he is Admiral Donald of the *Mahomet*, turned away like a servant, how does that make your lordships feel? A house divided against itself can't stand; and this gentleman has a scheme in his pocket — he will read it to your lordships — which will crack up the Empire of the Sea like an egg-shell! So I do hope, my lords, that you have not decided anything hasty about putting away Richard Hogarth: for unless he is liberated this night, it means sure and certain stoppage of everything tomorrow: and *that* means my ruin, and many another's beside —"

Now the Master called him to order, and addressed himself to O'Hara, who, in admiral's uniform and stars, all stately bows, grave smiles, in ten minutes had given guarantees, was a member, and in thirty had read a memorandum of a scheme of betrayal which everyone saw to be feasible.

Then the vote of death was annulled; and when the meeting broke up Hogarth was being lifted with bandaged eyes through the subterranean way to Market Street, where four men deposited him near the house-door, undid his ropes, said to him "You are free," and there he remained twenty minutes without motion, deadly sick, then rose, and, on finding the door, went wildly with dragged feet, tottered into a cab, and leant brow on hand.

As he entered the porch of his Berkeley Square house, Loveday rushed out to his knees with adoring eyes, having hardly hoped to see again that face of Hogarth, while Hogarth patted the bowed head, saying: "Do get me a meal, and let me hear what has been going on. . . . Oh, I am weary ."

And during the meal he heard all: of the Land Bill, the turmoil.

"Well, my God!" he exclaimed, "is there no drop of generous blood at all among those people? Never again do I trust them to make their own arrangements I When does this precious Bill have the Royal Assent?"

"Tomorrow, it is supposed."

"Really!" — he started: "and whereabouts is the Prince of Wales?"

"At Windsor tonight."

"Order the motor quick. I'll go."

He was soon off, and Loveday, listening to the dark story of Margaret's appearing and singing, and vanishing, accompanied him under a frosty moon, snow lying on village-street and hedge; but, travelling hard, they arrived shortly after one upon a Prince who, a wakeful man that night, sat conferring with Private Secretary and Attorney-General, he having assented to the introduction of the Land Bill, then been alarmed by the storm, and now was confronted with the responsibility of either giving His Majesty's assent, and earning execration, or refusing it, and taking a step unheard-of since William III.

In that state of embarrassment he was, when the Lord of the Sea was announced, and "It is with heartiest pleasure that I offer to your Lordship's Majesty my congratulations on this re-appearance," he said, greatly and gladly surprised, without at all seeming so.

And the two conferred till three, when a secretary, at Hogarth's dictation, wrote a document and its duplicate: a contract between Prince and King, giving pledges on each side, private, yet most momentous; and each, having signed both copies, retained one.

The next evening the Clerk in the Lords uttered those unusual words: "*Le Roy s'avisera*," and the country was thrown into transport by the news of the Royal rejection of the Land Bill, processions singing the National Anthem, bells ringing: and for a month the mention of a Royal name in any assembly brought the people to their feet.

Ministers, of course, resigned; and, as the Liberals refused office, writs for a new House were made returnable for the end of January.

XLIV

THE REGENCY

During the next month England was in a general-election turmoil; at the same time a Land Bill in the French Chamber,
and one in the Reichstag, was thrown out: whereupon a *ukase*
from the *Boodah* announced the raising of sea-rent to 5s. on all
ships over 2000 tons after the 1st February, the month of grace
over, the "screw tightening."

Already distress in England was great, coal being at three-
and-sixpence, bread at nine pence; a cry had arisen for the Union
of Britain with the Sea; and on the 27th of January a plebiscite
among the Trade Unions resulted in an affirmative vote of five
millions out of an electorate of nine.

Now, at this time the bulletins respecting His Majesty were of
a settled depression: he lived, but languished; and it was understood that the new Ministry's first act would be the appointment
of a Regency.

Then appeared a rumour: alterations were going forward at
Buckingham Palace on a scale of splendour new to Western man-
sions; the Prince of Wales had passed three days, from the 17th to
the 19th, in the *Boodah*: and the saying went that, on the night of
the rejection of the Land Bill, a compact had taken place between
the Prince and the Sea for a three years' Regency of the latter.

Excitement ensued, the matter becoming an election test: and
180 Labour Members, with 70 Liberals were returned pledged to
support a Regency of the Sea.

A definite coalition, meantime, had been announced between
the Jews and the Conservatives.

Never was election so rolled in dust and noise, in the result
the Jews having the casting vote: and if ever race was looked at
askance, it was they now by the British.

The session having been opened by Commission, a resolution
passed Lords and Commons that the Prince of Wales be empow-
ered to exercise the Royal Authority; whereupon the Prince at the
palace, having heard the Address, read a reply, sufficiently startling to the country, though well foreknown to those present: he
laid stress upon the new conditions of the world — that phleg-
matic eye, which had seen so much, lifting a moment in punctua-
tion to dwell coldly upon his hearers, then coldly reading again;
the difficulties, he said, which he was called upon to face on behalf

of His Majesty were not lightly to be undertaken, and his fuller answer would be contained in a proposal which he would make in the Lords as a peer of the realm.

The next night in a crowded House he read a speech distinguished by extraordinary dignity and severity: "My lords," he said at one point, slapping the table, though those eyes remained royally null: "when will your lordships learn to recognize the facts of life?" and, having proposed His Lordship's Majesty, the Lord of the Sea, to be Regent during His Majesty's illness, such Regency not to exceed a period of three years, he recommended a plebiscite.

No plebiscite was taken: for within some days the sense of the constituencies was revealed, and the Leader in the Lords received stern hints from the Liberal Leader, which damped pride: so their lordships abstained from Westminster, their Resolution being passed by just a quorum.

The country wondered at the ease with which the whole went off — not knowing that those who might have led resistance had a thought, and a prospect, inspired by one Pat O'Hara, which comforted them.

And now a Deputation of Five took boat in the *Prince George*, to wait upon the Lord of the Sea in the *Boodah* Throne Room, where the Lord President read the information that they were a Committee appointed to attend His Lordship's Majesty with the Resolutions of the Houses.

"We are instructed," he read, "to express the hope which the Lords Spiritual and Temporal, and the Commons, entertain, that His Lordship's Majesty, from his regard to the interests of His Majesty the King, will be ready to undertake the weighty and important trust proposed to be invested in His Lordship's Majesty, as soon as an Act of Parliament shall have been passed for carrying the same into effect."

He then read, and delivered, the Resolutions.

Hogarth replied, reading: "My Lords and Gentlemen, I receive the communication which your two Houses have instructed you to make to me with those sentiments of regard which I ever entertain for your two Houses. Deeply impressed with the necessity of tranquillizing the public mind throughout the world, I do not hesitate to accept the office and situation proposed to me."

So the Deputation departs; five days later twelve British battleships surround the *Boodah*, come to accompany the Lord of the Sea to England; and at eleven on the morning of the 9th, his yacht, borne in on the strong thunders of a royal salute, drops anchor in Southampton Water.

He had set so gorgeous a standard of luxury to Europe, that no one dreamed of making his entry into London an ordinary *fête*; and, as the procession traversed the triumphal arches of Piccadilly, he, swept to the gods in the lap of gallant sublimities, plumes, sabres, showering hoofs, squad-troops, outriders, showed to the Prince beside him and to the Czarowitz before him a miniature of Rebecca Frankl.

Some streets cheered — not all much: but during the illuminated night all London seemed to abandon itself to revelry.

The next morning Hogarth went in state to the Chapel Royal for certificate of Communion, attended by heralds, Sergeants-at-mace, sword-of-state, the Duke of York; and after "the service" communicated under a canopy at the hand of the Bishop of London.

Then, on the 14th, Lords and Commons had a final conference over the Regency Bill, when the Assistant of the Parliaments uttered the worlds: "*Le Roy le Veult*"; and on the 15th, the swearing-in day, a party of grenadiers with colours and fifes marched into the palace grounds, continuously to play "God Save the King"; while yeomen and ushers, together with servants-in-state of the Lord of the Sea, lined the great hall and staircase, lifeguardsmen lining a vista of state-apartments ending in a Blue-velvet Room, recently decorated; by 2.30 P.M. Privy Councillors commenced to arrive, till at 3.45 P.M. the Lord of the Sea sent Admiral Quilter-Beckett to the President of the Council, ordering his presence; and presently was himself seen coming up the vista, accompanied by his own household-officers, to the Blue-velvet Room where he sat at the table-head, the Royal personages on each hand, his own officers ranged on each side of the entrance-arch; and now one by one entered the full-dressed Councillors, with bows which he returned, taking seat according to precedence — Canterbury, then the Lord Chancellor, then York; and last came and sat a certain Mr. Forrest, Keeper of the Records.

Hogarth then rose and said:

"My Lords: I understand that by the Act passed by your Parliament appointing me Regent of this Empire, I am required to take certain oaths, as prescribed by the said Act: I am now ready to take these oaths ."

Whereupon rose the Lord Privy Seal, made a reverence, approached, and read, while Hogarth pronounced after him:

"I sincerely promise and swear that I will be faithful and bear true allegiance to His Majesty King George. So help me, God.

"I do solemnly promise and swear that I will truly and faithfully execute the Office of Regent of the King's Empire according to an Act of Parliament entitled 'an Act, etc.', and that I will, etc. So help me, God."

He then subscribed the two oaths, and after him the Privy Councillors, the Lord President first, as witnesses. It was then delivered to the Record Keeper, who deposited it in a box, while Hogarth presented his Lord's-Supper certificate: whereupon the Lord President bent the knee and kissed his hand, then the Royal personages, then the Archbishops, advancing in order on both sides.

It was a week of Hope, the turning over of a new leaf, so the spirit of festival reigned, and was deepened when the evening papers that day announced that a *ukase* of the Sea had reduced rent on British ships by 1s. 9d. per ton, and was heightened when during that and the following nights Hogarth dispensed three millions in fêting England: his illuminations having no resemblance to those sickly twinklings, tremulous at their own cost, previously deemed good enough for the jubilee-days of an empire; the people were astonished: ample and planetary his mind, his hand right royal, and London, bursting into light, flashed tidings of our earth to Mars. It was incredible then that any had ever wept, or would weep again; the bitterest foes of the Regent caught the contagion of world-gala; Europe flocked to London; theatres were gratis; the illusion of the comet of the final night was complete, her lurid rays sprawling 2000 feet aloft in stiff portentousness, prophesying Change, the parks all transfigured into universes of moons, crescents, stars, jerbs, Roman-candles, *pots de brin*, girandoles of rockets, pagodas, marquees, each tree a net of fireflies, while from five hundred and thirty balloons, with silent burst, snowed diverse fires.

The new reign opened with promise.

XLV

ESTRELLA, THE PROPHETESS

For three weeks a Provisional Ministry carried on the Government, confining itself to Supply; till, on the 3rd March, the Lord Regent succeeded in forming a Cabinet; and at 9 on the evening of the 5th for the first time addressed himself to the country in the House of Lords.

That night the world seemed hushed to listen, the peridom of Britain packing the Gallery with rainbow, and the peerdom those benches and cross-benches, red as massacre and the Scarlet Woman, where thronged 580, while to Charing Cross spread the crowd without. He, from the Throne, addressed them, and they, startled by the revelation of a caste chaster far than Vere de Vere, and a pride far more serenely throned than Hohenzollern, acknowledged him high-born . . . "Your lordships will not fail to perceive my will to invigorate some of our ancient epithets: thus, the First Estate of the Realm shall, during the present Regency, be veritably 'First', and in no case last;" anon he blew his bugle: "Let us play the man! — easy to say, hard to do: yet it was first said by an Englishman when the doing, I think, was hard enough, his martyr's shroud already rapt aloft in flame: *that* was magnanimous, my lords, I declare! *there* was the British Lion. . . ."

That same night a new Land Bill was introduced by Sir Robert Wortley, the Prime Minister — a bill drafted, criticized, and re-altered during two years by the legal experts of the Sea, proposing the "purchase" of Great Britain at a price of twice the annual value for inherited land, and seven times for land held by purchase: this to be paid in two and seven years respectively, without interest, lands yielding no revenue to become crown-lands from the date of the Bill, which was called: Land Department (Creation) Bill.

It passed first reading; but the question was: would the Jews vote for the second reading? Reluctant enough the Jewish members, but there were rumours that the Jewish electorate were instructing their representatives to repent and vote for.

And now spread far the League of Resistance, so did the Adair Street Society, its secret daughter, of which Admiral Donald (O'Hara) had now been elected Honorary Vice-Master, and whose Roll contained the names of an extraordinary number of Territorial officers.

The Society was busy: had building four yachts, all models of the Admiral's yacht attached to the *Mahomet*, which was called the *Mahomet II*; every dusk companies of 25 to 40 men drilled darkly in the back yard at Adair Street, some of them Territorial officers: in rotation they came, they drilled, over 1000; a top room piled with revolvers, swords, bowie-knives . . .

For the land-magnates laughed at the notion of submitting to the Bill: rather, said they, "rivers of blood." The mention by Hogarth of Ridley and Latimer they considered irrelevant; their fathers' heroic mood was a detail: not an entail.

In secret they met. Anarchists of the reddest hue.

One night when the Bill was approaching second-reading Frankl introduced Harris as a member; and wide-eyed stood Harris, though still cynical, with elegant walking-stick, hat cocked, and "I sye," he whispered, "are all these real, living lords?"

"Large as life," answered Frankl.

"Strike me dotty! The Lord said unto my lord, sit thou at my right hand" . . . the reason of this introduction of Harris being a relation which had arisen between the Army and the Lord Regent, who had been taking a startling interest in this branch of the services, had visited Aldershot, and held five reviews, flattering the soldier by private notice, shifting officers. By an Order in Council of the 3rd March, a reorganization was effected in the Army Board and Consultative Council, of the new men the Adjutant-General being General Sir Merrick Parr, uncle of Admiral Parr of the sea-fort *Shakespeare*, while the Commander-in-Chief and Inspector-General were the direct creations of the Regent, and the whole Headquarters Staff bound to follow him through thick and thin; and that "second reading" was near, which, if the Jews would vote against, well and good for Adair Street, but, if not, there remained either (1) the prompt execution of O'Hara's scheme without waiting for the four yachts, copies of the *Mahomet II*, which were slow in building; or (2) the knife of Harris.

But, as to (1), when three delegates from the Society had waited upon O'Hara in the *Mahomet* to urge immediate action, O'Hara had replied: "No, my lords, I cannot enter into this undertaking until preparations are complete, since the troops we send would never be allowed to land on the forts, if they arrived in ships not apparently our own. Your lordships cannot be more anxious than I to rid the earth of a devouring lion like Richard Hogarth, I do assure you; but, tut, is there nothing else meanwhile? Just let me introduce to your lordships a little young man whom I know" — he had summoned Harris.

But when the three delegates had gone, he had struck his brow, exclaiming: "Wretch that I am! — that great and good fellow, the fairest of the sons of men! . . . what a black depravity must be in this heart —" he had underlooked in the mirror, and cut a face; "but ah, Hogarth! this heart is in your net; and I loved the mother, too. . . ."

He had sought the altar, and that night had written piteously to Hogarth, appealing for fresh friendship and reconsideration of his sentence of dismissal.

So, at any rate, was Harris introduced to Adair Street, became its chief minister, and ten days before the second-reading debate had won, by O'Hara's recommendation, an *entrée* into the Palace as servant to a gentleman-usher-daily-waiter: and now he made bright the knife of the assassin, tending its edge as a gardener the tender sprout, the knife being his *métier* and forte, he despising the noisy, mediate, uncertain pistol, nor could use it, his instincts belonging to the Stone Age. But the days passed, and he could by no means get near to Hogarth.

One night he boldly penetrated to the royal antechamber with the knife under his waist-band, having passed the stairs-guard by a specious official envelope. As it was late, he thought it must be about the Regent's bedtime, having the vaguest ideas as to royal ways and bedtimes, Hogarth being then in a consultation with three of the Cabinet destined to last till morning. And Harris: "Can I see the Lord Regent?" with that lifted brow of perpetual surprise and alertness.

"You? Who are you?" asked a gentleman-in-waiting.

"That's neither 'ere nor there, if it comes to that. I'm Captain Macnaghten's man, then."

"But what is it you want?"

"He told me to give the Regent this 'ere" — showing the envelope.

"Weally! then, give it to me."

"He said I was to give it to the Regent's self."

"Then, go to blazes quickly, will you? and let Captain Macnaghten know fwom me that he has been dwinking."

Harris could not penetrate the ten-fold barrier; but he lay in wait; watched from some coign every Royal exit and entrance, careful that Hogarth never saw his face; and he cherished the knife-edge.

One night, four days before the debate, he stood by the Green Park railings, listless, smoking, when — he started: saw a hurried figure come out — face muffled — Hogarth! — alone.

Hogarth walked a little, entered a cab; Harris, in another, shadowed him.

Down Piccadilly, the Hammersmith Road, into the Addison: Hogarth alighted; Harris followed.

Now, at this time Hogarth had a spy, who presented him reports of the doings of Rebekah Frankl — a species of literature which the Regent found agreeable; and, as for two days Rebekah had, for some reason, been at a villa of Addison Road, this escapade of the Lord Regent was motived by his hope of catching there some glimpse of her, the house being small, he having seized his first chance of secret escape from state-affairs near midnight: and behind him, like the shadow of death, stole the assassin.

Hogarth, going soft up to the house, leaned aside from the frontage steps to peer; but Venetian blinds barred him from the least sight of the interior, though he could hear sounds, strange sounds, as of wailing; and, as the villa was in the midst of quite a spacious ground, well grown with trees and shrubberies, he stole round to the back, peered into an open door level with the garden, and within saw a doorway of twilight in the midst of darkness; had hoped to see a servant, who might talk gossip, or even contrive him sight of the Sacred Body; had ready bribe in hand: but nobody there. So, after some hesitation, he entered; and Harris, just then come to the house-corner on tiptoe, discerned him go in, ran on hot bricks to the door, and now distinctly saw Hogarth, who had passed through a kitchen, standing on three wooden steps before a doorway which framed a faint light in the room beyond.

On which a shivering of eagerness, quick as winking sheet-lightning, shook Harris' right knee.

Hogarth, meantime, having seen the chamber before him empty, in his headlong way had entered, and the guess now in Harris' mind was this: "It's a girl: a night out." . . .

He hesitated, Hogarth being once within the house and lost to him, but after some minutes dared to follow.

Hogarth, meantime, had seen that the light came from a death-taper, with which was a vessel of water for ceremonial purification, and a napkin, here being all the preparations for *tahara* (washing); and suddenly, in a near room, arose the clamorous dole of *shivah* (the seven mourning-days), Rachel weeping for her children, because they are not: a Jew was dead: "shema, Yisrael . . .": and this explained Rebekah's stay there, for the bereaved may not leave the house. A peer at the bed — a covered face — pierced him with a compunction like shame: here was *kodesh*, and he a desecrator with his earthy passion: so he turned to beat a retreat by the way he had come — when a faint sound that way, made by Harris; and, instead, he leapt lightly through a window five feet above the garden.

Some moments later Harris, entering on prowling all-fours, and seeing the bed-clothes hang immediately near, stole under; waited: no sound save the singsong lament; and "O Gawd," thought he, cynic even in his palest agitation, "there shall be weeping and wailing and gnashing of teeth." . . . But that Hogarth had not come to wail and gnash he felt convinced: if he heard no sound above him, that might be because of the sounds around; so he crawled barely out, and, kneeling, put up a most cautious groping hand, the bed being in the darkest part of the room; someone there: and swiftly as a dolphin twists to dart and snap, his knife was in a breast and instantly ready to strike its expected bedfellow.

But the breast was alone, the breast of Estrella, the Prophetess, four days dead.

Harris snatched off the face-cloth, peered upon a noble old visage, fixed now in trance, and said: "Well, I'm —"

Now he ran, but in the kitchen stopped wild-eyed. It I might be murder-he was not certain; at least it was out-rage, and he might be traced: there was the cabman who had brought him — his absence from the Palace — "Bah! it can't be proved. . . ." But still, if he were even arrested, and Hogarth got to hear of his presence about the Court — that would spoil all. He listened: all that part of the house a settled solitude, the servants themselves sitting *shivah*; and back he ran, seized upon the little old body, not now stiff, *rigor mortis* having passed, saw that the sheet was unstained, and snatched her away out to the bottom of the garden where shrubbery and holly-hedge formed a jungle.

Now he set to dig with hissing haste; and, even as he hissed and digged, he talked without pause, envenomed, heaping her sanctity with insult: "Old cat you . . . dust to dust and ashes to ashes, it is. . . . What you want to do that for? under you go in the cold, cold sod. . . . Who arst you to put your little finger in the pie? There's another one for you, fair in the gullet! Now take her up tenderly, lift her with care-and down she goes." . . .

Such were Estrella's *kaddish* and "House of Life." . . . As he had only the knife, and the work was slow, and in the midst of it an outcry from the house, the body missed, he stopped, listening, but without acute fear, knowing it improbable that they could dream of seeking in the grounds, and as a matter of fact their minds were a mere paralysis of holy wonder; so presently he had the little body in a two-foot grave, arranged surface and dead leaves to naturalness, leapt a wall, and got away.

Never did act of assassin have result so momentous: for though the predictions of Estrella had lately spread far among upper-class Jews, it was only on the day after her burial by Harris that her fame reached to each Jew under the sun.

It was given out that divine confirmation had been vouchsafed to her prophecies by the snatching of her body, like Enoch's, into Heaven, or by its burial, like Moses', by Jahvah: for when no explanation but one is extant, the brain fastens upon that, and embraces it.

And as Estrella, who, in life, had guarded her hard sayings for the few, had left papers revealing for her whole race what she had dreamed, like wildfire now ran her message among the Chosen.

Now Temple and Synagogue were crowded: rabbi and pawnbroker and *maggid*, clothes-man and *takif*, were infected; and there spread the cry (for the most part meaningless): "To Zion!"

It may be that the Jewish electorate were now too agitated with the near probability of Shiloh to interest themselves in any mundane question: at all events, it was during that rage that the Government-whips announced the certainty that the Jewish members would vote against the Land Bill.

Hogarth first heard it pretty late at night from the Prime Minister; and "Ha!-the Jews," he went: "so they have dared, these men? I never thought that they would! May God deliver me from His ill-chosen people — !"

"And ill-choosing, it seems, my Lord King."

"Quite so! But, Sir Robert Wortley, is it supportable this thing?" — a brand now on his brow — "an alien race in Britain opposing thus daringly not *my* will only, but the plain will of the people? And have I the air of one who will support it? Rather, I assure you, would I govern without a Parliament! But stop — perhaps I shall be found capable of dealing with these mischievous children of Israel. Give me a night: and tomorrow at noon come, and hear. Of course, this second-reading business must be postponed ."

And deep and wide, in lonely vigil, wrought the Regent's thought that night, till morning: of Abraham, Isaac, and Jacob, of tendencies, histories, soils, ports, railways, possibilities, race-genius, analogies, destinies; of Rothschild and I Solomon; of Hirsch and Y'hudah Hanassi; of the Jewish Board of Guardians, Rab Asa, and the Targum on the Babylonish Talmud; of the Bar-

bary Jews, the Samaritans, and Y'hudah Halevi; of the Colonial Bank, and the Karaite Jews. . . .

When at dawn he threw himself dressed into bed, he had resolved upon a very great thing: their expulsion from England, Pole and Hungarian, Baron and coster, and the little child at the breast, ten millions.

His eyes had closed toward sleep when, with a start, he remembered a prophecy uttered one evening in the *Boodah* Throne-room, and these words: "Richard, deal gently with my people. . . ."

Two nights later, with a retinue, he hurriedly left England-for Constantinople.

XLVI

THE ORDER IN COUNCIL

Three days before that setting-out, O'Hara's appeal for pardon had come under the Regent's notice: and as he had read, his eyes — once more — had softened, as he had thought: "It would be a great crime to forgive him the long list; but never mind — we will see." . . .

And he had meant to reply, but suddenly the Jews had swept O'Hara quite out of his mind.

He was away hardly two weeks: and when he returned, Palestine and western Armenia were his, all his acts of this period bearing resemblance in largeness and rage to the incredible forced-marches of Napoleon.

If one spreads apart the first two fingers, he sees exactly the country ordained by Hogarth for modern Israel: the first finger Palestine, looking upon the Mediterranean; between the fingers, the Syrian Desert; the second (longer) finger that Mesopotamia, "the cradle of our race" between the Euphrates and the Tigris, this opening upon the Persian Gulf, and the trade of the East.

The then population of this area was only 300,000 (Arabs, Turks, Jews, Greeks) in the Palestine finger, omitting Russian pilgrims to Jerusalem; while in the Mesopotamia finger — all that Hinterland of Palestine called "Turkish Armenia" — not 320,000 Armenians had been left by Khurdish rapine and Turkish atrocity: we may therefore say that the whole was an uninhabited land waiting for inhabitants.

The only things needed (according to modern notions) to make it immediately colonizable were roads and railways, and the Regent had not returned to Dover when both were making in Palestine, the Sultan, left thunderstruck with a chronic eye of scare by that visit, "lending his co-operation," consoled meanwhile by a Conversion Loan of thirteen millions out of Sea-revenue; to which add a grant-in-aid of fifteen millions to the emigrants, and the remark of Hogarth's Chancellor about this time becomes intelligible: "Your Lordship's Majesty's expenditure is exceeding revenue by 50 per cent"; so that Beech's was soon realizing considerably in bonds over Europe, and Hogarth temporarily poor — had stubbornly refused any Parliament-grant for the Regent's personal establishment.

And suddenly from the blue fell his bolt: at that same table of the Regent's oath-of-office assembled eighty-seven Jewish lords and gentlemen at noon of the 24th March, the first day of the month Nisan in the Jewish year 5699, ordered, each by himself, to the Royal presence; and the Regent, with the gravest eyes, both palms pressed on the table, in an embarrassment of compunction, rose and spoke with them — Rothschild and merchant-prince, Chief Rabbi, Manchester Chief Minister, Heads of the Alliance Israélite, Anglo-Jewish Association, Jewish Board, Jewish philanthropists, writers; and they could not believe themselves awake.

He began by speaking of himself, the fact of his power, with such graciousness, that all were affected, not by the power, but by the gentleness which wielded it: Providence had given him the disposal of the earth, and it was for him to do his poor best — a lonesome, sorrowful post; so that talking could never alter in anything the main point; but it could modify details: and he had called them to invoke their great administrative gift and expert counsel; he told of the exodus which he designed, the home which he had prepared them; recommended a Sanhedrim of Chief Jews to form the Provisional Government of the new State, with the Chief Rabbi as its head under the title of Shophet (Judge); would offer a contribution of £ 15,000,000 from his Exchequer toward an emigration and colonizing fund, and doubtless emigration bureaus would be at once established at principal centres; he would also hand over a Deed of Gift of this larger Judaea as between the Sea and the Jewish people to the Central Authority as soon as established; also, duplicates of the text of the Treaty as between the Sea and the Ottoman Empire. What he gave he gave, he assured them, with a free heart, without condition; except, of course, one: that no inch of the new land should ever "belong" to any particular Jew: for he gave, as Nature gave the earth, not to a hundred, but to all, living and to be born, occupiers to pay rent, not to any adventurer calling himself landlord, but to the Central Authority, representing all. This done, he would invoke with confidence upon their able race the blessing of Almighty God.

In tones so mellow did he utter himself, that for many minutes stillness reigned, every face pale.

Until a baron stood up with ashen under-lip, to say that such a scheme, it seemed to him, must remain for ever abortive, unless enforced by Act of Parliament —

But Hogarth checked him quick.

"No, my lord, not by Act of Parliament: the how your lordship may leave to me. I dare say you will see it in this evening's papers."

It was by an Order in Council!

"DECLARATION of the Court of Great Britain respecting the Order in Council.

"At the Court at Buckingham Palace, the 24th day of March, his Lordship's Majesty, the Lord Regent, in Council.

"WHEREAS His Lordship's Majesty was pleased to declare in the name and on behalf of His Majesty the King on the 23rd day of March: THAT if at any time, after the expiration of the three months following, any of the hereinafter mentioned trades, occupations, pursuits, or acts, shall be carried on or done within the United Kingdom of Great Britain and Ireland by any person being a person coming within the sense of the term "Jew" as hereinafter defined, THEN and thereafter such person shall be liable to the pains and penalties hereinafter specified."

*   *   *   *

No Jew might own or work land, or teach in any Cheder or school, or be entered at any Public School or University, or sign any stamped document, or carry on certain trades, or vote, or officiate at any public service, and so on: parentage, not religion, constituting a "Jew." Through Britain this piece of Russian despotism sent a wave of quiet gladness, and an epidemic of jest broke out, in club, factory, "Lane," and drawing-room: "You hurry up — to Jericho!" became the workman's answer to a Jew; it was remarked that the chimney of train and steamship would furnish a new pillar of cloud by day, and pillar of fire by night, to go before the modern Exodus; they were little to be pitied, for even Heaven was their mortgagor in land, with promise to pay — the Promised Land; a syndicate would be formed to "pool" milk and honey, and either Sharon or Salem would become the new Get-O at any price; being a rather Peculiar People, they would call the new Temple "the 'Ouse" (of Prey-ers), and make contango-day coincide with Passover. . . . But let him laugh that is of a merry heart: as for Israel, with weary breast and hunted stare he sandalled his foot for the final Exodus: yet not as them without hope. Already — some days before the Order in Council — the disappearance of Estrella's body, her daring prophecies, had led to the embarkation of 700 Jews for Palestine; and when the Regent's Edict gave startling confirmation of her prediction of "the Return," in many a million hearts thrilled the certainty: "the Day of the Lord is nigh!"

And with that their stoicism and organizing strength, they mutely turned to follow the finger of Destiny: their *takifs* (rich men), hard upon the unchosen, were, as usual, liberal to their own, the fund swelled, and a Committee left England for the accumulation of stores and implements; at the same time two Parliament Bills were passed in two sittings, empowering the purchase by Government of land "owned" by Jews on Land Bill terms, and quickening the machinery for the collection of debts due to Jews.

Whereupon, "You see," said the Chief Rabbi, "he drives us out: but he makes us aprons — if only of fig-leaves — to cover us. Let us bow to his rod, and thank him, and go: he is God's Minister."

So they went: the world's mercantile marine having been summoned, sea-ports were turned into caravansaries of gabardine and ear-lock: the Exodus began.

In the midst of which it came to the knowledge of the Regent that the house of Frankl was making ready for departure.

And now Hogarth rebelled against Heaven: self-forgetfully he did his best, and it returned and struck him dead: for what good, he thought, would his life do him, she always in Asia, he in Europe?

He wrote to her, a passionate hotch-potch of command and grovelling supplication: if she went, he would curse her; would go mad; would blaspheme God; would throw up everything; would die.

He had promised to go down to Oxford to receive a degree, and as up to the time of his departure she had not replied, he went half unconscious of himself and those about him.

Now, upon Adair Street the Expulsion had brought despair, the second-reading now assured, the Jews' vote over, and new writs issued; the second-reading debate was actually in progress at that date of the Oxford visit; and though the four yachts, copies of the *Mahomet II*, were being rapidly put together, the Bill, if at all pressed, must get through before they could be ready; nor could the House of Lords long delay its passage.

There remained Harris, so far ineffectual, but not therefore hopeless: so he, spurred, went down to Oxford.

But what Harris could not do was to get near to Hogarth: his task was, as it were, to pluck Venus from the firmament; but he mused, he mused upon her, with musing astrologic eye, with grand patience, fascinated by her very splendours, not without hope. When at 8 P.M. a banquet was served to 250 guests in the Radcliffe Library, the upper gallery being open to a crawling public to see the lions feed, Harris, watching thence the unattainable under the blue of the canopy — blue always in honour of the

Sea — thought within himself: "Ah, Mr. 76, you've got it all, ain't you? — for the time being. But 'ow'd you feel if I had a pistol now? Gawd! I can just see him nicely curl and kick. Worse luck, I can't shoot a bloomin' 'ouse."

But the opportunity was so exquisite, that he resolved to try — the exit reached, would run, get a pistol, and return; but at the door itself a hand touched his shoulder, and, with a twist of guilty scare, he saw — O'Hara.

"Good Gawd!" he whispered, "what you want to startle anybody like that for? Don't you know that the wicked flea pursueth every man, but the righteous shall escape his filthy snare?"

"What are you doing here, boy?" asked O'Hara.

"Thick-head! ain't I down 'ere after this precious Mr. 76?" — for Hogarth, if Monarch of the Sun, would have remained for Harris only a glorified 76, Colmoor being for him the reality of the universe, all else mirage, such stuff as dreams are made of.

"Well," said O'Hara, "come with me: want to talk to you" — he just come from the *Mahomet* through Spain and France, drawn to Hogarth as moths to a candle, his petition for pardon not yet answered; and he assumed that Hogarth's wrath still blazed, though, in fact, answer was only delayed by competition of greater interests, Hogarth having forgotten O'Hara; at any rate, O'Hara, with shrinking qualms, had come to Oxford, thinking: "I will try and get at him for one more talk — I am not afraid of your eyes, my son: tut! I've seen the great brow in a prison-cap. And the haughty beast still loves old Pat at bottom, I do declare. Be bold, be bold, but not *too* bold. . . . Well, I will! And, if I perish, I perish, and he perishes, too, so help me, God." . . .

And to Harris, walking by the towing path, he said: "No, boy, don't you. Not now. Tut! — those lords: they are only making you their tool. Don't you understand? Hogarth is robbing from them the land which they have robbed from the British people, and they naturally wish to murder him: but what have *you*, or I, to do with that? Let the thieves fight it out between them, while we enjoy ourselves, if we can. Weren't we happy in the *Mahomet*, boy — we two? Didn't you roll whole weeks drunk? That was better than Colmoor, eh, Alfie? And didn't I have my incense, my grapes, my little Circassian, and ten thousand pounds in yellow gold a year? Wasn't that all right? Well, we may have it again! — not in the *Mahomet*, perhaps, but somewhere. Do nothing — not yet: till I give the word. If you *must* kill, get a dog, or a horse, or an obscure old man, not the Regent of England —"

"Dirty old swine!" cried Harris, angry, "'aven't I forbid you again and again from making game of me? You're doing it now! You just try that on, and go up thou bald-head, it *is*!"

"But is this understood between us?"

"Old duffer! you are one thing today, and another thing to-morrow: there's no knowing how to tyke you. You're such a sinful old 'ypocrite, that you play-act before yourself, I do believe. What is it you do mean? You myke anyone sick of you; your incense and your burnt sacrifices are an offence unto me. This Mr. 76 once put a knife into me, and I mean to put another into him: 'ow's that?"

"Not now!"

"'Ow about your sweet friend, Frankl? I'm under contract with him, ain't I?"

"Better put the knife into Frankl."

"Into the pair of you, it strikes me!"

"Well, if you make the least attempt upon Hogarth now, you get not another shilling —."

"Bah! shut that — !"

But the threat won sullen consent; and when after the Banquet the Oxford guests had driven to see the illuminations, spoiled by boisterous Spring-winds, and when the Regent returned to his chambers, he caught sight of O'Hara amid the throng that lined the stair; upon which, after stepping up past, he stopped, twisted round, to say: "You, Admiral Donald?"

"If I might speak ten minutes with your Lordship's Majesty —"

"What about?"

Those bold eyes of O'Hara dropped.

"Well," said the Regent, "I will see. Come tomorrow — about five," and went on up.

The next morning the Degree was conferred in the theatre, Doctor of Common Law — "an appropriate one," the Master of Balliol remarked, "though 'Surgeon' would perhaps be the *mot juste*"; and thus at last Hogarth donned cap-and-tassel, though not Frankl's — a livery which drew from Harris the reflection: "Sweet beauty! — in his mortarboard." The nip upon the brow of the college-cap peak resembled the nip of the Scotch prison-cap, awaking memories: but the symbolism was different.

Meantime, the Regent's eye wandered, madness and folly in his heart, and fear, till at four a letter came, he having left Loveday at Buckingham Palace with instructions to open letters and send the One.

She had written:

"What you can expect of me I am unable to conceive. Have you not expelled me? Let us be worthy of our long friendship, and 'play the man'.... 'My exaltation to afflictions high'.... With prayers for you, I say good-bye: and will remember.

"REBEKAH FRANKL."

Loveday had added: "She left London at noon for Southampton. Purchas followed to spy. Machray's other detective waits in Palace for instructions."

As to the dinner in Christ Church Hall, and the Ball, which were to end the program of this last day, at four-thirty the news spread that the Regent had been taken ill.

"Have you not expelled me?" ... Was she angry? Did *she* not know that he meant well? Hogarth, breaking into a rage, leapt up, with, "I swear to God that not one step does she move out of this country — !" and rushed to a bell: a gentleman-usher came.

"What about going?"

"All will be ready in fifteen minutes, my Lord King."

"I feel bad: say ten minutes; tell the Lord Chamberlain."

"Yes. I might mention — did your Lordship's Majesty grant a ten minutes' audience to Admiral Donald for this hour?"

"*Who*? Yes, I think — Just kick him down the stairs! Or no — say I may see him some day."

This message, as the usher dashed through, was faithfully dropped at O'Hara's consciousness; and O'Hara said: "Hoity-toity ...!"

Bent-backed he descended to the Quadrangle, with a sense of defeat, rebuff, contumely, rage, but quite sprightly said to Harris, waiting beyond the Gateway: "Well, boy, how can we make a night of it? I feel that way."

"Seen Mr. 76?"

"Tut, no. Sharpen up that knife for his throat, boy!"

And Harris exclaimed: "Another chynge! Strike me silly! — what did I sye? Give me a new 'eart, O Lawd, it *is* — you grey-haired old duffer. Chopping and chynging, always the syme — to your old wife Jyne. I'd be ashamed of myself in your plyce. But sharpen up the knife, it *is*."

XLVII

THE EMIGRANTS

Late the same night the Regent received at the Palace a telegram about Rebekah: She had travelled alone to Southampton, where a landau at the station had awaited her, in which she had driven to a country-house near the Itchen named "Silverfern," two miles from Bitterne Manor, in which lived an elderly gentleman, Mr. Abrahams, ark-opener and scroll-bearer in the Synagogue, with his wife and two sons. The passage of these, and of Rebekah, was booked by the *Calabria*, Jewish emigrant-ship, to sail in four days.

Hogarth no sooner heard these tidings than he tumbled into crime: resolved to kidnap Rebekah; to break his own law for his own behoof: one of the basest acts of a King.

He had four days: and by the end of the second four men lay in wait round "Silverfern," one a sea-fort sub-lieutenant, one a detective, and two others very rough customers: a cottage having been hired by them for the reception of Rebekah in a dell a mile higher up the Itchen.

But something infects the world; and gravity badgers the bullet's trajectory; and a magnetic "H" disturbs the needle; and "impossible" roots turn up in the equation; and the finger of God is in every pie.

Hence, though the four ravishers lay in wait, and actually effected a seizure, the Regent did not get his girl.

None of the four had ever seen her: but as there was no young lady except her at "Silverfern," that seemed of no importance, so she had been only described to them as dark and pretty.

But on the night after Rebekah's arrival, there came to "Silverfern" a new inmate: Margaret Hogarth.

Her passage, too, was booked to Palestine.

For Frankl had said: "In expelling the Jews, he shall expel his own sister. Oh, that's sweet, after all!"

At this time Frankl's interest in Land Bill and England was dead, two interests only remaining to him: so to realize his share in the Western world as to reach Jerusalem loaded with wealth; and also, not less intense, to hurt Hogarth, to outwit him, to cry quits at the last.

It was hard — Hogarth being set so high; but he invoked the help of the Holy One (blessed be He): and was not without resource.

Why had Hogarth never had him seized, racked? What restrained the Regent *now*? That was a question with Frankl. Hogarth might say, even to himself, that Frankl was vermin too small to be crushed, that he waited for his sister from God; but lately the real reason had grown upon Frankl: it was because Hogarth *was afraid* of him! afraid that Frankl, if persecuted beyond measure, might blurt out the Regent's convict past, and raise a sensation of horror through the world not pleasant to face. Harris, O'Hara, Rebekah and Frankl alone knew that past, and the motives for silence of the first three were obvious; nor had Frankl whispered that secret even to his own heart in his bed-chamber, conscious of his own guilt in the matter of the Arab Jew's death, fearing that, if the wit and power of Hogarth were given motive to move heaven and earth, the real facts might not be undiscoverable: then would Frankl be ground to fine powder by the grinders. But if he was going to Palestine, what mattered?

Also, there was Margaret: she should go out as a Jewess.

She arrived at "Silverfern" in the charge of a Jewish clerk, and the Abrahams received her as an afflicted orphan, committed to Frankl by her father; she, like Rebekah, to go under their care.

Well, the evening before the departure, Mr. and Mrs. Abrahams, their two sons, Rebekah and Margaret, all go for a stroll — about nine o'clock, that morning one of the four ravishers having been to the house on some pretence, seen Margaret with Mrs. Abrahams under the porch, and noted her well, her grey tailor-gown, her brooch, her singing; and now, as all walked out under the moon, they were watched, the watchers, surprised at the presence of *two* young ladies, concluding that the smaller — Rebekah — must have arrived later: so upon the large and shapely form of Margaret their gaze fastened, as the party passed near their hedge of concealment, Margaret then remarking: "My name is Rachel Oppenheimer —" and Mrs. Abrahams with gentle chiding answering her: "No, be good: your name is Ruth Levi."

For during two years at the Jewish Asylum at Wroxham they had tilled into her shrieking brain, "Now, be good: your name is Rachel Oppenheimer," and one day she had said: "My name *is* Rachel Oppenheimer," and had been saying it ever since.

In fact, there was a real Rachel Oppenheimer, a dependent of Frankl's, at Yarmouth, who was rather mad, and when it had been necessary that Margaret should be out of the way in order to secure Hogarth's conviction, two doctors had examined this Rachel Oppenheimer, and given the legal certificates by means of which Frankl had put away Margaret; and she during two years of sanity in an atmosphere of lunacy had screamed for pity, till one morning she had shewed the stare, the unworldly rapture, and had started to sing her old songs.

After which, Frankl, hearing of it, and touched by some awe, had got her out, and kept her in one retreat or another.

But in all her madness was mixed some memory of his devilish heart, and every fresh sight of him inspired her with panic, she in his presence hanging upon his eyes, instant to obey his slightest hint: hence her beckoning down to Hogarth from that window in Market Street.

Now, on this last night of England the Abrahams party strolled far, two days like Summer days having come, on hedge and tree now tripping the shoots of Spring, the moon-haunted night of a mild mood: so from "Silverfern" lawns they passed up a steep field northward, down a path between village-houses, and idled within a pine-wood by the river-side.

The moon's glow was like one luminous ghost: and buttercup, daisy, snowdrop, primrose gathered Margaret, vagrant, flighty, light to the winds that wafted her as fluff, and tossed them suddenly aloft, and back they came to be tangled in her bare hair; and now she was a tipsy bacchante, singing:

"Will you come to the wedding? Will you come? Bring you own bread and butter, And your own tea and sugar, And we'll all pay a penny for the Rum."

"Poor Ruth!" — from Rebekah, an arm about her waist.

"There is such a huge pool which is wheeling," said Margaret, gazing at it with surprise, "and it goes hollow in the middle: my goodness, it does wheel! and there is a little grey duck in it ranging round and round with it, and this little grey duck is singing like an angel."

"Do you know where we are going to?" asked Rebekah: "to the land of our fathers, Ruth, after all the exile in this ugly Western world; and it is he who sends us, the fierce-willed master of men."

"My name," said Margaret, "is Rachel Oppenheimer"; and immediately, wafted like a half-inflated balloon which leaps to descend a thousand feet away, she sang:

"Happy day! Happy day! When Jesus washed my sins away . . ."

Then, woe-begone, she shook her head, and let fall her abandoned hand; and Rebekah, speaking more to herself: "Did you never hear of Hogarth, the King, Ruth? or see him in some dream in shining white, with a face like the face in the bush which burned and was not consumed?"

But now Margaret laughed, crying out: "Oh, there's a man riding a shorthorn bull that has wings; white it is: and up they fly, the bull pawing and snorting, all among the stars. Oh, and now the man is falling! — my goodness —"

She stood still, gazing at that thing in heaven.

"Well, what has become of the man, dear?" asked Rebekah.

"I can't make out. . . . But I should like to marry that man."

"Ah, if wishes were fathers, we should all have babies, Ruth, to say our *kaddish*."

"Oh, look — !" cried Margaret.

A rabbit had rushed across a path ahead, and she ran that way beyond a bend. . . . When Rebekah followed she had disappeared.

On Rebekah's outcry all set to search wood, path, river — she was gone; but after five minutes a voice a long way off in the wood, singing:

"O what a pretty place,   And what a graceful city. . . ."

on which the two youths flew toward the sound, and presently the rest, following, heard a shout, a cry, then silence, till one of the young men came running back, his face washed in blood: he had seen some forms, and, as he had approached, been struck on the brow, his brother felled. When all came to where the brother lay insensible, no sign of Margaret; nor could villagers and police, searching through the night, find her.

She had gone without surprise with her four captors, who had carried her to a cottage of boarded-up windows: and the same hour Hogarth had the news.

The next morning the four received detailed instructions at the village *poste restante*: the lady-attendant at the cottage was to ask the prisoner if she would go to London, try to persuade her, and, if she consented, make her sign pledge of honour (enclosed) to go without any attempt at escape during three days.

The men were surprised: for that Margaret was deranged they had seen at once, and supposed that the Regent must know it: what, then, could her pledge do? Their business, however, was to obey: and when Margaret was asked: "Will you go quietly to the Palace in London with us?" she answered: "Yes!" and sang:

"Here we go to London-town: Tri-de-laddie! Tri-de-laddie! See the King with his golden crown,   Tri-de-laddie, O!"

By noon the Abrahams and Rebekah were being tugged out of harbour, to the hand-wavings and god-speeds of seven emigrant-boats by the quay; but it was not till five that the Regent's emissaries could obtain a special train on the thronged lines; and not till after seven did they arrive with Margaret at the Palace-gates.

Now, that night the Lord Regent and the Prince of Wales were attending a banquet at the Guildhall, given in honour of sea-rent reduction on British ships, and at the moment when Margaret arrived Hogarth, already *en route*, thinking of Rebekah, muttered: "By now she is here!"

But since Frankl, on getting news of the disappearance of Margaret, had at once conjectured the hand of Hogarth, as Margaret was being handed from the cab at the Palace-gates, she saw two terrible eyes, and, snatching her hand free, flew screaming down the street — eyes of Frankl, who, conjecturing that hither she would be brought, had taken stand there half the afternoon, knowing precisely the effect upon her of the sight of his face; and said he: "You see, you haven't got her yet — though you *shall* have her to your heart's content. . . ."

As she could only run southward or northward, he had posted two motor-cars, one containing a clerk to south, the other Harris, to north, so that, as she ran, one or other should catch her, hustle her in, and dash away.

In fact, she ran north, right into the arms of Harris, her surprised guardians still ten yards behind; and "Quick!" hissed Harris, "come with me, or 'e'll 'ave you!" and was off with her.

Upon which Frankl drove to the Market Street house, where he found Harris and Margaret; and again, with screams, she sought to fly, though her first terrors gave place to a quiet subservience after some minutes of his presence.

"Oh Lawd!" said Harris, "she started singing in the car, you know. Sing me songs of Araby, it *is*. Enough to give anybody the sicks."

"You see this gentleman here?" said Frankl to Margaret.

"Yes," she whispered: "oh my!"

"Well, it so happens that very likely you are going to live in the same house as him — a big Palace with all gold and silver, where the King with his crown lives, and all. So while you are there, I want you to be his friend as if it was myself, and do everything he tells you, same as myself, in fact. Do you see?"

"Yes," she whispered, her large form towering above Frankl's, yet awe of him widening her eyes.

"What's your name?" said he.

"My name is Rachel Oppenheimer," said she.

"All right: come up and dress."

She followed him up to a back room, where was a lamp, a glass, etc., and on an old settee evening-dress complete, shoes, roses, head-wrap.

"Now," said Frankl, leaving her, he, too, in evening-dress, "I give you ten minutes to rig yourself out in that lot: a second more, and you catch it."

And in fifteen minutes they two were in a cab, *en route* for the Guildhall, Frankl, who had invitations for himself and daughter, saying: "You understand? you keep your eye fixed upon me the whole time — never mind about eating — and when I hold up my finger *so*, you rise and give them a little song. . . ."

It was a function intended to be memorable, the Lord Regent going in state, attended by 150 Yeomen, King-at-Arms, six heralds and all Heralds' College, to be met at Temple Bar by my Lord Mayor, that day made a baronet, with his Sheriffs and Aldermen on horseback; the Guildhall in blue velvet, the platform at the east end bearing rows of squat gold chairs, while a canopy of deep-blue velvet, lined with light-blue sarcenet, dropped ponderous draperies, tied back with gold ropes, over the floor; on the canopy-front being Sword and Sceptre, the Royal Crown of Britain, and the Diadem of the Sea; the canopy table and the other looking like a short and a long wine-banquet of the Magi in Ophir: present being members of the British Royal House, Ambassadors to Britain and the Sea, the two Archbishops, Ministers, the Speaker, Officers, Fort-Admirals, the Regent's Household, the chief Nobility, the City personages.

Farthest from the short royal table, near the foot of the long, where the dishes were *kosher* for a Jewish colony, sat Frankl, and opposite him Margaret; and that face of Frankl was pinched and worn.

He prayed continually: "May God be my Rock and my High Tower; may the Almighty be my Shield this night. . . ." while in two minutes Margaret had begun to be a wonder to her neighbours — heaved sighs, threw herself, beat plate with knife, hummed a little, yet conscious of wrong-doing, her eyes fixed upon Frankl.

"Oh, my!" her sigh heaved mortally, head tumbling dead on shoulder.

"Are you — unwell?" asked a startled neighbour, all shirt-front, eyeglass and delicacy.

"I see a long table with gold plates," she whined pitifully, "on every plate an eyeball dying. . . ."

Frankl controlled her with a glance of anger.

And in the second course after turtle, with a fainting prayer to Jehovah, the Jew clandestinely held up a forefinger; upon which she, after some hesitation, remembered the signal, and like a dart shot to her feet.

Now every eye fastened upon her, from Regent's and Prince's to the bottom, those near her, who knew her now, feeling a miserable heart-shrinking of shame.

With sideward head she stood some seconds, smiling; and she sighed: "My name is Rachel —"

But soon, her mood now rushing into sprightliness, she stamped, and with an active alacrity of eye, sang:

"Will you come to the wedding? Will you come? Bring your own bread-and-butter, And your own tea-and-sugar, And we'll all pay a penny for the Rum, Rum, Rum, We'll all pay a penny for the Rum."

The Regent had risen, while Frankl, calm now in reaction, gazed sweetly upon his face: the vengeance of a Jew — nor was he half done with vengeance. Certainly, Hogarth was pale: he had sought her long, and found her *so*. "Why it is my own heart," he thought, "and they have made her mad."

One moment a stab of shame pierced him at the reflection: "*Here!*" but in the next his heart yearned upon her, and he rose nimbly and naturally far beyond Lord Mayor and Prince, and the rut of the world. After a perfectly deliberate bow, he left his place, and walked down the length of the hall to her, amid the gaping gods, Loveday, too, and three others, when he was halfway, following.

He had her hand, touched her temple lightly, yet compellingly, healingly. . . .

"Dear, don't you know me? — Richard? — *Dick*?"

No, but at sight of Loveday some kind of recognition seemed to light, and die, in her eyes.

"Will you come, dear, and sit up yonder with me?" Hogarth asked, his face a mask of emotion.

Wearily she shook her head; and "John," said Hogarth, "take her home"; whereupon Loveday led her out, the Regent returning to the canopy.

Half an hour later he found it *à propos* of something to say to the Prince: "That lady who sang is my sister, Your Royal Highness — seems to have been subjected to gross cruelties, and has gone crazy."

The next morning everyone knew that she was the Regent's sister; and a man said to a man: "There is madness in the family, then. . . ."

XLVIII

THE SEA-FORTS

The second-reading of the Land Bill had passed by a 59 majority: and it would now have been easy work to hurry through
its remaining stages in a couple of weeks; but the Regent had
awaited the nation's verdict in the return of the 120 to fill the Jewish seats, sure of the result.

So the 23rd was a great night — the third-reading — the
majority 115 at 8 P.M.; and the next day, which was marked by a
very brilliant levée, the Bill was before the Lords.

This stage it might easily have reached four weeks before, but
had been shelved for the election of the 120: and in those weeks
the four copies of the *Mahomet II.* had been launched.

And suddenly — bad news from Palestine: news that there,
too, after all the safeguards, the greed of a few was working to
plant the old European wrong: for, the Sanhedrim being short of
funds for a railway, a syndicate of five merchant-princes had
offered to buy from it an estate between Jerusalem and the Jordan,
and when the Chief Rabbi had pointed out that the offer was
monstrous, in view of the terms of the Sea's Deed of Gift, a fierce
discussion had ensued, a schism; and although the syndicate's
offer had been rejected by 27, at the next session the defeated
leader, like some warlike Maccabæus, had surged with his faction
and a hundred Arabs into the Mosque of Omar where the Sanhedrim met, to cast those who did not escape by flight into prison
in the Pasha's Palace. In the hands of his clique the Government
remained.

Such was the news. . . .

It was followed in three days by a Representation to the
Regent, signed by 90,000 Jews in Palestine, the fourth name being
Rebekah Frankl's, they imploring him for their sinking ship just
launched, calling him "Father."

For though the Jews had been content to see that Europe
which they contemned parcelled out among a few, while the mass
of men hovered countryless — from this had arisen their lucre —
their mental quality was too rich in business shrewdness to tol-
erate in their own case any such Bedlam: yet they stood helpless
before the disaster, and only in the Regent was hope.

On that night of the arrival of their Petition, the Prime Minister and the Commander-in-Chief dined in the Palace, placid

men at the moment when soup began, the Regent's sky quite clear, for, though a rumour whispered that the Lords were designedly lengthening discussion of the Bill, this gave no one any concern.

During entremêts, however, a scribbled card was passed into the hand of the Commander-in-Chief, and, as he read, his eyebrows lifted. Craving permission, he hurried out, had some talk with his Director of Military Intelligence, and returned pale.

Afterwards, as they three sat on a balcony overlooking the lake, with cigars, the Regent said: "I have thought, Sir Robert Wortley, of sending out at once two thousand Tommies under, say, General Sir John Clough, to the help of those poor Jews. . . ."

Here the Commander-in-Chief cleared his throat, and in a strained voice interfered: "That is, my Lord King, if we ourselves have not need of every soldier of the line within the next week."

The Regent deposited his ash with peering eyes, puzzled.

"What does your Lordship mean?"

"Your Lordship's Majesty, I was summoned from dinner just now to talk with Major-General Sir Maurice Coppleston, who reports movements of armed men, just come to his knowledge, and now going forward on a considerable scale, all northward. He gathers that these can only consist of Territorials and Yeomanry Cavalry, of whom not less than twelve battalions of rifles and three batteries of artillery, officers and men, are now on the way to, or massed upon, York. How widely the movement may actually extend — God knows."

Silence now: Sir Robert Wortley suddenly whitening to the lips. Then Hogarth, in a very low voice, said: "They do not know me."

"If I may crave leave to retire at once —" from the Commander-in-Chief; and Hogarth gave consent.

Queer things, omens, doubtings, weird clouds, gathered about Hogarth that night. When at eleven he gave audience to Admiral Quilter-Beckett, arrived from the *Boodah* Quilter-Beckett said: "Strange the fine weather here: at sea it is quite rough, the *Boodah* well under foam, and that old *Campania* pitches so —"

"You have come, then, in the *Campania*?" — from Hogarth.

"Yes, my Lord King."

"And what about the yacht?"

"Oh, the yacht: in her I have sent the two hundred men to the *Mahomet*."

"*Which* two hundred men, Admiral?"

Quilter-Beckett stared.

"Your Lordship's Majesty has forgotten: I had instructions that you desired some interchanges among the garrisons, and had ordered the sending of two hundred of my men to the *Mahomet*, I to receive in return two hundred from her."

"And you have sent your two hundred?"

"Yes, my Lord King."

"Have you received the two hundred from the *Mahomet*?"

"They had not arrived when I left the *Boodah*."

"So that you left only one hundred men in the *Boodah*, with instructions to receive two hundred others?"

"That is so, my Lord King."

There was silence.

"But suppose I tell you that I have given no such instructions: will your heart — *leap*?"

Hogarth clapped a sudden hand of horror upon Quilter-Beckett's shoulder.

"My God — !" Quilter-Beckett started like a gun's recoil.

"Be calm, Admiral: it may be only some mistake. . . . From whence had you this order?"

"From — from the *Mahomet*, in the usual course —"

"Good night, Admiral; I would be alone."

At that very hour a world-tragedy was being enacted over the dark and turbulent ocean, and the immensest of Empires was sinking into the sea.

Darkly, quietly, with no mighty and multitudinous tumult of man.

That midnight the night-glass of many a mystified merchantman searched the murk for those coruscations with which the crescent of forts had constellated the Atlantic, the mariner's sea-rent waiting ready, with his ship's-papers, in his cash box: but no galaxy of lights glanced that night.

To some, before this, they had appeared, but, as the ship approached, had vanished, and it was as though the swarm of the Pleiades had been caught from the skies before their eyes. Long before dawn ships separated by three thousand miles had gained the assurance that this or that sea-fort no longer rode the familiar spot-had been rapt to the stars, had sunk, had somehow passed from being. Before this monstrous marvel the mariner stood dumb, and it was afterwards said that that wild night the terminals of heaven and earth were lost, that the storm-winds were haunted, in all the air lamentation, sobbings as for swallowed orbs, and the whisper: "It is finished."

Two days previously a telegram from Admiral O'Hara had

gone to all the forts in European waters, commanding an inter-change of 200 of their men with men of his own fort; and each officer in command, ignorant that the same instructions had gone to others, had complied: so that by the next morning, the 29th April, 1600 men from eight forts were converging in yachts upon the *Mahomet*. As the fort garrisons, originally numbering 500, had recently been reduced to 300, the others having been mostly drafted into the 2nd Division of the British Royal Marines, com-pliance with Admiral O'Hara's order left a garrison of 100 only at each of eight forts.

Toward five in the afternoon of that day, the 29th, 700 men, to the bewilderment of her officers, were in the *Mahomet* two of the fort-yachts having arrived upon a troubled First Lieutenant who was in command, all attempts to see the Admiral since the morning having failed.

But near seven the Admiral summoned the Treasurer to his *bureau* near the bottom, he being in dressing-gown and slippers, very slovenly, seeming either drunk or sick, his mouth gaping to his pantings, and anon his languishing eye shot dyingly to heaven.

"Well, you see how I am, Mr. Treasurer," he went, "seedy. Pain in this temple, trouble with the respiration, and a foul breath. Poor Admiral Donald, Mr. Treasurer, poor Admiral Donald. The fashion of this world passeth away, sir, and the Will of God be done! Sometimes, I pledge you my word, I almost wish that I was dead. There are things, sir, in this world — Ah, well, God help me; I feel very chippy. I wanted to ask you, sir, to let me see the books, and hand me over at once all unaudited and unsettled funds in your counting-house, though I'm not fit for affairs today, sir, God knows —"

"Sir!" cried the Treasurer, a hard-browed, bald-headed man with a fan-beard, savouring of banks and ledgers.

"Just pass them over, sir."

"Well, this is the most singular order I ever heard of!"

"Obey me promptly, sir, or, by God, I cashier you!" roared O'Hara, his raised lids laying nude the debauchery of those jaun-diced juicy balls.

"Be it so, Admiral Donald" — the Treasurer bowed: "but on the understanding that I formally protest against the irregularity, and report it to the High Chancellor."

He retired, and in half an hour returned with two clerks who bore books, himself a carpet-bag containing in cash-boxes £ 850,000, paper and gold, which he deposited on the Admiral's *bureau*, and, after again protesting before the clerks, went away.

Not far off by now were some of the other six fort-yachts, converging with their 200 upon the *Mahomet*, and as the Admiral had no intention of being put into irons as a lunatic in his own fort, at eight o'clock he stole from his apartments, dressed now, not in uniform, but in priest's robes and a voluminous cloak, bearing in one hand the bag, in the other a key.

Those lower depths of the *Mahomet* were an utter solitude, lit with rare rays; yet the Admiral journeyed through and up peering, skulking, pausing, hurrying, and, if by chance a light caught his face, it showed a horror of convulsive flesh, his body a mass of trembling, like jelly.

Now, the forts had been built to fight; and (since nothing is impossible), if they fought, they might fall into an enemy's hand: to obviate which, there was in a little room on the third floor a handle which opened by hydraulics a door in the fort's side on the fifth floor below, the existence of this room being unknown save to each Admiral and to four of his lieutenants, and its key kept in a spot known to these. This key O'Hara now had in hand; and as he pushed it into the lock, his jaw jabbered like a baboon's.

Night was now come; the sea rough; Spain lost to sight; the two emptied yachts on the way back to their forts; yonder the lights of the *Mahomet II.* lying-to; two officers in oilskins walking arm in arm, to and fro, on the roof; and said one: "Look at those waves there all of a sudden: they rather seem to be breaking on the wrong side of us."

Then they resumed their talk; and to and fro they walked, arm in arm.

Till now one with sudden hiss: "But-good Christ-just look-why, the roof's *leaning* — !"

At that moment an outcry and runners from below, shouts, a trumpet-call, were borne on the winds to them: for the Admiral had rushed up to the manned parts of the fort, all hell alight in his eyeballs, bawling out, "The boats! The *Mahomet* is sinking!"

In spite of which many perished, the survivors afterwards declaring that the tragedy mesmerized their nerves with a certain awe not to be compared with the terrors felt on sinking ships, the *Mahomet* affecting them like a being of life, like behemoth slowly dying, or some doomed moon. She gave them, indeed, plenty of time, though when the steel portals on two of her sides were opened, the sea washed up the steps, making the launching very delicate feats, and near the last the leaning was so marked, that there was difficulty in standing; and still in patient distress she waited while the waves like multitudinous wolves, trooped to prey upon her.

As the Admiral ran to the outer Collector's Office to embark, he was faced by the Treasurer, revolver in hand, and "Hand me over that bag, Admiral," he said pretty coolly, "or I blow out your brains."

O'Hara's mouth worked: he could not speak.

"Will you?" said the Treasurer: "no doubt you mean to hand it over to the proper authorities, but I prefer to do that myself. Be quick, you old dog!"

Whereat O'Hara, having no weapon, dropped the bag, and trotted wide-eyed forward to the thronged scene of the launchings.

There were more than enough boats, and though on the lowest side of the fort nothing could long be done, all had gone off, when the fort, having settled very low, looking for some time like a brawling cauldron and area of breaking waves coloured by her hundred lights, went down, and was not.

Whereupon the yacht, over a hundred yards away, was caught in the traction of her strong enthralment, and, like a planet, started into running round a region of sea which wheeled; while seven of the boats, rowing for life, were grasped, and dragged back, with a hundred and nine, into the deep.

"Toll for the brave. . . ."

As to the other boats, they arrived at Tarifa the following evening, with 583; but the Admiral ordered the *Mahomet II.* to Cadiz, where soon after midnight he landed, and, by negotiation with a "*Jefe*," in an hour had a train for Madrid. As he was about to step in, the Treasurer touched his shoulder.

"What, Admiral, off by land?"

"Yes, sir, as you know," said O'Hara, "for you have been spying my movements for the last hour. How childish to imagine that I have anything to fear, or want to escape! Why, I am bound for England — my only object in the land journey being quickness. I even invite you to come with me"

"All right, Admiral, I will. . . . If you be tempted to murder me *en route*, remember these" — a pair of pistols; and they set out at about the hour when the whole crescent of tragedies was over.

At six that evening a yacht, a copy of the *Mahomet II.*, had come to the Cattegat sea-fort to land 200 men who wore the Empire's blue-jacket, the name "Mahomet" on their caps — nothing to show that they were not genuine Mahomet men, though some looked rather sea-sick; but in reality they were young lords, stock-brokers, Territorial Officers, men-about-town, park-keepers, undergraduates, secretly armed with knife and revolver, and knowing, too, where the armoury of the sea-fort lay.

Meantime, three other yachts, all named *Mahomet II.*, were a-ply in the Atlantic, two containing 400 men each, one 600, each of the first two to land 200 at a fort at six, and her remaining 200 at the next fort by eight-thirty, serving four forts, the last to land 200 at each of three forts: so that by 10.30 P.M. each of eight forts, including the Cattegat, contained 200 enemies disguised as fort-men.

And punctually at eleven, in each, began perhaps the darkest massacre of history — no quarter given — and when the alarm went forth, whichever of the unarmed fort-men rushed to the dark armoury found the door fastened against him. Of two men in bed, talking together through an open door, one arose at the stroke of a clock and killed the other; some perished in sleep — all very quietly accomplished: a few shots, a few lost echoes in the vast castles, a few daubs of blood. And in no case did a single one, either massacred or assassin, escape alive: for, in every case, some one or other of the fort-officers — Admiral, Lieutenant, Com-mander — to prevent capture, opened the inlet to the flood in the very thick of the doom, went down with his muteness and his bub-bling, and the sea, a secret in its bosom, rolled over the Sea.

XLIX

THE DÉBÂCLE

All the next day, till near 9 P.M., not one syllable was definitely known of this tremendous fact by anyone in Britain: for though, early astir, the Regent telegraphed the *Mahomet*, all day he waited without reply.

At eleven the Prime Minister said to him: "Things, my Lord King, wear at this moment an aspect so threatening, that I see no escape from civil war, even if it be brief, except by the immediate forcing through of the Bill, and I stand ready — now — to propose you as new peers —"

"Wait," answered the Regent: "pass tonight the Bill should, but I think I shall effect that by myself going to the Lords, and listening a little to the talk."

A dark day, with an under-thought always, whatever the business, of one thing — the Sea. . . .

About 5.30, as was his custom, he went up a stair to pass along two corridors to the little cream suite in which lived Margaret, for whom the doctors now promised sanity, her forehead daily seeming to drink-in peace from the contact of his palm, after which she would comb his hair, he lying on a sofa, or taking tea; and, "Well, dear," he said, this last day of all, as her ladies retired to an inner salon, "how is the head?"

"I have seen you before," she replied: "what is your name?"

"Dick Hogarth. Come to me, and let me lay my heavy head on you. The heart of your friend bodes today, bodes, bodes; but is not afraid: a tough heart, Madge. Do you like me to press my hand upon your head like that?"

Then, weary of his moaning heart that moaned that day like choruses of haunted winds through desolate halls, he fell to sleep even as he mumbled to her, she, seated near his sofa, playing with his hair, his arm around her, faint zephyrs from the window fanning his head, waving down the valenciennes.

But now she tossed the comb away, hummed, became restless, disengaged her shoulders, rose, strayed listlessly, with sighs, and on finding herself in the antechamber, opened the door, went out into a corridor, leant her back, eyeing the floor; and next with a great sigh set to gazing upward, droning two notes, one *doh*, one *soh*. All was silent. But now a sound of voices that drew her, she moving into another longer corridor, with balusters which overlooked a hall below, and yonder at the stair-foot were two men in altercation, one a guard, to whom the other was saying "But I tell you the lydy herself arst me to go to her; it's an appointment, just like any other appointment. Do let a fellow pass!" and with mouth at ear he added: "_It's an affair of the 'eart! 'Ere's a sov — _"

"Couldn't, my friend, couldn't," the guardsman said.

But now Harris: "Why, there she is 'erself, so 'elp-! come out to meet me, as the Lord liveth!" — ran then toward where she looked over to send up the hoarse whisper: "I sye — didn't you tell me yourself to come — ?"

On which she nodded amiably, smiling, touching a rose in her bosom.

"There you are! What more do you want?" he said to the guard, who now gave him passage: and like a dart he darted, like a freed lark, or unleashed hound, fleet on the feet, with lifted brow.

"I sye!" he whispered her, all active, brisk as a cat, ecstatic — "where's 'e?"

"Who?" — she still at her rose, a memory straying in her that here was a friend, whom the Terrible One had bid her obey.

"Mr. — the Regent," he whispered.

"I don't know him. What is your name? *My* name is —"

"Oh, you muddle-headed cat! Don't you know the dark man with the black moles — quick!"

"*Sh-h-h* — he is sleeping."

"Gawd! is he though? Come, show me! I've got a old appointment —"

She led the way: the two corridors — the door — the room, he treading on air, brow up, eyes on fire, knife bright and ready; and eight feet from the couch she put out her forefinger, pointing, smiling, Hogarth's face toward them, his mouth pouting in sleep, bosom breathing, a breeze in his hair.

From the lips of Harris, in the faintest snake-hiss, proceeded, "Sleep, my little one-sleep, my pretty one — *sleep* —" and with a wrist as graceful as the spring of a tigress he had the knife buried in Hogarth's left breast.

Some instinct must have pierced Hogarth's sleep an instant before the actual blow, for while the knife was yet in him he had Harris's wrist; and the assassin fled writhing, so brisk a trick had cracked his elbow.

And blanched and short-breathed sprang Hogarth, but at once tottered, Margaret, open-mouthed, regarding him, till he suddenly cried out "Ladies!," and before they came had hurried out, drawing his coat over the place of blood.

In the second corridor he had to stop and lean, but then descended, striking all whom he passed with awe at his face, till he stumbled into his own drawing-room, and, as he fell, was caught by Sir Francis Yeames, the Private Secretary.

The wound had passed along the outer front surface of the second rib toward the scapula, injuring two of the branches of the axillary artery: so whispered the Resident Medical Attendant, while the council of doctors pronounced the condition "very grave," but not "dangerous" — a case for "judicious pressure"; and after a long swoon he opened his eyes; in the deeply-recessed series of windows, narrow and round-topped, now dying the twilight; the insignificant bed lost in a chamber of frescoes and vast darksome oils of battles and loves. And, suddenly starting, he asked: "What's the time?"

"Seven-thirty, my Lord King," answered Sir Martin Phipps.

"Ah, I remember: I was stabbed. Who did it?"

"It can only be assumed from the evidence of a guardsman that it was a servant in the Palace, called Harris."

"Aye, I think I saw his face. Does anyone know of the matter?"

"Very few persons so far. . . . The police are after Harris."

Now the Regent started, understanding that the condemnation of Harris would mean a revelation of the Colmoor-horror secret; and he said after a minute, "John, is that you? Will you go and have the whole thing quashed?. . . . And now, doctor, the wound."

"The wound is not what we call 'dangerous', my Lord King: ah, but believe me, it was a narrow shave."

"I dare say, Sir Martin: the outcomes of this particular world do arrive by narrow shaves; but they arrive, and life is an escape. At any rate, doctor, I shall be able to go, as arranged, to the Lords —"

The doctor smiled. "No, never that."

"I shall go."

And at once he leapt from bed, staggering headlong in the effort, to strike his head against a window corner, while all ran, crying out, to catch him, the doctor thinking: "Those whom the gods destroy they first drive mad."

So far not a whisper of the stab had reached even the Prime Minister or the Prince; but since the news of moving troops, and the reluctance of the Lords to pass the Bill, agitated all, London came out to watch his descent upon the Lords.

He went in precisely the spirit of a professor who steps to the chair, smiles, and takes the class; but as he drove down Whitehall, this thought pierced him with a keener point than the steel of Harris: "*The Sea . . . !*"

He did not know that at last a thousand transmitters, from Tarifa, from Frederikshavn, from many a ship, were thrilling the ether with messages as to the Sea.

Nor did he know that that day Frankl had whispered to some dozen people, with proofs and old newspapers, that convict past of the Regent.

And from his very first entering, when the Lord Chancellor rose, and the Regent made the bow, he was shocked by the scene of open insolence spread before him.

Everywhere the boldest eyes regarded him; he saw smiles of scorn, snarling visages, as, with reclining head and lowered lids, his eyes rested on the House: a hard gaze. Unfortunately, his pallor was perfectly obvious, and its significance, the stab being unknown, was misunderstood.

And up rose a young lord, who stammered unprofundities just below the region of lawn-sleeves to the right; and another with slow step, as if to music, came up the gangway, and spoke at the table; and another after him: and it needed sustained effort to understand what they said; the brain, as it were, would not close upon statement after statement so insignificant. But Hogarth would have endured till midnight, or longer, but for a growing doubt within him: "Am I bleeding? Shall I not certainly faint?"

And there was this other question: "To what greater daring of insolence will these impossible speeches rise?"

Suddenly, at five minutes to ten, in the very midst of a duke's speech, the Regent, with dizzy brain, was on his feet: there was a few moments' gasp and breathlessness; and then — all at once — it was as though a wind from hell swept through that House, whirling in its vehemence Regent, lords, Gallery, Black Rod, Clerk, Usher, and all; and every face was marble, and every eye a blaze.

The Regent cried: "Your lordships' eloquence —"

And as he said "eloquence," a voice that was a scream, a forward-straining form, a pointing finger: "Why, my lords, that man is only a common convict! — reprieved for murder — escaped from Colmoor. And all his forts are sunk!"

It happened that in the midst of this outcry, the Regent fell back afaint, the moles black, the face white.

Now, here seemed simple panic: and like a pack of dogs which rush to mangle a mongrel, they were at him pell-mell.

See now a shocking scrimmage, a rush and crush for precedence, surge upon surge of men jostling each other in a struggle to get near him, sticks reaching awkwardly over heads to inflict far forceless blows, and on his face the fists; a hundred roaring "Order!", fighting against the tide; three hundred shrieking, "Kill him!" "Have him done with!" "Dash out his brains!", and pressing to that job. Sergeant-at-Arms, meanwhile, Clerk-attending-the-Table, and the physician, had run to give the alarm; but it was by one of those miracles of wild minutes, when turbulent sprites appear to mix themselves in the business of men, worse — embroiling the embroiled, that through the throng in the street rushed the word that the Regent was being killed: and quick, before any fatal blow had been struck, the rabble were there in that chamber, having brushed away every barrier.

They imagined themselves come to save: in reality they came to kill — were, in fact, too many for the area of the room, so that men succumbed fast as by plague-stroke under trampling feet, and even after twenty minutes when sixty-seven lay mangled the scene of horror could not be said to be ended.

Early upon the irruption the physician, three policemen, a Reading Clerk, and the Bishop of Durham, had managed to extricate and drag the Regent out; and through the shouting of the outside crowd he was driven home unconscious.

L

THE DECISION

Somewhat before this hour Admiral O'Hara had arrived at Croydon, a lust, a morbid curiosity, now working in this man — having committed the ineffable sin, to enjoy its fruit by hearing what Richard Hogarth now said, in what precise way he groaned, or raved, smiled, or wept, or stormed; for he was cruelly in love with Hogarth.

All the way had come with him the *Mahomet*'s treasurer, with his bag of wealth — and two pistols.

So at Dieppe O'Harra had wired to Harris:

"Meet me at Croydon tonight, the 9.45 from Newhaven, as you love life. Most important. Shall expect wire from you at the London and Paris Hotel, Newhaven, not later than six, saying yes."

But at Newhaven he had found no answer — Harris, in fact, not having received the telegram, having already inflicted his stab, and fled the Palace.

Whereupon O'Hara, in an agony of doubt, had telegraphed Frankl from Newhaven:

"For God's sake find Harris. Make him meet me at Croydon tonight in the 9.45 from Newhaven. Do not fail."

Now, Frankl knew exactly where Harris was — hiding in the Market Street house. And he said to himself: "All right: it's got something to do with money, and a lot of it, too, with all this 'God's sake'. Suppose we *both* go to Croydon?"

Hence Frankl missed the joy of seeing the Regent mobbed: for at 9.30 he was waiting with Harris on the Croydon up-platform.

And as the train stopped, they two hurried into the compartment where O'Hara sat alone.

"You, my friend?" said O'Hara to Frankl.

"Large as life," replied Frankl: "I and the boy have already made it up between us for a third each: you a third, I a third, Alfie a third: that's fair; I keep the police off the backs of the pair of you, and you pay me a third. What's the figure?"

In one moment of silence O'Hara plotted; then his tongue yielded to the temptation of the great words: "Eight-hundred-and-fifty thousand, sir."

So after three minutes' talk Harris got out, and, as the train started, sprang into a first-class compartment in which was one other occupant.

Now, it was natural that the treasurer, carrying such a sum, should scrutinize any stranger, but Harris disarmed suspicion: his right arm, twisted by Hogarth, was in a sling, and he threw himself aside, and seemed to sleep, between the peak of his cap and his muffler hardly an inch of interval: so the treasurer, too, worn with travel, settled into a half-drowse.

Harris, however, like many of his type, was perfectly ambidextrous, often using the left hand by preference; and as the train passed Bromley, he darted, plunged his knife, streaked with the Regent's blood, into the treasurer's heart, and huddled the body under the seat.

No stoppage till London Bridge, where, with the bag, Harris left the train, Frankl and O'Hara trotting after his burdened haste; and, after two changes of cabs, the three arrived at the Market Street house.

There Harris laid the bag on the floor of an empty back room, where through a broken window came a little light, and the three stood looking down upon the bag, solemnly as upon a body.

Then suddenly Harris: "Come, gentlemen of the jury, let's have my share of the dead meat: and 'ere's off out of it for this child — only this blooming arm of mine! it's going to get me nabbed as sure as sticks. Never mind — trot it out, Captain! and don't cheat an innocent orphan, lest the ravens of the valley pick out the yellow galls of some o' you."

Neither of the other two, however, seemed anxious for the division; and after a minute's silence Frankl said: "The third of 850, I *believe*, is 2, 8, 3; how are we going to carry away 283 thousand without something to put it in? I vote, Pat, that we leave the bag here, and come and divide at midnight sharp. How would that do?"

"Yes," said Harris, "I think I see old Pat leaving the lot with me — what O! You know 'ow I'd fondle it for you, and keep it out of the cold, cold world, till you came back, don't you, you baldheaded priest?"

"Shut your mouth, boy. We can't take it away without something, as Mr. Frankl very justly observes. Aren't there some safes, Frankl, in Adair Street?"

"Right you are: and one, as I happen to know, empty. Who'll keep the key?"

"You, if you like, my friend. I'll keep the keys of the room-doors. And Harris will stand guard."

"The very thing," remarked Frankl.

So it was agreed. Harris took the bag; they descended to the cellar; then, striking matches, down three marl steps to the subterranean way made for Hogarth; and along it, forty feet, they stumbled bent, Harris gripped by each sleeve.

Then in the Adair Street Board Room they lit a candle, and in the room next it found the safes, the largest of which admitting the bag, Frankl locked its door, took the key; O'Hara then locked the room door, took the key; and at the stair-bottom locked another door, took the key; so that Frankl could not now get at the bag without him, nor he without Frankl, nor Harris without both.

Two then went away, while Harris, sprawling cynically on a solitary chair down in the parlour with straight open legs, awaited the *rendezvous* at twelve.

He had not, however, sat very long, when the taper at his feet glared on a face of terror at a sound of ghosts in the tomb that the house was, and he started to his feet, prone, snatching his knife — thinking, as always, of the Only Reality, the police. But he had not prowled three ecstatic steps when O'Hara stood before him.

"Oh, damned fool!" he went with infinite contempt and reproach, "to frighten anybody like that! What's it you are after now? Frighten anybody like that. . . ."

"*Alfie!*" — O'Hara whispered it breathfully as the hoarse sirocco, stepping daintily like the peacock. Tell it not in Gath! If Alfie rammed the knife into the marrow of Frankl's back at the moment when the safe was opened, then Alfie would have, not a third, but a half; and the thing was desirable for this reason: that a half is greater than a third . . .

Harris saw that: but he seemed reluctant, meditating upon the ground; then walking, hands in pockets.

"Why, boy, he is only an interloper," said O'Hara: "I meant the money to be divided fairly between you and me. Why should this Jew come in?"

"All right," said Harris: "I don't mind."

"And I know a little castle in Granada, Alfie, which we'll buy —"

"All right: you go away. It's agreed."

And O'Hara hurried away, took a cab, drove for the Palace; while Harris, left alone, sat serious, with sprawling straight legs, and presently muttered: "Blind me, I must be going dotty or something! p'raps it's this arm. . . ."

He had not thought of killing Frankl, until it had been suggested! — some class-habit, or instinct, of honour among thieves (which, however, his reason despised) . . . But five minutes after

O'Hara had gone he started alert, staring, with tight fist, and, "All right, you two," said he, "blood it is!"

He sat again: and again, after twenty minutes, the house gave a sound — Frankl, who had let himself in by the front door, each member possessing a key to that.

"Well, Alf," said he, "all alone? Then, we two can have a little chat between us little two."

And he stood and talked, while Harris sprawled and listened, Frankl's road to his end being more circuitous than O'Hara's, more hedged, too, with reasons, scruples, sanctions: but he reached it, pointing out that a half is greater than a third; also that O'Hara would be a continual witness against Harris' past, whereas he, Frankl, left England for Asia the next morning.

Alfie pretended aversion to bloodshed, but finally consented; upon which Frankl went away, and took cab for Scotland Yard: his idea being to have Harris arrested red-handed in the murder of O'Hara.

The streets through which he drove wore a singular aspect — of commotion, hurry, unrest, two dragoon-orderlies galloping past him at the Marble Arch, in Whitehall the tramp of some line-regiment battalion, and he said to himself: "He is going to fight it out with them, I suppose — Satan take the lot!"

At Scotland Yard he said to the Inspector in Charge, having given his card, that if two officers were placed at his disposition, he might be able to lead them to the arrest of a man long "wanted," who now premeditated another murder.

Meantime, O'Hara was in conversation with Loveday in the Regent's library, nearer the centre of which stood a group of four with their heads together — Prime Minister, First Lord, War Office Secretary, a Naval Lord; further still, a spurred General, cloaked over his out-stuck sword, writing, with a wet white brow; and, "I suppose he will want to see you," said Loveday, "if you have anything to say. But the doctors have first to be reckoned with: I suppose you know that he has been stabbed and beaten."

"Stabbed! by whom?"

"By Harris."

"No! When?"

"This afternoon."

"Ah! I did not know."

"It was by your recommendation, it appears, that Harris became Captain Macnaghten's servant," said Loveday with his smile, looking very gaunt and bent-down.

"Tut, sir!" — from O'Hara — "you are not my judge: I am here to see the Lord of the Sea, my King."

"Ah! — you still give him the title."

And now O'Hara, drawing his chair nearer to ask: "*How did he take it?*" stretching back the waiting mouth to hear that thing.

"The Lord Regent? Well, at eight-thirty he went to the House of Lords, where they beat him nearly to death on the throne, the gentle hearts, and the doctors forbade me to speak to him of the Sea; but his eyes seemed to question me, so I leant over, and told him."

"Yes — and whatever did he say?"

He said: "'What, old Pat?'"

O'Hara rose to stand by a hearth, black-robed to the heels and tonsured, and at the angle of his jaw some sinews ribbed and moved: not a syllable now from him.

"I am going in now to him," said Loveday: "if you care to wait here, I will see" — and passing through a palace pretty busy that night with feet and a thousand working purposes, went to sit at the sick bed, the doctors retiring.

"How is the pain?"

"The pain," said the Regent very weakly, "is nonsense: I am not going to be bullied by doctors, but shall do exactly as I like."

"And what is that, Richard?"

"There is a Normandy village, John, called Valée-les-Noisettes — white houses with an extraordinary sound of forest about, one of Poussin's landscapes, with a smithy under a chestnut precisely as in the poem; and the blacksmith is a charming man. I dare say someone will find me money enough to purchase a share of his smithy: and with him I shall work, starting for him before sunrise, with my sister."

Loveday, wondering if he was delirious, said irrelevantly: "I have to tell you that by five A.M. there will be 15,000 additional infantry in London, with —"

"Ah, I wish they'd lend them me to send out to those poor Jews, John. But, for myself — I was mad when I gave that order. It won't do! the world is addicted to its orbit, and relapses. I don't say that it will be always so, but it is now. As against the Empire of the Sea arises — Pat O'Hara; as against the brushing aside of these rebels arise — Germany, Russia, the hostile world. Consider the rancour of the nations at Britain's late advantages in sea-rent, try to conceive the scream of jubilation that rings to the sky tonight against her, and against me. Do you think I could *now* start a civil war in England? for the satisfaction of my own pride? I call God to witness that never for my own pride have I done aught, but that the Kingdom of God might come. I know that bitter tears will flow at the fall of the righteous man — many calling me 'traitor' for abandoning those ready to die for me. Yet it shall be. I never thought to fail, to fly, John Loveday, chased by such little fellows: but God has done it. Well, then, the smithy. You and all, therefore, will find enough to do tonight."

Loveday lifted a face streaming with tears to say: "The man, O'Hara, waits to see you."

"Really? Well, come, we will see him. . . ." and in some minutes O'Hara was there by the bedside, the eyes of the two fixed together, over Hogarth's face five oblongs of sticking-plaster, his head bandaged, and at a corner of O'Hara's mouth a twitching.

"Pat, did you betray me?" asked Hogarth.

O'Hara nodded: "Yes."

"Well, you may sit and tell me, and ease your poor heart."

And a long time O'Hara sat, going into the mighty crime, torturing details, revelling in the vastness of the horror, the sickness of the self-inflicted filth, and pangs of the self-inflicted scalpel.

"And why did you do it, my friend?"

"Because I worship you. . . ."

"Well, perhaps I understand you, crooked soul. But what will you do now?"

"We shall see. What will you?"

"I am going to France to live as a private person."

"Tut, you remain as simple as a child: the earth's not large enough to contain you, you couldn't now remain a private person for three weeks. Come, I have discrowned you: I will give you another crown, though I shall never see you wear it. Why not go to your own people?"

"Which people?"

"The Jews."

"Don't talk that same madness."

"My time with you is short, Raphael Spinoza" — O'Hara glanced at his watch — "in five minutes we part, never, I do assure you, to meet again. Listen, then, to me: you are a Jew. I knew your mother — the most intellectual woman, I suppose, who ever drew breath, the only one whom I have loved; and I should have known you merely from your resemblance to her at my first glance at you in Colmoor, though I had more precise data: the three moles, the bloodshot eye, for didn't I baptize you? haven't I rocked you in my arms? You know St. Hilda on the hill over Westring, which you found me examining that morning after our escape from the prison? I was priest there, three years, and twice I have confessed her — ah! and remember it! for when your foster-father wanted her to turn Methodist, she wouldn't stand that, and since she must needs be a *meshumad* (apostate), became a Catholic. Well, now, I once saw at Thring, and once in the *Boodah*, an old goat-hair trunk of yours: what is become of it?"

"I have it —" Hogarth was shivering, his eyes wide, and in his memory a strange singsong crooning of *t'hillim*, heard ages before in some other world over a cradle.

"Did you know that that trunk has a false bottom?" asked O'Hara.

"Yes."

"Oh, you knew . . . And have you never seen a bundle of papers under it?"

"Yes — I assumed them to be old farm-accounts. . . ."

"They are all the proofs you need concerning your birth; it is *my* trunk by the way — Ah, I must go!"

At the door he fastened upon Hogarth a last reluctant gaze to say good-bye, but Hogarth, staring wildly afar, did not turn his eyes, and O'Hara, with a sigh, was gone.

He drove to Adair Street, and, as he passed by a mews, Frankl, waiting there with two detectives, saw him by a street-light, but made no remark.

When O'Hara entered the house, he looked about for Harris, but Harris had gone to the lodging of a woman in James Street near, to arrange a hiding-place for the bag, passing out through the Market Street house; and O'Hara, opening the two locked doors, entered the safe-room, where he stood waiting, his forehead low, resting on the steel top; and now a sob throbbed through his frame, and his lips let out ". . . *so* lovely . . . so great. . . ."

Count a minute's stillness: and now the man's soul and being foundered in a storm of sorrow, and half-words borne on shivering puffs of breath, and choking groans, broke the stillness: "My Liege! Richard! my King!"

This died to silence; and now he roamed the room with furious steps, and lowering brow, and an out-pushed under-lip, until, deciding, he drew from his pocket a penknife, opened it, leant now one elbow on the safe-top, blade in hand, considered, considered, hesitating, then with lifted chin and the thinnest whimpering like a puppy, pretty pitiful, cut from under his left ear to the chin.

Certainly a hurt so shallow could never have killed, for the hand had been cherishingly restrained, and the thing was no sooner done than the priest, seeing that he did not die, ran horror-eyed, streaming with blood, shouting a hoarse whisper: "Help! help! help!"

But at that cry he sighed, fell back, and effectually died, his heart pierced by the knife of Harris.

And some moments later the face of Frankl, who bore a candle, looked in at the door.

"Is that all right, Alfie?" — in the weakest whisper.

"Come on in, and don't ask any questions," said Harris.

Frankl entered, peered upon the dead visage of the priest; then, the detectives being now behind the parlour-door below, with handcuffs, rose to run to summon them: but, to his horror, Harris was now before the door; he saw in the candlelight those eyes of Alfie fixed upon him: and he knew: before the least threat or movement by Harris, the Jew sent to Heaven a piercing shriek, his hour come. . . .

". . . dirty-livered Jew . . ." striking in the breast, and, as Frankl fell, he gave him one other in the temple, with "Down, down to hell, and sye *I* sent thee thither"; and to dead O'Hara near he gave one in the cheek, with "Go up, thou bald-head, it *is*": all in two seconds' space; and he was now about to turn anew to hack at Frankl, when his keen ear heard a creak; and he sprang up a spinning motionlessness — the Reality before him.

And instantly on the realization of that fact, he was submissive, reverent, as before the very Helmet of Pallas, goddess of Blue; and said he with sullen dejection, reverent of the Helmet, but easy with the man: "All right: you've beat me . . . I suppose it's that Regent-stabbing affair brought you: it was I did it all right."

When they went down, almost from the door a crowd gathered, pressing close, Harris' hands and front all red from O'Hara's throat; and when one policeman, big with the fact, whispered a gentleman: "You may have heard, sir, that the Regent was stabbed today — it's been kept precious dark, but the fact's so: this is the beauty as done it," like loosened effluvia that news flew — but distorted, largened — the stains were Regent's blood! — and beyond measure had the crowd spread ere it reached the Edgware Road.

There at the corner, as the officers looked about for a cab, and one blew a whistle, a man reached out and fiercely struck Harris on the face, while another shouted: "Lynch the beggar!"; and now arose a hustling, huddled impulses, and now in full vogue that grave noising of congregations when the voice of God jogs them; while Harris, excessively pallid, handcuffed, began to whistle; a number of other police now seeking the crowd's centre, but with difficulty; a cab, too, slowly making a way which closed like water round it: and when this had nearly reached him, Harris, in his eagerness to get in, sprang far toward it — and slipped. He never rose again: the crowd rolled over his last howl, and in the midst of a great row as of hounds, trampled him to a paste.

About that very time that better man whom he had stabbed, in tying up in bed a bundle of old papers, was saying: "Yes, I will go to my people." . . .

And by six A.M. he was up, in his study, dressed, looking quite owlish with his excess of eyes, which, however, danced at the first news of the morning — the arrival at Portsmouth of the *Boodah II.*, which had raced like a carrier-bird since 8.30 P.M. of the 29th, full of the news of the vanished *Mahomet*: on her being 200 marines.

After that he spoke through the telephone with various Government-offices, early astir that morning, till the Private Secretary looked in with the announcement that his train would be ready in ten minutes.

His last act in the Palace was the sending to the Treasurer at Jerusalem, for Miss Frankl, the telegram:

> "Be surprised, but believe: I am a Jew.
> "RICHARD."

Of the Household some fifty, catching wind of what was toward, offered, even begged, to go with him; but in general he refused, and set out with a suite of only seven.

They reached Hastings at twenty minutes to ten, where, to the disgust of all, the region of Central Station was found crowded; whereupon Sir Francis Yeames held a consultation with a local rector, and a dash was made to a private hotel near the pier.

There, looking from behind window curtains at eleven, Hogarth saw before a paper-shop:

FLIGHT OF THE REGENT

A minute afterwards he started backward from the splintered window.

Everything was known:

LIFE-HISTORY OF THE CONVICT HOGARTH
MARVELLOUS DETAILS

The street, to its two vanishing-points, was one scene of hats, mixed with upturned faces: and it was an aggressive crowd that gave out a sound.

Not till noon did the *Boodah II.* arrive; and then there was no setting out — all the front windows of the house now broken, and in the town a row like the feeding-time of lions, which uttered "coward," "murderer," "convict," "traitor." Hogarth had been put to bed, the two ladies were in a state of scare, Margaret anon crying on Loveday's shoulder, declaring that "*He*" (meaning Frankl) was in the crowd, and coming, coming, boring his way: she had seen him.

At last, near four P.M., a portion of the yard-wall at the back was broken down by the party, Hogarth was raised and dressed, and through the breach the party passed into another back-yard, then made beachward, Hogarth leaning on the arm of Sir Martin Phipps; but they had no sooner come to the Esplanade than they were surrounded, and when, on their attaining the pier, the pier-turnstile was closed against the mob, it was impossible to conceive whence so many missiles came. Once Hogarth stopped, faced round, looked at them, but now a pebble bruised his left temple, and he dropped, fainting.

Caught up by Sir Martin, Loveday, Sir Francis Yeames, and Colonel Lord Hallett of the body-guard, he was hurried, a hanging concave with abandoned head, to the long-waiting boat, and it was in a scurry of escape, out of stroke, that the oarsmen rowed away.

Yonder lay the yacht with her fires banked, and was soon under weigh.

She had started, when a harbour-master's motor-boat was observed giving chase, in her an officer from Scotland Yard who bore a bag, found by means of the key in Frankl's pocket in the Adair Street safe; on its clasp the name "Mahomet," and it contained £850,000: so that the yacht went wealthy on her way.

LI

THE MODEL

The voyage to Palestine was marked by two events: one the stoppage at Tarifa, where the five hundred from the *Mahomet* were, these, when taken on board the *Boodah II.*, making an armed force of 700; and then, toward sunset of the fifth day, a steamer exchanged signals with the *Boodah II.*, enquired after the whereabouts of the Lord of the Sea, received the reply "on board," and when she stopped it turned out that she had on board a Jewish Petition urging upon Spinoza to come and throw in his lot with them. And here again was that name of Rebekah, spelled now Ribkah.

For the news of his fall — the fact that he was a Jew — had created a mighty stirring in Israel, of wonder, of the pride of race.

By the seventh day the yacht was off the Palestine coast, and Joppa, seated on her cliffs, appeared over a foaming roadstead. But when a landing was effected, they were to hear that there had been a collision on the Jerusalem-Joppa railway, the line blocked, travel suspended; so, as the filthy town was congested, the Royal party took refuge in a great restaurant-tent, set up by a Polish Jew in gaberdine and fur cap, who vociferated invitation at the door. All was mud, beggary, narrowness, chaos, picturesque woe. Yet work had commenced: between the upper and the nether millstone a woman ground corn at a doorway; the camel passed loaded; the dragoman went with quicker step. In the afternoon Spinoza, wandering beyond the outskirts of the town, saw in an orange-grove, sitting before a roofless hut, six diligent two-handed Jews exhaustively drawing the cord of the cobbler; further still, and saw what could only have been a Petticoat-Lane Jew ploughing with a little cow and a camel: and he smiled, thanking God, and taking courage — had always loved this land.

The next morning he procured a number of clumsy waggons, with horses, asses, camels, and provisions; and his caravan set out, to travel all day over a plain, a "goodly land," the almond-tree in blossom, orange and olive, everywhere lilies, the scarlet anemone, he considering himself so familiar with the way, that he was their only guide, though the morning was misty; and through the plain of Sharon they wended over the worst roads in existence, until, passing into a country of rocks, they made out afar the mountains of Judæa, whose patches of white stone look like snow in sunshine, on the roads streams of wayfarers, tending all eastward to Jerusalem, lines of camels and waggons, pedestrians with wine-skins, mother and sucking child on the solitary ass, and the Bedouin troop; but Spinoza was all solitary among fastnesses on the third forenoon when he muttered nervously: "I must certainly have lost the way".

Thereupon he called halt, and the caravan turned back to re-find the road, Spinoza prying on camel-back foremost, clad now in the caftan and white robes of the Orient.

But all day the caravan wandered out of the track in a white sea of mist: no farmstead, nor cot, but the wild vine, and the wild fig, and twice a telegraph-tree, still with its bark on, and the abandoned hold of a bandit-sheik. Finally, near six P.M., Spinoza, finding himself in a valley-bottom, sent out the order to pitch camp: upon which the tents were fixed near a brook, waggons grouped around, and animals picketed to grass. Spinoza, the two ladies, and Loveday, then ate together at the door of one tent; after which he rose and strolled away, thinking how best to handle this crab of Israel.

He noticed that the mist was lifting a little; and suddenly, as he strolled, he stood still, listening: for remote tones of singing or mourning seemed to meet his ear — from the west: and in some moments more he saw the Mount of Olives — to the west, not, as he believed that it must be, to the east, he having, in fact, in losing his way from the coast, passed by Jerusalem to the north; and on the other side of the Mount of Olives, from its foot to the Brook Kedron, spread at that moment over the Valley of Jehosophat an innumerable multitude, covered in praying-shawls, many prostrate, many with the keen and stressful face of supplication lifted in appeal to God, that He would visit His people, and turn again in this latter day to His lost and helpless flock. Every child of Israel who could contrive it, at whatever cost, was there, since it was the prophesied day of — "the Coming."

But a bold woman, summoning her fainting strength, bracing her trembling knee, stepped a little up the hillside to fling high her hand as a sign — Rebecca Frankl, celebrated now through Israel as the elect of the sibyl Estrella; and at that signal the congregation, gazing keenly into heaven, lifted up their voice in meek song, singing the sibyl's "Hymn to the Messiah":

"The oceans trudge and tire their soul, desiring Thee; and night-winds homeless roam with dole, reproaching Thee; the clouds aspire, and find no goal, and gush for Thee, reproaching Thee."

"Thou scrawled'st 'I mean' in rocks and men, in trends and streams; the prophets raved, to sages' ken Thou shewed'st dreams; Thou shrouded'st dark the How and When in starry schemes, and trends and streams."

"The jungles blare, the glebe-lands low and bleat for Thee; the generations rage and go, agaze for Thee; creation travaileth in woe, with groans for Thee, agaze for Thee."

"Adonai, come! with crashing rote of chariots come; or moonlight-mild, alone, afloat, Messussah, come; with floods of lutes, or thundering throat, but come! O, come! Messussah come."

"The Arctics hawk-up their haunted heart, and raucous, spue; and north-winds, wawling calls, outstart, to droop anew; the clouds like scouts updart, depart, and truceless do, and droop anew."

"How long! They breeds have waited fain what sibyls ween; Thou scribbled'st in their secret brain 'I scheme; I mean'; the constellations stray and strain: Break out! be seen what sibyls ween."

"The pampas stamp and, nomad, low, reposeless, lone; raging the generations trow, and drudge, and drown; a anguished glance this latter woe throws to Thy Throne, reposeless, lone" . . .

Before them, above them, as they sang stood — a man.

Hard by a wall of that Moslem mosque, once a chapel which marked the supposed spot of "the Ascension," he stood, in an attitude of suspense, astonishment, his body half-twisted — Spinoza.

An instant, and he was aware of Jerusalem lying "as a city that is compact" before him — not to the east — to the west! Yet another instant, and he realized that the whole tract of humanity — man, woman, child — was on its face before him.

A faintness overcame him, shame, dismay; then, his blood now rushing to his brow, his mouth sent out the passionate shout:

"Not to *me!* Not to *me!* I am the Lord of the Sea. . . . !"

But when the people heard this, saw him, knew him, they remained in adoration. . . .

By a special ship they had sent him a petition to come; here he was weeks sooner than ship or airship could have conveyed him: and they took him as the answer to their supplication, the answer which Heaven willed, in the sure and certain faith that he would cure their ache, and the ache of the world.

An acclamation like the voice of many waters arose and rolled below him, and on the bosom of that tumult he moved among them into the Holy City, as darkness covered all.

*   *   *   *   *   *   *

He took the title of Shophet, or Judge, and for sixty years ruled over Israel.

It has been said that the initial "pull" over other nations possessed by Israel (in respect of the sea-forts remaining in the Gulf of Aden, Yellow Sea, Western Pacific) was the cause of his rise as of some thrice-ardent Star of the Morning and asterisk dancing in the dawn's dark: for the other nations, timorous of one another, made never an attempt to build; but, for our share, we insist that anyway Judæa was bound to become what she became — indeed, sea-rent after the Regency collapse was decreased at the three forts, and suddenly in the twelfth year of his judgeship Spinoza ordered its stoppage.

By which period the University of Jerusalem had become the chief nerve-centre of the world's research and upward effort: for in creating a "civilized State" — "proud and happy" — Spinoza did it with that spinning rapidity of the modernization of Japan, so that in whatever respects it was not a question of months, it was a question of not many years.

For, as in the soul of the Jewish people abode as before that genius for righteousness which wrote the Bible, and as the soul of righteousness lies even in this; Thou shalt not steal, therefore Israel with some little pain attained to this: whereupon with startling emphasis was brought to pass that statement: "Righteousness exalteth a nation."

For the promise says: "I will put a new spirit within them"; and this — very rapidly — found fulfilment.

Whereupon others fast, faster, found fulfilment, so that a stale and bitter word was in Pall Mall, saying: "The lot of them seem to have formed themselves into a syndicate to run the prophecies."

Again the promise has it: "I shall be with them"; and again: "They shall be a cleansed nation"; and again: "They shall fear Him."

The transformation was rapid for the reason that it was natural, seeing that it had been Europe only that, like a Circe, had bewitched them into beastial shapes, "sharks," and "bulls," and "bears," mediæval Jews, for example, having been debarred from every pursuit save commerce: so that Shylock was obliged to turn into a Venetian; and, in ceasing to be a Hebrew, became more Venetian than the Venetians, for the reason that he had more brains, ready to beat them at any game they cared to mention; but the genuine self of Shylock was a vine-dresser or sandal-maker, as Hillel was a woodchopper, David a shepherd, Amos a fig-gatherer, Saul an ass-driver, Rabbi Ben Zakkai a sail-maker, Paul a tent-maker: so that the return to simplicity and honesty was quickly accomplished.

And now, that done, behold a wonder: at the whirling of a wand the swine of Circe converted back to biped man; whereupon without fail whatsoever he does it shall astonishingly prosper: that succession of wits, seers, savants, Heines, Einsteins, inspired mouths, pens of iridium, brushes from the archangel's plumage, discoveries, new Americas, elations, sensations — in therapeutics — in aeronautics-beyond-the-atmosphere — in the powers involved in sub-atoms — in the powers, latent till now, involved in soul . . . for now each of millions was free to think, free to manifest his own particular luck and knack in discovery, having a country, foothold, not hovering like Noah's dove, urging still the purposeless wing not to pitch into nowhere: for the promise says: "Ye shall not sow and another reap, ye shall not plant and another garner," but in a land of gentlemen ye shall live, as it were to swellings of music, while a noble height grows upon your smooth foreheads, and the sum-total of the blending movements of your bodies and brains shall, as seen from heaven, appear the minuet of a people.

Within forty years mighty works had been done: forts, irrigation of deserts, reclamation of the Dead Sea, passionate temples clapped to the lower clouds about the perpetual lamp, and that baroque Art of the Orient which at the Judges progresses in Summer through the country would draw multitudes of foreigners to gape at so great pomp, at Corinthian cities full of grace and riches which had arisen to crown with many crowns that plain of Mesopotamia, and where desolate Tyre had mourned her purples, and old Tadmor in the Wilderness (Palmyra) had sat in dirt; to gape, too, at a Jerusalem which in twenty years had crossed the Valley of Jehosophat, and might really then be called "the Golden," a purged Babylon, a London burnt to ashes and rebuilt somewhere else: for the Shophet proved true Duke and Leader, born mountaineer, climbing from pinnacle to wild pinnacle, becking his people after him with many a meaningful gesture skyward and suggesting smile; and Israel followed his thrilling way, hearing always the Excelsior of his calling as it were the voice direct of Heaven. What no merits of his could give, the land which he had chosen gave, Mesopotamia pretty soon proving herself a treasury of mineral riches: here is bdellium and the onyx-stone; and where the streaming Pison, dawdling, draws his twine of waters over that happy valley of Havilah, there is gold — hoard stored from before the Eozoic, as misers bury for their heirs, in mine and friable quarry, rollick rain: "and the gold of *that* land is good."

Here was not merely progress, but progress at increasing speed — acceleration — finally resembling flight, as of eagle or phoenix, eye fixed on the sun: Tyre by the fiftieth year having grown into the biggest of ports, her quays unloading 6,700,000 tons a year, mart of tangled masts, felucca, galiot, junk, cargoes of Tarshish and the Isles, Levantine stuffs, spice from the Southern Sea; while Jerusalem had grown into the recognized school of the wealthier youth of Europe, Asia and America.

For it says: "The Kings of the earth shall bring their honour and glory unto her"; and again: "She shall reign gloriously."

And not Israel alone reaped the fruits of his own fine weather, but his dews fell wide. For it says: "They shall be as dew from the Lord"; and again: "They shall fill the face of the earth with fruit"; and again: "All nations shall call them blessed."

And so it was: for the example of Israel, his suasive charm, proved compelling as sunshine to shoots, so that that heart of Spinoza lived to see the spectacle of a whole world deserting the gory path of Rome to go up into those uplands of mildness and gleefulness whither invites the smile of that lily Galilean.

The mission of "unbelieving" Israel was to convert Christendom to Christianity: and this he did.

We watch the Judge coming down the Mount of Olives in the midst of a jubilant throng all involved in a noise of timbrels and instruments of music: for his life was simple and one with the life of his people. It is evening, all the west yonder a bewitched Kingdom charm-embathed, wherein a barge of Venus bethronged with loves and roses voyages on a sea of dalliance en route for the last Beatific — the last, the seventh, Heaven — whitherward gads all a pilgrim-swarm of enraptured spirits, all, all thitherward, Paul caught up with clothes aflaunt, and soaring eagle, Enoch transfigured, green hippogriff, hop of squatted frog; and thitherward trots with blinkings, bleating, the Ram of the Golden Fleece, the flagrant flamingos flap and go.

The Judge, hoary-headed now, in a robe of cloth-of-silver which rippled, had but now got home from a Pilgrimage; and the time was Simcath Torah, the Rejoicing of the Law, and the carrying of Candles, in the month. Tishri: silver his robe and silver his hair that hung round a brown and puckered skin, but silvery, too, his every tooth still, and his vigour good; and, as down the Mount of Olives he stepped, he saw Mount Sion and that Temple that he had piled, across whose roughened frontispiece of gold glowed in a bow, bold like the rainbow's, in characters of blazing sapphire and chrysoprase, that inscription:

"Y'HOVAH B'KOKMAR YSAD ARETS, CONEN SHAMAIM B'THBUNAH"

and, as he saw it, lo, buoyancy caught the old man's feet: for the cymballing and music had grown very fiercely hot, so that all the congregation reeled in dance; and as the lasso drops round the astonished prairie-horse and draws asprawl, so dancing caught and drew his foot, and he danced.

And his wife Rebecca, mother of many sons, prying from a window-lattice, writhed odd the eyebrows of the cynic, one beyond the other: for not with foot alone he danced, but his wrung belly laboured in that travail of Orient dancing; and she turned and smiled to Margaret Loveday a turned-down smile, implying shrug, implying girding, her eyelids lowered, yet indulgent of his nature's rage.

And not with foot and abdomen alone he danced, but his two balancing palms danced to the beat of the heat of the music's heart; and with heel and toe he danced. And as he danced, he sang, all apant, filling up with nonsense-sounds when the rhythm's imperative tramp outran his improvisation; and singing he danced, and dancing sang: with abdomen and arms he danced, and with toe and heel he danced.

And dancing he sang:

> My hands,
> be dancing to God,
> your Guide,
>   And peal my pipes,
>   and riot my feet,
>   and writhe to His Heat,
>   my tripes.
> So fair!
> With Rum-te-te-Tum
> te Tum,
>   And Rum and Tum,
>   and Rum-te-te-Tum,
>   and Rum-te-te-Tum,
>   te Tum.
> So fair!
> This freehold for seraphs free!
>   That flame! those skies!
>   and Blest is Her Name,
>   and blest are my eyes,
>   that see.

I'll dance,
I'll dance like a ram,
for fun,
  I'll smack the sun,
  I'll dance at the breeze
  I'll dance till I breed
  a son.
For Thou!
Thou bringest Thine ends
to pass:
  This hump so high,
  this lump and her sigh,
  Thou lead'st through the Needle's Eye.
'Tis well
the saurians sprawled,
and roared!
  'Tis well Thou art!
  and well that Thou wast,
  and well when at last
  they soared!
And well,
O well that Thou art
to be
  When seraph hearts
  will laugh by this brook,
  and break for the love
  of Thee.
Thy years
shall still by increase
te Tum,
  And dance and dance,
  With Rum-te-te-Tum. . . .

so, singing, he danced, and, dancing, sang; and their sounds grew
faint; and they entered into the City of Glory, and their sounds
failed. . . .

They took him for the Sent of Heaven, nor did the results of
his glorious reign gainsay such a notion: the good Loveday,
indeed, had the agreeable fancy that our greatest are really One,
who eternally runs the circle of incarnation after incarnation
from hoary old ages till now—the Ancient of Days, his hair white

like wool, quietly turning up anew when the time yearns, and men are near to yield to the enemy: Proteus his name, and ever the shape he takes is strange, unexpected, yet ever sharing the same three traits of vision, rage and generousness—the Slayer of the Giant—Arthur come back—the Messenger of the Covenant—the genius of our species—Jesus the Oft-Born.

www.ingramcontent.com/pod-product-compliance
Lightning Source LLC
Chambersburg PA
CBHW050036180626
46810CB00002B/741